Applause for

Limestone Concerto

Limestone Concerto is a masterful work that evokes fond and chilling memories of my home state of Indiana. Set in 1963, the political tension of that time seems eerily familiar in this gripping and delicate tale.
> — *B. J.* Sears, *Professor of Film and Television, Savannah College of Arts/Sciences; Sound editor on* <u>Amadeus</u>

Westfeldt dishes himself up a full plate and then manages this heap of incidents with impressive agility. [Westfeldt] … a master of narrative counterpoint.
> — *Wes Blomster, Boulder Daily Camera*

Instead of musical notes Mr. Westfeldt uses words in this concerto that describes cultural and personal conflict during a time of great political upheaval. *Limestone Concerto* is a virtuoso performance that will keep you reading through its thrilling finale.
> — *Sue Levine, Executive Director, Boulder Philharmonic*

Against the backdrop of assassinations, the Cold War and Civil Rights, Mr. Westfeldt composes a contemporary speech-song about classical musicians in the Crossroads of America. Read this smart up-tempo thriller with vintage champagne and a Bach *Partita.*
> — *Molly LeClair, Coauthor of* <u>Thinking and Writing in the Humanities</u>; *Instructor, Writing and Rhetoric, University of Colorado at Boulder*

The author displays keen insights into the mindsets and quirky personalities of those who inhabit the stages and the boardrooms of America's symphony orchestras.
> —*Tom Akins, Principal Timpanist, Indianapolis Symphony 1965-91*

Limestone Concerto

Wallace Westfeldt

MudBug Press
Boulder, Colorado

Published by MudBug Press, which is an imprint of MudBug CO LLC. PO Box 1316 Boulder, CO 80306-1316.

For more information, contact editor@mudbugpress.com or visit www.limestoneconcerto.com.

Printed in the United States of America.

ISBN: 0-9778197-9-5
ISBN-13: 978-0-9778197-9-9
LCCN: 2006921628

For Betty Weems and Izler Solomon

Second Edition Note:

Most of the readers of Limestone Concerto that I have talked to, see no need for a second edition. The errors in the first edition are considered minor or go completely unnoticed.

However, there were two readers who wanted changes significant enough to warrant a second edition. One was Maestro Vladimir Ashkenazy. The other was Professor Emeritus John L. Murphy. These individuals have spent an inordinate amount of effort and time suggesting changes for the second edition. In my early conversations with them, it was amusing to me that the suggestions from the celebrated pianist and conductor were literary, whereas the suggestions from the noted Shakespearean scholar were musical. Subsequent conversations were more closely aligned with their areas of expertise. It is my opinion that the changes have been seamlessly integrated into this edition and therefore do not need to be called out.

I am very grateful to the Maestro and the Professor for the time they invested to improve this novel.

Limestone Concerto

I   Molla di ottimismo
II   Estate calda lunga
III   Caduta dura vivace

Many of the chapter headings in Limestone Concerto include a musical suggestion. The reader may find that playing the music before, during, or after reading the chapter will enhance the experience. Chapters with no musical heading are intended to be read with silence.

Notes for Concerto:
July 1953, Quarry No. 5 – Southern Indiana
July 6, 1962 – Gorky Park
March 1, 1963 – Moscow

Concerto:
First Movement: Molla di ottimismo (Optimistic spring)

Second Movement: Estate Calda Lunga (Long Hot Summer)

Third Movement: Caduta dura vivace (Lively hard fall)

Notes for LIMESTONE CONCERTO:

July 1953, Quarry No. 5 – Southern Indiana

When a quarry dies, it drowns. As soon as excavation penetrates the aquifer, water is continuously pumped out while quarrymen harvest the limestone. Eventually natural forces overwhelm mortal efforts, and the quarry floods. Adult fish show up in a couple of days, somehow navigating a labyrinth of underground rivers.

The deeper sections are about one hundred feet. The rest of the depths vary according to underwater terrain which is a hidden chaos of partially cut blocks. Clean-cut limestone surrounds three sides of the abandoned pit. The sheer walls and the echo that goes with them conjure up an image of a swimming pool for giants. Compared to lakes and rivers in this area, the quarry water is clear, with ten to twenty foot visibility, and refreshingly cold on a hot, humid Indiana day.

"Jump, Jed," they hollered.

Jedidiah Norton wrestled with his fear of the unknown and the known. The unknown was what would happen after the sixty-foot freefall. Would he plunge safely into deep cool water? Or would that plunge be interrupted by an unseen block of rock? Or worse, a block that was atilt with gritty edge ready to tear into unprotected flesh? The known would be the merciless teasing from his friends.

Well, sort of friends.

i

They were dumb and cruel, but he preferred their company to the stuck-up music students his mom wanted him to hang out with. He needed their approval. Or did he? In another year, he would be at Indiana University and clearly they would not. Why did he give a shit what they thought? They were bullies, rednecks. Gar's dad was surely a member of the Klan. But Jed envied their power, their carelessness. He wanted to know their secret.

"Chickenshit," Gar said.

"Asshole," Jed said.

"Pussy," Lou said.

"Bedwetter." Jed regretted saying that. The dark silence on Lou's face solved his dilemma — a few broken ribs would be a minor penalty for the verbal transgression. Three steps and he launched himself into the air.

"I'll be goddamned," Gar said, "the faggot jumped."

It was a long fall, longer than any of them thought it was. When he hit the water, the splashdown echoed in the confines of the stone walls while they waited for him to surface.

"There he is," Lou said. "I didn't think the fucker had it in him." Jed was still too shaken from the impact to feel the cold. He only hit water, but it felt much harder. Cold crept in, bringing him back to his senses. He could hear the hootin' and hollerin' from above.

"Nice jump, for a pussy!" Gar yelled.

Jed swam to the opposite side, to a large block of limestone that was tilted and halfway submerged. He crawled out, perched himself on the rock, smiled, and saluted his buddies with a middle finger.

"Hey Gar, you ever jumped from here?" Lou asked.

"Can't say I have." Gar stared over the edge. This was a newly flooded quarry, and the distance to the water looked a lot farther after Jed's jump.

"Good thing we got that faggot fiddle player to test it," Lou said, smiling down at Jed relaxing in the sun.

Gar took off, arms flailing, mouth wide open trying to scream 'Go Bearcats,' but found no air to make the words. When he finally reached the water, his mouth was still open. He plunged deep and the water rushed in where his scream never came out. Bobbing to the surface, he sputtered and coughed as if a preacher had sneaked up to baptize him by surprise. Seeing loudmouth Gar in distress started Lou and Jed laughing. The laughter increased as the reverberating walls kept adding to the joke.

Lou, still laughing, took his leap. He landed pretty darn close to the recovering Gar, giving him another good dousing. Lou surfaced. Gar dunked him and held him underwater.

"Ya almost killed me, ya fuckin' commie." Gar released him and swam towards the stone block that Jed was on. Jed was still holding his sides at the slapstick scene. Lou beat Gar to the tilted platform and scurried up to join Jed.

"What's so fuckin' funny?" Gar asked. He looked up at his friends, who could barely talk.

"Great jump, Gar," Jed said.

"Wanna do it again?" Lou said.

"Fuckin'-A, man, that was a long way down," Gar said. He tried to crawl onto the rock, but the contagious laughter and his belly kept getting in the way. Jed reached out to Gar and they grabbed each other's wrists. Curling his toes on coarse limestone and bending his knees for leverage, Jed was able to pull Gar from the water but not far enough to get him on the rock. Gar's dripping body looked like poorly sewn tuck-and-roll upholstery. Lou took Jed's other hand, pulling Gar up farther. Just as they neared the center of gravity, Lou let go of the giggling duo and they fell back into the water.

When Jed surfaced, he found his own laughter drowned by the echoing cackle of Lou.

July 6, 1962 — Gorky Park, Moscow

Vladimir Khazar took his daily walk in "The Park of Culture and Rest" early in the morning. At this time of day and this time of year, lovers affectionately strolled among the fir trees enjoying a privacy compared to their cramped shared apartments. But he wasn't there to spy; just to be alone … or as alone as you could be in the Soviet Union. As the Ferris wheel started to turn and the boisterous summer crowd arrived, he exited the sanctuary at 9 Krymsky Val and saw the parked car.

The driver was standing next to the right rear door. He opened the door and stared at Vladimir. The citizens of Moscow had learned an entire lexicon of visual cues just to avoid saying the wrong thing when the wrong person was listening; the political inverse to the auditory sensitivity of a blind man. In this case, the cues were a black Volga, with chauffeur, parked in a no parking zone. Translation: It must be the vehicle of someone fairly high up in the party, perhaps a minister. In this country rank ruled. Those who had rank could do for themselves and others things that they would never dare speak of. And those of a lesser rank could only obey. Therefore, even though every muscle in his body wanted to go the other way, Vladimir got into the back seat of the car. Inside was a round man in a baggy gray suit. A large briefcase sat next to him under the protection of his arm.

"Happy birthday, Comrade Khazar," the man said without smiling. Vladimir was not surprised that the man knew his name or the date of his birth. He did not reply. The driver started the car and pulled away from the curb.

"You need not worry. This is a good day for you." The tension in Vladimir's muscles subsided as he realized the lowered threat level.

"Have we met?" Vladimir said.

"No. I am the Deputy Minister of Foreign Affairs. And it is probably a good idea that we not meet again." Vladimir's muscles retightened. Perhaps this man was not a threat, but something sure was threatening. The round man continued.

"So the Party has been good to you lately?" The question was rhetorical. Khazar won the Tchaikovsky Competition in May and became a Soviet celebrity. Along with the prize came benefits awarded to the artistic elite such as international travel and a spacious apartment to himself.

"Yes, but far more complicated," Vladimir answered. "I think there are more people listening to me when I practice *alone* in my apartment than in the concert hall."

The round man smiled at the pianist's impertinence. "Well, I'm afraid it's going to get more complicated ... but in a good way. You see diplomacy is complicated, too. Did you know that Jason Foster is coming to play here next year?"

"No, I didn't. He is a venerable pianist. I look forward to hearing him play."

"Perhaps you could compare notes?"

"If he so desires, it would be my pleasure."

"You miss the point. He doesn't desire it. He doesn't even know he is coming yet. The Party desires it. Or I should say *certain members* of the Party desire it. This Cold War with America is getting dangerously icy. We would like to take the chill off."

"I have no skill in this area," Vladimir said firmly.

The minister laughed out loud this time.

"You severely underrate the impact of your playing." The minister reached into his briefcase and handed over a gift-wrapped package. Vladimir stared at it, not knowing what to do.

"It's your birthday, go ahead and open it ... gently." Carefully not ripping the paper, Vladimir opened the present. After staring at it and then catching his breath, he looked at the minister.

"It is the original," the minister said. "An excellent copy now resides in the Music Conservatory.

"But how did you ...?" The minister stopped the question by putting a single finger to his pursed lips.

"After you have had time to enjoy it, I suggest that you give it to Mr. Foster when he comes to visit," the minister said. Vladimir nodded in agreement.

"Oh, and I almost forgot. You're going to America."

"What?" Vladimir had not absorbed the first surprise.

"You will be touring there in about a year from next fall, I think. Sorry it will take so long, but as you say, things are so complicated now."

The driver stopped the car outside Vladimir's apartment.

Vladimir got out, clutching the gift. He felt excited and anxious about what the future held for him ... not unlike the feeling he had just before going on stage to perform a concerto.

As he watched the Volga drive off, he said, "This *is* a good day for me."

March 1, 1963 – Moscow

Vladimir looked into the open briefcase and smiled at three cartons of cigarettes — Lucky Strikes, Winstons, and Camels.

"I didn't know which you preferred," Jason said.

"I enjoy them all." Vladimir grabbed the contraband. "Please, make yourself at home, while I get coffee."

Even by American standards, the living room of this third floor apartment was expansive. On the north side, six large windows overlooked the Moscow River. A full-sized concert piano was centered beneath the windows. Jason walked over to the keyboard. To his left was a desk littered with pages of sheet music, bound scores, and international magazines. He set his now-empty briefcase on the desk and looked up. Far across the river the Kremlin's governmental and religious spires poked through dank haze.

"What a lovely view," he said.

"Yes ... is even better when snow leaves."

Jason turned to see his host was back with the coffee. Vladimir was twenty-five and, despite the cigarette hanging out of his mouth, he looked fourteen. His translucent skin mimicked the complexion of his city.

"But is not view I want," he said, exhaling smoke through his mouth and nostrils. Jason gave him a curious look and started to ask why, but Vladimir interrupted him. "How did you like playing in our Bolshoi?" The diminutive Russian handed Jason a cup of coffee.

"The theatre is marvelous. The acoustics are superb."

"Yes, acoustics are always excellent in Moscow." Vladimir laughed. "Everything can be heard everywhere." He rolled his eyes and took a sip of coffee. "I understand that you are friend of Maestro Zellingari."

"An old friend. In fact, I will be playing with him in a couple of weeks. It will be the final concert of the ISO's regular season," Jason said.

"What concerto?"

"The *Emperor*."

"Would you like to see my notes?" Vladimir's excitement reduced his age to twelve.

"I would be honored."

The young pianist shook off the praise, put his cup on the sill, and turned to the desk. Opening the file drawer, he took out an object roughly the size of a dictionary, but half as thick. It was wrapped in a beige chamois and tied with a strap of the same material. He placed it on the table next to a *New Yorker* magazine. A bookmark with the handwritten letters ISOLZ was sticking out of the magazine. Jason recognized the issue.

Vladimir held a finger to his lips and said, "Let's start on third movement. I feel it is most neglected." While continuing to talk about Beethoven's 5th Piano Concerto, Vladimir opened the magazine to the bookmark. It was a review of the Indianapolis Symphony Orchestra's Carnegie Hall performance last year. Jason shook his head in confusion. The article had nothing to do with the concerto or the conversation.

"… that's why is important to hold back on the forte in beginning of movement. You must save some for finale," Vladimir said as he handed the *New Yorker* to Jason.

A portion of the review had been circled. Jason was still confused, but he smiled in fascination at this method of double communication. His ears gobbled up the musical insights, while his eyes tried to decode the mystery of the objects before him.

"I see. But you will have to show me more. How can you balance this restraint with the obvious intention for a dramatic transition from the second movement?" Jason asked, pointing to the unknown object on the desk.

"Excellent question," Vladimir said. "The conductor and pianist must be one mind during this moment. Look here, where bassoons hand G note to horns?

"Yes. And then they have to hold it *pianissimo* for three full measures."

"Until *rondo* starts. Beethoven is devil, I think." Vladimir shook his head and untied the strap.

"But a genius at allowing the instrument to emerge from the orchestra," Jason said.

Vladimir nodded and unfolded the chamois.

Jason looked at the beautiful cover but could not translate the Cyrillic title. He turned to the first page and recognized it immediately. But he had never seen anything like it.

"Notice the *firma originale* after the *cresecendo*," Vladimir said, pointing to the bottom of the page.

Jason's breathing stopped as he read the signature. Slowly, he scanned the page and turned another.

After several deliberate breaths and just one more page Jason said, "This is a remarkable ..." he chose the word carefully, "... insight."

Vladimir giggled like a ten-year-old and said, "You must show it to Zellingari."

"You would share something so valuable?" Jason asked.

Vladimir refolded the chamois around the treasure, retied the strap, and put it in the briefcase. Handing the case to Jason, the Soviet pianist said, "It is a gift."

I
Molla di ottimismo

— 1 —

MARCH 18, 1963 MONDAY

Alison's Studio – Indianapolis, Indiana

Music: Sibelius – Symphony No. 5

Alison's fingers were deep inside Leon's head. The clay was still too cold, but the morning light was the only good light in her studio. The room was on the third floor of the Tudor mansion, as far away from the maestro's study as possible so she could play music while she worked. But it was a dumpy studio. It needed more windows, and the ceiling was too low. She wanted a loft. The construction could start after the regular season finished and Leon was away guest conducting. Alison flattened his nose with a putty knife. Her stereo was within arm's length of the sculpting stand. She tweaked the volume of the symphony. The knurled knob had been smoothed by the clay from her hands. The floor of the remodeled room would be stuffed with foam to insulate her from the silence.

She scooped more clay for the cheeks. He had become jowly in the last few years, not unhandsome, but somehow anthropological. She had to be

1

careful that he didn't look like a gorilla. She tried to find the man she fell for in Aspen, Colorado. He was angular then, like Sinatra, but darker in skin and mood. Alison went to Aspen for two reasons: the sculpting classes and the Music Festival. Every weekend, she attended both concerts and soon focused on only one aspect of the orchestra, the conductor. He stood on the podium with arms that were as broad as eagle's wings for fourth movement finales. But then, during a second movement adagio, he delicately balanced the tempo of the entire orchestra with one hand as if he were a single-winged butterfly.

In Aspen, she spent long days working feverishly. She slept little but did not seem tired. And when she did sleep, she woke up smiling. She had the appetite of Ghandi. She felt short of breath. It's the altitude, Alison claimed, and she was right. Her heart was lifted away and she didn't care if it was the music or the man.

Leon Zellingari taught at the festival's music school during the week. After classes he would walk west towards the sunset and his apartment. The dirt streets were sprayed with oil to keep the dust down. The still air held the smell of both oil and blue spruces. On his right, a yellow bungalow bordered the cliff above Hallam Lake. Leon could hear the rapids of the Roaring Fork River beyond the lake. He marveled at his combination of fortunes: great smells, great sounds, great sunset, and a great orchestra. Aside from the fact that there was no baseball nearby, this place was a lot better than Indianapolis.

On his left there was a blue convertible with its lights on. The top was up but the door was unlocked, and his good mood spawned the good deed. Setting his brief of scores on the hood, which was still warm, he opened the driver's side door to turn off the headlights. Trying nearly all the other knobs first, he found the lights last. As the car-lights went out, a porch light went on.

"Hey, that's my car," a woman shouted from the small house.

Leon turned, startled. He could not see the figure behind the light. "Uh, the car lights were on. I was just turning them off."

"You broke into my car?"

"No, no, it was unlocked." Leon fumbled for an excuse and found one in the ignition. "In fact, I think the keys are in it." He walked to the door smiling.

Alison reached out to take the car keys and inspected the articulated fingers connected to his muscular hand. She had never seen that baton-less right hand in the midst of a mundane gesture, only in the glory of its profession. Her face lost its profiling stare. Snaring the moment, she took on a demure look of guilt.

"Why, I'm so embarrassed, sir, I thought you were stealing my car." Her drawl bloomed like magnolias. Leon laughed with his deep chortle.

"No, just walking by, sorry to disturb you," he said turning to leave.

"I am so sorry. Can you forgive me?"

"There is no need, really. Glad I could help. Good evening," and he walked back to the car to get his music scores left on the hood.

Alison only had to leave the headlights on one more night to get him to come in for a drink. This story was frequently told in public as one of coincidence. It made for good copy, thought Alison, smiling at the clay model she still held in her hands.

The smile was replaced by squinting determination. Leon's head and Edith Campbell's head had to be finished by the reception this weekend. Edith's was a bit owlish, but that should work. It was Leon's head that was giving her problems. She couldn't discover the discoverer, for that is what he was ... not a creator, not a composer, not an improver. If he were, he would improve the ending to this Sibelius; such a beautiful piece, such a stupid ending. "It's in the score," he would say. "I just have to find it." He's in the clay, Alison, find him. Find his hands, those arms, the smile, the chortle, find the music, the intensity, find the human, not the ape.

The heads would remain on permanent display at Campbell Hall. At least, Edith's would. Leon's would stay there as long as he did. If her plans for next season worked out, that wouldn't be so long. The thought reminded her. This week's soloist, Jason Foster, should be bringing the package with him today.

— 2 —

MARCH 18 MONDAY

Luncheon – Zellingari Home

Music: Bach, Concerto for Oboe and Violin in D minor

The Zellingaris frequently held luncheons for the guest soloist. These relaxed affairs were known as much for the food as the celebrities attending. When Alison moved to Indianapolis, she first went her home in Lousiana to find a suitable cook for the household. "Suitable" meant cooking elegant meals for parties of two to two hundred while maintaining the quiet that the maestro required. "Mary House is as quiet as a mouse," Alison's mom said. Mary was originally from Jamaica and discovered a culinary knack in the kitchens of the Garden District of New Orleans. She had learned silence and other dark arts on the island. Cooking for the Zellingaris was a tremendous stage. Her meals were as spectacular as a Puccini aria.

Mary never complained. But, if she did, it would be about Mrs. Zellingari's dual penchant for surprise and improvisation. Mary took today's example out of the oven. Shortly after she arrived for work this morning, Alison came down in her smock, collected five ramekins from the cupboard, and arranged them on the counter.

"Mary, Mr. Foster, his wife Maria, and Hugh are coming for lunch. Let's have Gazpacho and a bacon cheese soufflé."

"Yes, ma'am."

"Oh, and let's do something really special to the soufflé."

The muscles between Mary's shoulder blades tightened as she thought of how much she disliked that phrase. "And what would dat be, ma'am?"

"Let's hide a poached egg in the soufflé. I read about in a magazine."

"Excuse me?" Mary cocked her head.

4

"Yes, and make sure the yolk is soft."

Mary stared at the ramekins on the table and said quietly, "No way you can make da soufflé like dat, ma'am." But Alison had already left, leaving Mary alone to figure out how to defy the physics of eggs.

In addition to Mary's artistry in the kitchen, it was her somewhat pedestrian job to answer the door. She didn't mind it. She got to meet the faces that she would feed. Over time, Mary developed a cordial relationship with many of the musicians. She remembered Mr. Foster as a nice and handsome man.

She opened the door, and there was Jason, a pretty lady, and Hugh Morgan. Hugh was the first oboe of the symphony and a great friend of the conductor's wife. Mary was pretty sure that he wore makeup. He was a self-proclaimed gourmand and hoped that if the Zellingaris ever moved to Cleveland or New York, he would get Mary as a going-away present. Hugh loved Mary. She thought he was the devil.

"Mary, my sweet, it's been so long since you have fed me. You were in my dreams last night." She drew the sign of the pentagram behind her back as Hugh, the shameless, continued. What tantalizing treats do you have for us today? What delectable delicacies are in store? What culinary arts await our consumption?"

Mary ignored Hugh and said in her Jamaican rhythm, "Mr. Foster, it's good to see you, come in."

As they passed the threshold, the fifty-year-old Jason introduced his new wife, Maria, with adolescent pride. Mary mechanically rotated her head towards the much younger woman.

"Delighted to meet you, Mary. Did you know your reputation goes all the way to New York?" Maria shared her husband's sweet sincerity.

"Why, no ma'am, t'ank you. Mrs. Zellingari will be down in a minute," she said dutifully. With a little extra helping of pride, she retreated to the kitchen as Leon arrived to greet his guests.

Jason and Leon were old friends. They had gained popularity and success at roughly the same time. He was a traveling soloist living in New York, which afforded him a greater reputation than the musical director of a Midwestern orchestra could receive. Jason was instrumental in creating the season's guest performance at Carnegie Hall for the Indianapolis Symphony Orchestra. Alison made sure that Leon got the kind of exposure he needed. She created the *ISO to NY* promos that ended up on the desks of critics and musical luminaries. When they returned, she framed excerpts from the *Times* and *New Yorker* reviews and hung them strategically in Leon's study.

In the stonelike countenance of Zellingari, there was a barely contained joy of inspiration and concentration that supported the compelling force of his baton-less gestures. His attention to his players was like the devotion a soloist shows to his instrument. And, indeed, Zellingari had transformed a hundred individual performers into one voice that responded joyously to every command - Julius Harold, <u>NEW YORK TIMES</u>

I have been hearing some background chatter about the quality of the Indianapolis Symphony and its conductor Leon Zellingari. Skeptically, I went to Carnegie Hall to see for myself. What a magnificent surprise. I would never have expected the depth of tone, accuracy, and responsiveness displayed by this Midwestern orchestra. In addition, the choice of the Schubert was as bold as its interpretation was sublime. It made me proud as an American and generated a desire that some foreign countries, particularly Russia, could hear it. — William Winthrop, <u>THE NEW YORKER</u>

"Maestro, you are looking very well." Jason held out his arms broadly for their hug.

"You too, Jason, but not nearly as good as your wife," Leon said. "How are you, Maria? Is he treating you well? If not, I will make it very hard on him this week."

The really obnoxious aspect of flirting musicians is how self-amused it makes them, thought Alison as she reached the bottom of the stairs. "Jason, my dear, how was Moscow?" Alison hugged the pianist warmly and whispered in his ear, "*Did you bring it?*"

"Moscow was dreadful." As he spoke, he gave a nod to Alison's whisper. "It was cold, sparse, and lonely. Maria had to stay home for her show."

"Oh, you poor boy! No vodka, no caviar, no adoring fans?" Alison mocked.

"The music was sublime, the audiences intelligent, appreciative, and large. The state requires it." Jason answered.

"And, Maria, Leon is absolutely right, you do look lovely. Success agrees with you."

"Thank you, staying busy helped me forget about being so far away from Jason," Maria said happily and seemingly blind to Alison's artistic jealousies.

Maria recently had an exhibition of charcoals in Manhattan. Alison was sure that it was because Maria lived in New York and was married to Jason. Maria appeared unaware of all things ugly, including her own charcoal-stained hands and the clay permanently stuck under Alison's fingernails. "I hear we have two new pieces to look at," Maria said.

"As usual, Hugh has been opening his mouth too much," Alison said. "Perhaps he should practice more and talk less."

"And eat more," Hugh chimed in. "When's lunch?"

(Gazpacho is a Spanish and Portuguese dish. Like most peasant fare adapted for the United States, it tends to suffer in quality from impatience and carelessness. To distinguish it from a cold vegetable soup, one must find the freshest tomatoes, carefully hand chop the ingredients, and let it chill long enough — four hours — for the vegetal flavors to meld with the sherry vinegar. The Iberians call it "Ensalada Liquida." It is served on a hot day when the cool spiciness can offset the midday sun. Mary had seen better tomatoes, but she had a secret that added a unique elegance — sweet onions from Maui. Hugh knew a regular supplier of these and frequently shared them with Alison.)

While Alison served gazpacho from the tureen, Mary poured a Vouvray. She poured the wine slowly, hoping that someone would try the soup before she disappeared into the kitchen. Predictably, Hugh lunged at his bowl. He was enamored with all things oral. As he savored the individual flavors that the spicy broth unleashed, he slowly swayed from side to side as if he were in the midst of one of his oboe solos. Ignoring Hugh's reverie, the guests turned to their own soup.

Maria was the first to speak. "Mary, I lived in Spain for two years and had gazpacho once a week, but I never tasted anything like this."

"Thank you, ma'am," she said quietly and slipped back into the kitchen. Mary decided she liked Maria even though she did have dirty hands.

"Sometimes, we wonder who the real artist *is* in this house," Leon said to Maria, who was seated to his right.

"I don't," Hugh said to no one in particular.

Jason laughed. "It's a good thing he can play so well, eh, Leon?"

"No shit," Leon said, equally amused. Hugh's job security was in no way endangered or supported by the food favors and friendship he showed the conductor's wife. He was one of the top ten oboe players in the world and knew it. The table conversation turned to New York, common friends, and rumors about upcoming tours. They did not discuss this week's concert. Eventually, Jason asked about next season. "What are your plans, Maestro?"

"Well, first I have to find a new principal for the cellos."

"Oh no, Sazarin is leaving? Where's he going?" Jason asked.

"Cleveland," Leon answered. "Sometimes I think we are their minor league farm club."

"Well, that is a great loss, but that makes my letter to you all the more timely." Jason smiled at Leon.

"Yes, I meant to ask you about that. This Michael from Czechoslovakia, is he really that good?" Leon received recommendations for musicians every day and had developed a skeptical shield to protect him from the frequent hyperbole. He felt guilty about not giving Jason more credit.

"The name is Micaela, and yes, *she* is that good," Jason said.

"Micaela Miklos?" Hugh looked up from his bowl.

"The same." Jason said, nodding to Hugh.

"Oh, she's good, very good. She wants to come here?" Hugh was surprised.

"She doesn't like New York. The position in Cleveland is apparently taken, and I made sure she was in the audience during the Carnegie performance. She was impressed," Jason explained.

"With me?" Hugh grinned.

"Actually, she did mention you, but most of her praise was reserved for the maestro. 'Such beautiful hands, it makes you wonder why anyone uses a baton.' " Jason delivered the quote flamboyantly with eyes cast upwards and hands clasped together. Leon's attempt to keep his professional expression was belied by a muffled snort.

"I don't think I like her," Alison said. "Tell me, what does she look like?" Alison looked at Jason and Hugh in turn. Both declined to answer, and neither would look her in the eye.

"So she is *that* beautiful?" Alison drained her wine glass.

"Oh, Alison, she is simply gorgeous," Maria said. "And such a sad story."

"Really." Alison's voice reminded Leon of the gazpacho ... very cool and very spicy. He enjoyed her jealousy and did nothing to prevent it. In fact, he often found ways to encourage it.

"She is a Czech refugee." Maria went on, "During her escape, both her parents were killed. There is a rumor that she has a boyfriend back there, either in prison or dead. Consequently, her politics are significantly anti-communist. I think that is the reason she didn't like the New York crowd. She would fit in

8

great in Indiana. In fact, with her politics, story, and looks at the front of the stage, you will probably sell out every night."

"We already sell out every night," Alison said.

"Still, it's good PR. Right, Alison?" Leon grinned at Alison and then took on his normal serious tone and asked, "But, can she play and does she have the presence to lead her section?"

"And will she audition?" Hugh said. Leon auditioned everyone, no matter what their credentials and reputation were.

"She will and would like to," Jason said.

"Well, then, by all means. Darling, why don't you have the audition here and then we can welcome her with a special lunch from Mary," said the charming hostess.

"May I come?" asked Hugh, the insatiable.

"No!" Leon and Alison answered simultaneously. Jason and Maria laughed, followed by Alison and Leon.

Mary could tell from the sounds of conversation and silverware that they were almost done with the first course, although it didn't matter, because the bacon soufflés, particularly these soufflés, had their own timetable. The first course was cleared from the table. After serving the salads onto the large dinner plates, Mary brought in the individual ramekins on a tray and set them on the sideboard. Then, with hot pads, she delivered each one with its high crown. As the flutes received the champagne, Mary was again soaking in the compliments, even though no one had taken a bite.

Alison encouraged her guests. "C'mon, eat it now before it falls."

Maria went first, taking in a forkful of the crust and the moist inside. "It's like eating a cloud," she said, marveling at the light texture and rich flavoring. There was a pervasive aroma of some chile that she could not identify.

Mary saw the familiar question on Mrs. Foster's face and said obligingly, "Tabasco with a hint of dee Scotch Bonnet."

Alison and Mary anxiously waited for the first one to discover the surprise. Happily, Jason found it before Hugh. His fork had cut easily through the airy mass to meet the resisting egg. Without question or hesitation, he took a mouthful of soufflé and poached egg. The wonderful richness was offset by the bacon and the crust. It reminded him of having Blinis with caviar at the Russian Cafe. He looked at Mary with respect and saluted with open hand as one salutes a soloist.

Hugh was next. He was more impressed with the feat than the flavor. "My God, there is an egg in my soufflé." Everyone laughed at the unintended joke.

"No, I mean it," he protested. "There is a poached egg inside. This is not possible." He began to eat with rapture as Mary left the room.

"Seriously, Jason, how was the orchestra in Moscow?" Leon had conducted the London, Berlin, and Israeli philharmonics but never the highly acclaimed Moscow orchestra.

"As good as or better than their hockey team. There is definitely something to be said for state-supported arts," Jason said, shaking his head. "Every principal is capable of a stellar solo career in the US, including the oboist," glancing at Hugh's savage involvement with his soufflé.

"I don't suppose he wants to defect?" Leon said, failing to get a rise out of Hugh, who seemed oblivious to anything beyond his own hedonistic joy of Mary's food.

Jason laughed. He enjoyed watching his friend forced into tolerance of one of his stars. "No, no one, it seems wants to leave. Scientists, artists, and Olympic athletes are the new Russian aristocracy."

"What about the lack of programming freedom?" Leon asked, referring to the Soviet's restrictions against modern and particularly Western composers.

"Everyone complains about it, but they are not very serious complaints. Besides, they don't believe that we have the programming freedom we say we do. I told the concertmaster that next week I was doing the *Emperor,* sandwiched between Schoenberg and Stravinsky in the heart of conservative America, and he demanded a new interpreter. He simply could not believe that American conductors could program what they wanted."

"That concertmaster is closer to the truth than you might think." Hugh said, returning from the planet of food.

"What do you mean?" Jason asked.

Leon raised his left hand almost invisibly to Hugh, who immediately and silently deferred to the cue from his conductor. "We do receive certain pressures concerning the programming," Leon answered for Hugh.

"From the fundraisers?" Maria asked.

"To some degree, but the real problem is closer to home," Leon reluctantly went on. "It turns out that some of the members of our orchestra have rather curious political beliefs, considering they are card-carrying members of the musician's union. Micaela will probably find friends fast."

"You're kidding," Jason said.

"Unfortunately, no," Leon said. "It seems that the right-wing of the orchestra is more vocal in a Midwestern setting than it is on the coasts."

10

"But just as anonymous," the oboist said as he refilled his own glass with champagne; even Hugh's prodigious appetite wouldn't finish lunch today.

"You might as well know that these folks weren't delighted with your appearances at the Bolshoi," added Leon. Jason and Maria stared at the conductor.

"Honestly, it's just a bunch of fuss and feathers." Alison wanted to save more than the luncheon. Hugh's sexual preferences had caused him to receive individual and unnerving threats. "Every orchestra has a few huckleberries you have to ignore."

"I am sure that's true," Maria agreed. "Alison, tell us about your new commissions."

Despite the patronizing attitude, Alison welcomed the change of subject. "The Campbell Foundation has commissioned me for two busts to be unveiled at next year's first concert. One is a bust of Edith and the other is of Leon. The clay models are nearly done. We'll show them at the reception after this Saturday's performance. If they pass that inebriated review, they'll be recast in limestone this summer. Jed Norton, our second viola, studied in Bloomington and knows the quarries. I think he was actually born there. He's going to show me around."

"May we see them?" Maria was as bubbly as the champagne.

"They're not in a good state right now," Alison said.

"Yeah, one looks like a gorilla." Hugh had recovered.

"Hugh!" Alison was not pleased. Jason laughed hard.

"Oh, c'mon, Alison, just me," Maria said. "I am sure the boys have some bad puns they want to share."

"Not me," Hugh said, "although I do have some tasty jokes." Alison knew how tasteless these jokes were.

"I am persuaded," Alison said.

Maria and Alison left the table. The men sat looking at each other. "Excuse me, gentleman, I need to know how Mary made that soufflé," Hugh said, heading to the kitchen.

"Let's take a walk," Jason said to Leon.

Music: Bach, Concerto in D Minor for Two Violins

As soon as Maria entered Alison's studio, she took a flat silver case from her purse and opened it. Inside was a hand rolled cigarette. "Does anybody besides Hugh come in here?" she asked while lighting up.

"Not without an invitation. I didn't know you smoked, Maria."

"I don't. This is a joint."

"Excuse me?"

"A joint, pot ... y'know, marijuana." Maria took another hit and looked at Alison's frozen face and then the bust of Edith Campbell. "You better try some of this. You're beginning to look like Edith here."

"Maria ... I, uh, I never imagined you were ... could be a ..."

"Pot head? It's not as bad as all that. Christ, how do you think I stay so fucking bubbly?" Nothing Maria said helped Alison's temporary paralysis. Maria went on, "Relax girl, it's not contagious. A lot of people get high. A lot of people have champagne at lunch. Jason introduced me to it before we were married."

"Jason?"

"Yes, Jason," Maria answered. "He started smoking pot when he was having problems with his hands. I thought everybody knew that."

"Champagne is not addicting." Alison was trying to sync up with the conversation.

"Only because alcoholics can't afford it. Honestly, Alison, don't pretend to be stupid with me."

"What do you mean, you thought everyone knew?"

"Leon knows."

"Ridiculous."

"Speaking of Leon, Hugh is right."

"About what?"

"It does look like a gorilla," Maria said, studying the clay sculpture.

"Oh, shit."

"Don't worry, it's close. Something's just not right."

"I know. It's the cheeks. They're too jowly."

"No ... I don't think so. The cheeks are right." Alison and Maria stared at the sculpture. Maria moved close, closer, nose to nose, then back next to Alison. "Check out the eyes."

Alison stared at the piece intently. "They are too close together."

"Uh huh," Maria confirmed. "Once you move them apart, try smoothing the temples, and I think you will get your man back."

"Thanks."

"Don't mention it."

"How often do you get high?"

"Couple times a month, and more often when I travel."

"And Jason?"

"Not much anymore. His hands are better. We use it for sex sometimes."

"Really?"

"Oh yeah, very long, drawn-out sex."

"Can I try some?"

Maria handed over the joint and instructed Alison to inhale and hold it in. Alison took the joint between her fingers and gently brought it to her mouth. She puckered her lips as Maria had, sucked the cannabis in deeply — holding it in with a conspiratorial smile.

"Tastes good," she exhaled.

"Who cares? So tell me about the threats against Hugh?" Maria asked.

"Who said anything about threats?"

"If you keep acting stupid, I am going to assume you are trying to hit on me. Hugh always says more with his oboe and his silence than that wide open mouth of his. How bad is it?" The champagne and pot fueled Maria. She was considerably more brazen ... enjoyable, Alison thought.

"It's definitely worse this year. There has always been grumbling, but it's been louder, and more ... blatant, more contentious. There have been some personal attacks too," Alison said.

"Like what?"

"Someone put a note in Hugh's music. It said, 'Die you commie faggot.'"

"Jesus."

"Yeah, it was placed just inside the front cover during intermission. No one saw who did it."

"What did he do?"

"He grabbed it and stuffed it in his pocket. No one knew at the time. He had demanding solos for the second half and played them beautifully. After the performance, he came into Leon's dressing room shaking ... almost collapsed."

"What did Leon do?"

"He closed the next rehearsal to musicians and staff only. He talked for ten minutes and then told everyone to go home and practice. The musicians were silent when they left the hall."

"What did he tell them?"

"I don't know."

"Alison!"

"Honestly, he wouldn't tell me, but it sure scared the shit out of them, or most of them."

"Did the notes stop?" Maria asked.

"Nothing seems to be happening in the hall, rehearsals, or performances. There are still jokes during rehearsals. Jed and Hugh are pretty good at needling each other."

"Jed's the viola player?" Maria asked.

"Yep, he's a weird one, an Indiana native, fair talent, not great. I'm pretty sure he goes to John Birch Society meetings, but he and Hugh trade insults as if they were friends. I can't figure him out. He seems out of place."

"What did Leon mean about people being unhappy with Jason at the Bolshoi?"

"We got some crank calls."

"Threats?"

"Yep." Alison took another hit. "I wouldn't worry, Maria, these folks are all talk and no names. If they were really going to do anything, they wouldn't telegraph it, would they?"

Maria shivered, "I suppose not. Still, it gives me the creeps."

Music: Bach, Goldberg Variations, Aria

Jason and Leon walked in the yard skirting the crocuses that interrupted the patches of myrtle. The black walnut trees provided a great canopy for the sunny day. They talked some about the rehearsal plan for the week, but mostly about the quality of great orchestras and who was heir apparent to lead them. There was a growing tendency to select younger conductors these days. Leon would need another artistic break, like the New York trip, to move up the list.

"You know, they are still talking about the Carnegie performance," Jason said.

"Well, it'll fade eventually. It always does," Leon said. He had stacks of favorable reviews from all over the world. But reviews, like news, lost their shine quickly. Position is what really counted. No matter what miracles he worked with the ISO, it was still known as a second rate orchestra. Nevertheless, he was surprised by Jason's comment.

"What are they still talking about?"

"The Schubert, mostly. That was one ballsy move," Jason answered. He was referring to *Schubert's Ninth Symphony*. The work is not notoriously difficult for the orchestra or the audience, but it begins with a beautifully fragile horn solo. The French horn is the bane of conductors. Except for the top orchestras, horn talent is sketchy at best and their errors are easily noticed.

For the conductor of the ISO to open his Carnegie debut relying on the perfect execution of some twenty notes by one member of his orchestra, a French horn no less, was considered to be either extreme lunacy or a remarkable confidence. But Leon had Martha Collins for his principal horn. She had the talent and the chutzpah to pull it off.

"Not everyone knows about Martha's big brass ones."

"Yes, I guess so — another one of your hidden aces. Anyway, people talk about that performance as if it were the only time the ninth had been played in New York."

Of course, it wasn't. But the bold move by the Midwestern conductor with no baton captured the attention of critics, audience, and orchestra. Even Leon admitted that that particular performance was magical. Apparently, its luster persisted.

As they returned to the house, they found themselves at the front door next to Hugh's car.

"Leon, I have something for you." Jason opened the door and pulled out a large gift box from the foot well in the back seat. The box was sealed with tape. "It's something I found in Moscow."

Leon began to open the box.

"No, don't open it now. Save it for later, when you are alone in your study." The conductor complied with no questions.

When Leon and Jason came in the front door, their wives were very slowly descending the rest of the stairs. They appeared to be dizzy with laughter.

"Maria has solved all my problems, darling." Alison slid her arm around Leon's neck.

"Really, how kind of her." He enjoyed, but was somewhat embarrassed by, Alison's blatant affection.

"Yep, you are no longer a gorilla. You are a human." Alison and Maria shared an unquenchable stream of laughter.

"How gratifying to know." Leon was irritated with their inability to control the clanging noise of their private joke.

"Oh, yes, Maria shared her expertise with me. She is very generous."

"Sounds like you shared quite a bit of champagne too."

"Champagne? Nope, that's for alcoholics. We decided it's better to smoke pot."

"What?" Leon was accumulating confusion and exasperation in equal amounts.

"Don't worry, honey, I will explain later. By the way, Maria, do you think you could spare one or two of those?"

Hugh came out of the kitchen. "Time to go?"

Jason nodded and said, "We should get back to the hotel. Alison, thank you and Mary for a wonderful lunch. Maestro, I will see you at rehearsal tomorrow." The trio left.

Leon closed the door and turned to Alison, "I need to study some more today. Are you sure you are okay?"

"I am just fine. I only need to move your eyes farther apart and you will be okay, too." She retreated upstairs to her studio.

— 3 —

"Great music is heard in the heart long before ... and long after ... the performance." — Izler Solomon 1962

MARCH 18 MONDAY

Maestro's Study

Leon took the box to his study, set it on the side table, and plumped himself down in his burgundy chair. During the season, aside from rehearsals and luncheons, he spent most of his day sitting in that chair. Leon was a short man, swarthy in nature, but not small. The chair was enormous, big enough for two of him, or at least for him and a medium-sized child. It would have been a great chair for watching baseball. Instead of a TV, there was a music stand in front of the chair, and not one of those small fold-up ones. This one came straight from the concert stage and was sturdy enough to hold the really large scores. Today he was studying Stravinsky's *Firebird*. He lifted his right hand to count out the tempo. It was an elegantly silent movement, not unlike a magician's, but there was no audience, no assistant, and no sound. His hands were dirt brown dark with long fingers and the exercised shape of a violinist. Playing violin was his original career until the knuckles started to prematurely ache. You could still get him to play the fiddle on the right occasion with the right people.

He would sit in his chair for hours, studying the music. He never used a baton. He claimed it was because of a near accident that he had once, conducting the *Karelia Suite*. Swooping down with his right hand, he almost took out the viola's eye. "She had such pretty eyes," he'd say. "They were green-gray with gold flecks that sparkled in the stage light." His wife had come to realize that rampant flirting was a requirement for a conductor, even if there was no basis in fact. That was the case here. The story of the baton was just conductor's legend, good for program copy. Besides, he needed some answer for the incessant question, "Why don't you use a baton?" The answer was that it simply wasn't right for him. His hands had a force that the small stick would have muted.

Music was rarely heard in the conductor's study. The perimeter of silence extended into the living room and dining room. In the study, at his back, were lead-paned windows. Any outdoor noise was a restless audience to be ignored. His hi-fi was on his right on the bottom shelf of a floor-to-ceiling bookcase. Also in the bookcase were the infrequently played records and the frequently used three-ring binders containing his program logs. Every performance was timed to the second. His chair looked diagonally across the room, over a coffee table, to a four-foot high monaural speaker. Its main function was to hold up a few houseplants. Now and then, he would get up to put on a record to listen to *someone else's* performance of a particular piece. He only started the turntable for competitive purposes, and the music wouldn't be on long. He would compare tempo, the conductor's most precious commodity. The interpretation would be his own and cascade from this starting point.

This weekend was really going to shake the walls of Campbell Hall. It was always good to end the season with a dramatic piece like the *Firebird*. Good for attendance, season ticket sales, and fundraising. And with Jason doing the *Emperor* concerto in the first half, the huckleberries in the audience would suddenly be sad the season was over. There is a certain optimism that coincides with the season finale, the same kind of optimism that occurs at the beginning of the baseball season. After all, the Cubs *could* win the pennant this year. Baseball was one of the few subjects that made Leon smile. He played some as a child until his violin instructor said, "Hardballs and violin fingers do not mix. Choose one or the other." He picked baseball. His parents picked the violin.

Next month, he would be in Wrigley Field taking a much-needed break. The break would continue at Alison's family place in New Orleans. Then the summer festivals would start. He only had guest performances this summer; another reason to be optimistic. Less work, more exposure.

It had been a great year. The trip to Carnegie with the whole orchestra was a remarkable achievement. He was concerned about next year. That thought rattled him. Even though the program was done and it was good, it was not a step up from last season. New York took a whole year of preparation. No matter, he consoled himself, *We can rest on our laurels. Just do the music right … like the Firebird.*

Leon was annoyed at his scattered thoughts and refocused his attention on the work. After five minutes, he was distracted again. This time it was the object on the side table. It seemed to grow larger in the corner of his eye. He closed the *Firebird*, stood up, tossed it on the table, and used his pocket knife to open the bothersome box.

He reached inside, untied the strap, unfolded the chamois, and stared at the leather bound score. The score's title had been raised and gilded. Leon was trilingual. He was so fluent that he could nearly translate the title with his hands as they slid over the Cyrillic letters. They looked beautiful and felt valuable. This was the conductor's score for Sergei Rachmaninov's *Third Piano Concerto*, a prodigious piece, challenging for pianist and orchestra alike; twice as many notes as the *Second Piano Concerto*. Although he had only performed it once, with Byron Janis, it was quite familiar to him. It touched him deeply; one of the few works that he found himself totally involved with, both tempo and melody.

He took the score from the box. It seemed heavy. Opening the score, his eyes widened. It was handwritten, not printed. He scanned to the bottom of the page and gasped. There was the signature of Rachmaninov himself. The conductor was holding the composer's original work. It now seemed too heavy. Leon placed it in the music stand and sat down because he needed to.

His hand passed down the page as if he were caressing the first few bars. The notes appeared alive. They weren't moving around. Each one occupied a precise space in time and tone. But they weren't still either. Quarter and eighth notes floated in the beginning ripple of clarinets and bassoons *dum, da dum, da dum, da dum, da dum.* The supporting notes from the basses pulsed as they were plucked, *pizzicato.* And then, by the third bar, out of the muted swirl of strings, the thematic current of the piano flowed across the page in simple octaves. Leon read the instruction for the soloist — or did he hear it? … *commodo,* comfortable, play leisurely. Leon settled into his chair. He communed with concerto and composer for forty-six minutes.

The spirit of Sergei left the room when he closed the score. At the same time, new questions crept in. Why did Jason give this to me? Does he want to play it? He couldn't do that now — maybe when he was younger.

— 4 —

March 20, Mannlicher-Carcano, an Italian military carbine, was shipped from Klein's of Chicago to the Dallas Post Office Box of Alek Hiddel, also known as Lee Harvey Oswald

MARCH 23 SATURDAY

Concert Reception – Edith Campbell's Home Following Saturday Night Concert

Music: Mozart, Clarinet Concerto, K. 622 in A

The exquisite vintage champagne reminded Leon of eating crab claws at the end of the Lake Pontchartrain pier. He wanted to be alone with the aroma of spent shellfish. But even though it was rapidly approaching midnight, he was still on the job. These receptions were as important to the fundraising as anything else. The jewelry hanging from those drunken necks and puffy earlobes could pay for a season and a half. Besides, without Edith Campbell, there would be no funds at all — no concert hall, for that matter.

"Maestro! Congratulations! A spectacular finale to our greatest season." It was the chairman of the symphony board. Leon reluctantly turned to his boss.

"Thanks BoBo, I thought the *scherzo* was sloppy," Leon said.

"Oh yeah, maybe, but you'll fix it in tomorrow's matinee." This remark constituted pressure from Robert Delmonico, known both affectionately and derisively as BoBo. Chairman Delmonico was not capable of knowing when he was insulted.

"Well, paisan," BoBo was always trying to pretend that Leon was Italian. "... we are actually going to end up in the black for the first time since '59 right before the musicians' strike. Fabulous! I don't know how we will top it next year." Not entirely incompetent ... more subtle pressure for Leon. The Chairman said this loud enough for the music critic from the *Indianapolis Star* to hear. Leon thought of '59, the year these delightful grapes were harvested. He wanted another glass of champagne.

"BoBo, darling, leave my poor husband alone." Alison's charm was an irresistible force. "Can't you see how tired he is? After all, as my Mama used to say, 'art before greed.' Honey, you need a refill and there is someone I want you to meet," Alison said, whisking him away to the bar.

While getting his refill Leon said quietly to Alison, "Four things, darling: First, you can't say that to Robert. Think of him as the hand that feeds. Second, thank you for doing that ... I love you. Third, I doubt your mother ever said that. And fourth, who did you want me to meet besides the bartender?"

"Well, I'm sure if mother was ever sober she would have said that. Come with me, Shorty."

Alison slid her arm into the crook of Leon's left elbow and walked him towards the study that was empty except for a red-headed man in a black suit. "Leon, I'd like you to meet my old friend, Thomas Flynn. Thomas was the fellow I told you about who broke his leg skiing and spent the entire World Affairs Conference, including my big party, flat on his back in my bed."

"As one of your many house guests, right?" Leon said with mock jealously.

"I assure you, sir, that aside from some very questionable political arguments, everything was above board." Thomas' Boston accent was as thick but more Irish than the President's. "Nice to meet you."

"Unfortunately, what Thomas says is true. I am sure that his good behavior was only due to his incapacitation and not his charming hostess." Alison winked. "Now, besides your short stature, the two of you have something else in common. Why don't you talk, and I will go make sure BoBo isn't bothering Edith."

With fondness and frustration Leon watched Alison go away. He knew he was being set up. He had no clue what it was about, but suspected that it was in his interest. He thought it was about work, from which he definitely needed a vacation ... soon. He was also pretty sure that Thomas knew what was going on and was part of the setup. This guy's reputation preceded him. Thomas was a long-time friend of the Kennedys and an assistant to Adlai Stevenson, the U.S. delegate to the United Nations. Alison had been at it again. Leon wanted to know what was up.

"So, how did you like the concert, Thomas?" the maestro asked.

"It was marvelous. I particularly liked the Stravinsky. However, I must admit I tuned out during the *scherzo*."

"Alison told you to say that."

"No," he said.

Leon paused and stared at Thomas. "You know what this is about, don't you?" he asked.

"Yes, I do."

Leon waited him out.

"Maestro, what I am going to tell you is extremely confidential."

"You're making me nervous."

"Good, because you should be. You are about to receive a great opportunity. And as with all great opportunities, there are problems."

"You mean problems for me?"

"Yes."

"And Alison?"

"Maybe."

"And your main job, if I am not mistaken, is solving problems."

"In a manner of speaking." Thomas stopped looking at Leon in the eye.

"I take it you are not solving my problem, but rather using me to solve someone else's."

"You are correct, sir," Thomas said.

"Better tell me quick then, and don't call me sir."

"Very well. Two months ago, I had a meeting with Jack and Ambassador Dobrynin."

"Jack Kennedy?" asked Leon.

"Yes."

"I didn't think that we were speaking with the Russians."

"Now is not a good time to ask questions. By the way, they are Soviets, not Russians."

"Oh, sorry, go on."

"I will. We, and some friends at the Kremlin, are arranging a U.S. tour for Khazar. This tour is scheduled to begin next December as we kick off the re-election campaign."

"You are using a member of the Communist party to kick off the election campaign for the president of the United States?" Leon saw Thomas wince. "Sorry again. No more questions, I promise." Leon's eyes were starting to light up.

"We would like the tour to premiere with the Indianapolis Symphony."

Leon no longer needed a vacation. Vladimir Khazar, one of the world's premier piano soloists and winner of last year's Tchaikovsky competition, was going to have his American debut with the Indianapolis Symphony. This was exactly what Leon needed, the "step up" from last season. The "break" that could move him from being the "most underrated conductor" to the same level as Ormandy and Bernstein.

"This is fantastic, Thomas! He is truly a great artist. The concert will be an international event, the likes of which Indiana has never seen." Leon looked at Thomas, who was staring silently. He could see the other shoe was about to drop. He waited for the fall.

"Now we are getting to the sticky part," Thomas said. Leon's face transformed from elation to worry. "Vladimir is a friend of mine. Three months ago, I was in Munich and he was coincidentally at the State Opera House for a Chopin recital. We met briefly and privately in the hall after the morning rehearsal." Leon looked away as Flynn finished the explanation.

"It seems he wants to defect."

Hugh came into the study. "Maestro, you had better come back into the living room. They are about to do the unveiling." Leon did not respond.

"Come on, Leon, let's go see," Thomas said. "We'll talk about this much more in the coming months." All three walked to the living room with Thomas lagging behind.

"What the hell was that all about?" Hugh quietly asked. Still no answer from Leon. Walking ahead into the living room, Leon stopped at the bar to get a bourbon on the rocks. Hard liquor the night before a matinee performance was an unusual break in his routine.

If there were fewer than fifty people in Edith Campbell's living room, the space seemed out of scale. It was so immense that, with the antique furnishings removed, it served as a small concert hall. Around the perimeter of the room was a narrow border of exposed parquet. The center of this space was covered by an expanse of intricate fabric that cushioned both sole and soul. It was undoubtedly the largest Oriental rug most people had ever seen. To step onto the rug was a transition into opulence. Drinks were frequently held with two hands. Anyone who knew anything about antiques didn't risk sitting down in the carved wooden chairs. On the walls and at the ends of couches, museum-quality paintings and sculpture were on display. Hanging beside the entryway in a simple ebony frame was a little-known Picasso depicting romance in a kitchen.

The largest antique was at the end of the room. Built of solid rosewood in 1855, the Chickering concert grand piano was blessed with a shimmering, rich sound. Its ornate scrollwork was equally engrossing when the instrument was silent. Leon was not bothered by the fact that this piano cost more than the combined salaries of his first chairs, but he always looked the other way when guests rested their drinks or ashtrays on the instrument. Tonight, the piano was a pedestal for the clay busts, still hidden under their shrouds.

The unveiling was a combination of review and ritual. Undoubtedly, all responses would be favorable; the trick would be to sort out the cloying flattery from the honest critiques. There were only a handful of opinions that mattered to Alison, and truthfully, the only vote that counted was Edith's. She was pretty hard to read. She had one smile that included nearly all of her responses from, 'I really like that' to 'Tomorrow, I'm going to fire that son of a bitch.' She was elegantly ruthless. Her appreciation of art was knowledgeable and sincere.

The bumbling board president presided as master of ceremonies. "Ladies and gentlemen, may I have your attention, please?" He was ignored even though the guests were gathering. Once again, "Your attention, please, for the unveiling." The chatter continued until interrupted by a loud whistle that happened to be a concert A.

"Thanks, Hugh," acknowledged the chairman. Realizing the source of the whistle, the musicians laughed at their private joke. BoBo continued, "Tonight, we are privileged to be pleasured, er, I mean we have the pleasure and the privilege of being the first to see the most recent commercial, I mean, commissioned works of the Campbell Foundation." Now let's see, how shall we do this? Both at once or one at time?"

"Ladies first, BoBo," prompted a voice from the audience.

"Right, good idea." The chairman turned to the smaller head and with all his heart, hoped it was Edith's. Slowly, he lifted the cloth until he knew he had the right one, and then removed its cover with a flourish. As everyone cheered and clapped, Alison turned to Edith, watching intently for the all-purpose smile to appear. On the time-to-smile gauge, quicker was definitely better. Within the time it takes to play a quarter-note, Edith's face matched the expression of the applause. Alison unclenched her jaw and let her breath escape. You can't beat that, she thought. Alison's relief was total. She knew that Leon's bust was as good as Edith's — better, really. In any case, it didn't matter. The only one Edith would care about was her own. Alison got a friendly elbow in the ribs from Maria. "She likes it. Nice work, girl," Maria whispered.

"And now, for our fearless leader." Leon took another belt of his bourbon as BoBo whipped off the second cover. The obligatory applause and cheers ensued, but all that Alison noticed was the stunned silence surrounding her. Jason stood motionless, staring. Maria's mouth fell open. Worst of all, Edith looked lifeless, as if the head on her shoulders had been replaced by the clay model on the piano. It was a disaster, Alison thought.

Hugh broke the spell. "Where's the gorilla?"

Jason moved closer to the head. He reached out his hand to touch the bust. He turned to Alison. "This is the man who was on the podium tonight. You have really captured something here." Finally, Jason smiled. Alison was bowled over. She valued Jason's opinion tremendously. She never expected to get a personal review from him, much less a positive one.

"Maria helped me a great deal, you know," Alison said.

"Not with this, honey," Maria said. "This is much more than you showed me in your studio. It's spooky, as if he is on the verge of raising his hands to start a symphony."

"What hands?" Hugh asked.

"Shut up, Hugh," Maria said.

Edith inspected the piece like a jeweler. When she finished, she walked over and hugged Alison. "Simply marvelous, my dear. You have been underpaid. Would you be interested in more work?"

It is difficult to say thank you audibly when one is smiling so much, but Alison managed. Despite the free-flowing liquor, many of the guests perceived that something special was going on. They took their turns viewing the sculptures and mobbing Alison with questions.

Jason came over to the conductor who was definitely more alone than his likeness. "Must feel kind of strange," Jason said.

"Yes, it does, very strange indeed. It's funny, I don't think I see what everyone else sees in that head, but what I do see feels like home," Leon mused, and then changed the subject. "By the way, I have been meaning to ask you a question all week, but I was scared to."

"And what would that be?"

"I wanted to ask you why you gave me that score. But I was afraid you would say that you wanted to perform it."

"No fucking way. I can't take on that beast. Maybe when I was younger."

"Yeah, that's just what I was thinking," agreed Leon with a knowing smile for his friend. "It's the wrong question. The question should have been, 'Who gave you that score?'" Leon looked directly at Jason.

"A remarkable young pianist who lives in Moscow."

"Thought so," Leon said. "Thank you very much, Jason."

"Don't mention it." After a comfortable silence, Jason asked, "When's the last time you played the fiddle?"

"It has been too long." Leon grinned.

Jason and Leon proceeded to take over the piano area and started to play *Brahms Hungarian Dances*. Mrs. Campbell's reception was turning out to be one of the great parties of the year. Maria and Hugh headed to the bar. With two large snifters of warmed French cognac, they shared a pink Louis XV chaise.

"When was the last time you saw the conductor play the violin?" Maria asked.

"How about never," Hugh answered.

— 5 —

APRIL 4 THURSDAY

The Audition – Maestro's Study

Music: Puccini, Un Bel Di Vedremo, from Madame Butterfly

Leon preferred to conduct his auditions at home. His concert hall office was cramped. There were too many interruptions. And, if the musician didn't pass, better that they not develop an attachment to the grandeur of the hall or any orchestral personnel that happened to be around. Even though Micaela's credentials were spectacular, the audition was not just a formality. The conductor had a complex relationship with the members of his orchestra, more so with the first chairs. These were his captains. They needed to lead their sections. To do that, they needed to earn the respect of their own players, of all the other sections, and the conductor. He needed to hear Micaela play, he needed to see how she presented herself, answered questions, gave opinions, and, most of all, how they got along.

He never did get along well with Sarazin. The cellist was moving to Cleveland because of the symphony, the money, and ambition. Sarazin wanted to be a soloist, not just the principal cello in a better-than-average orchestra. He made all this perfectly clear, and Leon was only too happy to see him go.

He thought Sarazin was overrated and would never make it as a soloist. He regretted trusting Sarazin's credentials over his own instincts during that audition. Leon wasn't going to make the same mistake again. The orchestra was his instrument. He took care of it as if it were the last remaining Stradivarius.

This care was the magic he brought to the orchestras with which he performed. He was not a dictator by decree only, as were so many of his contemporaries. His power came from his complete attention to his players and the understanding that they were the medium from which the music came forth. When he had been invited to guest conduct *Also Sprach Zarathustra* with the famed Berlin Philharmonic, former home to such unparalleled conductors as Bülow, Nikisch, and Karajan, he was not intimidated. At his first rehearsal, he told the orchestra, "Guten Tag, I have *not* come here to conduct this orchestra. I have come here to play Strauss. Join me, bitte." From the first downbeat of that rehearsal to the standing ovation at the end of the performance, the orchestra behaved as if Johann himself were on the podium.

Whispers of that week traveled through the musicians' grapevine further than Leon, or his agent, ever knew, as far as Moscow and Prague. Those whispers and the performance at Carnegie were the reasons Micaela was here today. She had heard, "He doesn't conduct you … he plays you, and you'll feel better for it." She had seen him perform. Now, she wanted to play for him.

Micaela was born and raised ten kilometers north of Prague in the town of Klecany on the Vltava river. Until she was thirteen years old, she took her lessons there. Frequently, she was given passes to hear the Czech Philharmonic. At thirteen, she was admitted to the conservatory at Prague and studied there until she was a member of the Philharmonic. Her parents subsequently moved to Bratislava on the Danube. She became first chair within three years at the age of twenty-two, but her blazing advancement would go no further under the communist-controlled art scene in Czechoslovakia. She longed for more experience, a wider selection of material, not necessarily the same exposure that a soloist would get, although she wouldn't mind that. Her desire to move on was borne out of curiosity, not ambition. She wrote frequently to her parents of her frustration. They arranged for her defection.

They had rebellious friends in Bratislava, and the Philharmonic was traveling there for guest performances in the spring. Her parents came to watch the first evening performance and afterwards took her out, ostensibly to celebrate. They brought her clothes, food, and money. They told her she could be smuggled on a boat upriver to Vienna. But, she would have to decide to go right then, leaving her parents and cello behind. Realizing that this might be her only chance, and deeply moved by the trouble her parents had gone through to make this happen, she said yes, barely able to see for the tears. She made the short trip across the border without incident and was in Vienna before dawn.

Within forty-eight hours the Soviet KGB arrested her parents. Deciding to make an example to prevent further defections, the KGB executed them before the end of the week. The depth of Micaela's depression upon hearing the news might have been terminal had it not been for the support of the musical community in Vienna. She was able to borrow a cello and was given a seat in the Vienna Symphony Orchestra immediately. Within two years, she moved up to second chair and made an impression on many visiting conductors and soloists, including Jason Foster. He heard some of her story and wrote to Maria in New York:

Darling,

I have just met the most amazing cellist in Vienna. She is from Prague and defected a few years back. Her defection, I hear, brought about the demise of her parents. She plays beautifully on a borrowed and inferior instrument. She can afford no more. Yes, she is beautiful, too, which is why I am writing this letter right away to assuage you from any mistaken jealousy as I plan to help improve her position. I hope she can be our guest in New York next year, and perhaps attend Leon's concert at Carnegie with us.

With Maria's approval, Micaela was able to make the trip to New York. The added bonus of hearing Zellingari in concert was fulfilling beyond her imagination. She knew immediately that she wanted to work in America.

Except for the last part, Micaela repeated this whole story to Leon when he had simply asked her to recite her credentials. Leon didn't pay attention to resumes; he found them lacking in scope and complexity. He always wanted to hear someone's story from start to finish without abbreviations or omissions. He felt the same way about the music he performed. Program venues frequently made him compromise, but he always resisted doing just the fourth movement of *Beethoven's Ninth* or just the overture to *Nozze de Figaro*.

Micaela had come in, set up the cello, and placed her music in the stand in front of her chair. She was ready to play. Instead, for thirty minutes, with arms draped over her instrument, she told her story. Now she was silent. She felt awkward. She did not intend to be so forthcoming. This was supposed to be a musical audition. She wasn't expecting a job interview. Leon was silent, too, but not uncomfortable. He was impressed with her story, but even more so with the telling of it. He was still absorbing the performance — the sound of her accent, the intensity of her eyes, her calm body language. If he had to make the decision right now, without hearing a note, he would say yes, and he was certain of all the reasons why. He was equally certain not all the reasons would sit well with Alison. Micaela was a striking woman. Now, if her playing could match her reputation …

"I am sorry I speak so much. I have not had many auditions." Micaela's Slavic accent seem to heave with her ample breasts.

"Don't apologize. You have brought some music to play?"

"Yes," said Micaela, smiling. "I start with the Dvorak?"

Leon nodded but was disappointed. Why did cellists applying for an orchestral job always start with one of the relatively few concertos for cello? It was probably the last thing he was interested in. He wasn't looking for a soloist, but for a musician and a leader, not necessarily in that order. His preconceived distaste evaporated within seconds. First of all, she didn't select the virtuoso section but the *adagio* and was playing it slower than he had ever heard it before, hanging on to the notes as if she were physically holding them up in the air. The phrase ended exactly when she came to the end of the bow. She had a deft touch.

"Shall I go on?" Micaela asked.

"No, I'd like to hear that again," Leon directed. He wanted to measure the exactitude of repetition. She performed the section again, with no discernible difference.

"That's fine. Please go on with your other selections." For the next forty minutes, Micaela played a variety of familiar cello highlights, including virtuoso sections, with no response from Leon. At the end, she said, "That is all I brought today." Leon stood up and slowly paced across the room.

"Have you ever performed Rachmaninov's *Third Piano Concerto*?" he asked.

"Yes," she answered, pushing her eyebrows together. It was an unusual request for a cellist. Leon walked some more. He went over to the shelf beside his chair and picked up Jason's gift. He turned a few pages and placed it in Micaela's stand. She stared at the handwritten score.

"Where did you get … ?"

"A friend." Leon cut her off. "Please start three bars after letter D. I will give you the tempo." Leon gave her the downbeat for the cello passage about three minutes into the first movement. He stood above her where she could see him and the music at the same time. The handwritten notes seem to move in time with his right hand; she played on. The conductor used his left hand with fingers curled as if holding the neck of a violin to ask for more feeling. She responded. The notes on the page pulsed in front of Micaela. Leon reached over from the opposite side of the stand and turned the page. She continued to play, or someone did, she thought. Leon stopped suddenly, lifted the score from the stand and put it away. Micaela stared blankly ahead wondering what had just happened.

"Micaela, thank you. That was marvelous. How long are you staying in town?"

"Until I find out if I get position."

"Excuse me?"

"I stay until I find out if I get position," she repeated. "This is only position I apply for, the only one I want. I like to know now. Do I get position?" She looked at Leon with a desperate but determined firmness.

"Well, normally we discuss terms with your agent."

"I do not have agent."

Leon stared silently for a full minute. She was perfect.

"What do you know about me?" Leon asked.

"I know you are great conductor. In Europe, some say you are reincarnation of Nikisch. I know you are dedicated to quality and integrity of the music. It is said that you are stern but also kind."

"That's flattering but not altogether true. At least it's not that simple."

"Vhat do you mean?" she asked.

"Behind the Iron Curtain, you had propaganda and politics. On this side of the curtain, we have publicity and politics. Micaela, you are a remarkable cellist, fully capable of leading our section. But you are more than that. You are a story. And there are people inside and outside the symphony organization who would exploit that story for their own personal gain."

"Vould you be one of those people?"

"Yes. With great care and protection, but yes, I would," Leon answered.

"So you are honest as well." Micaela turned her gaze to the windows behind Leon and thought for a moment. Bringing her attention back to him, she said, "My parents give lives so I could do this. I see no reason to keep secret."

31

"You will be required to do interviews, photographs, that sort of thing," Leon warned.

"I have no experience in this."

"I will be there to help you and make sure that it doesn't distract from your job."

"So … do I need agent?"

"Next Tuesday, I am having a special meeting of the principals to discuss changes to next year's program. Would you care to join us?" Leon smiled at her with the certain knowledge that she would need an agent before long.

— 6 —

APRIL 4 THURSDAY

Turtle Soup – Zellingari Home

Music: Dvorak, Concerto for Cello and Orchestra, Op 104.

Since working for the Zellingaris, Mary had prepared dinners and luncheons
to rival the White House or cruise ships. She had never heard of most of the
dishes and didn't like a good many of them. She had accomplished delicacies
such as Bouillabaise, Beef Wellington for six (one rare, two medium rare, and
three well-done), escargot in puff pastry cups with fennel (she still couldn't
believe anybody ate those), Salmon Chaud Froid, and Poisson en Croute. Then
there were the exotic dishes like Quail Roasted in Grape Leaves with Truffles
and Lambs' Brains with Remolade. The way Mary figured it, given a good
recipe, there was a reasonably good chance that it would come out good, if you
like that sort of food.

The biggest problem she ran into besides Mrs. Zellingari's rampant
creativity was finding the ingredients. Fortunately, or unfortunately for Mary,
the necessary—sometimes very rare —ingredients were always found. Found
by Mrs. Zellingari with help from Hugh. Today's lunch was no exception.

"Mary, the maestro is auditioning Micaela Miklos this morning. We will
have to be especially quiet. Afterwards, we will serve her lunch."

"Yes, ma'am. And what will you be wanting?"

"It will be simple. Just a quiche and soup will do nicely."

33

"What kind a soup?"

"Turtle soup," Alison answered.

"Turtle soup, ma'am?"

"Yes, Mary, you must have made it in New Orleans."

"Yes ma'am, I did do dat, but I ain't got no turtle meat," Mary said.

"Oh, I forgot to show you." Alison went to the milk box by the door and picked up a cardboard box that was resting there. Inside was a two-pound turtle. "Hugh had this shipped straight from Louisiana. It's a Green Turtle; it will be just perfect."

"Ma'am, the turtle is moving."

"I should hope so. You are supposed to use fresh turtle meat, aren't you?" Alison said and left the room.

Mary looked at the turtle and said, "Your day is going to be a lot worse den mine and my day is already bad."

She trussed its hind legs over a one inch dowel rod. The rod spanned the shelves on either side of the sink so that turtle was hanging upside down. Then, she cut the head off as close the shell as possible. The flesh quivered constantly during the two hours it took to drain the turtle.

While waiting for the turtle to finish, Mary made the quiche and set the table. The swinging door from the kitchen to the dining room had a squeak. Mary opened it only far enough to slide through, stepping over the hardwood to the carpet. She placed a small towel between the door and jam before moving over to the sideboard. Because the maestro's study was near the dining room, Mary had to prepare the table in silence. It took Mary sixteen minutes to do a formal table setting. She liked it. It was like playing hide-and-seek. She removed the candelabras from the table and brought out the white lace tablecloth. Holding the two corners, she turned and threw the cloth high and down the table, watching it float down. After straightening it, she selected the spring placemats for five. The maestro would sit at the head of the table near the kitchen door. Mrs. Zellingari would be at the other end with her back to the living room. Miss Miklos would be on the conductor's right facing the French doors with the best view of the yard and gardens. The doorbell rang. It was Micaela. Mary escorted her towards the maestro's study. He met them halfway, in the living room. Mary returned to the table.

The cabinets to the sideboard opened easily and quietly. Mary selected salad plates for the quiche, butter dishes, soup plates, and chargers. The Royal Doulton china was white with blue trim. As she set them down on the placemats, she visualized the food. The soup would take center stage. A wedge of quiche would be on the upper right, the butter dish on the upper left. Recently Alison had found a butter pat mold in the shape of a treble clef. Mary decided she would place a basil leaf underneath to highlight the shape. Next came the silverware.

The silverware drawer was the trickiest. She handled the pulls gently so they would not clang. She lifted and tugged to the right to unbind the side of the drawer. It came out cleanly. She heard Micaela talking to the maestro. She couldn't make out the words, but she loved the sound. Mary turned to hear better and removed her support from the drawer. The settling drawer squeaked like a bad woodwind. Damn, she thought. Oh well, it's open.

The Italian silver setting consisted of knife, fork, butter knife, soup spoon, and coffee spoon. She laid the silver down piece by piece. The sound of a cello replaced the sound of Micaela's voice.

It was time for the wine glasses. They were in a beautiful glass cabinet with sticky doors. Holding the left door firmly with the flat of her hand she gently coaxed the right door open without a sound as Micaela played a Bach sonata. Mary smiled. Mrs. Zellingari would want her long and ultra thin stemmed wine glasses. They looked as if they had been made with Saran wrap. She brought them carefully to the table, one by one so they didn't touch. They made a beautiful tone when they did. Shoot, she almost forgot the napkins, located in one more troublesome drawer of the antique sideboard. Not distracted this time, she silently pulled open the drawer. The napkins were folded into fans and arranged at the top of the settings. Mary surveyed her work and returned the candelabras to the center. Satisfied, she placed her hand in the gap the towel made for the kitchen door and opened it just enough to slip back through to the kitchen and then eased the door closed.

While the quiche cooled, she returned to the turtle. With a sharp knife she removed the shells, carefully avoiding the gall balder. If the gall bladder was pierced, its contents would poison the turtle meat. Alison stepped into the kitchen when Mary was in the midst of this surgical procedure.

Without looking up Mary asked with a wistful and twisted grin, "Mrs. Zellingari, is Hugh coming for dee lunch?"

"No, he's not. But I will tell him you asked about him. Hugh is so fond of you." Too bad, Mary thought, she could have killed one bird with one gall bladder. After washing the rest of the entrails and the turtle meat thoroughly in cold water, she placed them in a stockpot and boiled them gently for ten minutes. Then, she tossed the entrails in the garbage while saving the water for stock. Expertly, she chopped the turtle meat into half-inch dice, along with onions and ham. In a cast iron skillet she browned the onions and turtle in lard. As if following a voodoo ritual, she gently mixed in garlic, thyme, bay leaf, cloves, and ground allspice, then, vigorously, stirred in three tablespoons of a cold roux along with two tablespoons of filet powder. Mary poured the stock in over the mixture and brought it to a boil. For one hour, she slowly stirred the soup, adjusting the seasoning with salt, pepper, and Tabasco. In the middle of this final stage, she cracked open the dining room door to mix the sounds of the solo cello with the earthy aroma that swirled in the kitchen.

— 7 —

APRIL 4 THURSDAY

Trip to Oolitic – Southern Indiana

Music: Williams, "American Collection" Theme

The taste of the exquisite soup was completely submerged by the distractions permeating Alison's attention. It was getting close to 1:30 in the afternoon. Alison had forgotten to tell anyone that Jed was picking her up after lunch to drive down to the quarries in Lawrence County. Both Mary and Leon would frown at this oversight. Mary would just be her cantankerous self, but Leon would be particularly upset because the late lunch would mean a premature meeting of a new member of the orchestra, a principal no less, with one of the second section minions.

Alison always sat at the end of the table that gave her a view through the hallway to the front door. She now divided that view with her wristwatch and the irritatingly beautiful Micaela Miklos. The innuendos of her beauty had been severely understated. Although poorly dressed in a loose gray skirt and pale blouse slightly frayed at the cuffs, Micaela had a vast array of fortunate female features that would no doubt have a dizzying effect on most of the male members of the orchestra. During the concerts, dressed in her formal black gown, long legs draped around the cello and black hair cascading down her back, she would be a public sensation.

Jed drove his freshly washed Oldsmobile station wagon up the driveway to the front door of the Zellingari house and stopped. The house and grounds were impressive but not ostentatious. He had once been invited to the

37

maestro's previous house before the marriage to Alison. Things had definitely improved for his boss since then: pretty wife, more money, better contract, flashy gigs in New York and Berlin. Jed was six feet tall, blue eyes, sandy blond hair, and lean. He was attractive even though his eyes were close together. His skin was terminally pale and, no matter how much he washed, the smell of paint thinner remained with him. Aside from the principals and women with working husbands, the members of the orchestras all required second or third jobs to make ends meet. Jed's second job was as a house painter.

The entrance to the house was on the passenger side of the car. Getting out of the Olds, he walked around to the front door and rang the bell. Alison saw Mary go to the door. When Jed smiled, people were either charmed or chilled. The combination of his cheery demeanor and his close-set eyes allowed simultaneous interpretations of the sincere or sociopathic. He knew how to be charming. But he meted out those charms in a miserly fashion, as if he were protecting a limited supply. He saved them for important situations like girlfriends, girlfriends' parents, or the social events that were sometimes required of a member of the symphony orchestra. When Mary opened the door, Jed provided only the smallest of smiles for the black maid.

"May I help you?" Mary said.

"Hi, my name is Jed Norton and I have an appointment with Mrs. Zellingari." Mary was chilled. Without responding, she closed the door. It was not unusual that she did not invite him in. In all but the very worst of weather, Mary was not to allow people in that she didn't know or that she hadn't been informed were coming. It *was* unusual for her to simply shut the door in their face. Mary walked to the dining room.

"Excuse me, Mrs. Zellingari, were you expecting a Mr. Norton?" Mary interrupted the lunchtime conversation as if important and unpleasant news had arrived.

"Yes, Jed. Mary, please show him in. Leon, you remember Jed is taking me down to Bloomington today to meet his friends at the quarry to talk about limestone for the sculptures," Alison said. "What great timing. He can meet Micaela." Alison could see immediately that Leon was not pleased with this "fortunate timing," nor was he buying her attempts to get out of the musical *faux pas*. What if Micaela had not passed the audition? And even though she did, this was not the way he wanted to introduce her to the other members of the orchestra. First, she should meet with the other principals, then her section, and finally the orchestra at large. To begin with a "member of the section," a rather average viola player, and a troubling one at that, disrupted his plan.

His orchestra was a complex stew of tradition, hierarchy, politics, and aspirations. What he did on the podium was only half the challenge. Alison's connection with Hugh was not threatening because she developed it long after Leon had become Hugh's maestro. But Micaela had only just become a member of this musical mélange. Alison had meddled inside her husband's domain.

Mary opened the door and gestured for Jed to come in. "Please follow me," she said stiffly. Mary led Jed to the dining room, and Alison got up to greet him. "Hi Jed, so good of you to come. We are just finishing. Would you like to have some coffee with us?" Alison asked.

"That would be great, thank you." Jed's stretched his face into a smile that even the father of a daughter could love.

"Mary, would you bring coffee for Mr. Norton?" Mary replied with a nod and grumbled her way into the kitchen.

Leon took over Alison's introductions. "Jed, I would like you to meet the newest member of our orchestral family, Micaela Miklos, who will be replacing Sarazin next season."

Jed had heard about Micaela. Everyone had. They had heard about her talent, her beauty, snippets of the story of her escape. Everyone was quietly rooting for her audition, hoping they would get a chance to meet her, hear her play, and play with her. Somewhere deep inside of him, Jed drew in an invisible breath. He was startled not by her beauty, but by her look. Not her looking at him, but the look of her. Like an impressionist painting, it didn't matter whether you were near or far, there was so much to see, to devour. Her look was as rich with experience as it was with beauty. It was a look you could enjoy staring at all day. He realized in that single beat of time that if he had to watch her play without hearing a note, it would be extremely satisfying. He bent slightly to shake her hand.

"Very pleased to meet you. There was a rumor going around that you might join us. A happy rumor at that," Jed said.

"Jed plays in the viola section and is an Indiana native. He is here today to introduce Alison to the quarries down south. Alison intends to cast my old face in limestone, that is, a sculpture of my face," Leon said. "She is also working on a bust of our major benefactor."

Mary returned with the coffee. They served French Market coffee from New Orleans at the Zellingaris'. The added chicory gave off a distinctive aroma that Mary was counting on to disguise the rather large amounts of Tabasco and salt that she had added to Jed's cup. Leon gestured for Jed to sit. He responded to his director immediately.

"So … you are musician *and* tour guide?" Micaela asked. Alison was sure that Micaela had tweaked up her Slavic accent just a bit, a flirting technique that Alison was very familiar with. Leon and Mary were not the only ones surprised today. Clearly Jed did not plan to be having coffee at the maestro's house nor to be chatting with the new principal cellist, whose feminine wiles seemed to be directly focused on him. He thought he was just being asked to show the conductor's wife some holes in the ground. He shamelessly enjoyed Micaela's incapacitating gaze. She laughed at his apparent stupor.

"Perhaps, you try your coffee?" she smiled. Her smile, which contained the comic and tragic masks simultaneously, did nothing to help Jed's bewitched state. However, he was able to hypnotically pick up the coffee and drink as directed.

The doctored coffee transported Jed to a different kind of distress. His soulful gaze was replaced with a puckered mouth, bulging eyes, and an unintelligible request for help. Alison called for Mary to bring bread. "Sorry, ma'am, all out of bread, how about some nice iced tea?" Jed nodded with desperate silence as the capsicum salt mixture seared his mouth. Mary quickly provided a fresh glass as if she had anticipated the situation, which she had. Earlier in the week, Hugh had delivered some rare Japanese horseradish. He called it wasabi and said it was to be used with raw fish. "Ma'am, who eats raw fish?" Mary asked. "Why, the Japanese do." Alison replied to Mary's contorted face. After delivering the coffee to Jed, Mary decided to try out the ghastly green condiment and dissolved a heaping tablespoon in his soon to be requested iced tea. The tea was a little cloudy but she doubted Jed would notice. When she returned with the glass, Jed quickly grabbed for the tea and drained the glass with great relief. The cool refreshing beverage put out the fire in his mouth. As he enjoyed the relief, he became dimly aware that the tea tasted … well … foreign. This awareness was obliterated by the fumes of the horseradish rushing to his nasal passage and back of the throat. His entire respiratory system was being reamed by a vegetal brushfire. The contents of his sinuses were about to leak out of his eyeballs. Except for a slight wandering of his head, Jed's body was frozen in place as if any sudden movement would break the containment field of his skin. He was possessed by involuntary pathetic gasping.

The anxiety spread from Jed to everyone else in the room except Mary, who was simply impressed with the effects of the wasabi. Micaela was particularly attentive and concerned as she provided napkins to soak up the moisture exuding from Jed's head. It was doubtful that he could have enjoyed the soothing Slavic cooing from the blur of his anaphylacticly impaired senses. As the anxiety increased, the effects began to wear off and soon Jed, along with everyone else in the room, began to calm. Mary mercifully brought clear cool water, which Jed smelled before drinking.

"It must have been an allergic reaction," Alison said, embarrassed.

"I don't have any allergies," Jed said with disdain.

"You do now," Mary mumbled on her way back into the kitchen.

"Are you okay?" Micaela asked with sincere concern and a doe-like gaze that Jed took in with a deep breath through his newly cleansed sinuses.

"Yes, I'll be fine." Jed smiled warmly as he easily slid back into his earlier amorous reverie.

"I am relieved," Leon said. "When were you planning to depart for the quarries?"

"We should go now," Jed was slow to reply while still looking at Micaela. "The forecast is rain, Mrs. Zellingari."

"I'll get my coat and the bust, but first I have to speak with Mary," Alison said. Jed rose and said goodbye to Micaela and the maestro. Alison went into the kitchen where Mary was cleaning dishes. She started to confront Mary but noticed the freshly baked bread on the cooling rack. Mary turned and saw her boss looking at the bread. "I thought it would be too hot to serve it to him," she said, staring Alison directly in the eye. Alison started to speak, but was halted by the stare. She looked away and left the kitchen by the door near the coat closet. As she left, Mary said, "Ma'am, you best be careful wid dat mon."

The driveway was one lane and Jed's station wagon was temporarily blocked by a US Mail truck. The postman was coming up the steps with a delivery. Jed was at the door waiting when Alison arrived, carrying a large rectangular box with Leon's head inside.

"Jed, would you mind signing for it, while I put on my coat?" Alison asked. Jed signed and the postman handed over a brown package tied with string. It was addressed to

חַצֶגְנ Zellingari.

The shipper's address was in Cyrillic, but Jed recognized the characters, CCCP. The hammer and sickle stamps were unmistakable.

"Thank you," said Alison as she took the package. "Could you put the bust in the car? I will give this to Leon, and we will be on our way." The postal truck was backing out now, so Jed got in the station wagon and waited for Alison. She came back shortly. Jed started the car and backed down the driveway just as it began to drizzle. He was silently preoccupied.

Alison, still embarrassed about the coffee incident, was not comfortable with the silence and began to chatter aimlessly about the sample sculpture, dimly aware that no one was listening. Eventually, she looked over at Jed. "I'm so sorry about the coffee. I don't understand what happened."

"I don't think your maid likes me," he said.

"Mary? That's crazy, she doesn't even know you. Are you sure you're okay?"

"Actually, I'm fine. I don't remember when my sinuses have been this clear. Maybe I will start putting paint thinner in my iced tea." He grinned and glanced at Alison. It was a gracious reply and Alison was charmed. They traveled Highway 37 south of the city, and the drizzle turned to a downpour.

"Have you lived in Indiana all your life?" Alison asked.

"Yep, born and bred Hoosier. Rarely been out of the state. Went to Chicago a few times, Florida on spring break, and took a vacation once to Disneyland. I suppose if the music school wasn't so good in Bloomington, Mom would have shipped me off to some music college out east. I did spend a summer in Aspen once, under the maestro. But I believe that was before you met him."

"How come you didn't go back?"

"I wasn't invited," he deadpanned.

"Oh," Alison said quietly. She felt like an idiot for asking the question. How many times was she going to embarrass herself in front of Jed today?

He waited two beats and started to laugh, "Don't worry, Mrs. Zellingari, I was just teasing. I told the maestro that I couldn't afford it. I couldn't make enough money out there to support the expense of the trip. It's better to paint houses in the summer." The Indiana drawl was familiar and so was his sense of humor.

"Please, call me Alison."

"Well," he paused, "Alison," and after another long pause "at least outside Campbell Hall and your house." There was something enormously clever about this man, she thought, both appealing and unnerving. She remembered that even Hugh called her Mrs. Zellingari at the concert hall.

"You're right, that would be better," she agreed. "So, where exactly are we going today?"

"My hometown. Ohhhlitic, Indiana. Limestone capital of world," Jed said as if he were head of the Oolitic chamber of the commerce.

"You don't say." Alison giggled.

"I do say. And so will everyone else say when we get down there. In fact, some Ohhhlitics might say it to you more than once." Jed laughed and Alison joined in.

"I take it you don't miss your hometown?" she asked.

"No. Yes. Aww, I don't know. Moving north from southern Indiana is kind of an evolutionary journey. I visit from time to time. I left after high school and everyone else stayed. A bunch of my high school buddies always come up for the 500, and we get together in the infield for old times sake. In fact, you are going to meet two of them today."

"Really?"

"Yep, Lou and Gar."

"Gar?" Alison smiled.

"Garth is real name." Jed laughed, "... but Gar fits him much better. Anyhow, Lou and Gar worked the quarries during the summer and after high school they started their own business, F & W Limestone — Lou Flesher and Garth Watkins. It's a relatively small limestone company. They do some architecture, but lately they have been specializing in artwork. They hired away some of the better carvers from Victor and Indiana Limestone, regular artistes del gesso. Apparently those companies don't do enough ornate work to keep a good carver interested. Lou and Gar are surprisingly successful."

"Why surprising?"

Jed laughed. "Tell you what. Why don't you ask me that on the way back?"

Music: Meyer, 1B, from Appalachian Journey

They were south of Bloomington. Alison and Jed had been trading stories about college. Jed went to Indiana University because of the music school and Alison had gone to Colorado University for the mountains and skiing. Jed said that when he moved from Oolitic to the dorm in Bloomington, it was as if he had been transported to another planet that was only twenty minutes away. Alison had become interested in the arts and started staying in Aspen during the summer. As they compared their paths to Indianapolis, the rain abated, revealing the lushness of an Indiana spring. Jed turned off of the highway and headed down a side road. The quarry entrance was visible a half mile away on the left. The gate was bracketed by two large Teutonic-styled eagle heads with F & W embossed below on the pedestals. As they passed through, the sun came out. The office was another quarter mile from the entrance. Jed parked in the visitor's space.

The reception area was tiled with polished limestone. In the waiting area, the chairs were not cheap but tasteless nevertheless. On the walls were photographs of the plant operations and maps of the quarry grounds. The grounds covered five hundred acres, the sign said. There were also pictures of buildings and sculptures done by F & W. Jed and Alison approached the receptionist. On her light-blue formica counter was a paperweight-sized limestone gargoyle.

"Hi, Jed Norton and Mrs. Zellingari to see Gar and Lou."

"Mr. Flesher is at the querries, but I believe Mr. Watkins is expecting you. Just a moment." The receptionist buzzed Gar's office. "Mr. Watkins, Jed Norton and Mrs. Zellenyari …" she said stumbling on Alison's name.

"Zellingari." Jed helped.

"Zellingari to see you, sir," she finished. The receptionist looked up and said, "He'll be right out." Alison was inspecting the gargoyle just as Garth Watkins came blustering in. She jerked at the resemblance. Gar's small head and large ears seemed to be attached to the rest of his body by a military style collar with a snap under the thin black tie. The existence of a neck was only implied. He was wearing black pants and a white short-sleeved shirt. He had two waists. One was located where his belt was buckled. The actual location was concealed by the second waist, where the buttons on his shirt stressed to the point of popping. Neither his height nor his nose had grown with the rest of his body since high school. With gapped-tooth grin and a powerful handshake, he welcomed Jed.

"Hey, Jed, glad you finally made it. We were getting worried. Did the weather slow you down?"

"Hmm, yeah. Gar, this is Mrs. Zellingari. Alison, meet Garth Watkins, part owner of F & W Limestone, better known as Gar."

"Pleased to meet you, ma'am." Looking at the ground, Gar squeezed Alison's hand, trying to be gentler than with his buddy. Alison tried not to wince with pain and nodded her head. "Mrs. Zeelin…"

"Call me Alison."

"Thank you," Gar said, relieved, but not enough to look her in the eye. "Alison, welcome to Ohhlitic, limestone capital of the world."

"Is it really?" Alison smiled.

"Why, yes, it is, ma'am. Did you know that 2.7 million cubic feet of Indiana limestone is querried every year?"

"No, I never knew that."

"That's right." Gar continued, "And did you know that Indiana limestone can be querried and milled with greater efficiency, in terms of energy consumed, than most competing building materials?"

"Gar ...," Jed was trying stop him, but Alison was enjoying the pitch.

"I had no idea." Alison's charm prompted him for more.

"Absolutely." Gar was getting worked up now. "In fact, the Empire State Building, right there in New York City, is made out of Indiana limestone."

"Well, I'll be darned. Your limestone?"

"No, no, no. That was before we came on the scene. Actually, we specialize in smaller projects, county courthouses and the like."

"And art," Jed said.

"Yeah, yeah, art. And that's why you're here, isn't it?" Gar said, as if he'd just remembered where he was. Alison couldn't tell how much of this country bumpkin act was real, but she didn't care. It reminded her of times long ago in Lousiana.

"Hey, college boy, how ya doin?" Lou had just come in covered in quarry dust and mud. He wore a short-sleeved T-shirt and jeans. He was extremely fit, taller than Jed, and had the long biceps of a basketball player. He had almost made the sectionals for the Oolitic Bearcats. Where Gar's smile was twisted, Lou's was handsome and infectious.

"Lou! Whatcha been doin', mudwrestling?" Jed said.

"Nope, we thought we lost another hole to the floods. It's been really bad this year. None of the farmers have been able to plant along the bottoms. Did you see all the bean blossoms coming down?" Lou was shaking his friend's hand firmly.

"Lou, meet your new client, Mrs. Zellingari."

"Call me Alison, please."

"Pleased to meet you, ma'am. My name is Lou Flesher. Is this your first time to Ohhlitic?"

"Yes, it is."

"Well, welcome to the limestone capital of the world."

"Thank you," Alison said, stifling the laugh. "I thought it was Oolitic? Gar and Lou grinned at Jed.

"It is," explained Jed. "Oolitic comes from the Greek word oolite, meaning eggs and stone. Limestone is a sedimentary rock composed of minerals, along with the small shells and eggs left behind when this area was covered by an inland sea." Gar and Lou looked at Jed as if this were the first time they had heard the definition. It very well could have been.

"But around here, they say Ohlitic. Down in Bedford, they say Ohhhhlitic.

"Mrs. Zeel ... I mean Alison here wants us to do some art for her," Gar said.

"Yeah, I know," Lou said without looking at his partner. "Did you bring the bust down with you?"

"It's in the car," Jed answered.

"Then, let's drive over to the foundry. Gar, why don't you ride with Jed, and Alison can come in my truck," Lou directed. When Gar and Jed got in the car, Gar asked, "Ya doin' your boss's wife, Jed?"

"Shut up."

"'Cause you know it's not smart to do the boss's wife. Not that I would blame you. She's kinda cute. But it ain't smart."

"Shut the fuck up."

"She seems right friendly to you. I bet if you wanted to do her, she'd let ya." The drive to foundry was short. Jed got out holding the box with Leon's head in it. They walked to the side of the foundry building, stepping on limestone bricks to stay out of the mud. There were works in progress, finished works, and mistakes — abstract sculptures, wildlife, historical scenes, heads, torsos, all done with extraordinary detail and craftsmanship. Alison was frankly surprised by the graceful forms that had been achieved with the limestone medium. Originally, she had envisioned the busts in something more traditional, like marble, but Edith had insisted that it be Indiana limestone, and it looked like that might be a good choice.

"These are beautiful," she said, to no one in particular.

"Yeah, we nicked some pretty good cutters from the big boys," Lou said.

"Here, take a look at this one," Gar was pointing out a bust of an elderly gentleman. It was an uninteresting head, but extremely well done. The initials RW were stamped on the unfinished base. "We did this for some friends in Washington."

"Who is it?" Alison asked. Lou and Gar looked at each other for moment.

"It's their grandfather," Lou said. "I think John Welton's his name. Never met him actually. They sent us a model, just like yours."

"Who's RW, then?" Alison asked.

"RW?" Lou echoed.

"Yeah, the initials on the base."

"Oh, yeah, well, that's, uh, … the client. Robert Welton, his son." Lou said as Gar's shoulder protrusion nodded in agreement.

"Let's see what you brought," Lou said to Alison. Gar opened the box and took out Leon's head. He placed it on the bench next to Welton. Welton's head with its strict Aryan features presented a striking contrast with the Sephardic Jew. They discussed the process of turning Leon's head into limestone and how long it would take. Alison explained that she had another head, roughly the same size, and would bring it down when she came back to review the casting. Fees and schedules were arranged, and soon it was time for Jed and Alison to leave.

Once past the city limits, they drove by a John Birch Society billboard that said "Impeach Earl Warren." Alison had an astute and well-connected interest in politics. Her father had trained her young. He had made quite a bit of money in Louisiana oil and gas. He had discovered that it was useful to have friends in office. He contributed to both the Republicans and the Democrats. He leaned to the right and his daughter to the left, which provided enjoyable political debates between the two of them. Alison's dad convinced her that she could always learn more by asking questions and carefully listening than by talking too much. Alison's mother thought it was unbecoming for women to talk politics. Over the years, Alison inherited her father's extensive connections as well as his skill at subtle inquisition. She knew a lot about Earl Warren. Not only was she a personal friend of Justice Byron White, but she fondly remembered the delight on Thomas Flynn's face when he delivered an analysis of the benefits of Earl Warren for liberal issues.

Earl Warren had been a dogged, crime-fighting district attorney for Alameda County, California, which included Oakland and Berkeley. He had tried hundreds of cases, from murder to window-breaking, and despite his reputation for using melodramtic courtroom tactics, he had never had a case overturned by a higher court. He had been the Republican governor for three successive terms. Eisenhower wanted a strong conservative leader on the court. Because of Warren's credentials and the fact that he was liked on both sides of the congressional aisle, Eisenhower's advisers assured the president that this would be an easy nomination and a successful one for the Republican party. Their homework was terribly incomplete. Warren's bipartisan support was a result of his centrist-to-liberal views. He was so centrist that, in 1946, he ran for California governor unopposed because he won both the Republican and Democratic primaries. Warren had campaigned for universal health care, and the only election he ever lost was when he was vice presidential nominee on the Dewey ticket against Harry Truman. His performance and votes on the court had been decidedly liberal, including the ruling that racial segregation in public schools was unconstitutional. Thomas' delight in getting what amounted to being an unintended gift from the Republicans was surpassed by his extreme hatred of ultra right-wing groups, such as the John Birch Society, which were still basking in the glow of recent McCarthyism. The Supreme Court was currently deliberating over the constitutionality of school prayer, so the JBS had paid for numerous billboards, bumper stickers, and had even developed a "Warren Impeachment Kit." Now seemed like a good time to verify Alison's preconceptions about Jed's political leanings.

"Don't you think it's odd that the Birch Society has it in for the Chief Justice?" Alison asked. "After all, he was a Republican governor appointed by Eisenhower."

"Not really," Jed said, suddenly alert. "The man has all but replaced the phrase 'One nation under God' with 'One nation under the Supreme Court'."

That was easy, thought Alison. Clearly this second fiddle house painter had some strong political opinions. She ventured further, "You mean their interference with our public schools?"

"Yes, exactly! What right does he have to interfere with our neighborhood schools? To force integration when there is no need? Pretty soon they will be bussing white kids to Crispus Attucks High School, and they won't even be allowed to pray for their lives."

The Court hadn't ruled on school prayer yet. In February, they had heard arguments from the nation's most famous atheist, Madalyn Murray (O'Hair), protesting prayer in school. Alison decided it wouldn't be a good idea to bring that up now. After waiting for Jed's last comment to settle in the car, she changed the subject.

"So, it seems that Gar is short for more than Garth."

"Yeah, he was called all sorts of things. Gargoyle, Girth, Gargantuan," Jed said.

"Must have been rough."

"He didn't seem to mind."

— 8 —

APRIL 4 THURSDAY

The Package – Maestro's Study

Music: Tchaikovsky: Elegy

Leon looked at the first line of the address,

חתן צֶ גּ Zellingari.

The last time he had seen his name like that it was literally "in lights" on the marquee when he conducted the National Symphony in Israel. Then he looked at the return address. He read the Russian Cyrillic and knew that the three-foot box was from Khazar. Profoundly curious, he hastily cut the packaging string and removed the outside paper, preserving the section with the Moscow address. The box was made of thin balsa which he easily separated by hand, revealing a black case for a viola. Leon picked up an envelope that was on the outside of the case. The envelope had been taped closed, as if it had been opened and resealed. He read the enclosed letter.

> *Maestro,*
> *If you please accept these as token of expectation of our future collaboration. ~~They~~ It has been in my family for long time and are dear to me. I am understanding you are fond of playing this instrument in past life. Please keep safe so I hope we can enjoy it together in future. --VK*

Leon opened the case. He scratched his head, surprised that Khazar was misinformed about the viola. Perhaps it was just a translation problem. Leon took the viola from its case and was again surprised. It was an unremarkable instrument; hardly worth playing, and it was heavier than it should be. He tapped the top. The sound was dull and dead. He tried looking in the F holes for a name, but it was too dark inside. He tapped the top some more. It was definitely muffled. Something was absorbing the sound. He shook the instrument. Nothing happened. He looked closely at the ribbing around the sidewall where it connected to the top. Then he looked at the same ribbing for the bottom. It did not have the same color. He found a seam and picked at it. This section of the rib started to peel away from the bottom sidewall. He could see something inside. He continued to delaminate the rib and removed it. The backside of the viola lifted off easily. Someone had put a false wall around the F holes. In the belly of the viola was a black felt bag with the Star of David sewn into it and another envelope laid on top. Leon picked up the envelope and slowly turned it over in his hand a couple of times. This envelope had only been sealed once and had the initials *LZ* on the front. He put it aside for the moment and opened the bag. Inside was a black yarmulke with silver trim. The prayer shawl, or *talit*, was white with complex black and silver embroidery surrounding the black letters of the talit prayer. The four knotted fringes, *tzitzit*, included one blue thread. It was a beautiful and elegant piece. The remaining contraband consisted of two small leather boxes with straps. Leon had had a formal but not orthodox Jewish upbringing. He had seen these boxes used before. They were called *tefilin* and contained portions of the *Torah*. Worn on arm and head by traditional Jews during worship, they were said to contain great mysticism and power. *'And thou shalt bind them for a sign upon thy hand, and they shall be for frontlets between thine eyes.'* Leon smiled as he remembered the line from Deuteronomy. Jewish mystics focused on achieving an immediate personal encounter with a *Greater Reality,* called *devakut.* Clearly, there was another devoted side to this great pianist. He opened the envelope and read the letter.

> *Maestro,*
>
> *It is difficult for us to communicate without censorship in the Soviet Union. I sincerely apologize if this instrument of faith has posed any problem for you. By the same token, I hope that this package has arrived safely and without trouble into your hands, as its contents are dear to me. They were gifts from my grandparents for my Bar Mitzvah.*
>
> *I have looked forward to our upcoming meeting for so long and so many reasons. The opportunity to play Rachmaninov with the great Zellingari is worth the trip alone. But as you know, that is not the only reason I am coming. The thought of living in a strange land, where I am free to play, think, and*

pray as I please is tremendously invigorating. Yet, I dread it as well, for I will be in exile from my homeland, part of the continual Diaspora of our people.

I am hoping that you can keep these items in a safe place until that time when we can meet freely face to face.

Shalom,

VK

Apparently, Vladimir's command of the English language was better than he would have people believe, Leon thought. He put the envelope down and looked at the accoutrements of his tribe. Carefully unfolding the talit, he draped it across his shoulders, fastening it with the talit clip. Gently, he placed the yarmulke on his head. Then he strapped one leather box to his forehead, with the straps hanging down around his neck. The other leather box went onto his left bicep, wrapping the strap around his forearm seven times and six times around his fingers. Without *Torah*, but with hands clasped in front of him, he prayed for Khazar's safe journey. As he chanted and deepened his concentration, he felt lifted and comforted by the shawl, as if he were wrapped in the wings of God.

— 9 —

APRIL 9 TUESDAY

Campbell Hall – Indianapolis

Music: Satie, Gnosienne No. 4, Nicolas Gombert (Sanctus) and Magnificat Secundi Toni ("Renaissance" for the modern hall)

Micaela took the bus to the Butler University campus. She was early for the meeting because she wanted to explore the hall. Leon had given her a tour the afternoon of her audition, but it was too short and the experience was drowned in the business of signing papers and meeting Delmonico. The chairman of the symphony was her first disappointment since she arrived. Despite his permanent grin, he seemed insincere and officious. He reminded her of so many high-placed party members in Prague, but not as bright. The bus dropped her off about a block away from the hall, where the residential neighborhood gave way to the open campus. Briefcase in hand, she crossed the street and walked leisurely towards the large rectangular blocks that comprised Campbell Hall. Framed by an easy spring day, she was struck by how modern the building was. The halls she had played in were steeped in history, and their architecture reflected it. Campbell was just a year old. It was built with the influence of Lincoln Center, as opposed to Carnegie Hall. The minimally finished limestone was barely interrupted by long inserts of glass, giving views to and from the various lobbies. The overall impression was of a building much larger than its actual size, and it reduced Micaela's significance as she vainly tried every locked entrance door. Finally, an elderly custodian came to her rescue.

"May I help you?" the custodian asked as he opened the door.

"Yes, thank you," said a relieved Micaela. "I am here for meeting of principals of orchestra."

"Ah, you must be Miss Miklos. My name is Allen. Maestro Zellingari told me to look out for you. You know, you are quite early." Allen offered a grandfatherly smile, which made it clear that he was custodian for more than the building.

"Yes. I was hoping to look around?" Micaela replied sheepishly.

"Good idea. Do you need directions?"

"No … I mean, yes. I do not know where meeting room is, but I like to go just inside … for now."

"Follow me." Allen led her through the east side of the hall lobby, unlocked two sets of doors until they were backstage. He brought her into the hall from stage left. "Please make yourself at home," he told her. "You can use those stairs to explore the seating areas. If you need anything, just call my name and I will hear you. Would you like me to come get you when it is time for the meeting?" said Allen.

"Thank you. Yes, that is wonderful. Thank you … much," Micaela was very happy to have met him.

The oversized impression of the building carried over into its interior, which appeared cavernous compared to other music halls. The stage was particularly expansive, and seemed more so because the orchestral shell had been taken down at the end of the season. Campbell was a multi-use facility, built for stage productions as well as the symphony. Some said it couldn't be done, that its diverse plan would be a compromise. Although the arguments continued after the building was finished, most were convinced that it was an unqualified success. Leon was particularly happy with it, partially because it was the best hall he had ever called his home, certainly much better than the termite-ridden Marat that the Shriners rented out. But mainly, he relished the modern acoustic science that had been applied. The hall was part of his instrument. The shell had been specifically designed to push the sound out and up to the audience. It was adaptable, suiting a chamber orchestra as well as *Beethoven's Ninth* with full chorus. Once the sound left the stage, it was gently absorbed by the floor audience, which had no center aisle for unwanted reflections or audience traffic. The side walls of barely porous limestone caressed the sound, allowing it to proceed undiminished higher and farther. Finally, at the top, were adjustable plywood acoustic planks that had been painted gold and that balanced every last audio reflection in the hall. These planks, or clouds, as they were called, assured that the hall was "live" enough so that even the softest *pianissimo* could be heard in the last row of the third balcony and the full force of the *fortississimo* could be felt.

Micaela walked slowly towards center stage. The sound of her shoes on the hardwood did not echo, but seemed uncommonly live. She rotated left, taking in the box seats, three tiers of balconies, and the overwhelming ocean of red velvet seats on the main floor, and then looked up at the gold acoustic clouds.

"To ye velki misto," she said out loud, trying to absorb the enormous space. Like her shoes, the sound of her voice was live, carried, but not echoing. Everything in America is so large, she thought, this time silently. She took the stairs that Allen showed her. A third of the way up the main floor, she entered the row and proceeded to the center seat. The view from the audience was rare but not unfamiliar. Most recently, she had been in Carnegie. And, her oldest musical memories were from the audience when she went to see the Philharmonic in Prague. Those early trips with her mother and father were how her comfort on stage had been established. Unlike many performers, Leon included, there were only a few butterflies in her stomach before concerts, no throwing up, no irritable tirades about trivial details before walking on stage. The concert hall was her playroom. She was safe and secure. Maybe a little less secure now. This was an awfully big playroom. She sat quietly, absorbing the silence and the room, remembering her first concerts in Prague, from the audience and then from the stage, then imagining the concerts to come in this hall, from this audience and then from this stage. She remembered her parents in the audience in Bratislava, and then dreamed them here to Campbell Hall.

"Mama, where's the best seat in the theatre?"

"Well, baby, the second best seat is located in the center of the main floor about a third of the way up. You can see very well, and the music has traveled far enough to blend together."

"But, Mama, where is the *best* seat in the house?"

"Oh, the *best* seat. Sorry, I thought you meant the best seat that we might possibly sit in. You see, the best seat is reserved for angels." Micaela's mother turned and pointed upwards towards the back of the hall. "If you draw an imaginary line from the top rear of the hall all the way to the back of the conductor's head and then move back along that line over the audience about fifteen meters, that is the best seat in the house — the angel's seat."

"Do angels really sit there, Mama?"

"Oh, yes, darling. They do. You can't see them, but when the music is really good you can feel their joy. And then when the music is really, really, good, it is said that the conductor sits with them."

"Miss Miklos, it is time," said Allen from center stage in a conversational voice. Micaela heard him as clearly as if he were standing in front of her. Her head had been turned straight up to the angel's seat. She wiped her face with the back of her sleeve and returned to the stage.

— 10 —

APRIL 9 TUESDAY

Meeting of the Principals – Campbell Hall Conference Room

Music: Schubert: Symphony No. 9 in C Major, D 944, Third Movement, Scherzo - Allegro Vivace

This was a special meeting for the upcoming season. Original programming had been set and promoted during the second half of the current season in order to sell tickets. But with the news about Khazar and the hiring of Micaela, it was clear that there would have to be changes. Aside from Leon, there was a minimum of six other participants: Eric Solomon, violins/violas and concertmaster; Hugh Morgan, oboes and *de facto* leader of the rest of the woodwinds; Martha Collins, first French horn, representing the rest of the brass section; Sam Kiton for the percussion; Hermann Wangler for the bass section; and now Micaela Miklos for the cellos. Other first chairs were invited but not required to come. Today, Mario Cicero, the dashing and promiscuous first flute, was in attendance. Robert Delmonico was invited but, as usual, was given the wrong time and place.

As they gathered in the tight conference room, they all made a particular effort to introduce themselves to Micaela. Her arrival was a twofold blessing: one, the musical grapevine is powerful and they had all heard of her skill; and two, they were rid of the arrogant and acerbic first cello, Sarazin.

Leon, as usual, arrived five minutes late, expecting everyone to be in their seats ready to start. Mario was tardy due to his enrapture with Micaela, but rushed to his chair as soon as the maestro came in.

"I assume you have all had the opportunity to meet our new first chair for the cellos." Everyone nodded. "Good. Micaela's timely arrival bodes well for next season. She will also be the main topic of our opening concert. But first, I want to review where we are as a symphony orchestra. Last season was the most successful season in the history of the ISO. It was the most successful in terms of ticket sales, fundraising, and critical acclaim. Because of the trip to New York, we are now being recognized around the world. Admittedly, we are still ranked below the big three in the United States and the big six worldwide, but our progress has been tremendous. The basis of that progress is the work you do. The focus, the quality, the attention to artistry, and the long hours of practice allow this to happen. For this, I thank you deeply. It will be hard to surpass last season's success, but not as hard as you might think. You see, quality breeds quality. One of the reasons Micaela is with us today is because she saw the Carnegie performance. I have received more audition requests, as you all know too well, than ever before. We have momentum, and we are going to use it. We are going to modify two of our eighteen weekend concert pairs this year. There will be two highlight events. One will be our Thanksgiving Concert featuring Rachmaninov's *Third Piano Concerto*."

"Who's the victim?" Hugh asked.

"Khazar." A low whistle and excited murmurs went around the table.

"I didn't know he was even coming to America," Eric said.

"Nobody does, Eric, and we have to keep it that way for a while."

"Where's he going to open?" Hermann asked.

"It's gotta be New York," Martha said. The table nodded but Leon did not.

"Philly?" Eric guessed, but still there was no affirmation from Leon.

"That leaves Cleveland," Hugh said. Leon shook his head. He thoroughly enjoyed the ensuing silence at the table. It was as if no one dared to confirm the fantastic news for fear of jinxing it. Finally, the perpetually dour Hermann spoke.

"Are you telling us that Vladimir Khazar, the darling of the Soviet Union, is going to start his first American tour here?" he asked, with a perceptible crack opening in his stone face. Leon nodded. The silence was replaced by giggles, chatter, and outright laughter.

"Bernstein, Ormandy, and Szell are gonna go nuts," Hugh said. "How did you pull this off?"

"There were a lot of people involved." Leon ducked the question. "Until we go public with this, it is extraordinarily important that you keep this a secret, or it could kill the whole deal. I am only telling you now so that you will not be surprised when the news comes out and so you can review your sections' work for the Rach III. The concerto is demanding on the orchestra as well as on the pianist and, needless to say, it must be done superbly." Leon scanned the table for acknowledgment and agreement. "Okay, now let's move on to the second highlight pair, which actually comes first. As you know, the soloist for those concerts is Luca Giarrizzo. This will also be Micaela's American debut. What you may not know is that both Harold and Winthrop expressed an interest in reviewing us on our home turf. Given the correct program, and the combination of Luca and Micaela, we should be able to get at least one of them to fly out here for opening night. This would be a perfect start to the season. Our reputation would pick up just where we left off at Carnegie."

"You want to showcase Micaela," Eric said.

"Yes, but not as a soloist, simply as leader of her section," Leon said, looking directly at Eric.

"And Luca's doing the Paganini for the encore?" Eric asked.

"As usual," Leon answered.

"*Don Quixote*?" Hermann suggested.

"The New York critics would like it but not *our* house on opening night. I want the house standing when the *Times* and the *New Yorker* are scribbling their final notes."

"Thank you," said Micaela, much relieved. Strauss' *Don Quixote* is a difficult and complex work that is very nearly a cello concerto. The table laughed at her relief.

"You could open with the Tchaikovsky's *Andante Cantabile*," said Hugh.

"Whatcha tryin' to do, put us out of work?" Martha pitched in. Hugh's suggestion was part of Tchaikovsky's *String Quartet No. 1*. The orchestral arrangement included only Violins I & II, Violas, and Cellos.

"No, I was just thinking of Eric and Micaela banging it out on stage front." The male chortling around the table amplified Hugh's intentional but unfortunate phrasing.

"Poorly put, but I tend to agree. What do you think?" Leon looked at Eric and Micaela for confirmation. They both nodded easily.

"It will undoubtedly confirm the strength of our string section. May we ramp it up a bit?" Eric asked Leon.

"Yeah, push the crescendos and we will not be doing the Bernstein tempo, it pours like ketchup. I want the whole thing out of the bottle in under seven minutes. Micaela, you'd better let your team know that this will be an auspicious beginning for them. You will probably need an off-season rehearsal. Put the pressure on them."

"Sounds like fun," Micaela said with calm excitement. She knew it would be good to be in America under Zellingari, and this meeting was confirming it.

"Okay, everyone, we have the opening. We will use the chamber orchestra set-up. Then everyone else can come on stage for the concerto. Don't worry, Martha, we will make up for it in the second half."

"Why wait for the intermission?" Martha interrupted hesitantly.

"You have a suggestion for the concerto, Martha?" Leon asked with reservation, since Martha was not hesitant about anything.

"Well, I was just thinking," she said, a lascivious grin coming over her face, "if Micaela isn't too tired from *banging* Eric, maybe she would like to bang Luca with the *Brahms Double*. No offense, darlin'." Micaela turned her head and did not respond, nor would she have been able to because of the ensuing cat calls and laughter around the table. Martha's suggestion was not only crass, it was impossible.

"Giarrizzo won't do the double," Eric said. "He barely tolerates being interrupted by the orchestra, much less being upstaged by a cello."

Hugh nodded, "Yeah, too bad, though — there are some nice reed solos."

"And some tasty naked horn bits, too," Eric said staring at Martha. Martha looked back with a grin.

Micaela was painfully aware that Leon had been silent after Martha's suggestion. Her resentment towards Martha's unkind words was completely submerged in the fear and excitement that the maestro was seriously considering the idea. She was sure that this was a bad idea. *Very* rarely was a principal given the chance to do a concerto. It would alienate a premier soloist and the concertmaster, her colleague, immediately. She felt the conductor's head turn towards her. She was not ready for her cue. Neither was anyone else.

"Are you up to it?" Leon said. The table went silent. Hugh's mouth opened. Eric snapped his head in surprise towards the conductor. Martha was trying to hide her grin.

"Sounds like busy summer. Of course, I would like willing partner," Micaela answered.

"I will take care of Luca," Leon said.

"Can we watch?" Hugh whined, and everyone except Eric laughed.

"Actually, I was meaning study partner for concerto," Micaela, said looking at Eric, who was looking at no one.

Eric eventually returned his attention and said, "It would be my pleasure, Micaela." Leon was happily surprised that Micaela had a deft hand in politics as well as music, even though he knew this was going to cost him big with Eric. He would find a way to make it up to him, perhaps when Khazar came.

"Okay, that's about 35-40 minutes. The first half is done. And I have just decided on the second half ... Copland."

"*Appalachian Spring*?" Mario asked.

"In the fall?" Hugh countered.

"*Rodeo*?" Sam, the percussion leader, said hopefully.

"Yes, *Rodeo*, but it isn't long enough. We will add *Billy the Kid* on the front end," Leon said.

"Ooo, doggies, vee are havink' a hoedown," Hermann said. The combination of his German accent and the cowboy slang sent everyone laughing.

Leon continued, "A New York composer for the New York critics, enough tasty licks for every section in the orchestra, excitement and great melody for the audience — this concert is not only going to sell out, but everyone, and I mean *everyone,* should go home smiling." Although agreement was not required, everyone at the table nodded with sublime confidence. The meeting dissolved with excited chatter. Most of Micaela's new colleagues took the time to provide good-natured commiseration for her daunting challenge.

Eric came over to her and said, "Welcome to America."

"Thank you, Eric. I am grateful you help me with the Brahms. It is good of you."

Eric nodded. "I think you will find this an unusual orchestra. We are not without our politics and jealousies. On the other hand, our leader has created a spirit here where each one of us is willing to take one for the team."

"Excuse me, I do not understand." Micaela was not familiar with the sports idiom.

"Sorry," Eric said. "Let's just say, all for one and one for all."

Just then BoBo came through the door carrying his tedious budget reports and season attendance statistics. It was as if someone had given the signal for dispersal.

"Where's everyone going?" BoBo asked. Leon took him by the elbow.

"Sorry, Robert, the meeting has just concluded. Didn't you receive the time change?"

"No, I didn't and I have these reports to give you from last season," said the frustrated chairman.

"Darn it, we must make sure you get the correct time next time. Unfortunately, everyone has to go now. It looks like we will have an exciting season ahead. Why don't you let me fill you in this afternoon?"

"You know I can't do that. I have the school board meeting for the Music Memory contest."

"Of course, that's right, I forgot. And I have to go to Chicago tomorrow. Tell you what. Leave the papers with me. I will review them and we can get together next week," Leon said.

"But what about the PR plan for Micaela?" BoBo whined. With Leon's glance, Micaela knew that was her cue to get out the door while she could.

"Yes, I have been working on some ideas with Alison. I think you will be very happy with it. We can go over that next week, too."

"You've been working on it?" BoBo was now exasperated. "But that's my job!" Nearly everyone was gone now, and Leon continued to pacify BoBo. It was a necessary but continuously tedious task for the maestro.

Music: Sibelius, Symphony No. 5 in E Flat Major, Op. 82 Third Movement, Andante Mosso, Quasi Allegretto

Now knowing what she would be performing, Micaela decided she wanted to view the hall again. Even though opening night was six months away, the excitement of her opportunity placed a goofy grin on her face. The conference room was on the third floor of Campbell and, as she turned left to go to where she thought the stairs were, there was a single door rather than the expected double. She opened the door to an auxiliary control room area for the stage spotlights. She was lost. She turned to retrace her steps, stumbling on a large instrument case for a trombone.

"Hello, Micaela." Years behind the iron curtain and on stage had taught her to stifle any evidence of being startled no matter what she felt inside. Her eyes were just now adapting to the low light and she swallowed as she recognized the voice and the face in the shadow. With relief, she looked at Jed and said, "Hello. Good to see you again. I am glad it is you. I am lost in my new home. Can you help me?"

"I would be delighted." And he was. "Where do you want to go?"

"I was going home. But wanted to see hall … see it again before going. That's how I become lost."

"No problem. In fact, there is pretty good view from right over here. Follow me." Jed led her to a door on the opposite side of the control room that accessed corrugated metal stairs.

"Here, take my hand and hold on to the railing." Micaela took his hand. He gave it a reassuring squeeze and guided her up the stairs to the catwalks that connected the spotlight stations. They were among the clouds now, hanging above the back of the main floor in front of and slightly above the third tier balconies. Micaela had never before seen a concert hall from this point of view. "Užasne," she gasped. "You can see everything from here."

"And nobody can see you, especially when the spots are on," said Jed. The height was unnerving and exciting at the same time. Micaela squeezed Jed's hand with delight and to be steadied.

"Are you lighting director, too?" she teased Jed.

"I did some of the lights for high school plays. I was just showing some old friends around. Probably get in trouble with Allen, if he knew I was here. We'd better go. What brings you to the hall today?"

"I had programming meeting."

Jed hesitated. "So, I suppose you can tell me what changes we're going to have?"

"I could. It's quite good. First …"

"No, I was just joking. Eric will want to be the one to tell us first," Jed interrupted.

Micaela paused and then gushed, "Thank you. I need no more problems with Eric. You have saved me twice today. You have more talents than viola. Do you play trombone too?" They were coming to the place where Micaela had stumbled. The only light in the control room was from the open door.

"No, ma'am, that's mine." This time Micaela's training failed her as the troll-like Gar stepped out of the shadow and picked up his case. She squealed. The subsequent appearance of Lou was a soothing contrast to being surprised by Gar.

"These must be your friends," Micaela said.

"Yep. Gar and Lou, please meet Micaela Miklos, she is the newest star in our orchestra," said Jed.

"Sorry to scare you, ma'am," Gar shook hands.

"Don't worry, Miss Miklos, Gar scares everyone," grinned Lou.

"Gar and Lou are old school friends of mine. They were up here for a local band concert and took the time to come see where I work," said Jed.

"How nice," said Micaela. "What instrument do you play, Lou?"

"Aw, I just came along for the ride. Don't get to see Jed so much anymore. Just wanted to visit. Plus the 500 is coming up and we need to finalize plans."

"The 500?" asked Micaela.

Jed laughed. "Guys, Micaela is new to the United States and doesn't know about the race."

"Sheesh, you'd have to be a commie or from Mars not to know what the 500 is," said Gar.

"Well, I'm not from Mars, but from Czechoslovakia, does it count?" Micaela smiled. Jed and Lou laughed. Gar stood open-mouthed. Jed looked at Gar and said, "Micaela is a refugee. She defected to Austria a couple of years ago."

"So, you are not a commie?" Gar asked. Micaela's expression went dark and deep as the question seemed to wound her.

"No, stupid, in fact, she has considerably more reason to hate them than you do," Jed said.

"Really, why's that?" asked Gar, the clueless.

"Because they executed her parents when she left," answered Jed. Although Micaela was used to taking care of herself, she looked at Jed with a deep appreciation for his defense.

"Those godless bastards," Gar said. He said it without any real regard for Micaela's tragedy. Gar found the fact more triumphant than sad.

"Shut up, Gar," said Lou as he looked at Micaela.

"What ... What'd I say?"

"I really must go now," said Micaela.

"I'll lead you out," Jed said.

"Nice to meet you, hope to see you again," Lou said. Jed led Micaela out and down to the lobby.

"Are you all right?" he asked.

"Yes, I am fine," she answered. "I must go home now. Thank you for explanation upstairs. It felt odd being suspected communist."

"I'll bet. You sure you're okay?" Jed pressed. Micaela smiled much more broadly now; she was enjoying his concern.

"Yes, very fine, but I must go. Thanks again, for everything." She shook his hand and walked out the door. Jed stood for a moment watching after her and then returned to his friends. When Jed was gone, Allen came to the doors to check that they were still locked.

— 11 —

U.S. SUB MISSING WITH 129 – Chicago Tribune, April 11

APRIL 10 WEDNESDAY

Wrigley Field – Chicago

Music: Dvorak, Slavonic Dance in E Minor, Op. 72. No. 2

When Leon stepped out of the taxi he had taken from O'Hare, he paused to survey the scene. Normally, when going to and from cabs, Leon moved quickly and with purpose, like a predator closing on his target. But whenever he was on the sidewalk outside of a ballpark, particularly Wrigley Field, his tempo slowed. He looked up at the red and white sign, "Wrigley Field Home of the Chicago Cubs," savoring its impending sanctuary. Inside those walls was another dimension, shielded from all the details and logistics of his complicated life. As he walked through the arch at gate 10, there seemed to be a change in the air pressure. Sounds of the crowd and vendors hawking food and programs were not so much heard as felt as they passed through him, gently reaming out the detritus from his normal life. He inhaled the smell of dank cement, hot dogs, and beer, and his body, mind, and soul received a much-needed cleaning and detailing. This trip to Wrigley in the early spring was his annual tune up. He was in the transition area between the outside world and the ballpark itself, where he needed to pick up three things: scorecard, hot dog, and a beer. The trio acquired, he proceeded into the inner sanctum. He had two seats three rows behind the first base dugout and in from the aisle on his right, so his view would not be interrupted by people going up and down the stairs. Being a celebrity has benefits. These were comp tickets. Alison never wanted to go, which was fine with him. He liked being there alone. The extra seat gave him space to put his jacket and to move around, although he didn't need the space today; it was freezing and the crowd was sparse. He took the inner seat, leaving the aisle seat open to his right.

The Dodgers batting practice was just finishing. He settled in and started to fill out his scorecard. Sandy Koufax was pitching for the Dodgers and Bob Buhl for the Cubs. Being a fan of the slender southpaw from L.A. meant that Leon had a conflict of interest. Koufax hadn't finished or won a game since last July. It would be interesting to see how his sore hand was doing. He was hoping Koufax would be back in form, but not enough to beat the Cubs. As players started to line the base paths, Leon's focus wandered to this morning's conversation with Luca. It had been predictably difficult.

Although Gianluca Giarrizzo was born in San Francisco, his high-pitched voice was pure Brooklyn gravel.

"You must be feeling great, Leon," he said. "I hear you got rid of that putz Sarazin and snagged Miklos. I don't think they would have allowed that trade in baseball."

"Word travels fast. Anyhow, it wasn't a trade."

"On the grapevine it is. The news is all over and Szell isn't happy about it." Luca's grin reached through the phone.

"Wait 'til he starts working with the guy. I guess I won't be guesting in Cleveland anytime soon."

"Aw, don't worry about it. If you keep this up, you won't need it. Why'd you call? Just to brag?" Luca asked.

"I wanted to talk about the program next fall."

"You want to change it?"

"Yep."

"Well, you know me. I'll play anything anywhere." This boast was effectively true. Once Luca gave a Master's Class at Rice University and challenged the students to ask him to play whatever they liked. His remarkable repertoire did not fail him. He specialized in taking on the truly difficult pieces. He was the first to play the famed and fiendishly difficult Bartok *Solo Sonata*. Luca also recorded all twenty-four of Paganini's incredibly difficult "*Caprices*." Paganini was his favorite encore selection for tours.

"That's great. I want to change it to *Brahms Concerto for Violin and Cello*." Leon waited for the reply, and at least a full measure of silence passed.

"Are you fucking nuts?"

"Calm down, Gianluca."

"Calm down! Damn … it isn't even correctly titled. It should be Concerto for Cello and stupid fiddle player who gets suckered into ruining his career. Shit, even when Heifetz recorded it, people only remembered the cellist."

"Piatigorsky," deadpanned Leon.

"Thanks for reminding me," Luca said with disgusted sarcasm.

"Come on, you know it's a good piece."

"I don't give a shit. I am a virtuoso soloist, not a sidekick to … who is the cellist gonna be, anyway?" Leon was really hesitant to answer that question, and his delay provided Luca with the answer.

"Oh no," Luca realized. "You can't be serious. You want me to do dueling strings with your first chair?"

"The audience will go nuts."

"And she gets the 45 and I get a peashooter. This is suicide for me."

"That's bullshit. You are invulnerable. Besides, the critics will consider it uncommonly gracious and sensitive of you."

"I am neither gracious nor sensitive. Christ! Have you seen her tits? No one will even notice I'm on stage."

"Sure they will. She won't have stage front. She will remain with her section. And for the encore, you can do your precious Paganini." Leon had nearly exhausted his arguments.

"This is crazy, Leon. Why don't you just have her duel with your concertmaster and I'll take the week off," Luca pouted.

"Ah, c'mon. It's really not that bad. I'm sure I can get a New York critic there, and you can show him that you are much more than a technical specialist." That was Leon's final salvo.

There was silence on the line and then Luca asked, "Who from New York?"

Leon was relieved. He had him hooked. "Winthrop or Harold." These critics represented the *New Yorker* and the *New York Times* respectively. The *Times* was considered to be more of an authority, but the *New Yorker* had broader appeal outside of the city.

"Why would they come?"

"They both went ape over our Carnegie performance last year and have expressed a desire to see the ISO in its natural setting. What better time than the season opener with the famous Luca and the mysterious Czech cellist?"

After a thoughtful silence, "Well, I'll tell you what. You get either one of those hacks in the audience and I'll be there. I'll even play "Back Home in Indiana" if you want. By the way, Micaela is single, isn't she?"

"Luca, you can't afford another ex-wife. You'd better stay at our house."

"Tell Mary I want spinach gnocchi."

"You got it."

"And you got me, old friend," Luca laughed.

Leon was actually swooning with the way next season was shaping up when
the public address system woke him from his smug reverie. "Welcome to the
friendly confines of Wrigley Field." He stood up for the National Anthem
realizing that his mind was not actually in the place he intended it to be. He
started to take in the ivy walls, ignoring what he considered to be the worst
work of a bad composer. Soon after the anthem was completed, the Cubbies
ran out on the field for their warm-ups. Leon made a final check of his
scorecard. Leading off was Brock in right field. Then came the shortstop,
Rodgers, Williams in left. The new cleanup hitter was the third baseman,
Santo, followed by the previous cleanup first baseman, Banks. In the sixth slot
was the centerfielder, Mathews. Then came the second baseman, Hubbs,
followed by the battery of Bertell and Buhl. The Dodger bats would have to
do it from the bench. Three starters were sidelined: *Tommy* Davis, last year's
RBI leader, Maury Wills, the record base stealer, and Bill Skowron, the former
Yankee, were all injured. Buhl was ready now and the L.A. leadoff hitter and
centerfielder, *Willie* Davis, got in the batter's box. Davis stole 32 bases last
year, second to Maury Will's record shattering 104. Better keep him off first,
Leon thought, as he took a sip of beer. On the 1-2 count, Buhl hit Davis in the
foot.

"Rats, you had 'em," Leon jeered as Davis trotted to first. The second
baseman, Nate Oliver, was up and went down swinging on fourth pitch. He
never touched the ball.

"Way to bring it, Buhl," Leon cheered. Wally Moon, the Dodger
leftfielder, came to the plate. A 250 hitter last year, Buhl came right at him
with a fast ball, strike one called. On the second pitch, Davis took off and stole
second easily. Bertell's throw was off-line and late. Moon swung and missed
at the next pitch outside. On the 0-2 count, Moon expected a ball and Buhl
froze him with a fast ball inside, strike three called.

"All right, Buhl! Now keep it down for Frank," Leon knew his baseball,
which included knowing that the rightfielder, Frank Howard, had 119 RBIs
and 31 homers last year. The wind off the lake wasn't going to help. The first
pitch was low, ball one. The big right-hander stepped out of the box to get his
sign from the third base coach. Back in the box, Buhl checked Davis' lead
from second. At the top of his windup, Davis took off for third. Howard swung
at the high and outside pitch. Bertell snagged the pitchout and fired down to
third.

"You got 'em!" Leon yelled. However, the throw was wild and sailed into left field as Davis trotted into home.

"Sheesh, it's 1 nothing and L.A. hasn't even touched the damn ball." Leon was happily riled and took another sip of beer. The cold air was showing someone's breath to his right.

"Little cold for that beer, don't you think?" Leon knew by the sound of the voice who it was, but still turned in disbelief to see Thomas Flynn. Leon stared for a moment, then turned back to the game to watch Howard fly out to finish the top of the first.

"We have to talk," Thomas said.

"Did Alison tell you where I was?"

"No, I didn't ask her."

"Then how the hell did you find …," started Leon. "Never mind, I don't want to know." He still wasn't looking at Thomas. He was concentrating on Koufax's warm-ups, as if they might erase the presence of the interloper.

"You received a package recently," Thomas stated. There was no response from Leon. The Cubbie rightfielder Brock was coming to the plate. "A package from our young soloist, I believe."

"You gonna tell me what's in it?"

"Nope, I don't really care. Well, at least I don't think I do. I am more interested in who knows you have it."

"Why? … All right, nice shot!" Brock got a hit.

"Because I found out you had it from an unexpected source."

"Who would that be, the CIA?"

"No, that would be an expected source. This information came from Robert Welch," Thomas said, expecting some response.

"Who's he?" Leon asked.

"He is the founder and president of the John Birch Society," Thomas said quietly and observed some sort of jolt in Leon.

"You communicate with them?" Leon was incredulous.

"It's kind of a one-way communication," Thomas answered, and Leon eventually nodded his understanding. "So, can you think of anyone you know that might have told them?"

"No one in my house. What about the postman?" Leon shaded his immediate suspicions.

"Could be. The point is that they are interested and somehow close to you. We have to act before they do and keep the initiative." Thomas had been putting some thought into the John Birch Society involvement. The realization that Thomas was spending so much of his valuable time on this situation was itself unnerving, much less the news. Koufax fanned the 6'3" Andre Rodgers, 1 out.

"What did you have in mind?"

"Publicity. It can be the greatest protection in the world."

"And the greatest pain in the ass," Leon added.

"We need to start leaking the news. Why don't you start by telling your staff?"

"Already did, but I told them to keep it a secret."

"Will they?" Thomas asked.

"They will try, no doubt. However, a phone call would probably get it out of them. 'Hello, John Doe from the *Indianapolis Star*. I heard a rumor about a Soviet soloist coming in November. Can you confirm this?' " The lefthander Billy Williams grounded a curve ball into a 4-6-3 double play. "Damn," Leon said.

"Okay, what about musician friends in New York?" suggested Thomas.

"That shouldn't be too hard. What is it exactly that we are worried the John Birchers might do? They seem all talk to me."

"That's the problem. We don't know what they are doing or might do. Jack hates surprises."

"Name dropper."

Thomas laughed, "Some sense of humor is intact."

"Yeah, this is getting really funny. Both the government and anti-Semitic groups are monitoring my mail and whereabouts. I'm fighting with the soloist six months before the concert. My concertmaster is pissed off at me. My wife seems to be developing a strange new habit. And now I have a mysterious little Irishman showing up uninvited at my baseball game."

"Sounds like you need a vacation," Thomas said.

"What the hell do you think this is?"

"At least Koufax's hand seems to be all right."

"Yeah, I suppose so. Could be a long day for the Cubs." Leon's attention was returning to the game. Thomas bought a couple beers and they settled into the rest of the game, which turned out to be mostly a whiffing bee. During the course of the game, Leon found out that Thomas was a baseball fan too, and between planning how to leak the news to the press, they discussed optimistic predictions for the Cubs this year. Leon also shared some behind-the-scenes music lore, including his recent conversation with Luca. Thomas listened intently and was very amused at the dynamics.

"This Micaela Miklos," Thomas said, "she is quite the cellist, then?"

"Oh yeah, she is very good," answered Leon. After a silent moment, "Would you like to come to the opening?"

"Yes, I would, schedule permitting. That would be great."

"You can be our guest in the box, if you like. Or is that too high-profile for you?"

Thomas smiled, "No, no, that's really not a problem. In fact, it would be a good setup for the image."

"Yours or the president's?"

"I don't really have an image, Leon. What I meant to say is that it would be a good setup for the image we are trying to create for Jack if he comes to the concert in November."

Leon tried to concentrate on the game. Both Buhl and Koufax were on today. The Dodgers scored another unearned run on a passed ball by Bertell in the fifth inning. It was the bottom of the eighth with one out, and Brock swung at strike three. However, it was a wild pitch in the dirt, and he reached first. Two singles later Brock scored, and Leon was still silent, although Thomas was cheering loudly. When the duo of Santos and Banks struck out and grounded out respectively, Leon finally said weakly, "He's coming to the concert?"

"Maybe, or maybe just Jackie without the President. The scheduling is tough. He will have started early campaign trips in Texas the week before Thanksgiving. And we are not sure how close he should be to the defection. At any rate, Jackie is very keen on the idea. If it is done right, we could capture the Midwest early," Thomas explained. Leon stared at the field slack-jawed. Thomas went on, "Of course, these things have a way of changing at the last minute, so it is extremely unwise to tell anyone."

"Then why did you tell me?" Leon asked.

"If the president and/or the first lady do attend, it will require a great deal of last-minute preparation, and I didn't want *you* to be surprised."

"Thanks," said Leon, almost inaudible as the game was winding down.

"Cheer up, Maestro, you know it's going to be a great season." Thomas patted Leon on the back firmly. Final score L.A. 2 and Chicago 1. Koufax had ten strikeouts and Buhl six with two unearned runs.

Thomas took out a business card and wrote a phone number on it. He told Leon that if he had any concerns or new information that he thought was important, he should call him any time. Despite his mysterious nature, and the fact that Thomas was two for two in completely shocking Leon, the conductor was starting to trust the Irishman's intentions. He felt reassured about having the number.

Music: Stravinsky, Le Sacre du Printemps, Introduction

They parted ways outside the ballpark, and Leon took a cab to the Drake Hotel, where he was looking forward to a cold martini and a hot bowl of Bookbinder's red snapper soup downstairs in the Cape Cod Room.

"Welcome back, Mr. Zellingari, sorry about Bertell," the doorman greeted Leon.

"Yeah Freddy, it was a shame. Buhl pitched a beauty. So did Koufax. God, it was cold," said Leon as he searched for a tip for the doorman.

"Not as cold as Santos and Banks, I hear," Freddy said. Leon couldn't find any money for the tip.

"I'll have to catch you later," said Leon.

"No problem Mr. Zellingari. As usual, your bag arrived earlier from O'Hare. I will send it right up." Leon was well known and well liked at the Drake. He always stayed there and preferred to eat at the hotel whether he was in Chicago on business or to watch the Cubs. Check-in was routinely fast and cordial. He was still numb from both the temperature and the news. Soon he was thawing out in the hot shower of his suite. In front of the full-length mirror he looked at his spindly-legged, naked self. He turned sideways so his right side faced the mirror. The muscles along the right shoulder blade of a conductor are more pronounced, as a result of the extra effort and repetitive motion of the "tempo" hand. In Leon's case, this musculature was exaggerated because he didn't use a baton. He hunched over more and started pacing in front of the mirror. At each turn, he straightened himself a little more as if imitating the snapshots of human evolution. Eventually, he straightened himself as properly as possible and, with a naked grin, he said out loud, "Playing for the President — you've got to be kidding." Then he let his body go slack, into an exaggerated Quasimodo-like stoop. With towel-dried hair, wilder than Beethoven's, he closed one eye, looked in the mirror, and mocked out loud in his best imitation of Charles Laughton, "Sanc-tu-ary, Mr. President, sanc-tu-ary." By the time he left the bathroom, he was randomly chortling at his good fortune. He called the restaurant. The maitre d' answered, "Yes, Mr. Zellingari?"

"I'll be down in fifteen minutes. Is that okay?"

"Certainly, sir, Gabriel is ready for you. Sorry about the game, sir."

"The what? Oh yeah, damn shame." Leon hung up and began to dress, humming the introduction melody to Rachmaninov's concerto. He was still singing in the elevator when the familiar attendant said, "Boy, did Bertell blow it today."

"Yeah, he sure did," Leon said with a smirk. "At least Koufax's hand is okay." Leon was at the restaurant within ten minutes of his call. He was taken to his table immediately, and as he sat down, his martini arrived. He consumed half of it before Gabriel reached the table. Gabriel was from Guatemala and a very proud waiter. When he first waited on Leon years ago, he was offended because the conductor appeared not to acknowledge any comments he made in Spanish. This was a frequent problem for Leon. His physical appearance and dark olive skin tone were frequently misinterpreted as Italian, Mexican, even Arabic. Aside from Italian music notation, he knew none of those languages. Members of those ethnic groups would presume that Leon knew their language and would incorrectly judge him to be a snob. It was more than a language problem in the South, where he was frequently mistaken as a chauffeur, the waiter, or the doorman (particularly when he wore his tails). In time, Gabriel's misunderstanding was cleared up, and they began a polite friendship. Leon always requested him when he ate at the Cape Cod Room. Eventually, the request was no longer necessary. Leon began to pick up a little Spanish, in part because of some touring in Mexico. He enjoyed eating alone at the Drake's famous restaurant. He was largely undisturbed and the food was very good. They used all homemade stocks — no bases — and had excellent seafood.

"¿Ola Gabriel, que tal?" Leon said.

"Bien, Maestro, gracias. Que Lastima por la basebol."

Surprisingly, Leon smiled broadly, "It was really a good game, though. Buhl is looking sharp."

"But the Cubs lost, didn't they?" Gabriel asked.

"Yeah, yeah, you win some and you lose some," answered Leon. His uncharacteristic giddiness after a loss confused the familiar waiter completely. Leon drained his martini. "Bring on the Bookbinders and the wine list."

"Yes, sir. Esta noche, tenemos Tiburon. They tell me it was swimming off the Cape yesterday."

"Sold." Gabriel started to turn away when Leon continued, "Anything else you recommend, Tengo mucho hambre."

"Fresh morels con fettucine."

"I'll have a half-portion before the shark. Gracias, Gabriel." Leon was done ordering his feast, at least until dessert. He was trying to remember the last time he felt this good. It didn't take long. It was after the final rehearsal of the Schubert for Carnegie Hall. He knew then that the evening performance was going to be special, just as he now knew that this next season, still so far away, was going to be incredible. He fondled the heavy silver and stared at the charger in front of him, embossed with the Cape Cod logo, grinning deeply to himself. The sommelier arrived at the table.

"Mr. Zellingari?"

"Yes?"

"Someone brought this by for you. The corkage fee has been paid." He displayed the bottle to Leon, who recognized it immediately. Anyone could see it was champagne, but only a few would be familiar with the label. It was Vintage Krug. Krug only produces a Vintage when a crop has exceptional characteristics. This bottle was 1959. Leon was inwardly salivating.

"There's a card, sir," said the sommelier. Leon took the card and read the vintner's description.

> *"Krug Vintage is like a concerto, a joint venture between our Krug style and the personality of a certain year. The year is the soloist but the orchestra remains Krug."*

Then underneath, Leon read the handwritten note.

> *May our joint venture be as deliciously successful as this wine. -- TF*

"I'll drink to that," Leon said.

"Excuse me, sir?"

"Nothing. That will be perfect with my dinner tonight. Please open it and pour a glass for yourself and one for Gabriel."

After tending to the maestro, the maitre'd brought a glass over to Gabriel who looked at it and asked, "¿Es seguro los Cubs perdido hoy?"

— 12 —

MAY 8 WEDNESDAY

Breakfast Overture

"**Micaela is a charming** young woman, don't you think?" Alison said to Leon over breakfast.

"Uh huh," Leon replied from behind the sports section of the *Indianapolis Star*. "She can play the daylights out of that cello."

"Well, she'd better, considering the opening program." Alison paused. before inserting the second needle. "How did Eric take it?"

"Better than Luca." Leon put down the paper. He'd had his fill of the box scores and Alison's subterfuge. "What's up, Alison?"

"Whatever do you mean?" she asked, tweaking her drawl. The amount of extra attention that Micaela was getting from Leon was not uncalled for, but not acceptable to the wife of the conductor.

"You know that won't work with me, darling. Tell me what's on your mind." Leon waited. Alison sipped her coffee and made him wait a little more.

"I was just thinking that Micaela has been spending a lot of her time planning for next season and really hasn't had a chance to get to know Indianapolis."

"That's not necessarily a bad thing," Leon said. "What did you have in mind?"

"The 500 is coming up."

"That's a great idea. I got an extra ticket from BoBo this year. She can come with us."

"My dear, she has seen too much of *us*. The point is she needs to see other people, perhaps other players besides the principals. After all, you want her to get along with the *whole* orchestra, don't you?" Leon rubbed his face with both hands. He was being out-maneuvered, and he didn't even know why.

Picking up his cup of coffee he said, "Sure … whom did you have in mind?"

"Jed."

"Jed!" Leon's coffee cup hit the saucer firmly. "You can't be serious. You want her to be introduced to Indianapolis by a second-fiddle John Bircher?"

"It's just the 500. She will be introduced to the whole city in later in the summer. And Jed knows the 500; he goes every year."

"Yeah, to the infield orgy."

"Honestly, Leon, you're a sensationalist. I was talking with the Kohn's..."

"Who are the Kohn's?"

"Our neighbors." Alison squinted.

"Oh yeah, right."

"Anyway, they went to the infield last year and said it was fine. Besides, Jed's not that bad."

"Are you speaking of music or politics?" Leon asked. He thought it was rhetorical question.

"You told me he was playing better." Leon didn't reply. "But I was speaking of politics. Yeah, he's a touch too conservative, but who isn't around here?"

"Why can't she go with the neighbors?"

"They're not members of the orchestra, silly." Alison smiled.

Leon was losing the battle and not happy about it. Last year, he was looking for excuses to fire Jed. He would only do so for musical reasons. But he couldn't. Jed was getting better and obviously working at it. It would send the wrong message. Furthermore, good strings were not that easy to find. Leon thought that Alison was wrong about Jed's politics. Jed came from southern Indiana which is just as *deep south* as anywhere else in America.

"I don't like it." Leon folded his arms.

"You don't have to be involved. I can set it up it without you."

"I don't doubt that," Leon said. Alison said nothing but stared at Leon over the breakfast table with an intensity of purpose that began to wither Leon's resolve. His shoulders slumped. "Okay. But I don't want to know anything about it. And be sure he takes her in a car and not on that damn motorcycle."

II
Estate calda lunga

Wallace Westfeldt

— 13 —

MAY 30 THURSDAY

The Indianapolis 500

Music: Bach, Suite No. 1 G Major, for Unaccompanied Cello, Courante

The hard rain and hard drinking started after the race. The drenching didn't help the soybean farmers, who were already flooded along the bottoms, but it did help wash away the refuse of 300,000 fans. The drinking didn't wash away anything but was inevitable. The beers during the day were baked away by the sun and Micaela's company. After Jed dropped her off, he and the boys had plenty of stamina for the obligatory shots. They celebrated Parnelli Jones' win. They argued over the future of the Offenhauser-style race cars that had been winning the Indianapolis 500 for the past decade and a half. Gar and Lou, mostly Gar, felt that Parnelli proved that the roadster was here to stay. Jed was pretty sure that Jones had been cheating on the yellow flag and that the Scottish rookie, Jim Clark, was a superior driver in a superior car. It would only be a matter of time before he drove into Victory Lane. Jed went on to insist that the "Offy's" days were numbered, and pretty soon there would be nothing but these imported bullets with their whining, high-rpm engines winning the biggest spectacle in auto racing.

As Gar chased a shot of Jim Beam with his thirtieth beer of the day, he said, "Ain't gonna happen. Can you imagine some foreigner sitting in the winner's circle drinking milk? It ain't right. They won't even drink it. They'll want that champagne or something. It ain't American." Gar wiped the beer foam off his lips. "And if it ain't American, it's most likely anti-American and someone should do something about it."

"Like what, Gar?" Lou asked.

"I dunno, like get rid of 'em."

"What do you mean, 'get rid of them'?" Jed laughed.

"Aww, let 'em race in their own countries," said Gar. This argument had actually started earlier on race day, when Jed brought Micaela to the track and was explaining the race and race cars to her. The fact that Micaela was at the 500 with Jed was a great surprise to him as well as to a great many other folks.

The next day Jed woke up to a wave of Indiana humidity. He wished it were colder and darker to soothe his hollow bones and thin skin. He would have stayed in bed, but he had to piss like a racehorse. He stood up. The effects of the alcohol-diminished blood pressure made him unsteady. After the bathroom, he made his way to the kitchen for a large glass of orange juice. The brief potassium relief led him to the front door for the morning *Star,* as the first of the only two good side effects of a hangover set in, hunger. Jed started the kettle for coffee and tossed the bacon in the cast iron skillet. After the Wonder Bread was in the toaster, he slipped the eggs into the hot grease and turned them as soon as they set up. The kettle whistled. He plopped the over easy eggs and soft bacon undrained on the plate. He put a little butter on the toast and lots of Strawberry Rhubarb Preserves from Dillman Farms, just north of his hometown. As he stirred the Folgers Instant in his coffee cup, he unfolded the paper.

"JONES WINS FASTEST '500' " said the *Star*'s headlines, along with two article heads, *"Shatters Track Record with 143.137 Average"* and *"Mighty Offy Record Challenged By Lightweight Lotus."* In between the articles, there was a picture of Mr. and Mrs. Parnelli Jones waving to the Victory Lane crowd.

"Now, that is one ugly wife," Jed muttered. True, Grayce Jones was porcine enough to threaten his appetite and libido, but the pervasive aroma of the bacon took over, and he devoured his breakfast. Skimming the news, he noted that Clark had complained about Jones advancing during the yellow. He finished the paper in the bathroom and started to clean up, ending with a long shower where he could enjoy the second pleasurable side effect of a hangover. He had an unfamiliar obstacle to his masturbation. He couldn't think of who he wanted to fuck. The only two women in his mind right now were Grayce and Micaela. The fact that Grayce's image remained in his head was terribly annoying in any case, but particularly so in juxtaposition to the beautiful and exceedingly sexy Micaela. He had spent the whole day with her and had a great time. She was funny, charming, voluptuous, and he was pretty sure that she had enjoyed the day and his company. Micaela was a perfect target for a little shower-time fantasy. She certainly was adventurous enough. When he rode to her apartment, she had no qualms about straddling the back of his motorcycle. Indeed, she smiled with delight when he handed her his spare helmet. She slid her Japanese straw hat to her back cowboy style, strapped on the helmet, hitched up her khaki capris, and got on. He had been concerned that the infield partying, for which the infield of the Indianapolis Motor Speedway was so infamous, would be too low-class for someone with her sophistication, and she might be stuffy. On the contrary, she seemed uncommonly comfortable and continually curious, asking genuine questions about the cars and the race. When Gar teased her about her accent and the Japanese hat that indeed looked goofy, she said, "At least ve don't drink mouthvash for beer where I come from."

Gar's grin vanished. "Did she say mouthwash?" he asked, his eyes widening.

"Actually, I think she said mouth*vash,* Gar," Lou's grin was bigger as he stepped closer to Micaela. "So, Micaela, you say the beer is stronger in Czechoslovakia?"

"Yes, in Czechoslovakia, Austria, all of Europe."

"Tell me, Micaela, do they drink a lot in Europe?" asked Lou.

"Oh, no," added Jed softly. He knew where this was going.

"You mean compared to here?" replied Micaela. Lou nodded his head. "I guess I don't know, ve don't usually drink this early in the morning unless it is champagne. But yes, I guess ve drink a lot."

"Well, Micaela, around here, and especially on a hot race day like this, we think it is important to stay lubricated," said Lou.

"Like the cars," said Micaela.

"Exactly. You catch on quick. In fact, we have a method for assuring lubrication called the Oolitic Funnel Chug."

"C'mon, Lou, give her a break, she's new around here." Jed said.

"Relax, Jed. I think Micaela has the experience to take care of herself. Gar, bring out the funnel." Micaela gave a single nod of agreement. Gar handed Lou the funnel and continued, "Okay, what we have here is your standard wide-mouth funnel for changing the oil in your car. As you see, we have inserted the small end into this rather long clear plastic tubing, just the right size to get ... well, to get your mouth around. While holding the open end of the tube up, we pour one, maybe two cans of beer into the funnel. Then the Chugger …"

"Chugger?" asked Micaela.

"The drinker gets down on their knees and tries to drink or chug, as we like to say, all of the beer as fast as possible."

"I see. Maybe that's vy your beer is tasteless," smiled Micaela. Jed winced and Lou laughed. Gar was beside himself.

"Mebbe you'd like to try it?" Gar stared at her.

"Indeed, I vould. Sounds fun. After all, it is important to stay lubricated, right?" The boys were too surprised to nod. "Vould it be possible to get demonstration first?" she asked.

"No problem," said Gar. He took the church key hanging on a string from his belt, opened a can of Schlitz, and handed it to Lou. Gar held the business end while Lou poured the can in slowly to reduce the foam. When the can emptied, Gar got on his knees while holding the opening closed with his palm. He tilted his head back and put the tube in his mouth. Gar had the ability to hold open his throat and could drain the tube as fast as gravity would allow. He drained it quickly without spilling a drop.

"Marvelous," Micaela cheered. "That was fantastic. You are indeed a virtuoso." She clapped her hands in delight.

"A what?" Gar was confused.

"An expert," Jed explained. Gar's gargoyle grin returned. He had never before been called an expert.

"My turn," said Micaela, like a schoolgirl. This time Gar prepared the funnel end, and Jed held the open end of the tube closed for Micaela as she got on her knees in the infield grass.

"Ready?" asked Jed. Micaela nodded. Jed held the funnel close to her mouth and then took his hand away. She started to drink. She could not hold her throat open like Gar, but she could swallow and swallow. About halfway through the tube, Lou opened another can of Schlitz. Jed was watching Micaela closely and did not see as Lou started adding more beer to the funnel. Lou stopped at about half a can and Micaela continued to swallow, with small amounts of beer spilling down her cheeks and onto the shoulders of her capped sleeved blouse, until she finished the whole tube. By this time, they had drawn a cheering crowd, and Micaela held up her hands in triumph as Jed smiled and said, "Brava, Micaela," giving her a napkin to wipe her face. Gar put his hand on Jed's shoulder and leered, "Boy, that chick can chug."

"Shut up, Gar," said Jed.

'Shit,' thought Jed as the memory of Gar's lascivious comment spoiled the shower moment for him just as the hot water was running out. He stayed in the cold shower, rinsing and clearing his head.

Music: Bach, Suite No. 5 C Minor, S. 1011 for Unaccompanied Cello, Sarabande

After he dressed in a white t-shirt and shorts, his long night and large breakfast called for a nap. But it was time to practice. There would have been more efficacy if he waited until the afternoon when he was steadier, but morning practice was an old habit that he was loathe to break. When he was younger, the mornings were best because there was no conflict with his friends, who, by and large, really didn't understand his dedication to the music. Music was something that you did in school, not every day, and certainly not in the summer. He began the session by washing his hands in warm water. The chair and music stand were already set up. He wiped the strings of the viola, sat down, and proceeded to do twenty minutes of scales, starting slowly and evenly. "Always start *lento* and *legato*," his instructor had told him. "Never practice mistakes." The warning still echoed in his head as he built his tempo gradually and carefully to *allegro*. There would be no *presto* today. Having no specific performance to prepare for, he moved on from the scales to the Goldberg Variations. It was a holiday, as well as off-season, so he would only practice for an hour. He got through fewer than half of them — not bad, really — considering his still somewhat mushy mind. After practice, the nap seemed less attractive. His home began to look small and dreary. He needed to get out. Leaving his helmet, but grabbing his dark glasses, he set out as if he were late for rehearsal.

Jed purchased his '61 Indian a year ago. Everyone knew that these new *Chiefs* were actually British machines made to look like the American classic. The original motorcycle company nearly went bankrupt in '53. Nevertheless, the throaty Enfield engine felt good, as did the muggy air pressing on his face. Not really knowing where he was going, he ended up at the Eagle Crest reservoir, cruising the roads inside the park looking for place to stop and walk. It was crowded. Even though the 500 was a party for several hundred thousand *white* people, the whole city gets caught up in the event, starting a month beforehand. There are parades, school contests, daily news, the qualifying rounds, celebrity sightings, and society dinners. The day after the race is a citywide hangover, and much of the city seemed to be at Eagle Crest fishing, sailing, rowing, barbecuing, and generally trying to figure out what they were going to do with the rest of their summer.

Jed ended up at one of the docks where various small boats, cheap fishing poles, and volleyball nets were available for rent. He parked his bike and made his way through the multifarious multitude to the water's edge. In the middle of the reservoir was a single sculler pulling gracefully through the still water and passing a small sloop with limp sails. Even the weather seemed hung over. Looking back on shore, he expected to hear more noise. There were families, couples, kids playing, but all their noise seemed attenuated, like a dead concert hall, where sounds and emotions are insulated by the forces of humidity and thick fabrics.

The social textures of Indiana were inherently separate. And most of Indiana preferred it that way. Only in basketball, the orchestra, and parks like this was there a blending of the races and classes. These institutions required the deference of acceptance, even in the absence of interaction. He began to feel uncomfortably insulated and out of place. Unlike everyone else around him except the sculler, he was solo. No one smiled at him. No one said "hi." And he offered nothing as well. Being alone was not an unusual state for Jed. Being alone in a crowd was. He left the crowded bank for a walk in the woods.

He slipped into the forest as if it were the center seam in a stage curtain. The single-file trail meandered through the twisted trunks of the springtime woods. Solitude was complete, even though the masses were just yards away. The shade transformed the humidity from something oppressing into something that soothed his skin, which had been scoured thin by alcoholic pollution. He went deeper, craning his neck to absorb the beauty. There were mottled bark sycamores, buckeyes and boxelders, chestnuts, black walnut, pines, hackberrys, hawthorns, willows, hornbeams, and tulips — the Indiana state tree. His ability to identify them was spotty. He would have felt better if he knew them all.

He had learned about trees from a class at Camp Culver, located north of Indianapolis on the shores of Lake Maxinkuckee. It was an extensive facility, including athletic fields, modern buildings, barracks, dining halls, and an open-air chapel of rough-hewn logs. Separating these buildings were well-tended grounds and the lake, where a variety of water sports were taught. The summer camp housed about 200 boys from ages nine through thirteen. Jed was nine.

He was terribly excited to be there. The catalog promised all kinds of activities, adventure, and, being an only child, he looked forward to enjoying this fun stuff with guys his own age.

During the first day of orientation, Sunday, the camp counselor outlined the week's schedule. He finished by announcing that there would be a Vespers service for everyone at 4:30 in the chapel. He also said that for any Catholics, there was an additional service at 5:30. Jed was terrified. He hadn't heard of Vespers, but he knew what a chapel was. He had been in one once ... only once, for the wedding of his babysitter. Since it was clearly assumed that he was supposed to know what to do and how to behave, he felt unprepared, as if he had forgotten his homework and it was due in an hour. He was desperate and alone. He stared at the floor, not knowing what to do.

A smaller boy from South Bend noticed that Jed's demeanor had changed from initial excitement. When the meeting finished, he came over to Jed and said, "It's okay to be Catholic. I'm Catholic, too." Jed knew nothing of the difference between Catholics and Protestants, but he didn't care. He needed to be something now rather than nothing. He accepted the boy's kindness and religion without hesitation. The boy left to tell the counselor that they were both Catholics. As it turned out, they were the only Catholics in that barracks.

Vespers service lasted between thirty and forty-five minutes and, to Jed's relief, he didn't have to do anything but listen and enjoy the beautiful setting. He didn't hear many of the words or understand them, but he did kneel and move his lips during the Lord's Prayer. The boy and Jed sat together. At the end of the Vespers, nearly everyone rose to leave. Jed didn't know what to do. His fallacious acceptance was now going to get him into more trouble. He would certainly not be able to fake the Catholic service. There were so few Catholics remaining in the chapel.

The counselor saw the look on Jed's face. He came over and said with a smile, "You're not really Catholic, are you?"

"No, sir, not really," Jed said. Without looking at his new friend, Jed and the counselor left, leaving the boy from South Bend alone.

Now, 17 years later, Jed walked alone in the woods. Eventually, he came across a black-barked smoke tree. The labyrinth of its multi-trunks stood out from the mosaic of surrounding trees, as well as its own foliage. Following trunk and limb, the gnarled tree seemed to grow before his eyes, extending itself like the jointed leg of a spider.

A cloud passed overhead, extinguishing the friendly dapples of sunlight. The smoke tree grew larger in the darkening light, and Jed looked down for his path. It was gone. He turned behind him to retrace his steps, but there were no steps to retrace. An endless variety of trees concealed his view, and there was no contrast to find the small footpath. The muscles between his neck and shoulders tightened. The creeping panic annoyed him. He knew he wasn't lost, just misplaced a little. Enough walking in any direction would bring him out of the woods in a short time. He should be enjoying this spot. But as his mind wandered, the place became less beautiful and more threatening. The soothing shelter had become oppressive. The fantastic diversity had become intimidating. This was no better than the crowd and, in fact, worse, because of the unpredictability of nature. What if it stormed, hailed, or lightning struck? He saw something dark, moving quickly a few yards to his right. His experience and intellect were no match for the irrational fear that there was a wild animal close by and that the animal was approaching him now. He used the formerly fearsome smoke tree to screen his presence. Pretty soon the animal emerged from the curtain of bushes.

"Hi Mister, what'cha hidin' from?" said a small black child carrying a fishing pole. Fear was replaced by relief, which in turn, was replaced by embarrassment and irritation at his own stupidity. He resented the boy's carefree presumption and then sloughed it off to the low intellect of his race. Nevertheless, the boy had a certain cherubic charm. That and his dignity required that Jed be cordial.

"Nothing, just getting a better look at this tree," Jed replied lamely. "Catch anything?"

The boy proudly held out his stringer of four bluegills and one catfish while discounting his yield, "Aw, I usually do better, but these will fry up nice."

"What did you use?"

"Worms on a bobber," the boy said, as he started to walk back to the docks. Jed followed. They emerged from the forest at the parking lot, and Jed went to his bike.

"Is dat your'n?" The boy was wide-eyed.

"Yes, it is." The motorcycle rider smiled.

"Kin ah sit on it?" The boy asked, putting down his pole and stringer.

Jed stiffened. Then, for reasons he would not be able to explain to his friends or himself, he picked up the boy and put him on the saddle. The boy reached forward for the handlebars but, since his feet couldn't reach the pedals, he started to fall to the kickstand side. Jed caught and steadied him.

"Thanks." With Jed's help to reach the handlebars, the boy was nearly prone over the gas tank. "How fast does she go?" he asked with unquenchable excitement.

"Don't really know, but I had it up to 80 once. I don't like going much faster than that." The boy let out a low whistle and was going to ask another question when he interrupted himself,

"Hey, I know you. You're the guy with the fat violin." Jed reeled at the recognition. The boy went on,

"Yeah, what did you call it — a vee ol..."

"Viola," said Jed.

"Yeah, that's it. You came to our school last year. You 'member?"

"What school do you go to?"

"I went to PS 27."

Jed did remember. As part of its musical outreach program, the Symphony would send small ensembles to the local schools. He had volunteered once in order to gain more visibility with the orchestra. He eventually volunteered three more times.

"On nineteenth, near the park?" asked Jed.

"Yep. That's the one. Going to high school next year," the boy said proudly.

"Congratulations. Where?"

"Hopefully, Shortridge. Gotta take some summer classes at Crispus Attucks, though."

"Horace!!!!" came a loud mezzo-soprano yell from the picnic area.

"Eek, gotta go, what's your name?" Jed helped him off the bike.

"Jed Norton."

"Well, I guess you know mine now. See you around." The boy picked up his fish and gear and went running to his family. Jed started his bike and rode off.

— 14 —

JUNE 2 SUNDAY

Wine Lessons – Micaela's Apartment

Music: Haydn, Concerto for Cello and Orchestra D Major, Op. 101

Jed spent a good part of the holiday weekend on the back of his motorcycle. It wasn't so much a tour of his home state as it was but an attempt to ream out a sense of anhedonia. He had learned the word in college: *a psychological condition characterized by the inability to experience pleasure in normally pleasurable acts.* He wished had never learned the word, which now hung on him like a wooden sign, warning others to stay away. No matter how many miles he rode, he couldn't shake it loose. At the end of his ride on Sunday, for no known reason, he felt anxious to get home. Parking his bike, he bounded up the stoop to his brick duplex. The phone was ringing. He fumbled with the lock and caught the phone in time.

"Hello," he panted.

"Hello, Jed?" Instantly identifying the voice, he took a deep breath, loosened his grip on the phone, and spoke with pleasant deliberation.

"Hello, Micaela."

"Did I call at bad time?"

"No, not at all. I just got back from a ride and rushed to catch the phone."

"Now, you are catching breath."

"And now it's caught. How are you?"

"I am fine. I had wonderful time at race, and I have been trying to call …
but no answer. Did you go away?"

"No, but aside from practice and sleep, I have been out on the bike most
of the time. Kinda of touring my home state."

"Practice on holiday, how good of you," Micaela said, sarcastically. For
professional musicians, there were no days without practice.

"Yeah, right," Jed said. "But considering the partying after I dropped you
off, I am not sure it has been very effective."

"Hee, hee. So you and your friends had late night?"

"Most definitely too late. 500 foolishness I suppose."

"I see. Vell, I vanted to express my thanks by cooking authentic Slovakian
dinner, but perhaps ven you still need recover," Micaela said. Her words
drifted inside of him in big blocky letters dripping in a syrup of accent that
drowned the anhedonia .

"No, no … recovery is complete … really." Jed laughed.

"Are you sure?" asked Micaela, echoing Jed's amusement.

"Yes, I am sure. I don't even know what Slovakian food is, but I would
love to try it."

"Then, is settled. Come over … seven o'clock?"

"What should I bring?" asked Jed.

"Some vine. A red for menu," answered Micaela.

"See you at seven."

"Bye bye," said Micaela.

"Bye." As Jed hung up the phone, his euphoria was quickly replaced by
panic. Wine? He knew nothing about wine. Plus it was Sunday on Memorial
Day weekend, so many stores were closed. Jed rifled through the yellow pages
looking for ads about wine. Finding none, he chose the friendliest ad.

"Hoosier Buddy Liquors."

"You're open?"

"Always, we're your buddy."

"Do you have any red wine?" asked Jed.

"Yes, and white."

"Any imported?"

"Dunno. Just a sec. Hey, Melba," the clerk shouted in the store. "We got
any foreign wine? We do? Yessir, we do, and it's got a cork in it."

"Great, tell me how to get there." Jed took down the directions. In the meantime, he had time for a little practice and a lot of cleanup.

Jed arrived at Micaela's apartment house early. The Hoosier Buddy's Liquor Store was considerably out of the way, so he had left with plenty of time. However, there was no traffic on this holiday, so the trip was quicker than expected. He had found a Hungarian red called Egri Bikivar, hoping that it was close enough to home to make Micaela feel appreciated. He drove around the block a couple of times, trying to use up time. He finally gave up and parked his bike. The vestibule to the apartment house had stainless-steel-framed-glass inner and outer doors. Inside the vestibule, he scanned the brushed steel mailboxes and found "M. Miklos Apt 3B" and pressed the button next to it.

"Hello?" her accent was clear even through the primitive electronics.

"Hi, it's Jed."

"Jed? You are early," she said.

"Yeah, sorry." Jed looked at his watch. Shit, he was at least thirty minutes early. "I'll come back later."

"No, no. Just a minute and I buzz you in," she said.

Jed paced the tiny confines of the vestibule, annoyed with his own impatience. Five seconds later he heard the grating buzz of the electric lock and went through the inner door. Micaela had a third-floor walkup. At the landing of the second floor, Jed slowed down. She's going to think I am always out of breath, he thought. He checked himself over. His clothes looked brand new, because they had hardly been worn. He had formal wear for the concerts, painting clothes, jeans and t-shirts for casual. Several months ago, he did make a trip to the local preppy store, Roderick St. Johns, to buy some *in-between* stuff. The button-down herringbone seemed fine, the brown slacks survived the ride. However, the left Bass Wejun had scuff marks from the Indian's shift lever, which he brushed off. The hallway to her door had been upgraded to that rundown modern look that new apartment buildings achieved about six months after completion. He stood at her door and knocked sharply on the wood veneer. Micaela opened quickly. She was wearing a light blue silk bathrobe with Japanese flower designs embroidered on it. She held it tight, just below the convergence of her clavicles. Her hair was pinned up, and still wet. He could see the drops of water glide down her neck and dampen the collar of the robe. He had noticed the extended length of her neck before. It was like Audrey Hepburn's but proportional to her more athletic frame. The color of her skin was a translucent white that seemed to flow into the loosely fitting robe.

"As you see, you *are* early," she said.

"Sorry," smiled Jed. He could not conceal the insincerity of his apology. Micaela grinned back, "I vill be bit longer getting ready. Please make yourself at home. There is corkscrew on kitchen counter and Lowenbrau in ice box." Micaela slipped gracefully away to her bedroom as Jed stepped in. The experience of stepping in was more immersion than entry. The aromas wafting from the kitchen enveloped everything in their path, including him. Although invisible, their strength was tangible. He had not the experience to identify the overriding carrier scent. Sweet Hungarian Paprika had been used liberally for the main course, *Paprikas Csirke*. But his ignorance did not prevent him from realizing that Micaela was an experienced, if not tidy, cook who had been working hard on this meal. As he took three steps to the kitchen, the portents of sensual delights multiplied.

Unbagging the wine and placing it on the counter, he opened the fridge looking for a beer. There was a six pack of green bottles of imported Lowenbrau. Taking one out, he inspected the label, realizing that this was what Micaela had been referring to. He tried to imitate her pronunciation, "Loenenbrowch," but failed. Using the other end of the double-handled corkscrew, he uncapped the beer, scraped off the dirty bits from the sticky lead cover, and took a pull. As the heady German pilsner went down, he winced, "Acck, I guess I prefer mouthvash?" Slowly pouring most of the brew down the drain, he looked over the sparsely furnished apartment. The kitchen was open to the dining room, where a card table had been set, complete with candles, and flowers. He stopped pouring when Micaela came in. She was wearing a rosehip-colored, faded paisley sundress with a rounded neckline. Aside from a gold locket around her neck, there was no jewelry and no shoes. Jed drank the rest of his beer and smiled at her.

"You like the Lowenbrau?" she asked.

"It's great," he gritted.

"Liar," she laughed. "Let's try your vine instead. Vhat did you bring?"

"I hope it's okay. I don't know a lot about wine, but it's red and close to where you come from," Jed answered. Micaela read the label and laughed hard.

"Indeed it is. This is perfect. For main course ve are having *Paprikas Csirke,* which is Hungarian." Still looking at the label and laughing, she asked, "Do you know vhat Egri Bikivar means?" Jed shrugged. "I tell you later." She winked … or did she? Jed couldn't tell. He took the bottle to open it. Micaela fetched the two glasses from the dinner table and set them on the boomerang-patterned formica bar that separated the kitchen from the dining area. Jed poured her and himself a full glass. Micaela looked at the glass and then at him.

"Jed, I am *wh*ondering, can you help me *wh*ith a question?" she asked deliberately, working on her 'w's.

"I'll do my best," he replied.

"Vhat exactly is Hoosier?

Jed laughed. "You mean besides being a person from Indiana?"

"Yes." Micaela moved around to the other side of the bar to work on dinner. Jed started to trade positions. "No, stay," she said. "You can help. Chop these tomatoes."

"Vhat is a Hoosier?" Jed repeated in her accent as he fumbled with the tomatoes. "Well, as you may have noticed, America is a big country. As big as Europe, depending on what you include." Micaela nodded her head. Jed continued "While most of us speak English, there are groups of people who have different accents and colloquialisms."

"*Wh*at's colloquialism?" Micaela asked.

"It's a different word or set of words for a common idea or phrase. For example, I might say there's not enough room in this kitchen to swing a cat."

"Hmmmm. You're saying my kitchen is small?"

"Exactly, and if it were much smaller I wouldn't have room to change my mind."

"Vhat? Oh, I get it," Micaela laughed. "If it is even smaller, I could not *wh*ear my clothes. Is that it?" Micaela now laughed at her own cleverness.

"Well, sort of." Jed winced. "The problem is that you just made that up. Colloquialisms aren't made up. They just exist."

"Somebody had to make up sometime."

"Perhaps, but nobody ever knows who did. And no one ever takes credit. Okay, let's move on. In this part of the country that we call the great state of Indiana, we have our own style of speaking and colloquialisms that denote us as Hoosiers. The word Hoosier is actually a derogatory term applied by our neighbors, who could not understand whether we were saying 'Who is here', 'Who's your', or 'Whose ear'," Jed tugged on his ear on the last phrase.

Micaela nodded. "But could not they figure it out?"

"Yes, I suppose they could or should. But that's not the point or the more amusing irony, which is … despite the fact that this was an insult, we Hoosiers took on the name as a prideful identifier of residents of this state." Micaela stared, perplexed.

"What you should be saying now, Micaela, is: 'Why in tarnation did they do that? Are they just dumber than a box of rocks? Gosh o' mighty, they better find some tall grass to hide in when the fool killer comes around.' " Micaela's slack jaw turned into loud laughter as she enjoyed Jed's exaggerated imitation.

"Jed, you must teach me to speak Hoosier," Micaela said.

"It would make me as happy as a hog in a field of acorns. And you can teach me to chop tomatoes."

She took the vegetable from him. "No I will teach you how to pour wine. It is much easier."

"Okey doke," he said before draining his glass. "I'm ready for the first lesson." Micaela took the bottle. "First, you must handle wine vith care. It was made vith ... *with* care and should be treated with respect. Gently pour glass no more than half full, maybe less, so it can breathe. At the end of pour, turn bottle one quarter so it does not drip on outside of glass." Micaela demonstrated the procedure. "Now, drink with respect, too. Hold glass by stem, not bowl — do not cloud beauty with unsightly fingerprints. Swirl glass gently to unleash smell from grapes and sip wine, holding in mouth so all flavors can be enjoyed." Jed did as told.

"And mighty fine smell that is, ma'am. Or as we like to say ... ayr-oh-ma. And you're right, it would be a lot more purty if there weren't all these dad-gum fingerprints on the glass. Gee whillikens, who put those there?"

"I vill never keep up," Micaela giggled. "Dinner is almost ready. Help me with plates." Jed actually did make himself useful and found himself developing an extraordinary appetite. Micaela grabbed hot pads and took the roasting pan with the Chicken Paprika out of the oven. After testing doneness, she added a little salt and asked Jed to light the candles. She brought the plates to the table and told Jed to sit. She returned to the kitchen for the bread and the bottle of wine. Jed was motionless but nearly salivating in his seat.

"Eat," she commanded. Jed obliged. As he took the first bite, he was painfully aware of Micaela watching him and was ready to provide any compliment necessary, despite how bad it might taste.

"This is delicious!" he said.

"You look surprised."

"No, I mean, yes. I mean, I really had no idea how good this was going to be." With a mouth-filled grin, Jed shut up and started to devour his dinner.

"Thank you," Micaela said as he gobbled. Soon Jed looked at his plate as if someone had stolen his food. Glancing up at Micaela in the candlelight, he apologized for ignoring her. "It's just that this is so good," he explained.

"Vould you like more?" she cooed.

"Oh, yes, please." Micaela cut half of her portion and gave it to Jed.

"Are you sure?" Jed said.

"Absolutely. Please. Eat," Micaela insisted. When Jed was finally done, Micaela said, "Did you have enough?"

"Yes, it was fantastic. What did you call it?" Jed asked.

"It doesn't matter. Time for another wine lesson." Jed looked at Micaela with expectation. Micaela took the bottle of wine and filled her glass to the brim. Jed looked curious. Grabbing the glass firmly by the bowl, pausing for a moment, she looked at Jed and then tossed the entire contents in Jed's face. Jed sputtered in disbelief. Micaela stood up went around the corner of the table, rotated Jed's chair a quarter turn, and then straddled him. Grabbing his wine-wet face in both hands, she kissed him deeply and fiercely, inhaling the mixed aroma of Jed and the Egri Bikivar. Jed's multiple surprises started to evaporate like uncontained alcohol. He responded to her passion as a familiar and devoted addict. The intense sexual intoxication threatened the stability of the chair. He stood up with her and gazed down. She craned her neck upwards, eyes nearly closed, stretching the length of her body and legs. There were tiny tears tinged with red from the wine that transferred from his face. He held her head gently in his left hand and brushed the tears from her cheeks.

She opened her eyes at him, and he asked, "Are you okay?" He felt himself falling into the wells of her eyes.

She smiled and said, "Please come with me." She led him by the hand to the bedroom.

Hours, days, weeks, but truly minutes later, Jed lay staring at the ceiling with Micaela comfortably crooked in his left arm. She was watching her own hand gliding along his pale stomach, watching his ribs rise and fall slowly with his breathing.

"I hope you don't think I am too aggressive." It was not a question, but Jed took it as one anyway.

"Actually, I am having hard time thinking now at all," he joked. "But if I were capable of thinking, I certainly wouldn't think that."

"Really?" she said. "What vould ... would you think, then?"

"I vould think ..." he said teasing her accent. "I vould think that you vere fantastic."

"Aww, that is too easy," she said as she pinched him hard.

"Ow, that hurt. And that *was* too aggressive."

"Tell me what you really think," Micaela insisted and turned her head upwards towards Jed. He looked at her and again felt her eyes pulling at him, twin sources of gravity. He stared until she started to turn away.

"Okay, ma'am, this is what I really think," with thick Hoosier accent. "I think you really got your rhubarb up."

"My what?"

"Around these parts, when a woman is, well, acting and feeling the way you are, we say she has her rhubarb up," Jed explained, continuing with the accent.

"What is a rhubarb?" Micaela asked.

"Well, it's a plant, sometimes used in pies. It's also a fight. And it is a condition that a woman sometimes finds herself in," he answered dryly.

"Really, that's what you think?"

"Yes," he answered. Micaela shook her head and turned away. He turned her face back towards him and repeated, "Yes, that is what I think." Pausing to hold onto her eyes with his own, he continued, "And I really, truly am amazed about how good I feel. And I don't remember ever feeling this way before. And I don't want to be any place else in the world but here. I have never ever had more pleasure looking into someone's eyes as I do yours. And I really think you *are* fantastic." He continued to hold her gaze until she smiled and relaxed. She turned onto her back. He started to kiss her shoulders and said, "I was also wondering if, even though I have to get up early and go to work," pausing for another kiss, "if I might stay the night."

She stretched her arms above her head and said softly, "Yes, you may."

"And, perhaps, we could have an encore," he pressed.

"Yes, we could do that. After all, it seems I have plenty of rhubarb." Laughing, they fell into each other again.

Jed woke up first and knew instantly where he was. However, that knowledge did not lessen his awe and disbelief. He could have been impressed with himself that he had just spent the night with the first chair of the cellos. That would be several stations above him in the hierarchy of the orchestra. But, in fact, it wasn't himself that he was impressed with at all. It was her. It wasn't that she was unlike any woman that he had been with, it was that she was unlike any person he had been with. He looked at her, feeling certain that he knew her well and not at all at the same time. He wanted to wake her up and ask her questions, and he didn't even know what those questions were.

Her peaceful sleep stayed his exuberance long enough for him to get dressed and gain the bearings of his responsibilities. He really did have to get to work early, he thought, as he put on his watch. *I'll leave her a note.* He went into the kitchen to find paper and pencil.

The kitchen was a disaster that could not be overlooked. While starting to clean up, he chuckled at the mess and the memory of her throwing the wine on him. He wondered what it would be like to live with someone messier than himself that *he* would have to clean up after. The fact that he was wondering about living with her froze him in mid-rinse. He was shaking his head in disbelief at himself when he heard, "Good morning." Micaela had risen and was wearing the same Japanese silk bathrobe that she greeted him in, the night before.

"Good morning." He grinned so wide it hurt. "You look great," he said with sincere intensity.

"Ahhh." she shook off the compliment. "Vhat are you doing?"

"Just cleaning up a bit before going to work. Actually, I am little late."

"Don't worry, I vill take care of it. I have to get going, too. I have to be over at Eric's in a couple hours."

"Eric?" Jed said, surprised, which Micaela noticed with enjoyment.

"Yeah, I wanted to practice with you before moving up string section." She said this into Jed's ear with a quick flick of the tongue. Jed understood the tease, but because Eric was his boss, and he didn't like him, and he was still trying to figure out what to do about liking Micaela so much, he had to force his laughter.

"Better be careful where that bow has been fiddling around."

Micaela picked up on the acid comment and decided she'd better explain.

"Eric is helping me study for opening performance. I am doing Brahms Double with Gianluca Giarrizzo," she said, taking the dishes out of his hand and giving him a warm hug. The hug was more effective than the explanation and Jed held onto it with great pleasure.

Then what she actually said sunk into his brain. "The *Brahms Double Concerto!*" he exclaimed and she nodded. "With Luca!" he exclaimed again and she said,

"You repeat well, Jed."

"On your first night?!" Now Micaela turned her head and eyes down.

"Yes," she said softly.

"That's unbelievable. How did they get Luca to agree to that? What an opportunity for you!" Jed was sincerely excited for her.

"Yah, so much opportunity."

Although Jed had never had such an opportunity as a performer, he could empathize with her fears immediately.

"Don't worry," he laughed. "You will do fine. Eric will be a great help. He may be a prick, but he is a tremendous violinist and teacher. Listen closely to him. Besides, you have plenty of rhubarb for the performance."

Micaela appreciated having Jed in her corner. "I am beginning to vonder what word really means," she said.

Jed laughed and dried his hands with a dish towel. Seeing the bottle of wine from last night, he asked, "Speaking of which, you never told me what Egri Bikivar means."

Sliding her hand along his arm she answered, "Bull's Blood. Now get out of here. I must clean up." She kissed him.

"Yes ma'am," he said. Then he muttered loud enough for her to hear, "I think I better get a case of that stuff." He walked out the door to the sweet sound of her laughter.

—15 —

"Is it not strange that sheeps' guts should hale souls out of men's bodies?" — Shakespeare, <u>Much Ado About Nothing</u>

JUNE 3 MONDAY

Eric and Micaela's First Study Session – Eric's House

Music: Bach, Sonata No. 1 for Solo Violin, G Minor

Lugging her cello up the porch steps, Micaela heard Bach's *Sonata No. 1* coming from within Eric's house. Show-off, she thought. There was a note on the door that said to come in. She became aware that the sound was somehow unusual and saw Eric in his living room. He was in the midst of the *Presto*. Not surprisingly, her entrance would remain unacknowledged until the end of this final movement. Taking advantage of the situation, she put her cello down and paced in front of Eric like a child trying to shake the concentration of the Buckingham Palace Guard. She stopped the game immediately when she noticed the source of the unusual sound. This was not an ordinary violin. Rarely do you see ornamental scrollwork on the bridge. There was no chin rest. The bow was dramatically cambered in order to make it easier to play chords and single notes simultaneously. It was a baroque violin, a period instrument playing the music of its period. Eric played it with very little left hand vibrato, yet the sound produced an ethereal reverberation, as if it were in a small chamber hall inhabited by the ghosts of Bach and Martin Luther. Eric finished the sonata.

98

"What lovely instrument," said Micaela.

"Please hold it."

Micaela did as instructed and took the instrument with two hands and held it with care. Even as a cellist, she could tell that it was unusually light. She removed one hand and pantomimed how light it was. She brushed her other hand over the strings. They were not the standard metal. She looked at Eric.

"Catgut," he replied to the unasked question. He continued to describe the instrument. "It's light because the woods are thinner. So thin, in fact, it is tuned a half-tone lower. That makes it very responsive and easy to initiate tone."

"That must be a great asset for Bach Sonati," Micaela said.

"Yes, although they are still impossible," Eric grinned. "The dynamic range is somewhat limited. If you play it too hard, the sound will break. Any orchestra would overwhelm it."

"Vould ... would you mind doing the Adagio?"

Eric took the rare instrument back to play the first movement of Bach's *First Sonata for Violin*. Besides being a composer and pianist, Bach also played the violin. He must have been very good, considering the difficulty of these pieces. It is said that they have never been played correctly and only exist in their purest form on paper. The combination of chording and single notes sometimes seem better suited to a piano than a simple four-stringed instrument. The Adagio is as difficult as it is delicate.

Eric started, and Micaela quickly slipped into closed-eye reverie at the mournful tune. Just as quickly she opened her eyes to reassure her visual sense that there was only one instrument playing. The illusion of two instruments was marvelous, and she returned to her trance for the rest of the selection. At the end, she opened her eyes and thanked Eric.

"Okay, let's get to work." Eric put away the baroque and got his Stradivarius while Micaela unpacked her cello. They set up the music for the concerto and tuned their instruments. "I will alternate between the string section and Luca's part to keep a frame of reference. You focus only on the cello concerto." Eric counted out the tempo and started the dramatic beginning vocalizing to give his single instrument more emphasis 'Daaa de da, Daaaa de da, Da de da Da de da ...'. Then came the opening cadenza for Micaela. Eric watched closely through the solo. Then, together, they vocalized the wind section that separated the opening cello from the opening violin. Eric took hold of the part with vigor, and soon the cello and violin were musically interlocked in glorious Brahms. Eric stopped them when the longer orchestral interlude began.

"Let's jump ahead to two bars before letter J." They shuffled their sheet music to the spot and then began again with Eric's cue. They continued in this manner throughout the first movement. Once in a while Eric would stop and suggest small changes in the dynamic, "Try making that *crescendo forte* steeper at the end, 'da da Da, Da, DA'." Micaela responded dutifully and beautifully. At the end of the first movement, they took a break.

Eric laughed, "Well, if Gianluca doesn't walk off the stage after the opening, this should be quite something."

"What do you mean?" asked Micaela. Eric continued to laugh quietly and then took a long drink of his water.

"Micaela, you really are getting the most out of that crummy cello. One can only imagine what's going to happen when they get you a real one."

"But what did you mean about 'walking off the stage?'"

"I will try to say this as politely as possible. Your approach to this piece is appropriately and perfectly erotic. Luca is, how shall I say this … more pornographic? Yes, that's it — both in his playing and in his life. On stage, he will want to objectify you but will fail if you play like that. How he reacts to that failure will be interesting to see."

Micaela was confused, "Are you saying I have to tone it down?"

"No! Never. Lay it on during the first rehearsal. That'll give him two or three chances to figure out what he's going to do. And the rest of us can enjoy the fireworks." Eric raised his eyebrows to support his mischievous smile. "Now, let's get back to it."

— 16 —

Monk Commits Suicide by Fire In Anti-Diem Protest — June 11

Civil Rights Leader Medgar Evers Assassinated in Mississippi — June 12

JUNE 12 WEDNESDAY

Public Relations Meeting – Bobo's Office

Music: Vivaldi, Spring - First Movement, from Four Seasons

BoBo had the largest office in Campbell. Behind his walnut desk were his framed certificates of education, including his highly prized MBA from Ball State University. On the walls were some watercolors and one trophy-sized large mouth bass that he caught in Brookville Lake in Franklin County, south of Muncie. Today the three visitor chairs would be occupied by Leon, Alison, and Micaela. Normally, his secretary would use one of those chairs. But she was sick, and because Micaela was such an important part of this year's plan, she had been invited too. The absence of his secretary would only keep BoBo more in the dark than usual. His ignorance was not a functional concern because Alison and Leon did all the substantive work anyway. This year, BoBo had added a brand-new stereo to the office with a Gerard turntable. Just before the ten o'clock meeting, he put on the Concerto "Spring" from Vivaldi's *Four Seasons.*

Outside the door, Micaela could hear the sound and said, "Mě vynechte."

Leon said, "Ah, not a Vivaldi fan, are we?"

"Il Bach castrato," answered Micaela.

Leon laughed and then winked. "Careful, Micaela, Chairman Delmonico knows *some* Italian." Leon opened the door and led them into the office.

"Welcome, everyone. So good to see you." Delmonico greeted everyone with vigorous handshakes.

"Robert, I see you have a new acquisition." Leon was nearly shouting over the Vivaldi.

"Doesn't it sound marvelous?" said BoBo. Leon nodded in agreement.

"Is it too loud?" asked BoBo. "Maybe I should turn it down a bit." Leon answered for them.

"Actually we need to turn it off for the meeting. It is hard for musicians to concentrate when music like that is playing."

"You're right," agreed BoBo. "It's so beautiful. It's distracting. You should really consider programming it some time."

"Why?" said Micaela rhetorically. Both Leon and Alison had to cover their amusement.

"Excuse me?" asked BoBo, looking at Micaela with the possible, but unlikely, understanding that he had been insulted.

"Vhat I mean to say is … why is it necessary ven you have such a beautiful record player. It sounds, how do you say it … not dead?" said Micaela.

"Oh, yes, you mean live. Good point, Micaela. It is almost as good as live music. Boy, if stereos keep on getting better, you will all be out of a job," BoBo laughed. Leon forced a thin smile. Alison and Micaela didn't even bother.

"Just kidding, you guys," said BoBo. "Okay, we'd better get started. It's time to raise the bar. We need to do something really, really huge … bigger and better than all the other orchestras. And I think we can do it. We just need to think outside our normal frame of reference. Come up with something new and exciting and … er, large, something where everyone will feel the impact. Does anyone have an idea?" Alison, who had been patiently enduring BoBo's intro, handed out a typewritten plan consisting of an idea list, abstracts, and schedule. The ideas had been categorized into either musical news or society news. For example, reviews, musical stars, and programming news fell into the category of music only. Opening night, audience celebrities, parties, guest lists, Micaela, Vladimir, and Gianluca were always good for stories in the society pages. The ideas were all marked as either local, national or international news items. BoBo attempted to pore over the pages, nodding his head in feigned understanding.

"Would you like me to go over the plan by idea, schedule, or just the highlights?" asked Alison.

"Why don't we start with highlights and then we can flesh out the details," suggested BoBo. This meeting would start and end with the highlights.

"Fine, then let me start with Micaela, because she is certainly one of our brighter highlights of the season. We have arranged for her to do two columns for the *Indianapolis Star*. This will be a venue in which she can tell behind-the-scenes stories of the symphony and also introduce herself to the community of Indianapolis. The first column will be later this summer and is primarily a 'Hello Indianapolis' column or 'How I spent my summer vacation'."

"How I spent my non-vacation," Leon interjected.

"Yes," Alison agreed, "she will address all the work she is doing in preparation for the opening performance. And the following column, due out two weeks before opening, will detail her own and general concert preparation. Before her columns start, and for the columns to be of interest, Micaela needs to be introduced to Indianapolis. This will be done by a special presentation and a background story on Micaela's musical and personal history."

"Her personal history?" asked Bobo.

"The tragic assassination of her parents and her escape from Czechoslovakia," said Alison evenly.

"Oh yeah, sorry."

"What is special presentation?" asked Micaela. Micaela had been briefed by Leon and Alison on nearly all of this material, but not the presentation. Alison deferred to Leon.

"The Campbell Foundation has decided that if you are going to play in their building, you should be properly equipped." Leon presented Micaela with a picture and written description of a cello. Micaela caught her own breath but was still able to whisper,

"The Baudiot. It's not possible?" She looked at Leon and he nodded.

"Baudiot, who's Baudiot? I thought they were going to get her a Stradivarius," blurted BoBo.

"Most of the Stradivarius' are named after their earliest known owner. This particular cello was made by Stradivari in 1725. Shortly after that, it was acquired by Baudiot, and until very recently it was owned by one Gregor Piatigorsky."

"How much is it worth?"

"About three times the cost of your house." Leon's answer produced a leering smile on BoBo.

"How could he part with this?" asked Micaela

"Well, he has two, plus an Amati. Of the three, he thought this one would fit you best. He said he was glad it was going to a good home. It would seem that your reputation is quite widespread," Leon smiled and continued. "Micaela, before accepting this gift, you must first test it. Make sure that you and the instrument are a musical fit. It will arrive within the week."

"I don't know how to accept or refuse such a treasure," said Micaela.

"Eric and I will help. It will be fun to check it out," reassured Leon.

"If she *does* accept," Alison continued, "it will be formally presented by Edith Campbell on the fourth of July weekend, and Micaela's complete story will run as a sidebar, setting up her columns."

"Thank you," said Micaela to no one in particular.

"I have a question," BoBo said. Everyone waited. "No offense, Micaela, but you don't speak English so good. How are you going to write these columns?" Alison put her hand on Micaela's arm and answered for her.

"Actually, Micaela can speak and write very well. She just has a charming accent," Alison said in her thickest drawl. "But with all such pieces, they will be reviewed and edited before submission."

"That sounds very good. Like I said, no offense."

"There are a number of local events that both Leon and Micaela will attend together and separately so that she becomes a household word. Leon, you are on tap for the all the Ladies Luncheons again." Leon sighed in frustration.

"Maybe Micaela should go instead," said BoBo, trying to be helpful.

"No. Micaela will not be going to ladies-only events. She will do better with the men," corrected Alison.

"Seems like you have thought of everything," beamed Bobo.

"I have more," said Alison.

"More! Alison, you are incredible," said BoBo. She continued, ignoring the fact that he had shifted into his well-known hyperbolic mode.

"We have invited the New York critics to opening night. It looks like Winthrop is definite. The rest are all maybes, which probably means no. In addition to the opening performance, the busts will be unveiled during intermission. Although this is a local story, it is very important that Winthrop witness the event. Can you see to that, Robert?" Leon wasn't sure, but he thought he saw Alison bat her eyelashes when she made the request of Robert.

"Consider it done."

"And we need another favor," Alison said, once again directing her well-trained wiles at BoBo.

"Anything," said BoBo.

"We need to leak to the press about Khazar."

"What about him?" asked BoBo.

"The fact that he's coming," said Leon.

"I didn't know it was a secret," said BoBo. Alison and Leon looked at each other in disbelief.

Leon looked closely at BoBo and asked, "Robert, have you had recent conversations about this?"

"Well, yes," he answered sheepishly.

"Who?" the maestro pressed.

"Corbin called a couple of days ago."

"That would be Corbin Blomster, the columnist from the *Star*," Leon filled in.

"Yes."

"What did he want?" asked Leon.

"He just wanted to know if there was any news about next year's season," answered BoBo.

"And you told him … ?"

"I told him that Vladimir Khazar was doing his America debut with us in December." Leon was becoming silently apoplectic at the stupidity of his chairman. Alison was completely amused and turned to Leon.

"Consider it done, honey."

— 17 —

JUNE 25 TUESDAY

Jed and Micaela – Quarry No. 5

Music: Ravel, Daphnis et Chloe, Pantomime

The beach towel did not provide a significant cushion between the hard limestone and Micaela's stomach. The slab was at a shallow angle and disappeared into the cool quarry water a couple of yards below her feet. Her hands supported her chin as she stared at the cut quarry stone. She turned her head slightly as the coarse surface came into focus. She could see the seashells— smaller than the half moons of her closely manicured fingernails— embedded in the oolitic rock. The discovery of the shells allowed her to decode a myriad of other unknown shapes, frozen fossils of miniature life that was once covered by an inland sea. The sheer multitude of shapes thawed and softened her platform. The frequent shell spirals optically resurrected the movement of the long-dead creatures. Swirling in the noonday sun that warmed her bare back, the fossils increased her sense of melting into the primordial morass.

Jed swam to the tilted block. With an amphibious stride, he walked out of the water to where Micaela was sunbathing. He put on his dark glasses, picked up the basket of fried chicken, and stood over her, drying slowly in the humidity. It was Tuesday, June 25th, and the quarry was deserted.

"How do you say picnic in Czech?" he asked. Micaela surfaced from her carbonate immersion and turned over, ineffectively covering her breasts with her left arm. She rose to the sitting position, held her other hand as a sun visor and squinted up at the dripping silhouette.

"Pik Nik," she answered.

Jed laughed quietly. He was going to offer her some fried chicken. Instead, he put the basket down on the cut shelf a yard above her head and knelt down beside her on the towel. She reached over and took off his dark glasses. She laid them down on the edge of the limestone stage to her right. The glasses fell over the precipice, gently rattling on the abrasive surface until they disappeared into the water. Jed made no move to save them. He looked at her through her eyes. Micaela laid back down and let her arms fall to her side. Jed placed his palms on the towel on either side of her head and lowered himself down so that his first contact was her lips. The initial ease of the kissing and lovemaking they had discovered on that first night at her home had been augmented by practice. He lowered himself further to feel her breasts against his chest. Like her kisses, her breasts rose up to meet him, and they found the perfect point of pressure that made them feel that their skin was copulating before they were. She slid her hands up his forearms to his biceps, flexed to protect her from the hard limestone. Her hands continued on to his shoulders and down his back to the waistband of his trunks and then forcefully shoved them down below his hips.

He broke off the still-firing kiss, rose up to rest his arms, and moved his kneeling position between her spreading thighs. She was wearing a black string bikini tied on either side with a bowknot. He pulled at the tag end of each bow, releasing the front triangle. He slid his hand across her uncovered womb. She arched, moaned, spread her legs further, and hooked her heel high up against the back of his thigh, pulling him closer. He descended again with hands in the push-up position as she guided him inside her.

Jed was breathing hard from the athletic effort of holding himself up as well as the excitement. "It's okay," she said. "I can take it." Jed lowered himself, now resting more of his weight on her body as her body began to wrap more around his.

The world returned to them through the echo of Micaela's cries in the amphitheater of the quarry.

— 18 —

"Ich bin ein Berliner" — John Fitzgerald Kennedy at the Berlin Wall,
June 26

JUNE 26 WEDNESDAY

The 1725 Baudiot – Campbell Hall

Music: Saint-Saens, Concerto No. 1 for Cello and Orchestra A Minor

Allen knocked on the door to Leon's office.

"Who is it?" replied the unmistakable basso voice from behind the door.

"Allen, sir. It's arrived."

"Fantastic! Please come in." The maestro's voice moved up a few tones in
pitch and friendliness. Allen entered the small sanctuary where he knew that
Leon and Micaela were meeting to discuss program notes and the upcoming
presentation of the cello. He tried to remember when he had seen Leon in the
office so much. It certainly wasn't in the summer. That was the time for most
of his guest appearances.

But this year the conductor had canceled his guest appearances for the
music festivals in Flagstaff, Tampa, San Antonio, Rochester, and Mexico City.
He was still planning to appear at the Hollywood Bowl, San Diego, and
Aspen. London had fallen through, and no one knew why, or at least no one
was telling, but Leon had instigated all the other cancellations himself, and he
had good explanations prepared for the public and the players behind the
scenes.

When Leon heard that the Flagstaff season had to be shortened because of
budget problems, he immediately called to suggest that they cancel his
performance. His gracious offer was in no small way influenced by the recent
news that the brilliant violin soloist, Michael Rabin, with whom he was
scheduled to perform, had botched a performance due to a weird combination
of lithium, dexadrine, and miltown.

"Botched?" Luca had laughed. "Well, that's one way to put it. You might say destroyed, mutilated, or mangled."

"Luca, you exaggerate."

"No, I don't. I was there. Three times in the first movement, the orchestra had to wait for him. Twice in the second, he had a series of arpeggios that one orchestra member called 'klinkers on parade.' The cadenzas were a complete joke. He would just stop half way through most of them. But that is not the worst part. During the pause between the second and third, the orchestra waited while he pulled a handkerchief from his coat pocket to wipe his brow. Apparently, his pill bottle was wrapped inside. The bottle flew out of the handkerchief, hit the stage, and scattered pills of all shapes, sizes, and colors."

"Oy. How embarrassing," said Leon.

"Yeah, for everyone, Leon," Luca said pointedly. "First, the audience gasped. When Michael went down to gather his pills, there were boos and giggles."

"What did Szell do?" asked Leon.

"Pretty much nothing. He waited him out. One of his violins started to get out of her chair to help. He waved her off, and she sat back down. They eventually finished the concerto, bowed to pathetically polite applause, and Szell escorted him off the stage."

"What a shame. What a disaster," said Leon.

"Yes, it was," agreed Luca. "You know, years ago, when I heard him play Kreisler's *Recitative and Scherzo,* I almost put down the fiddle."

"I remember. But instead, Michael showed you how Kriesler did the *saultando* bowing on the triple chords."

"Yes, he did. I owe him a lot … more than you do, but I wouldn't play with him now," Luca said.

The other cancellations had less dramatic, but still plausible justifications. Nevertheless, it was uncharacteristic of Leon to cancel, particularly Mexico City. Allen had heard that the orchestra was of much lesser quality than originally reported, but the maestro was known for getting remarkable performances from lesser ensembles. It was not like him to back away from a challenge. Besides, Leon liked going to Mexico.

The other reason Leon gave Allen for spending extra time in the office was the "infernally noisy and expensive" remodeling going on at home in Alison's studio. An extremely plausible story, thought Allen, but it still seemed that an inordinate amount of work was being done in the office this summer. Several times a week there were meetings about the upcoming season. Most of them were about the programs and the extra study sessions going on. Others were about publicity opportunities. It was as if the season had never ended. The news about Khazar had been leaked and was receiving attention from the press. There was a lot of promotional activity planned for Micaela and the cello, but Allen felt as if his boss was purposely leaving something out … something important.

"Good morning, Miss Miklos," Allen said, as he entered the room.

"Good morning, Allen, it is good to see you." Her small smile barely concealed the anticipation building within her.

"Allen seems to always bring me good news," Leon said.

"It's the privilege of my position. I assign other people the task of bringing the bad." Allen winked. "I have taken the liberty of uncrating the instrument."

"Is the hall cleared?" Leon asked.

"Yes, sir. I have set up two stations and an additional chair for you. Eric is waiting downstairs." He looked at Micaela. "He is quite anxious for you to open the case."

"As am I," Micaela said. "I would like to wash up."

"Please," Leon said, waving her on. "I will meet you on stage. Allen, make sure the doors are locked."

Micaela soaped up her hands and washed them in warm water, remembering her first lesson at the conservatory in Prague. She had entered the instructor's study and had begun to unpack her instrument.

"Stop," the instructor commanded. Micaela froze.

"Give me your hands," he said. Micaela held out her hands, palms up, to the instructor. He grabbed both firmly in his own.

"Go wash them in warm water," he said.

"But they are clean."

"Perhaps, but they are cold. You wouldn't leave your bow in the snow, would you? From now on, keep your hands warm, and wash them before every practice, lesson, or performance. Those ten fingers are far more valuable than that piece of overvarnished maple you have there."

I wonder if he would say the same thing today. She laughed to herself. These hands were about to handle an instrument crafted more than 150 years ago in Cremona, and had been touched by a legacy of excellent cello players. The most recent was the great Gregor Piatigorsky. Her pangs of unworthiness were overwhelmed by a swell of desire to play the Baudiot. She had had a good cello in Prague. But that seemed long ago, and she had adapted to her often-criticized, current cello. In fact, she had grown fond of it. She knew its quirks, its strengths, and its weaknesses. But it was true, it had many weaknesses.

Eric and Leon were waiting for her when she walked onto the stage in the empty hall. The case lay on its back, unopened, next to a chair and music stand. Micaela hesitated.

"What *are* you waiting for?" Eric whined. Micaela didn't answer.

"What scares you most?" Leon asked gently.

Micaela slowly turned her head to the maestro.

"What if I don't like it?"

The conductor beamed at the delightful presumption of this reply. Truly, Micaela was a musician first and last.

"Well, then, I will see that it is returned, and we will find you an instrument that you do like," he said.

"How could one return so generous a gift?" she asked. Eric's breathing was becoming audible.

"Don't worry, I have done it before," Leon said. "Now, I think you should get on with it before Eric passes out." Micaela's and Leon's laughter bounced off the walls of the hall. Eric joined in weakly.

Micaela sat down next to the case, unfastened the latches, and raised the lid. The instrument was darker in color than she expected. When she took it out of the case, there was an envelope underneath. She handed the envelope to Eric and assembled the end-spike.

Eric removed the papers and found that they contained a written history of the known owners and documented restorations. He read from the recent restoration notes.

"In 1725, at the age of 81, Stradivari made two celli. 'La Belle Blonde' is light and elegant. The 'Baudiot', is dark, red, and ruggedly masculine. The Baudiot has had comparatively few restorations. Recently the end-plug for the end-spike was redone and has clearly been done before. The internal sound-post was in good shape, but since we had to replace the right and left corner blocks, it was changed at the same time. Small work has been done on the end-plug and prufling which seems uneven by design. Additional polishing and evening has been done on the fingerboard. Surprisingly, the belly (top) required nearly no work at all. In fact, it seems to be as close to its original

condition as any instrument we have worked on. This may explain some if its unique tonal characteristics. It is extremely responsive to tone initiation and has extraordinary sustain. The instrument's history of players and owners is fairly well known and included in the certificate of authenticity. The original owner is unknown. The cellist and composer Charles Baudiot acquired it in the early 1800s. It was sold by his widow shortly after his death. The instrument is a seminal example of the modern cello and has been well cared for. – Alfred Hill, Hill & Sons W. E., London"

After adjusting the length of the end-spike, Micaela let the cello rock back between her knees. She had purposely worn a light cotton dress for the occasion. Reaching around the belly she tightened the frog on her bow. She then slid the bow across the open A string while turning the tuning peg with her left hand. After repeating the procedure with the other three strings, she briefly looked up to return the smiles of Eric and Leon. Slightly tightening her knees on the sides of the cello, she began to play a series of scales.

As with any great work of art, one cannot nor does one want to absorb all of its characteristics instantly. Great art has great depth, and it is the process and the experience of exploring its layers that is sublime. The scales serve to loosen the palate of the musician and chambré the instrument itself. During this sonorous sampling, the musician learns the current mechanical characteristics of the instrument, including required pressure on the strings, responsiveness to *vibrato*, and fingerboard action. Starting at a moderate tempo and in the midrange, the musician evenly works toward the limits of the instrument, exploring both pitch and speed, as hands and strings find their own intimate connection.

Even though these initial steps were more mechanical than musical, no one in the room could ignore the inherent quality of this instrument's tone. The notes began to seep into the listeners like an audio bouquet. An instrument of this quality has so much to display, one cannot sense it all at once. In fact, some say it takes years.

Micaela moved from the scales to the Sarabande from Bach's *Suite No. 4 for Unaccompanied Cello*. The switch to music also divides the roles of the hands. Eventually, the left hand becomes the left-brain servant of the player, while the right hand becomes a servant of the heart.

There is a profane and moot debate about who is in a better position to hear the music, the cellist or the listener. The voyeur can quite correctly argue that the instrument is designed to be heard by someone sitting or standing in front of it. The projection of tone combines with the visually intertwined musician and instrument to provide a uniquely sensual and cerebral experience. Micaela, completely draped over the Baudiot, would empirically argue that the music penetrates her clothing and then caresses her knees, thighs, pelvis, stomach, breasts, as well as her hands, and eventually merges with something very deep inside her. She stopped her playing and sat staring straight ahead.

"Well?" asked Eric. Micaela was motionless.

"I had no idea," she answered softly. She could see that the conductor and concertmaster wanted her to continue. "Even though I know it's not so, the belly wood seems paper thin and too weak to hold strings … but it does. I feel vibrations before hearing them. It startles me … the action is flawless. And the tone … I don't know what to say … it moves me. It moves me very much. But there is something else, something hidden." She paused again. "Was it like this with your Strad, Eric?"

"Yes. And I am still discovering it." Eric opened his violin case. "A connoisseur once tried to explain to me the difference between a very good wine and a great wine. He said to me, 'You can talk about a very good wine all night. But a great wine talks to you.' " Micaela finally smiled.

"Well, Maestro, I am not sending this back. Come on Eric, let's show off for boss." Eric sat down like a child who had been waiting for his favorite ride in the carnival.

Leon watched his Strad-struck stars play the daylights out of the Brahms Double. He shook his head, smiled, and muttered, "Poor Luca."

— 19 —

JUNE 28 FRIDAY

Stump Shooting – Near Oolitic

Music: Bo Diddley, 500% More Man

If necessity is the mother of invention, then beer and boredom are the parents of stupid tricks with firearms. The young men of Oolitic had developed a particularly quaint midsummer custom of stump shooting. The ingredients for this event included but were not limited to:

1 case of appropriately named *Colt 45 Malt Liquor*
4 one-gallon milk jugs and funnel
6-pack of sterno cans
1 high-powered deer rifle, in this case a .3006 with scope
1 box of 200-grain cartridges with hollow point bullets
Sandbags
5-gallon can of gasoline
1 lighter
1 flashlight
1 tree stump, preferably in an open field with no neighbors
A moonless and rainless night
A pickup truck with a loud radio

By the time Gar and Lou had made it to the field, they had already gone through half of the Colt 45 case and showed no sign of slowing down. Gar parked the company's gray Dodge pickup and left the lights and radio on. Peggy Lee was singing *Big Bad Bill,* and Lou waited until Gar stepped out of the truck before switching the radio to a blues station out of Chicago.

"Goddamn it," said Gar. "Not that nigger music again."

"Relax, Gar, it'll grow on you," said Lou.

"That's what I'm afraid of. Oh well, you get the can. I'll get the jugs," said Gar. A small hoist with flaking orange paint was attached to the left rear of the truck bed. It was used to lift hay-bale-sized blocks of limestone. When Gar leaned over to get the jugs, he rammed his head against the over-hanging arm of the crane.

"Shit-fuck." Gar staggered.

"I swear, Gar. When the dumbshits get together, they must call you stupid," Lou said, as he picked off flakes of paint from Gar's forehead. Lou opened the tailgate and easily lifted the heavy five-gallon can of gasoline in one hand, while getting the funnel in the other. Gar grabbed the milk jugs, and they both walked to the front of the pickup to make use of the headlights. Lou was singing quietly along with the radio,

> *Now I am a man*
> *Made twenty-one*
> *You know, baby*
> *We can have a lot of fun*
>
> *I am man*
> *I spell M-A-N ... man*

Gar knelt down, opened the jugs, and Lou handed him the funnel. Lou unscrewed the cap to the gas can and started to pour.

"Hey, nigger lover, see if you can get it in the funnel this time," chided Gar.

"Now, Gar, no reason to call anybody names. It's just a guy bangin' out some blues. It don't hurt no one."

"It's the devil's music being played by the devil's horde. You should be more careful. You know how at the last meeting they were talking about how the commies were planting subli ... er, sublimim,

"Subliminal."

"Yeah, those kind of messages in our brains as part of the conspiracy."

"I don't think the commies know Bo Diddley."

"How do you know? Maybe they already got to your brains with this music. It's dangerous, I tell ya. And we ought to do something about it."

"We are doing something about it, Gar."

"Baloney. All we do is go to the meetings and talk, talk, talk. We need some action."

"Like what?"

"Hell, I dunno. Mebbe we could get rid of a few niggers and Jews."

"Like, how many?"

"Aw, kill'em all. Indiana would be a lot better place to live." The milk jug started overflowing and covered Gar with gasoline.

"Aww, Goddam it," said Gar.

"You are dangerously out of control, boy." Lou had stopped pouring and was waiting for Gar to get the next one ready amidst curses. Once the jugs were full, they both opened another can of Colt 45. Lou took out one of the cans of sterno. Gar got a jug. They turned off the truck lights, grabbed a flashlight, and walked out into the field. This area was being considered for development and was therefore recently clearcut. But the stumps hadn't been pulled yet. There were so many stumps available, it was hard to pick just the right one. It had to be about two or two-and-half feet high, big enough to hold the milk jug and preferably about fifty yards or more from the shooting location, which was usually next to the beer and the truck.

"Still going on vacation without the family?" asked Lou.

"Yep. Gonna see my cousin in Kentucky. He doesn't like people much."

When they finally wandered to a suitable stump, it turned out to be closer to a hundred yards. Gar put the jug on the stump. Lou looked around and pointed the flashlight at the truck.

"Ain't this a bit out of your range?" said Lou.

"Nah, I can do this easy. C'mon, light the can."

"Okay, but let's get another jug and set it behind. Two for one."

"Now you're talking," grinned Gar and went off to get another jug. When he returned, he was cursing and there were some more orange flakes stuck on his forehead.

Lou took out a pocketknife, opened the can of Sterno, and set it on the ground next to the stump, below the milk jug. He reached for his Zippo and waited for Gar. When Gar returned and put the new jug behind the other, Lou lit the Zippo and said,

"Better back away, Gar, you still smell like gas." Gar quickly stepped back a yard into the darkness. Lou lit the Sterno, backed up a few steps, and then turned with the flashlight for the truck.

"I'm going first," said Gar, starting to load the Winchester.

"Good, shoot first and drink later — maybe you'll actually hit something," Lou said, as he opened a couple more 45s and turned up the radio, which was now playing a medley of Muddy Waters tunes starting with *Baby Please Don't Go*. Gar threw down a couple of sandbags and settled in, trying to find the lit Sterno can in the scope.

"Can't find it, it must of blown out," he complained.

"Yeah, it's a fucking hurricane out here," said Lou. "You're pointed to the left of it. Come right about half a hoe handle. More … more, do you see it now or are you pointing at the sky?" Lou said.

"Nooo … got it," said Gar.

"Okay, now raise the barrel slowly so the flame is just off the bottom of the scope and let your eyes adjust. You should see the outline of the jug." Without warning Gar jerked the trigger. The bright yellow white flame from the end of the barrel and the concussive sound of the cartridge firing caught Lou by surprise.

"Jesus Christ, you clod!" yelled Lou, dropping his beer and belatedly holding his now ringing ears.

"What?"

"You're supposed to give a warning."

"How come it didn't work?" asked Gar

"Because you missed, stupid."

"Lemme try again."

"You've got to be kidding me. You shouldn't even be allowed to hold that rifle." Lou stood above Gar imperiously, waiting for him to give it up. Eventually, Gar staggered up and handed Lou the rifle.

"Now get me another Colt. You made me spill mine."

Lou knelt down, put the safety on, raised and slid the rifle bolt back to eject the spent cartridge and load another into the breech. He then slid the bolt back and down, inserting the cartridge in the barrel. He stared into the darkness, letting his eyes readjust until he could locate the Sterno flame. Gar was back with his beer. Lou took a sip and then gave it back. "Hold onto it for a moment," he said, as he got down into the prone position with the barrel of the rifle nestling into the sandbags. With his cheek on the stock, he found the small flame in the scope. Slowly, he moved upwards until the flame just disappeared behind the limb of the scope sight. Flicking off the safety, he waited. In this light, the cross hairs were not perceptible, so as the jug's outline became visible, he centered it in the circle of the scope. He raised the barrel until the jug was in the bottom of the scope to account for trajectory drop.

Quietly exhaling the word "Now," he squeezed the trigger. The thunderous sound and barrel flame were completely overcome by the event of the hollow-point bullet hitting the milk jugs full of gas.

The speed and impact of the distorting bullet made the jugs explode and the gas vaporize. The little can of Sterno became a detonator. The resulting angry orange fireball was enormous and cast a light that was too bright to read by, but illuminated the beaming smiles of Gar and Lou. A second later, a shock wave arrived that triggered those smiles into laughter and catcalls.

"Nice shot!" said Gar.

"Thanks. That was a lot of gas."

"Do you ever miss?" asked Gar.

"No."

— 20 —

JULY 2 TUESDAY

Never Dive Alone – Quarry No. 5

Music: Puccini, Sola, Perduta, Abbandonata, Aria from Manon Lescaut

Lee Minkson was a Navy demolition expert during the war. Operating around Tulagi island north of Guadalcanal, he saw more action than anyone would have volunteered for if they knew for what they were volunteering. He excelled as an underwater commando. Without even trying, he could hold his breath for more than two minutes and was extraordinarily calm in crisis situations. He won the Navy Cross for saving a mission that nearly went disastrously bad, when enemy soldiers discovered members of his team setting charges on a dock for Japanese small craft. He used his skills to remain unseen while finishing the job, blowing up the dock, and, in the ensuing confusion, rescuing his team.

After the war, he opened up the Bamboo Quarry, a dive shop on South Walnut in Bloomington, Indiana. Besides filling tanks and selling equipment, Lee taught scuba classes. His students primarily came from the university, and most of them were jocks from the Phi Delta Theta fraternity house. The Phi Delts arranged for the indoor classroom, which was a swimming pool and chalkboard. The local quarries were the outdoor classrooms. It was a tough class, based on his rigorous Navy training.

To start the first class, Lee would throw all the equipment into the deep end of the pool and tell his students to go put it on. Then he would casually stroll about the three sides of the deep end, watching the manner in which each student would inevitably fail. He could quickly assess a number of physical characteristics about each student, such as how well they could swim or how long they could hold their breath. More importantly, he could observe what he called their crisis personality, how they reacted to an unforeseen and threatening challenge. In five minutes of watching this exercise in underwater futility, Lee learned more about his students than they knew about themselves.

When the exercise ended, he would call them out of the pool and instruct them to take a seat on the floor around the chalkboard. His six-foot-two-inch frame towered over the sitting, shivering students. Lee rubbed his square, grizzled, burr-cut head and said, "At the end of this class, we are going to a shallow quarry about twenty-five to thirty feet deep. If you can accomplish in under two minutes, without surfacing, what you failed so miserably at today, you will have passed this class. If not, give it up. Take up surfing or something." Lee would then flip the freestanding blackboard and point to the prewritten tenets of his class. "I have four rules: Number one, always listen to me. Number two, take care of your equipment. Number three, solve your problems underwater. Number four, never dive alone. If you do not follow these rules, I will either kick you out of class, or you will not pass. Either way, I won't have to deal with you again."

Lee looked at each member of his class, checking for understanding and syncing up his analysis of their previous underwater test with their reaction to his boot camp introduction. Once his personal assessment was complete, he would begin the class with equipment instruction.

Lee loved to dive alone. He was just as comfortable underwater as he was on the surface. Between the war and his business, he had spent thousands of hours underwater in all kinds of surface and sea conditions. The extensive and bulky scuba equipment bothered him about as much as a pair of eyeglasses. On Tuesdays in the spring and summer, the Bamboo was closed, and he never missed a chance to take a solo trip to the quarries. Not that the quarries were such an exciting place to dive. Despite their apparent clarity from the surface, they were a bit murky underneath. The underwater terrain was a dull, rectangular ruin of fallen limestone blocks. There were some fish in the quarries, bass and carp mostly, and he always brought his spear gun so that he had a reasonable explanation for the trip, if anyone should ask. But the real reason for his excursions had nothing to do with the fish or the location.

He just longed to be by himself, isolated and shrouded in the weightless robe of water. When he took his classes to the quarries, they had dive plans, objectives, exercises, stopwatches, and compasses. When he went by himself, he would just descend, find a spot to hover, cradle the spear gun, watch the emptiness, and listen to his own breath. Every once in a while, a fish would enter the emptiness and inspect the bubbling, still diver. The last such fish would go home with him.

This Tuesday began as an overcast day. It had rained most of the weekend, making the quarry water murkier than usual. Lee preferred it that way. He decided to visit one of the older, larger quarries — an old friend, really. From the spot where he parked his blue Econoline van to the quarry entrance was about one hundred yards of southern Indiana jungle. There was a thin but well-traveled path to the low side of the quarry edge, and a shorter path to the high side from which local rubes and IU students full of too much juice would jump. One of these days, one of those boys is going to jump in the wrong place and crack his head open, Lee thought. He slung the frame holding his twin air tanks over his left shoulder and his duffle with the rest of his equipment over the other shoulder.

Emerging from the huckleberries and jack trees in full sweat and arriving at the water's edge, he dumped his tanks and duffle on a large limestone block that was tilted and halfway submerged. He saw a glider plane soaring silently overhead. He had been inside a glider once. It wasn't silent at all. The air slamming on the Plexiglas canopy made a roar. Opening the duffle, he took out his mask, rinsed it, and then spit in it, rubbed the saliva around, and left it to dry. Next he took the can of talcum powder and liberally coated the inside of his quarter-inch wet suit, except for the hood, and then powdered his booties. Finally, he took the U.S. Diver regulator out of its case and fastened it to the twin 50-cubic-inch air tanks. The 100-ci total would give him an hour dive, easy, depending on his depth and exertion. With regulator and tanks tested, he did a final mental equipment check. He did not want to be on the surface in a wetsuit on this hot day for long. Checklist complete, he changed into his bathing suit and put on the wetsuit, booties, hood, wrist depth gauge, underwater dive watch, wrist compass, and twelve pounds of lead weights. In addition, he strapped onto his shin a scabbard holding his underwater dagger. Grabbing fins, facemask, and spear gun in one hand and the tanks in the other, he shuffled down the limestone block. Carefully, he put the scuba tanks halfway into the water so that they were still resting on the block. Then he walked into the water and put on his fins and mask. Swimming back to the block, he dragged his tanks and regulator into the water with him and put them on. He took a compass heading on a point directly across the quarry and did a final check of his air supply.

Letting the surface of the water fold over him, he descended to about fifteen feet. Locking his left arm with the compass at a right angle to his right arm, which was pointing straight ahead, he followed his compass heading slowly to the other side of the quarry. At the quarry wall, he marked a large X in the algae with the tip of his spear gun and descended another thirty feet and made another X. It was dark, and the overcast day made it darker. He probably should have brought a light, but he had been in darker situations where a light revealing his location would have been disastrous. At this depth, the cold fresh water compressed his wet suit to the point that it required a slight but constant kick to hold his depth. He turned from the wall and took a bearing forty-five degrees from his return heading, then slowly moved into the emptiness. Visibility was less than ten feet. A block of fallen limestone suddenly loomed out of the darkness. It was resting on another, creating a convenient chair that faced back towards the wall. Lee took a seat and lay the spear gun down next to him on the limestone. A cloud of sediment stirred up from the surface of the rock and enveloped him. He remained still, waiting for the dust to settle.

The sound of breathing underwater, in and out through a regulator, had two distinct aspects. The inhale sounded like being in a small cave of plastic. The exhale added the sound of bubbles. They seemed louder and more disruptive than they actually were. Lee remembered how he had often wished for a bubbleless regulator when he was on nighttime operations behind enemy lines. The bubbles added slightly to the chance of discovery, but, more importantly, they blocked out any other sounds that might be present, such as the high-pitched whine of small craft overhead. Lee had learned to mix in intervals between his breaths so he could hear better underwater. Although this had the added benefit of conserving air, it had to be used carefully, since it tended to build up carbon dioxide in the lungs.

Up above, the sky was clearing, allowing more light into the quarry and below the surface. The dust had settled, and Lee had remained still for a good ten minutes. To his left a large carp became visible. Lee stopped his breathing, enticing the fish closer. The fish came within five feet and displayed its prehistoric face. Lee exhaled a plume of bubbles, which shooed the fish away. The sun was penetrating deeply now in auroras that waved in the murk of the quarry. As one shaft of light pierced the water, he glimpsed an object between him and the wall.

Size and distance were tough to gauge in these conditions. A crawfish right on the facemask could look like a sea monster. Once, off Savo Island, on a moonless night in crystal-clear water, Lee had mistaken an enemy sub for a whale. Fortunately, he'd heard the propellers between breaths. This object between him and the wall was only visible for a moment, until a cloud passed overhead.

Lee became intensely alert. One of the reasons he was so adept in a crisis was because he could detect the crisis before it was there. The hair tingling on his arms and the back of his neck were not symptoms but signposts and adrenalin injectors. He always used both to his advantage. He stopped his breathing and elevated his stillness to that of the limestone. He stared in the direction where the out-of-place object had vanished, waiting for the light to return.

The light shaft came in at an angle, slowly revealing the top of the object. At first it appeared like a bas-relief on the wall, a monochromatic visage. As the light increased, the full figure became apparent and Lee could see that it was a sculpture. His warning system started to shut itself down, and he moved to inspect the edifice more closely. As he left his chair, he wondered, why would a sculpture be down here? He really wished he had that light now. As he approached the figure he thought, "This is one ugly piece of work, no wonder it was sunk." When he got close enough for the gargoyle-like face to fill the visible area of his mask, he was able to see the pupils and iris of its eyes. This time the adrenalin alarms went off without warning, and Lee uncharacteristically screamed so hard that he blew the regulator out of his mouth. Jerking his head back and using his arms to swim, he distanced himself from the human being that, for an instant, seemed alive. He finished screaming when he ran out of air, at which point Lee executed the side roll maneuver to recover his regulator. Coughing some accidentally inhaled water into the regulator, Lee began to recover his sensibilities as well. The human being was indeed dead, and was just as harmless as he had been as an extremely ugly sculpture. After checking his watch, depth, and remaining air pressure, Lee began to inspect the scene and the body. There was no external evidence of impact to indicate that the man had jumped and hit a submerged rock. Considering that the man's body seemed as grotesque as his face, Lee was relieved that he was fully dressed. Fully dressed? Inspecting the man's back, Lee saw that his hands had been taped together, and there was a rope around his chest. He descended to the legs and discovered that they had also been bound. Another rope had been tied to the ankles. He followed the rope down another eight feet, where it was tied to a cinder block that was resting on the bottom. Leaving his spear gun behind, Lee slowly ascended and surfaced into bright sunshine.

Puccini Aria:

Sola, perduta, abbandonata...
in landa desolata!
Orror! Intorno a me s'oscura il ciel...
Ahimè, son sola!
E nel profondo deserto io cado,
strazio crudel, ah! sola abbandonata,
io, la deserta donna!
Ah! non voglio morir!
No! non voglio morir!
Tutto dunque è finito.
Terra di pace me sembrava questa...
Ahi! Mia beltà funesta,
ire novelle accende...
Strappar da lui mi si volea; or tutto
il mio passato orribile risorge,
e vivo innanzi al guardo mio si posa.
Ah! di sangue s'è macchiato.
Ah! tutto è finito.
Asil di pace ora la tomba invoco...
No! non voglio morir... amore, aita!

— 21 —

JULY 3 WEDNESDAY

Fischer's Fine Flowers – Between Bedford and Oolitic

Music: Stravinsky, Rite of Spring – The Sacrifice, Ritual Action of the Ancestors

Fred Fischer had three businesses. It was sometimes hard to tell where one business ended and another began. His wife wanted him to have three different business cards, but Fred was frugal and only had one. It said,

Fischer's Fine Flowers
Mortuary Services and Death Investigations

The storefront, Fischer's Fine Flowers, was located across the street from the Brooks Public Cemetery. The cemetery served both Bedford and Oolitic, as did Fred himself for both mortuary services and death investigations. Fred enjoyed the drive to work every morning. He always took the long route around three sides of the cemetery. This route allowed him time to consider the colorful beauty of all those headstones and flowers, most of which he had supplied. It also permitted him the superfluous task of "checking out the competition." Superfluous because there was no competition, nor was it likely that there would be any. Fred Fischer had bought the little house across from the cemetery fifteen years ago after putting in semesters as a premed student at Indiana University. Between his proximity to the cemetery and his high school friends on the city council, he was pretty much assured most of the Continual Care contracts, most of the mortuary contracts, and, as it turned out, a fair amount of walk-in traffic. He had started the business with his sister, Eunice.

Both Fred and Eunice were certified death investigators as well as morticians. Their licenses were framed and hung proudly next to the cash register in the flower shop. The only family member who knew anything about flowers was Fred's wife, Myrtle, who spent more hours at the shop than anyone else.

When Fred arrived at the shop in the mornings and got out of his car, he would survey his domain with great pleasure, enjoying the aroma of the flowers that Myrtle had already put on display around the parking lot and along the entrance to the shop. As he entered the store, he would take another deep breath that violated his previous reverie with the stench of KOOL cigarettes burning in one or more ashtrays. This violation would be the first in a series. Myrtle was a chain smoker.

It was Wednesday morning, and Eunice was supposed to be helping Myrtle prepare the day's arrangements for the continual care clients, an ever-increasing source of recurring revenue. Myrtle liked to call them "The Giving Dead."

"Where's Eunice?" asked Fred, putting out one of the cigarettes smoldering in an ashtray on the counter.

"She's in the mort. We got a new one last night," Myrtle answered, without looking at him. She had a KOOL wedged in the corner of her mouth with an inch-long ash at the end. Smoke was trailing up over her horn-rim glasses as she worked over the arrangement. The ash fell on top of the flowers like confectioner's sugar. She blew the ashes off of the yellow mums with a cloud of smoke.

"Anybody we know?" Fred asked, casually.

"Yep, the Watkins boy."

"Gar?"

"Yep, the fat boy is a goner. Scuba diver found him in querry number five."

"Really?" Fred was surprised. "Those boys been in and out of the querries since they were pups. Even if Gar hit his head, you'd figure he'd float to the top."

"Kind of hard to float when you got a concrete block tied to your feet," grinned Myrtle, as she expertly flicked her still-lit cigarette butt through the greenhouse side louver out into the parking lot.

"You don't say."

"I do say," said Myrtle. "And I'll tell ya sumptin' else. I may not have one of those fancy certificates y'all got, but I am pretty sure this was murder. You better commence upon your investigation."

"Who found him?" asked Fred.

"Some Navy guy from Bloomington. The sheriff said he was a war hero. Although they said he was shakin' like a shirt in a hurricane when he came down to report it. Number's on the bulletin board."

"Why's Eunice working on him now? Don't she know this a criminal investigation?"

"Yeah, she does. She's being careful. She was just worried that he was bloatin' up too quick and might make a mess." Myrtle laughed, coughed, and lit another cigarette all at the same time. "I told her, we've been worried about that for years."

Fred started to head over to the mortuary, but then turned back to the office. The thought of seeing a drowned and bloated Gar inspired him to make some calls first.

"Good morning, F & W Limestone. May I help you?"

"Yeah, give me Lou, please. Tell him Frank Fischer's calling," After a couple of minutes Lou picked up the phone.

"Hey, Frank, what can I do you for?"

"Seen Gar lately?" Frank asked.

"Not since some Stump Shootin' on Friday after work. He went on vacation. What's up?"

"He's dead."

"Say again?"

"Gar's dead, Lou. They fished him out of the querry yesterday."

"Goddamn it," said Lou. There was a long silence on the phone.

"You still there, Lou?"

"Yeah, I am still here," he answered. "Which one? Which querry?"

"Querry number 5. Why?"

"No way. He's been swimming in that place a hundred times. I mean, when we were kids, we used to jump there all the time. No way even dumb Gar could drown there," Lou was angry.

"You have a point, Lou. You see … the thing is … someone tied a cinder block to his legs." Fred waited through a long silence before Lou spoke.

"Poor dumb bastard. Do you know who did it?"

"Nope, we are just starting to look around. Got any ideas? Fired any cutters lately?"

"No. Anybody Gar knew, wouldn't do this. On the other hand, he could be pretty mouthy in the wrong crowd, if you know what I mean."

"Yep, I think I do. I suppose that is a possibility we will have to look into. Just the same, you might expect lots o' questions on this."

"Thanks for the heads-up," said Lou.

"I'll call you back when I get more information. I suppose you want to tell his family."

"Not really," Lou said. "But I will."

Fred asked Lou to call if anything that would help the investigation came to mind and then hung up the phone. Myrtle walked in and asked how Lou took the news.

"Okay, I guess. Sounded pretty angry."

— 22 —

JULY 5 FRIDAY

The Brightest Star – Indianapolis

Music: Gershwin, Prelude No. 1

When Alison came down the stairs, she saw Leon's briefcase by the front door and then walked into the kitchen. He was seated wearing dark pants, blue blazer, and a white shirt. Mary had served English muffins with her homemade strawberry rhubarb jam, but they were untouched.

"Good morning, Mary," said Alison.

"Good morning, ma'am," answered Mary with a sidelong glance at the maestro, who was so engrossed in the morning paper that Alison's arrival received the same attention as the toasted and now-cooling muffins. The fact that her husband was not traveling much this summer was initially exciting for Alison. The fact that he wasn't around much even when he was home was irritating in the extreme. But the unopened sports section reminded her of all the reasons that he might be preoccupied and quenched her instinct to pick a fight. Instead she read out loud from the sports section.

"I see the Cubbies won both games of the double header yesterday." There was no response from Leon. "Wow, that's a four-game sweep isn't it?" Still nothing. "It looks like Koufax is leading the National League in *touchdowns*." Finally, she gave up and asked, "So what did Corbin say?" Leon began to read from the *Indianapolis Star* society section …

The guest of honor at Edith Campbell's Annual Fourth of July lawn party this year was Leon Zellingari's newest and brightest star, Micaela Miklos.

Alison cringed.

Miss Miklos has recently moved to Indianapolis from Vienna, Austria, to become the new first chair for the Symphony's cello section. The red, white, and blue occasion featured music, dancing ,and flags attached to or hanging from any stationary object. The patriotic theme was mirrored on the tables by bouquets of irises, red roses, and calla lilies. During the outdoor dinner, Mrs.

130

Campbell introduced Miss Miklos to Indianapolis society and presented her with a new cello as a gift from the Campbell Foundation. Not exactly new, the priceless Stradivarius was made more than 150 years ago. Miklos lost her own cello when she escaped from communist Czechoslovakia four years ago. She has been playing on borrowed instruments ever since. However, the loss of her cello was insignificant compared to the loss of her family, which also occurred during that daring escape. In her eloquent acceptance speech, she not only thanked the Campbell Foundation and the ISO, but expressed her extreme gratitude for being able to work and live in the United States of America. She reinforced this sentiment by saying, "It is my wish that, one day, I may be a citizen of this great land of the free." Judging by the thunderous applause to this comment, her wish seems a certainty.

After dinner and fireworks, the strikingly attractive Miss Miklos was asked what she enjoyed most about Indiana. After Zellingari and the ISO, she made mention of the 500, swimming at the quarries, and rhubarb pie. We asked if she had met any eligible men since moving to Indianapolis. Her answer, "This cello is so good, who needs a man?"

"She didn't." Alison said, with her eyes closing.
"She did … and there's more," Leon continued.

We asked her what her idea of a perfect man would be and she said, "Someone not too smart and not too skinny."

Mary laughed out loud.

Despite the arrival of the cello, the Star *has learned that a certain young man from Lawrence County has been added to her list of favorite things about Indiana.*

Leon tossed the section of the paper in Alison's direction.
"There is a strikingly good picture of the strikingly beautiful if somewhat mouthy Miss Miklos," Leon said.
Alison's head was in her hands. "You know, it's not fair that they pressed her at the end of the party. After all, there was all that wine, and everyone was so relaxed." She paused and added hopefully, "On the whole, it's a pretty good story." Leon nodded silently, without smiling.
"Isn't Jed painting Micaela's apartment house?"

"Yep," answered Alison, without looking up.

"What an interesting euphemism," Leon said. Alison laughed hesitantly. Leon stood up from the table and said, "I have to call Micaela and then see Eric."

"I'll call Edith and see how she's taking it," Alison said.

Taking the sports section with him, Leon left for the phone in his study, and Alison went back upstairs to get dressed. Mary cleared the table of the half drunk coffee and uneaten English muffins with their coagulated butter.

Gershwin: Prelude No. 2

These days Jed would wake with a quiet anticipation of seeing something so desirable that there was no drag of sleep to pull him back. As he gazed at the sleeping Micaela, the only thing that would push him out of the bed and get him dressed was his schedule. It was hard to leave, but impossible to stay. Micaela made it harder by talking her landlady into, and contributing money for, repainting the apartment house. He would paint in the mornings when it was cool and the weather was stable. On most days, she would practice while he painted. Climbing the ladder with brush and pail, he would hear her ascending through the scales. Then, he would exaggerate his brushstrokes, keeping tempo with the following sonati. After lunch, he would go home to practice while his work dried. At the end of the day he would always find himself back at Micaela's home. Wednesdays and Fridays were different. She studied with Eric on those mornings. Jed and Micaela would linger over breakfast and the morning paper. Then she would go, and Jed would paint at a non-musical pace.

On the morning after Edith Campbell's lawn party, Jed quietly dressed in his work clothes and decided to introduce Micaela to gas-house eggs. After cooking the bacon, he made a little-larger-than-yolk-sized hole in a piece of bread. He laid the bread in the skillet and let it soak up the bacon grease, then cracked an egg into the center of the hole. After the egg set a little, he turned the egg-embedded toast to cook and soak the other side. When it got crispy on the surface, he served it with the superfluously drained bacon, along with a glass of concentrated orange juice and coffee. Micaela kissed him. He went outside to get the paper. She and Jed sat down to eat just as the phone rang.

"Hello."

"Micaela, this is Leon."

"Good morning, Maestro," she said, suddenly wide awake. An early call from the boss is as good as a cup of coffee.

"Are you studying with Eric this morning?" he asked.

"Yes, in about an hour at his place."

"Good, I need you to be late."

"Excuse me?" she said.

"Have you read the paper this morning?"

"No, I was just about to." She looked over at Jed who had separated the front section and was reading the front page. She walked to the limits of the phone cord to reach the newspaper lying on the table. Upside down, she could see her own picture on the top half of the society section. "Oh no, something is wrong?" Jed followed her gaze and smiled when he saw her picture. He tossed the front section aside and unfolded the society pages.

"Nothing that can't be fixed. Just show up about forty-five minutes late. It will give me time to talk to Eric," Leon said.

"I don't understand."

"You will. I'll call you later. Bye." Leon hung up. Jed had just started to read the article when Micaela ripped it out of his hands. She only made it as far as the first sentence,

"To je nemožne!" she said as she threw down the paper and started shaking her head. Jed picked it back up.

"What's wrong?"

"What's wrong?!" she fired back at Jed. "Ty idiote, what do you think Eric is going to think about 'Zellingari's brightest star'?"

"Who gives a shit what he thinks? You *are* the brightest star."

"*I* give shit. He is spending summer helping me with the concerto, preparing for Luca, and now is publicly demoted by someone who hasn't given one performance."

"Relax, Micaela. He'll get over it." He reached over to soothe her and she shook him off and waved him away with another Czech profanity. "C'mon, let's read the rest of the article." Jed began to recite the article, inserting his own complimentary commentary. Micaela paced with her arms folded, trying not to smile when he got to her patriotic comments. She was actually starting to calm down when he got to her comment about the cello being better than a man.

"Uh oh," said Jed.

"What?" asked Micaela.

" 'Better than a man'?" he quoted.

"It's just joke," she said, looking away.

"That's why I am laughing so hard," he said. "By the way, there are a lot of other people around here who might not think it's so funny either."

"Why? I have only been sleeping with you." Micaela turned to him and added, "So far."

Jed glared but moved on. "Many folks around here will consider it crass."

"Vhat is crass?" she asked.

"Vulgar — insensitive."

"Oh yes, like Martha?"

"Exactly," he said.

"No one complains about Martha."

"Martha doesn't get quoted in the papers." Then it was his turn to dig. "After all she's not our *brightest star*." Micaela was pacing by the bowl of apples and picked one up and threw at him. Jed ducked.

"What is with you? You just got all kinds of good PR, a fantastic new instrument, your boss is nuts about you, and you're worried about hurting another prima donna's feelings."

"I am not prima donna!"

"So far!" he said. "Eric will get over it. Leon will throw him a bone, and you guys will be practicing again by noon while I paint your fucking house." In the middle part of this phrase Jed had tried to be conciliatory, but a crescendo of resentment marked the end.

"So that's it … you're jealous," she said.

"Absolutely! But not of that wimpy Jew," he shook his head. "The good get better, and the great get greater, and the rest of us fight for scraps of practice time to keep up." Jed turned, stormed out the door, and rode away on his motorcycle.

"Hovno!" shouted Micaela. Then at her self, "*I* am the idiot." She looked at her watch. There was plenty of time before going over to Eric's, but not as much time as she wanted. Inwardly she rehearsed the upcoming groveling session while she scraped the cooled white bacon grease and coagulated eggs into the trash.

Beethoven Piano Concerto No. 5 in E Flat Major, Op. 73, Second Movement – Adagio un poco mosso

Leon walked up the stone steps of Eric's small house, briefcase in hand. The day was already warm, and he could hear the sounds of Eric's violin through the screen. The violinist let the doorbell ring a few more times before he stopped. He did not get up. He just said, "Come in."

Leon let himself in and stopped at the arch where the entryway opened to the small living area off the kitchen. Eric was only mildly surprised that Leon was at the door instead of Micaela.

"Would you like some coffee?" Eric offered.

"Yes, I would," Leon said. Eric got up and Leon followed him to the kitchen. Leon sat down at the table. He saw that the newspaper had been thrown to the floor. Eric poured the coffee into large mugs and brought them to the table. He sat down with his foot on the society page.

"How are you feeling?" Leon asked.

Eric tapped his foot on the 'Brightest Star' headline.

"I am feeling a wee bit dimmer today," Eric answered.

Leon waited.

"The worst part is, I can't get mad at anybody. Working with her this summer has been a career highlight for me. God, she's good. But when I read the paper this morning, I just wanted to move on, to go somewhere else where I could be the brightest, where I could have the opportunities she is going to have. You know you're going to lose her, don't you?"

"Yeah, if I can keep her for two years, that would be great."

"Is she coming here later?"

Leon nodded and said, "I asked her to be about forty-five minutes late."

"Good. Even though I was relieved to see you, I was disappointed," Eric said. He wistfully waved to the living room. "You wouldn't believe the music that goes on over there."

"Eric, I need to discuss the Khazar concert." The maestro was cuing his concertmaster. It is a unique characteristic of the performing arts that the performer can recover professional poise in almost any situation. Eric turned his eyes to his director and didn't even feel the ghostly disappearance of his self-indulgence. There are rewards for such skills.

"I want to do something different and, well, American, for the second half."

"Okay," Eric said evenly. "May I ask why?"

"I was hoping you would. And I want to tell you, but you have to promise me that you will tell no one else," Leon said.

"Sure has been a lot of secrecy this year. Of course, I will keep it confidential."

"It is very likely that the first lady of the United States will be attending the Thanksgiving weekend concert." Leon let the words settle and then continued. "And there is a possibility that she will bring her husband."

"You're kidding!" Eric said. Leon shook his head. As the news soaked in and the caffeine flowed through his bloodstream, Eric's excitement became evident. "What did you have in mind?" he asked quickly.

"*Gershwin Preludes*," answered the maestro.

"Khazar is going to play both halves?" Eric was incredulous.

"Nope," replied Leon. "Have you seen this?" Leon reached into his brief case, brought out some sheet music, and handed it over to the wide-eyed concertmaster. Eric took the papers. It was an unbound score of the *Gershwin Preludes*. Actually, it was a handwritten draft, clearly unfinished. Eric scanned the notation, noticeably confused. Leon chortled and then explained.

"This is an arrangement of the three *Preludes* for violin instead of piano. Micaela asked me to look at them." Eric looked at the signature on the work.

"Jed did this?" asked Eric.

"Hard to figure where he got the time, and it is very good work."

Eric scanned the pages.

"Would you care to play these for Mrs. Kennedy?" Leon asked.

Eric just beamed his answer.

Fauré: IV. Allegro Molto, Quartet in G Minor, Op. 45

Jed's grip on the handle bars was undetachable. The roaring motorcycle fueled his fury at the unfairness of his position. He worked hard as a musician and a painter to make ends meet. Because he had been spending so much time with Micaela, he had to squeeze his practicing into shorter and shorter spaces. In the meantime, she studied every other day with Eric and practiced daily at her house while he painted. And now, with absolutely everything going for her, she was whining about the feelings of that other fortunate fiddler. Only the belligerent and the whiners move up, he thought as he turned on to the interstate ramp.

Rush hour had faded, so he throttled up to about eighty miles per hour. Without helmet or goggles, the thick Indiana air blasted him in the face, wearing away the dirt clod of his irritation. Shortly, he slowed down and exited Interstate 65 somewhere near Meridian. He turned south and then backtracked west, wandering through unknown neighborhoods. Cruising down 11th, he stopped at a red light. Across the street to his right he saw Crispus

Attucks High School. As he became more cognizant of surroundings, he became painfully aware that the neighborhood had already noticed him. At this time of day there were some white faces, but they either belonged to summer school teachers or deliverymen, and Jed was clearly neither of those.

In the right lane, next to a playground, Jed waited for the light to change, which he began to think was stuck. He tried not to look at the crowd of young basketball players who had stopped their game to gather near him.

From somewhere on his right he heard, "Hey Honky!" That was enough for him. He let out the clutch and turned right onto West Street. He had barely made it past the high school when he heard the short burst of a siren behind him. Even though it was daytime, he could feel the flashing red light against his skin. Jed pulled over.

The ball players came over from the playground to enjoy the incident. Amidst the incessant catcalls, Jed heard, "License and registration please." Jed turned and looked into the mirrored sunglasses of the white cop who had his ticket book open. Jed smiled and reached to his back pocket. When his hand arrived at the empty pocket and froze, the cop, the gathering crowd, and Jed simultaneously had their own realizations. The crowd erupted, delighted and laughing.

"That boy is in a heap of trouble." "Yessir, officer, running a red light, driving without a license. You gotta real live criminal here." "He could be dangerous." "Yeah, better put that ticket book away and cuff him." "Hey, Franklin, didn't I see his face in the post office the other day?"

"Shit," Jed said.

The crowd continued, "Oooowee, foul language, too. That boy's goin' to jail. No doubt about it." "Too bad he forgot his wallet, he can't afford to bribe officer honky here." At the last comment, the cop turned to the crowd.

"All right, that's enough. Get outta here. Show's over." The crowd and comments slowly dispersed.

"Thank you," Jed said, with extreme politeness.

"What's your name?"

"Jed Norton," he answered obediently to the sunglasses.

"Where do you work?"

"I play viola for the Indianapolis Symphony." The cop took half a step back and looked him up and down. Realizing he was in his work clothes, Jed added pathetically "I also paint houses on the side." The cop put the ticket book away.

"You play the what?"

"The viola. It's like a violin … only bigger," Jed said, as the cop started to reach for his handcuffs.

"Well, Mr. Viola Player, you can get off the bike now. And while I put these bracelets on you, why don't you tell me what the fuck you are doing down here in this total eclipse?" Jed was about to answer but was interrupted by a roundish boy turning the corner.

"Hi Jed, what's happening?" the boy shouted out. Jed turned and saw a familiar face.

"Hi Horace. Well, I'm having some trouble here. My fault really, I left without my wallet."

"And the man's putting you in jail? That's cold." The cop stopped and looked at the boy.

"You know this man?" he asked.

"Sure do, that's Jed Norton, he plays for the Indianapolis Symphony. Came to our school once for a special concert. I also went fishing with him at Eagle Crest." The cop put the handcuffs away.

"Buddy, I don't care who you are, but you shouldn't be down here like this. I want you to follow me 'til we get to 34th Street, and then you can go wherever the hell you should be. Got it?" Jed nodded. The cop walked back to his car. Jed kick-started his motorcycle, looked over at Horace and said "Thank you." Horace smiled.

The replay of his fight with Micaela cascaded through his memory as he turned north from 34th Street. He sorted through the regrets and resentment that he had tried to blow out of his head with the ride. It was their first fight and, like a coffee stain, it left a bitter residue. He became interested in the fact that, although he was practicing less, he was becoming a better player. His irritation began to diminish, and the increasing regrets overwhelmed the remaining resentment. As he returned to the scene of the quarrel, he tried to formulate a plan for achieving forgiveness. Cleaning the kitchen was not an option. He found that it was unusually immaculate. Micaela must have worked off some of her anger in there. Perhaps, if she just found him working on her house when she came back, that would be enough. He retreated to the outside and set about opening cans of paint. The day was already hot. Before he started, he went back into the house to get something to drink. Refreshed by the cool tap water, he decided that a fresh pot of coffee might warm up a reconciliation. He assembled the sparkling coffee pot and filled it with Folgers and water.

As he waited for the familiar sound of the percolator, he scanned the rest of this morning's newspaper, which Michaela had neatly stacked, unread, on the kitchen table. At the Local section he froze. "**OOLITIC QUARRY OWNER DROWNS.**" He had to read the article twice. Sentences like, *Ex Navy Seal discovers Watkins's body at bottom of the Quarry No. 5. The condition of the body suggests foul play was involved,* and the quote from Fred Fischer, *"In these cases, it is standard procedure to start the death investigation with friends and acquaintances"* numbed Jed's comprehension. Eventually, he let the paper drop from hands, left the house, and rode home to change clothes before driving to Oolitic.

For Micaela the morning had been a series of unexpected events and moods. When she arrived at Eric's, she was completely thrown off by his upbeat demeanor. First, she thought he was putting up a front. But soon she had to conclude it was sincere, unassailable, and its source unknowable. On her way back home, she found she still had a reservoir of guilt, only now it was filled with her unfair and unkind words to Jed. Prepared once again for some light groveling, she was disappointed that Jed's motorcycle was not there. Disappointment gave way to irritation when she saw the scattered paint cans. Irritation gave way to anger as she entered her unlocked home and smelled the overcooked coffee. "Ňouma" she muttered. She turned off the coffee pot and started to clean up the mess of newspapers. On the top of the mess was the local section with the headline that halted her breath and doused her anger.

— 23 —

JULY 10 WEDNESDAY

Ladies Luncheon – Woodstock Country Club

Music: Vivaldi: Concerto for Strings, RV 151

Leon selected the blue paisley ascot. He tied it loosely, with an overhand knot. He stuffed it into the top of his crisp, white shirt with top button unfastened. The blue blazer neatly finished the ensemble. As he stood inspecting himself in the mirror, Alison walked behind him and deftly removed the ascot with a twist and a tug.

"Alison!"

"The summer's too hot for an ascot, darling."

"Well, I'm not wearing a tie," he said, as he started to button the top button.

"You don't have to," she cooed and returned to the back of his head. Gently, she shooed his hands from the top button and straightened his collar.

"These girls will love seeing your neck. It will make them feel closer to you. Besides, this look is more dramatic … short, dark, and handsome." She laughed.

"Are you sure that this isn't too informal?"

"That's the point, silly. After all, you are the celebrity, not them," Alison answered. Leon didn't really understand.

"Do I have a choice?" he asked.

"Nope."

"Well, then, I'd better get the car," said the resigned maestro. Leon left the room and stopped by the study to pick up his briefcase.

He drove the Royal Crown Chrysler with the two fingers of his left hand, his body slouched against the door. He stopped the car at the gate to the

Woodstock Country Club. The guard took a long look at Leon and then bent over to see Alison in the passenger seat. He started to say something, then stopped and waved them on. At the entrance to the main building, a black attendant opened the car door for Alison. Leon's presence was ignored. He got out by himself, picked up his briefcase, and walked around to where Alison was waiting. He looked around for someone to give the keys to. Another black attendant, seeing the driver's confusion, came over and spoke to Leon.

"Just take it around the back of the building and park it near the kitchen. They'll bring lunch out to you," the young man said, trying to be as helpful as possible. While Leon stared at the young man, Alison slid her arm inside of Leon's and kissed him on the cheek.

"Let's hurry, darlin', or you'll be late for your speech."

Leon held the keys in front of the attendant's face, dropped them and walked off with Alison on his arm. The attendant caught the keys and stared at the departing couple.

"Nice control, honey. I'm proud of you," Alison said.

"I'm not. But who was I going to hit? It wasn't his fault," he said, irritated. "You know that kid is going to dent my car."

"You could hit the guard on the way out. I'm sure he still doesn't understand why I was in the front seat," she suggested.

"Good idea. Let's see how the talk goes." He summoned a smile. Leon and Alison entered the arched portico of the country club as the young man carefully parked the conductor's Chrysler. At the end of the parking space there was a cement post placed to protect the honeysuckle bushes. Gently, he pushed the left taillight into the post until he heard it crack. Smiling, he shut off the car and returned to the front.

From the hallway leading to the banquet room, Leon could hear Eric's quintet playing Vivaldi's *Concerto in D Major* above the din of ninety Indianapolis society women. As he turned the corner into the banquet room, he was surprised to see Micaela, because the members of the Ladies Luncheon eat and drink Vivaldi. On the other hand, he did not expect but was not surprised to see the addition of Jed to the ensemble. Leon gave a passing wave to Eric, and he nodded his head in reply.

The luncheon was on its last course as Mr. and Mrs. Zellingari were escorted to the dais. They were offered coffee and dessert. Alison accepted both. Leon took only water. When the concerto ended, the chairwoman called the audience to order. Introducing the Zellingaris, she decided to forego the usual litany of Leon's musical exploits. Instead, she took advantage of her friendship with Alison and told the story of how the maestro came to meet his wife in Aspen. It was not a serious transgression, because the story had been told publicly before, but it was certainly not what the maestro expected. It added to his existing discomfort for these events, which amused the quintet, particularly Micaela, no end. As the conductor took the podium and held the lectern, his short stature seemed reversed. The casual look of his open shirt caused one listener near Micaela to whisper to her neighbor.

"I'd leave my car lights on for that man until the battery went dead."

The title of Leon's talk was "The Myth of the Conductor." It was a little over the head of most of the audience, but they didn't care. It would be followed by a question-and-answer forum. Leon began:

"Good afternoon, ladies. Thank you for having me here today." Alison looked out among the sea of Aqua-Netted beehives and recognized proudly that more than several ladies would be happy to have him just about anywhere. "Even more importantly," Leon continued, "thank you for your continued support and generous contributions to our Indianapolis Symphony Orchestra. Without your contributions, we would not be able to enjoy the world-class music and visiting soloists that grace the stage of Campbell Hall each year. Indeed, you would not be able to enjoy the excellent rendition of Vivaldi that you've just heard from Eric Solomon's quintet." Leon paused for the automatic applause and standing bows of the quintet.

"Eric is the first violinist and concertmaster of our symphony. Eric, would you please introduce the members of your ensemble?" Leon directed.

"With pleasure, Maestro," Eric obeyed. "On violins we have Ashley Hall, just acquired from the San Diego Symphony. She is second chair and will be sitting next to me at concerts. Also, Gregory Walker, principal of 2nd violins. On viola, we have Jed Norton. And, as a special treat, you are hearing the first United States public appearance of our new principal of the cello section, Miss Micaela Miklos." Micaela tapped her bow on the cello.

"Oh, yes," continued Eric. "Micaela wants me to point out that this is the American debut of her new cello as well. You may have read about the generous donation of this Stradivarius from the Campbell Foundation this summer." Additional obligatory applause followed Eric's introductions, along with much neck craning in order to get a look at the fabled Miss Miklos.

"Thank you, Eric. I understand your program is over for the day, so you may leave if you like, or stay and learn something." Leon winked. No one in the quintet gave even a hint of going anywhere.

"The subject of today's talk is 'The Myth of the Conductor.' Not infrequently, I am asked, What does the conductor, or maestro (as he is sometimes respectfully and disrespectfully called) do, exactly? And by implication, Is the conductor really necessary? Wouldn't a simple metronome do the job, cost less, and be more reliable? Of course, this last question comes up every year when I negotiate my contract with the board.

"To understand the answer to this question," Leon resumed, after the polite laughter, "you must first understand that there was classical and orchestral music before there were conductors. In fact, you heard some today. Antonio Vivaldi was long dead before the first professional conductor, Hans Guido Freiherr von Bülow, appeared on stage in the mid-1800s. Long before von Bülow, there were maestros di capella, or chapel masters, whose job it was to beat out the tempo with a roll of paper or short stick. Then came composers who directed and played their own music. In the case of Beethoven, when his hearing had become completely useless, the orchestra would take their cues from the keyboardist. Or in some cases," he said pointedly, towards Eric, the first violin."

"Orchestras of the time faced a two-fold problem. As the music became widely distributed and more and more scores became available, they needed a musical director, someone to decide what would be played when, as well as who would play it. At the same time, the music was becoming more complex, and the need arose for a conductor who steered the presentation into a cohesive and coherent musical experience. In addition, conductors like von Bulow and Arthur Nikisch began to add something else to the music ... interpretation. Just as the concerto soloist will interpret Rachmaninov or Chopin, the conductors were taking whole symphonies to new heights of expression. And, in fact, the orchestra became the instrument of the conductor, just like that Stradivarius cello is Micaela's instrument.

"But I haven't answered the first question, What does the maestro actually do? Some will enjoy telling you that the maestro simply listens to the maestra," he said, looking at Alison and spawning the expected laughter, noticeably louder from the quintet.

"Actually, I think the question is better asked, How does the maestro play his instrument? Well, like the musicians playing for you today, first, the conductor must select his instrument. It may surprise you to know that when Miss Miklos was offered this very valuable cello, it did not mean that she would automatically be able to accept it. First, she needed to try it out, to see if it would play properly for her. In the same way, I have auditioned each of our eighty-five musicians, some more than once. Second, the conductor must study the music. Long before rehearsal, he must study the music, note for note, looking for all nuances of expression. Third, he must practice with his instrument. For each one of our concert pairs, there are at least four rehearsals of three hours or more. And finally, he gets to perform the music.

"People develop the misconception that the conductor is unnecessary in performance. I have heard people say that once you have done the rehearsal and you have practiced, all the orchestra has to do is play the notes. When I hear this, I am depressed and amused. I am depressed because music is much more than just playing notes. If that were the case, you wouldn't even need an orchestra; I am sure a machine could do it. It is amusing to me, because there is nothing more exultant than performing with a fine and responsive orchestra. Notice I used the word responsive. The truth is that this orchestra can play without me. The fact that they respond to my direction regarding tempo, dynamics, and expression is an indescribable joy." At this point Eric stood and raised his hand.

"Apparently, my concertmaster needs to interrupt me. What is it, Eric?" asked Leon.

"Maestro, I must clarify an important point. While it is true that we can play without you, it is also true that we don't sound nearly as good." Eric grinned. Small laughter ensued.

"Thank you, Eric, but I assure you, that comment will not increase your salary," Leon said to larger laughter. He continued, "I have brought with me today a very special piece of music." Alison handed him his briefcase. Leon opened it, took out the Rach III score, and held it up. Even at a distance, the fine leather binding and gilded lettering broadcasted value and beauty.

"I am holding the conductor's score for Rachmaninov's *Third Piano Concerto* which will be performed by Vladimir Khazar and the Indianapolis Symphony in our last November pair. This particular score was handwritten by Sergei Rachmaninov himself. I will be happy to show you details of it after the question-and-answer session."

"I can't wait to see that," Eric whispered to his group.

"It's very beautiful. The handwritten notes are magical," said Micaela. The rest of the quintet turned to Micaela with questioning and jealous looks.

"He showed it to me at audition," she explained. The quintet turned back to the speaker. Only Jed smiled.

"I am not going to pass it around now. I don't think any of you could tolerate the embarrassment and the cost of a spilled cup of coffee."

144

"Each one of our Indianapolis Symphony musicians must practice at least two hours each day. That practice, plus rehearsal and performance time, adds up to over thirty-five hours a week for what is often less than minimum wage. Most of our orchestra members require other jobs to make a living. Some teach music, while others, hold trade jobs, like Jed Norton here, who is a house painter."

"I have really fair rates, too," Jed shouted. Leon ignored Jed and the laughter.

"If you consider this a digression to let you know that you are getting your money's worth, you are only partly correct. It is also so that you know that I know what they do, and I understand why they do it. And to the best of my ability, I will try to take care of them. But I don't take care of them … my instrument … for altruistic reasons. I take care of them because I, the maestro, am a slave.

"I am a slave to the same master the orchestra serves. Where composers revel in the joy of creation, we play in the light of discovery. Each time we play or study Brahms, Bach, Mozart, Prokofiev, or Rachmaninov, we discover new layers in these fantastic works. These layers inspire us to practice harder. These layers inspire us to play better, to feel more deeply, and to provide performances that inspire you to return again and again. It is what governs us and it's what lifts us above our mortal coil.

"So the myth of the conductor is that he is the maestro. The maestro is actually the music." He lifted the Rach III score high. "And we are glad to serve it."

While the topic was a bit weighty for much of this audience, they responded to his dramatic delivery, and provided Zellingari with yet another ovation. After the audience settled down, the chairwoman stood beside the conductor to present the questions, which had been filled out on three-by-five cards and collected towards the end of his speech.

"Our first question is, 'Do different conductors have different signals for their orchestra?' " recited the chairwoman.

"Excellent question. I am afraid it requires a fairly long–winded answer. I will try to be brief. Yes, each conductor has his or her own style. To varying degrees, an orchestra must learn its conductor. But this is not as hard as it sounds. First of all, it all begins with tempo. This is the downbeat, the first signal from the conductor, and the methods are more common than variant." Leon demonstrated the hammer fall of the downbeat. "By the way, without tempo, there is nothing. As my mentor Leopold Stokowski once said, 'If you give good tempo, great things can happen. If you don't … well, they will still play the piece, but your presence is really unnecessary.' "

"Next are the individual cues that may be necessary for a particular performance. These are largely self-explanatory and learned on the fly during rehearsal. For example, if I want the strings to provide more expression, I will do this." Leon curled the fingers of his left hand as if holding the neck of a violin and pulled it towards himself with increasing force. "The subtler signals can also be learned during rehearsal but more often develop over time as the conductor and the orchestra gain experience with each other."

"Next question. 'Your house must be constantly full of music. Do the neighbors complain?' " Leon deferred to Alison.

"Actually, our house is quieter than most. The maestro studies in silence and is rather demanding that the silence not be interrupted. Exceptions occur when a guest soloist is staying at the house or we are having a reception for the concert. The soloists usually practice there for several hours. And the receptions sometimes go on until the wee hours of the morning."

"Here is an interesting question that might be apropos. 'What kind of stereo do you have?' "

"I don't. I have a monaural record player, and I really don't know what brand it is. As Alison intimated, I rarely listen to records. The music I study is in here," he said, pushing his finger on the cover of the score. As the questions got more and more useless, the answers became more interesting but more technical. Pretty soon, the only listeners were the quintet.

"And here is our final question for the day. 'What would you like written on your tombstone?'"

"You're next." It was an unfortunate comment, made more so by Leon's delight and the raucous laughter of his musical cohorts. He did not intend to be hostile; it was just an awkward attempt at humor to what he thought was an inane question. Leon apologized to the chairwoman. Leon continued to apologize to Alison all the way home. He didn't even notice the cracked taillight until Alison had disappeared into the house and he was turning off the light in the garage.

— 24 —

"... a collection of wealthy businessmen, retired military officers, and little old ladies in tennis shoes." — California Attorney General Stanley Moss, talking about the John Birch Society

JULY 16 TUESDAY

JBS Meeting – Public School No. 70

Music: Wagner, Die Meistersinger von Nurnberg , Prelude to Act 1

Lou met Jed and Micaela at the gym door of Public School No. 70. The trio entered the small, grade-school gym, which had a stage at one end so it could double as an auditorium. Inside, the only interruption to the institutional beige motif was the school color purple curtain, the Indiana State flag, and the American flag bracketing the stage. All 275 folding chairs had been set, but it wasn't enough. The latecomers had to stand around the edges and at the rear of the hall. At 8:00 PM sharp, a middle-aged woman with grey-streaked black hair and a huge twinkle in her eye behind her chain-bound glasses came to the podium and spoke sharply into the microphone.

"Ladies and gentleman, my name is Betty Stalcup. I am a fifth-grade teacher here at School 70 and president of the Indianapolis chapter of the John Birch Society. The July meeting is now called to order. We have one order of business tonight and that is our guest speaker. Please welcome our founder, Mr. Robert Welch." The applause was quite loud with additional cheering, but not universally through the room. Some at the meeting, like Lou and Jed, knew who this man was. For many, like Micaela, it was their first visit. Welch nodded his head in appreciation of the reception and then raised his hands to quiet the crowd.

"Thank you. And thank you, Betty. May I assume that all your monthly meetings are this well attended?" The audience laughed on cue. Betty returned to the microphone.

"You can from now on, sir." Renewed cheers came from pockets in the crowd.

"That's good to hear," Welch said, with his grandfatherly smile. He put his hands on the podium and began his speech. "You know, when you are 63 years old, you are often asked if you have any regrets. As I tour John Birch chapters in America and see how effective and large they are becoming, it is hard to have any regrets. But I do. Let me explain by reading a quote from Major Pedro Diaz Lanz, former chief of Fidel Castro's air force:

'If there had been even one chapter of the John Birch Society in Havana prior to 1959, working to expose Castro as Robert Welch was at the time, Cuba would not have fallen to Communism.' Major Lanz defected from Cuba in 1959, and I met him last year in Miami. The major, like thousands of other Cubans, had fallen for Castro's propaganda and worked tirelessly to bring him to power. To this day, he regrets his ignorance and naiveté. And to this day, I regret we did not start the John Birch Society much, much earlier. But we have started! And we are growing! And we will have NO MORE REGRETS! We will defeat the communist horde and all enemies of freedom and America!" The fervent cheers of the crowd were infecting the newcomers. Lou, Jed, and Micaela smiled joyously at each other.

"I am going to assume that many of you in the audience are attending your first meeting of the John Birch Society ..."

"But not their last," someone yelled from the floor. Welch smiled and continued.

"... and are wondering who is John Birch and what it is exactly that we do. This society was formed just five years ago, in 1958. It was named in honor of Captain John Morrison Birch. Captain Birch had the simple desires for his life that we all do. At the age of 26, in the same year of his untimely death, he expressed them in this writing, '… to live slowly, to relax with my family before a glowing fireplace … to enjoy a good book … to reach the sunset of my life sound in body and mind, flanked by strong sons and grandsons …" He was not able to realize those desires. His dedication to God and country compelled him to fight communists in China, who had violently killed so many of his faith. John Birch fought successfully behind enemy lines for many years. In April of 1942, with his considerable talents and skills, he was able to see that Colonel Doolittle's bomber crews made it safely to Free China. Then, Birch stayed in China as an intelligence analyst and acted as the eyes of the 14th Air Force. He is credited with aiding in the rescue of scores of downed pilots.

"In 1945, this American war hero, to whom so many owed their lives, was shot in the leg, bound, and then executed with a single gunshot to the back of his head. His murderers desecrated his body. This tragedy was unforgivably compounded by our own U.S. government's political shenanigans. In an effort to depict the Red Chinese as innocuous 'agrarian reformers,' our *fearful* leaders suppressed the news of the unprovoked murder of Captain Birch. John Birch is an example to emulate, not a political embarrassment to be hidden. If we can rediscover some of our sounder spiritual values in the example of his life, and learn essential truths about our enemy from the lesson of his murder, then his death will cease to be a tragedy.

"The mission of our society is to honor John Birch by continuing to fight the communist enemy at home and abroad. And the weapon we will use to defeat the communist horde will be truth. As a government and a people, we can no longer afford to fuel the fire of misplaced sympathies. We need to put the blame were it righteously belongs — at the foot of the communist horde. No longer will our government, under the political guise of 'peaceful co-existence,' be able to hide the atrocities and repression of communist governments, like the murdering of families of communist refugees." Jed stole a quick glance at Micaela's reaction. He decided then and there to never play poker with that woman.

"No longer will the communist influence and corruption be swept under the carpet. No longer will we be drawn into unholy alliances because of the myth of the Holocaust. No longer will we allow the liberal and Jewish-based propaganda to go unchallenged. No longer will our leaders be ignorant and naïve. We will inundate them with the truth about communists, the forced mixing of the races, and the self-interest of certain non-Christian organizations." While the crowd continued to ramp, many members' applause notably abated, including Micaela's.

Debussy: Nocturnes - Nuages

After the meeting, Micaela, Jed, and Lou stopped at a local dive named Hutch's Hooch. Lou ordered a pitcher of Pabst Blue Ribbon. Jed found a booth. Settling into the cushioned bench, Micaela said, "I am so sorry to hear about Gar." Lou and Jed nodded silently. "Do they have any idea who did it?" Lou's shook his head slightly while looking at the table.

"Do you remember Fred Fischer?" Lou asked.

"Yeah, your old squirrel-hunting buddy," answered Jed. "Didn't he open a mortuary?"

"Yep. He also does death investigations."

"Has he turned up anything?" Jed asked.

"I dunno. He keeps changing is mind. He sure does ask a lot of questions. First, he thought that maybe Gar ran into the wrong crowd and started mouthing off."

"Certainly a possibility with Gar," Jed said.

"Yeah, right. He could always say the wrong thing at the wrong time. Anyhow, Fred is not sure about that anymore. He can't figure out how they could have thrown big ol' Gar over the edge of the querry without him banging into something."

"That would be tough," said Jed.

"Plus, he had the cinder block tied to him. Fred said there weren't enough nigras in Lawrence County to do that."

"Lots'a of people outside of Lawrence County know about that quarry."

"That's what I said. Anyhow, now he thinks that he was dropped."

"Dropped?"

"With a truck and a crane."

"You can't get a crane in there," Jed said.

"Actually, you can — a small one on a pickup would fit. Fred found some tire tracks." Lou took a long drink, wiped the foam off his upper lip, smiled at Micaela, and changed the subject.

"Micaela, what did you think of Mr. Welch?"

"Very impressive man. Very impressive speaker," she answered, unwilling to add anything more to her review.

Lou waited for a moment and then pressed. "Aw c'mon, Miss Future American Citizen, you must have more to say than that?" Micaela turned and looked at Lou. Jed knew her well enough by now to know that it was not likely she would back away from Lou's challenge.

"Okay. I have civics question." She smiled back at Lou. "Why all the anti-Semitism? I thought the American ideal included freedom for all religions." Lou started to answer, but Jed interrupted.

"It is important to differentiate between members of the Jewish faith and some of the leaders of the Jewish people who espouse self-serving propaganda. For example, there are several reliable texts that clearly explain that the number of Jews killed by the Germans was grossly exaggerated."

"Really. How was such 'reliable' information created?" she asked.

"It's quite interesting," Jed started to answer.

"I'll bet," said Micaela, staring at Lou.

Jed continued past the interruption. "Several experts were sent to study the crematoriums and gas chambers at Auschwitz and Birkenau and, using mathematical models, proved that it would take about fifty years to kill that many Jews."

"Experts in vhat?"

"Many of our states use the gas chamber for capital offenses. And most of our mortuaries provide cremation services. There are plenty of knowledgeable people in this area," answered Lou, smiling. There would be no more smiles on Micaela's face that night.

"In other words, you are saying that American death engineers have concluded that German death engineers are not as good as we thought," she said.

"I have never heard it put that way, but that is essentially the truth," Lou replied. Micaela's head was propped up by a triangle of her forearms and hands. Her eyes went from wide-eyed to closed and wide-eyed again. Jed looked around for objects within her reach.

"The truth," she said calmly, then with more volume, "I doubt that is truth … essentially or otherwise. But let's just say that your death experts are correct and the numbers are … too large. Maybe Nazis only killed one million."

"Two hundred fifty thousand, tops," Lou said. Micaela separated her strong hands, opening and closing them as if looking for something to grasp. Jed pushed himself deeper in the Naugahyde of the booth.

"Okay, let's just say they exterminated a *mere* quarter million." Micaela's face was twisted in her attempt to keep in control. "Does that mean that Nazis are not so bad, and somehow it is Jews' fault?"

"No, no, no, you're missing the point, Micaela," Jed said. Micaela snapped her attention to Jed. He wished he hadn't opened his mouth. But once started, there was no turning back. "Nobody's saying the Nazis are not guilty of horrible things. It's just that Jewish *leaders* exaggerated the situation so that America would align itself with the greater evil of communism. And they are still doing so," Jed said, hopeful of Micaela's understanding.

"The communists … the ones who killed your parents," added Lou.

"I know who fucking killed my parents!" she said. The shock of the profanity did not compare to the force of the accompanying arm gesture, which sent both the pitcher of beer and her glass flying towards the nearest table where two guys in John Deere tractor hats stared, open-mouthed. The glass shattered on the floor, the pitcher rolled, and Hutch's Hooch regulars were lightly doused with beer. The tractor hats rose, ready to fight.

The manager, in a white apron, appeared between the table and the booth, told the tractor hats to calm down, sit down, and gave them a towel. He then turned to the booth and said,

"You all can leave now."

"Vhy the fuck should ve leave?"

"Lady, we don't appreciate that kind of language here, much less throwing glasses around. You've had enough. Now you have to go."

"I have definitely had enough. May I use rest room before going?"

"As long as you don't throw anything. If you do, I'll have you arrested." Micaela scooted out of the booth and stomped off. The manager looked down at Jed and Lou and said, "You can wait for her outside."

Outside, Lou was quietly laughing and said to Jed, "Yer girl can sure blow her cork."

"Christ, Lou, whaddya expect?" Jed said painfully.

Lou stared at his friend for a moment and then said, "You know, college boy, think I'll skedaddle. You tell your pretty girlfriend that I am sorry and I had no call to say that about her parents. Okay?"

"Too chicken to tell her yourself?"

"That must be it." He winked at Jed and left.

Soon after, Micaela came out of the tavern.

"Lou's gone?" she asked.

"Yeah. He apologized for his crack about your parents. He thought he would be safer if I told you."

"Doesn't seem like kind of man who is concerned about safety," she said.

"Well, you don't seem like the kind of girl to start a bar fight," Jed laughed alone. Changing the subject he asked, "Is your hand okay?"

"What? Oh yes. It is fine. I didn't really hit glasses as much as I scooped them out of way." They paused in a complicated silence, and then Micaela said, "I want to go home now."

"Okay, let's go."

"I want you to go to your own place," she added. Jed did not respond. After he paused to absorb the instruction, he opened the car door for her. On the way over to Micaela's apartment, there was no conversation. Jed parked the car in front of the walkway to her door.

"You belong to this anti-communist society, don't you?" Micaela asked.

"Yes, I do."

"And you believe their *truth*?" She looked over to Jed with the question. He nodded that he did.

"I was hoping you might want to join us," he added. Micaela stopped looking at Jed and spoke to the windshield.

"I belong to different society. It is society of refugees. Membership is much more difficult to achieve. But once you are member, you are member for life. As member, you learn many things about fellow refugees. They become like … family. With their help, you determine what is true and what is not. Like family, you defend each other. Your John Birch Society does not speak for me or my family. Please leave us alone." Micaela got out of the car and walked to door. Jed waited to make sure she was safely inside.

— 25 —

"How do you feel about this Soviet Negro Republic, Governor [Rockefeller]? With Atlanta, perhaps as its capital? And Martin Luther King as its 'president'? And all of the cruelty and horror that would be imposed both on the white people and the colored people of the South — who were living together so peacefully with such steadily improving relations until May 17, 1954?" — Robert Welch, from August John Birch Society Bulletin

AUGUST 1 THURSDAY

Meeting with Lou and Betty – Jed's Home

Music: Ravel, Rapsodie Espagnole No. 1 "Prelude de la Nuit"

The coffee was a mistake. It just added to Jed's anxiety. Why did Lou and Betty Stalcup want to meet with him? Why at his house? Ever since he broke up with Micaela, he had avoided the Society. Were they coming to scold him? That would be sheer bullshit, he thought. But the thought did not diminish the guilt lurking in his psyche. He put some chips and dip on the coffee table.

Lou and Betty arrived together. Lou was dressed in T-shirt and jeans. Betty had on her schoolteacher suit and the permanent smile that accompanied her chewing gum. Her eyeglasses, hung by the ever-present chain, rested on her chest.

"Hi, Jed, long time no see," she said when Jed opened the door.

"Hi, Betty, hi, Lou, come on in." Lou headed straight for the kitchen, got a beer out of the icebox and proceeded to make himself at home. "Help yourself, Lou," Jed chided. Betty had come into the room and was intently surveying the surroundings. She walked over to the bookshelf, put her eyeglasses, on and inspected the book titles.

"Can I get you anything, Betty?" Jed asked.

"Yes, you *may* get me something," she corrected, without looking at Jed and still perusing the library.

Jed waited and finally had to say, "What may I get you?" Betty turned with a gum-smacking smile,

"How about a Coke … in a glass … with ice."

"Comin' right up," Jed said, going to the kitchen. Lou came out and sat on the couch, while Betty chose the easy chair.

When Jed returned with Betty's Coke, she said, "Quite an interesting collection of books you have there, Jed."

"Thanks."

Betty snickered. "That wasn't necessarily a compliment. I just meant there was some pretty avant-garde stuff on that shelf."

"I'm not sure what you mean, but much of that was required reading," he said, annoyed with his own defensiveness.

"College requirements, you mean." She snickered again.

"Yeah, college," he said. Lou and Betty both looked at each other and then ate some chips. "What do you guys want?" asked Jed.

"Good, straight to the point. I like that. Lou said you were a man of action. But since we hadn't seen you for a while, I didn't know for sure." She wagged her head.

"Know what, for sure?" Jed asked.

"Well, you know … if you were still with us. Still wanted to fight the communists. You are still with us, aren't you?" Betty asked. Jed nodded, but not firmly.

"Yes, if by fighting you mean telling the truth." Jed said.

"That's exactly what I mean, Jed. You do listen well. I always tell my fifth graders how important it is to listen well to succeed. I was just worried a little because of your environment, y'know?"

"No, I don't know. What environment are you talking about?"

"You know, all those Jews and liberals in the orchestra. It must be tough to work and listen to them whine every day. Especially if you are a good listener, if you know what I mean."

"It's not that much of a challenge, really," Jed said.

"Whatever you say. Here is the thing. Lou and I read in the papers about this commie coming over to play with you guys."

"Khazar?"

"Yeah, that's the guy. We were wonderin' …"

"I don't think he really cares about politics," Jed interrupted.

"It says in the paper that he is a member of the communist party," she said.

"They all have to be, or they can't tour." It was Jed's turn to correct.

"Okay, this commie Jew is going to be a big thing, right?" Betty plowed ahead. "Lou and I were thinking, what a great time to pass out some leaflets telling the truth about the communists. Maybe do an ad in the paper or something warning the public about his arrival."

"Warning them about what?"

"The commies are comin', Jed. C'mon, try to keep up," Lou scolded.

"They … I mean, he is coming to play Rachmaninov. He's not coming to sign you up for the party," Jed said.

Betty shook her head. "You've been away too long. You see, this is the way it always starts. He's gonna come and make nice and play some pretty music and then the public is gonna say, 'Hmm, I guess those communists aren't so bad.' We need to be there and remind the public about communist infiltration and atrocities. It's not about him, it's about the American way of life. We just want to keep the record straight and hand out some harmless leaflets."

"And an ad or two," added Lou.

"Yeah, an ad or two," Betty popped a chewing gum bubble.

"What do you want from me?" Jed shifted uncomfortably in his seat.

"Not much. We just need to know when he's coming, where he's staying, when rehearsals are. Stuff like that."

"Why?"

"Boy, you sure do ask a lot of questions." Betty laughed.

"They taught him that in college," said Lou. No one said anything until Jed asked his question a second time, with a palms-up hand gesture.

"We just want to make sure that we get the timing right. After all, it wouldn't make any sense to pass out leaflets at Campbell Hall if he wasn't there, right? By the way, that is where he is playing, isn't it?" Jed nodded.

"We also need to know how many people are with him," said Lou.

"How many people?" asked Jed.

"You don't think these guys travel alone, do you? They have Russian secret service guys with them. KGB, I think they're called. Well, we even hear that they are sometimes forced to marry wives who are members of the KGB," said Betty. Jed sat silently.

"C'mon, Jed, are you going to do it or not?" asked Lou.

Eventually, Jed said, "Okay. But I don't want my name to go with it. It could cost me my job."

"Those Godless bastards," said Betty. "Jed, we owe you one. This is a courageous thing you are doing. If you are ever ready to talk about it, we will make sure your story is told. Even though it is a school night, I would like to celebrate. Do you have any more beer?"

"Sure he does," answered Lou. "I'll go open a round." Lou was back quickly with three Schlitz.

"To the concert," Lou offered a toast. They all tapped the necks of their beer bottles. Betty stood up and walked over to Jed's practice area.

"So this must be where you practice?" she asked.

"Yes," answered Jed.

"It looks like you're doing some writing, too?"

"Sort of. I'm finishing a project I started in college. It's an arrangement of the Gershwin *Preludes* for violin. We are going to perform them in the same concert," Jed explained.

"Gershwin, he's the *Rhapsody in Blue* guy, right?" she asked.

"Yeah, that's right."

"I like that guy," she said, smacking her gum. "So you have to write all the parts for the orchestra?"

"No, just the conductor's score. Someone else will transpose and print the individual parts for the rest of the orchestra." Betty looked closely at the sheet music, then pointed to the individual staffs.

"I see, so that's what a conductor's score is. This is how the conductor knows when to point to different persons to play," she said.

"It's a bit more complicated than that. But you get the idea."

"It looks complicated. Does the conductor ever not use a score?" she asked.

"No, not really. They probably could if they wanted to. After all, the soloists play their concertos from memory. But it would take considerable time and preparation, and conductors have to do so many different programs, they don't bother to memorize them."

"That makes sense," Betty said. Lou had joined them to look at the sheet music.

"Is that what they were talking about in the paper?" Lou asked. Jed looked puzzled. "You know, some special score that your boss got hold of."

"Yeah. He's got the original score for the concerto that Khazar is going to play. Hand-done by the composer, very valuable. He's quite proud of it."

"You know what?" Betty's face lit with realization. The guys shook their heads. She went on, "Remember that package you told us about last spring?"

"You mean the one that the maestro got from Russia?"

"That's the one," said Betty. "I'll bet that was the score we're talking about."

"You're probably right," Jed nodded.

157

"Well, that's a hoot," said Lou. "We thought it was some secret papers from Russia or something. Turns out it was just music." Betty and Lou looked at each other and started to laugh.

III
Caduta dura vivace

— 26 —

SEPTEMBER 19 THURSDAY

Luca Rehearsal – Campbell Hall

Music: Brahms, Symphony No. 2 in D, Op. 73, First Movement, Allegro Non Troppo

The ISO performed Saturday night and Sunday afternoon. Typically, the orchestra would have rehearsals Tuesday, Wednesday, Friday, and Saturday. Monday and Thursday were days off. It was expected that those days would be used for individual and section practice. For extremely demanding programs or opening night, there would be a fifth rehearsal on Thursday. Because it was an extra rehearsal, there were several acceptable excuses for missing it. The musician's union would always complain, and those complaints would always be sent to Robert Delmonico. On Tuesday, Leon would start by running through all the program pieces except the concerto from start to finish. After each run-through, there would be discussion, primarily with, but not limited to, the principals. Voices with heavy accents of Texas, Brooklyn, Germany, Italy, Czechoslovakia, Asia, and the Midwest would speak in Italian, English, mathematics, and a classical skat to describe phrases.

"da dA DA Di da DE dum?"

"No, Hermann, I want Da Da DA DI DA de dum," the maestro would answer. Body language, usually a nod, would confirm the change, and Hermann's basses would take their pencils to the sheet music to make the note. The pencils were also used to deal with the incessant discrepancies between the conductor's score and the musician's sheet music. Inverted phrasing, different time intervals, even wrong notes, were a constant nuisance that required the free form interchange that Leon encouraged. Nevertheless, only

161

those who were extremely secure in their positions would offer corrections to Leon's errors.

"Maestro, three bars after the letter G, isn't it *crescendo forte*?" Martha said, more as a statement than a question. With a frustrated exhale, Leon flipped back through the pages of the score to resolve the discrepancy. He found none. He had conducted it incorrectly.

"From now on, I will conduct it that way," he said. The orchestra chuckled. The dress code for rehearsals was informal. For nearly everyone, the weather or the part-time job determined the dress code for the day. That is, everyone except Leon. He had an unalterable pattern that increased in formality as the week wore on towards the performance. You could tell what part of the week it was by the maestro's clothes. On Tuesday, he would wear a blue Chicago Cubs sweatshirt. On Wednesday, it was a grey Cubs sweatshirt. On Friday, it was a dark blue button-down from Roderick St. John's, with sleeves rolled up to the elbows. On Saturday, it was a white shirt with Windsor collar. The sleeves stayed down, but he left the top button unfastened. On all days, he wore black patent leather shoes and black pants with a gold watch and chain.

He would always enter the orchestral shell from stage right. If he was on the outside of the shell, stage left, he would walk around the back of the shell before entering his domain. The shell itself was not just a visual backdrop, but an acoustic device as well. It had been designed, with Leon's approval, to blend the music and send it outward to the audience.

The informality and openness of rehearsal never meant that it was disorganized or inefficient. Tuesdays were particularly demanding. Leon had the dizzying ability of conducting and verbally instructing at the same time. During the run-throughs, he would frequently shout instructions about the section just played, while continuing to conduct the rest of the piece. Second chairs would struggle to keep up because they had to alternate between playing and leaning forward with pencils in hand to record the conductor's comments. There was audible relief when Leon pulled his watch from his pants pocket and announced that it was time for one of the breaks required by the union. Despite the pace, rehearsals were fun. Yes, they had to perform for their peers and their boss, but klinkers (bad notes) were laughed at, jokes (usually vulgar) were made privately and publicly, and those not rehearsing at the time played a high-stakes game of cribbage in the wings. The relaxed atmosphere was akin to batting practice before a baseball game. There was even a small audience for most rehearsals. Anywhere from five to twenty "civilians" might be scattered in the first thirty rows of the hall. This privileged audience included significant donors, music students, soloists' spouses, local or visiting politicians, and Alison. There were exceptions to the rehearsal's normal demeanor. If rehearsals didn't progress to the conductor's satisfaction, Fridays would be extremely unpleasant, and orchestra members would warn each other before going on stage. For example:

"Better not drink that coffee, Hugh," Eric said, knowing a particularly difficult rehearsal was coming..

"Aw, shit, bad Friday?" Hugh asked.

"Yep, Allen's already closed the doors," Eric answered.

On bad Fridays, Allen would clear the hall. The orchestra was sealed from the rest of the world. Bathroom breaks occurred on the conductor's schedule, not nature's, nor the union's.

Other exceptions would occur depending on the personality of the soloist. Some were barely tolerable prima donnas, which meant that during their rehearsal time, backs were straighter, comments were kept to a minimum, and the cribbage game disappeared to the dressing room. On the other hand, some soloists were as fun as a class clown. Luca was one of these. He liked to show off. He liked to crack jokes. He always flirted with the prettiest orchestra members. If Leon got too serious, Luca would tease him, to the sublime delight of the orchestra.

The first rehearsal with the soloist was usually on Wednesday, unless it conflicted with the soloist's touring schedule, as was the case with Luca. Because this was the week before opening night, it was convenient to move him to Thursday. Even musicians who were not scheduled to play during the concerto found an excuse to be on stage or in the hall. No one was going to miss the first meeting of Luca and Micaela.

"Maestro, we are getting a large number of attendance requests for Thursday," Allen reported to Leon at the beginning of the week.

"I'm not surprised."

"Do you want me to close it?" Allen thought he was anticipating the conductor correctly.

"No. In fact, make sure everyone knows, especially Gianluca. Perhaps a partial house will encourage him to behave himself," Leon said. By the time the day came, a sizable audience had developed, including Edith Campbell, who needed no invitation or permission to attend.

Without Micaela's knowledge, an inordinate amount of attention had been given to her introduction to Gianluca Giarrizzo. Leon, Alison, and Eric had

163

debated whether it should be backstage, on stage, at the soloist's dressing room, or in the maestro's dressing room. They had even argued about what she should wear.

The maestro halted the fruitless debate and said, "How they are introduced is meaningless. How they meet in the music is what counts." Even if Micaela had heard this, it would have done little to quiet her own anxiety about the introduction. She frequently interrupted study sessions with Eric to pester him about how she should look, when to arrive, what to say.

"You should be more concerned with the opening cadenza," Eric counseled.

"That is the one thing I am not worried about." Micaela's musical confidence was truly intimidating.

Eric put down his violin and gave in, "Okay, here's my advice. Don't go to his dressing room. It shows subservience. Dress as you are now — comfortable, ready to go to work, and not too provocative." Micaela surveyed herself in surprise. She was wearing an oversized, high-necked top, a loose cotton dress, and flats.

"Surely, this is too informal?" she asked.

"Not for Leon's rehearsals. You will get the feel of it on Tuesday and Wednesday. Now, as Leon said, you will be sitting with your section, not stage front. So when you arrive, go to your chair, ready with some additional instructions for your cellos, and let him come to you."

"What if he doesn't?" she asked.

Eric laughed. "Then the sun will rise in the west."

On the day of the rehearsal, Micaela laid out on the bed the same clothes she was wearing when Eric gave his advice. As she stared at them with complete indifference, the black strapless performance gown that Alison had helped her find howled out at her from the open closet door. Shaking her head at the sartorial incongruity, she tossed the conservative top onto the floor in the corner. Instead, she selected a form-fitting, spaghetti-strapped purple top with a low, curved neckline. After she dressed, she looked at herself in the mirror.

"I'm comfortable, ready to work ... two out of three will have to do," she said. Adding a cardigan for the weather, she left for rehearsal, overladen with cello and briefcase.

Even though this was only her third rehearsal with the ISO, Micaela knew things were different as soon as she came through the stage door. Allen was there, storing the instrument cases backstage in neat rows. Normally, this exercise was saved for the performance. During rehearsals, cases were scattered haphazardly anywhere, including the first few rows of the hall. But there was no room for that today.

Allen helped her unpack her cello, bows, and accessories, and she walked to her chair just to the conductor's right. All of her section members were already seated and warming up. She set up her cello. Her chair was in its normal location at the foot of the podium, stage left. But because she would be doing the concerto, the music stand that she normally shared with her second chair was off-center to her right. It was an odd view for her, neither orchestra member nor soloist, but more like a player-coach. She turned to give her second chair an extra bow.

"I won't need this today, but I want you ready in case I need it Saturday night. Also, let's turn music stand more towards you," she barked. Hearing her own voice, she said, "Sorry, I'm a bit a jumpy today." Her second smiled and nodded with complete understanding. They continued to discuss performance details, such as whether Micaela would be on stage or enter with Luca for the concerto, who would hold the Baudiot, checking to make sure that the rest of the section had their music, and what to do if section members were absent or late. Her second suggested, "We can always shoot them later." Micaela enjoyed the levity.

On the other side of the stage, the affable Luca entered after Leon. While moving towards the podium, Luca shook hands with the many members of the string section. He waved at Hugh and Martha. Eric's newly acquired second chair was exquisitely tanned and had blonde hair that ended right at the waist of her hip-hugging, bell-bottom pants. Luca froze at her chair.

"Tell me you can play as good as you look," Giarrizzo said. The orchestra laughed.

"Better," Eric replied. The orchestra laughed harder.

"Uh oh ... then she must do the Brahms," Luca teased. She tried to hide behind her violin.

"Gianluca, please don't make me move her to the percussion section," Leon admonished, good naturedly.

"My apologies, Maestro," Luca said, while bowing to the totally embarrassed violinist, whose face was no longer tan but red as a sunburn. She raised her head from behind the violin, nodded to Luca, and he blew her a kiss. Luca turned and walked deliberately to the other side of Leon's podium — to Micaela, who was taking off her cardigan while still talking with her second. Most of the orchestra members were still warming up, but there was an audible decrease in volume.

"Miss Miklos?" he said. Micaela turned, handed her cello to her second, and stood up from her chair to shake hands.

"Mr. Giarrizzo, it is a great honor and pleasure to meet you." Her respectful demeanor was completely lost on Luca and everyone else within earshot. And the perimeter of earshot had expanded to the limits of the hall the moment Micaela stood up. From the point of view of the audience, the leering Luca and the busty Micaela were framed by the uncharacteristically silent and staring orchestra. Like the playbill of a melodrama, the frozen scene was at best comic and at worst shocking. Alison, who was seated next to Edith, did her best to stifle her amusement at the speechless Luca.

Without looking at Alison, Edith said quietly, "I hope you found her something more modest for Saturday night." Alison sunk deeper into her chair as Luca recovered.

"Actually, it is rumored that the honor is mine." He openly scanned her body. "Clearly, the pleasure already is mine. Call me Luca." Micaela made no reply. Luca continued, as the orchestra recovered its sensibilities as well. "Is this your new treasure I heard about?" he asked, pointing to the Baudiot.

"Yes, it is. I am quite fortunate. It was previously owned by Gre…"

"I know who owned it. Tell me, have you had time to become compatible?" There was a gauntlet's warning in Luca's question. Micaela stiffened and stared at the somewhat shorter Luca.

"Yes, quite compatible." On the other side of the podium, Eric rolled his eyes.

Leon interrupted the conversation. "Luca, are you ready?"

"Ready, Maestro." Luca retreated to his side of the podium, and Micaela sat down. Leon signaled for Hugh to provide the concert A for everyone to tune to.

When silence returned, Leon said, "From the top, please." Leon raised his arms and held for a second, then provided the downbeat. The no-holds-barred beginning of the *Brahms Double* did nothing to relieve the tension of the first meeting between Luca and Micaela. Like a soundtrack for a black-and-white Western, the music provided dramatic ammunition for this duel.

The orchestra loudly introduces the concerto with a skip-stairs descent from E to E in A minor, followed by a quick ascent in triplets of all the notes in the same scale. Then the cello gets the first shot. It is a long, low, and lengthy solo, providing ample opportunity for disaster or, as in this case, a demonstration of a remarkable cellist and cello. The tension of this minor is elevated by delicate use of the tritone (Eflat). The music is not just heard but felt, in the vibrating of a deep and most human chord. The opening cadenza is incongruously but smoothly interrupted by a switch to A Major, highlighting clarinet and oboe.

This switch allowed Luca to tease himself into the piece with the delicate violin. The brilliance of Brahms permits the soloists to approach each other from the extremes of their instruments, as well as the major and minor keys. Soon they were merged, demonstrating their common ground and delightful differences.

Two minutes into the first movement, the orchestra's part provided a lengthy break from the breathless opening duel, during which the unsmiling Luca used his handkerchief to wipe his brow and violin. When the soloists began again, this time with the orchestra, it was once again Micaela who got to lead, with Luca following. Luca broke a string.

"Aw shit," said Luca, handing the violin to Eric. Eric passed the violin to his second to restring and offered his own to Luca.

"NO! I'll wait!" the soloist said loud enough for everyone to hear. Because it was a rehearsal, Leon was obliged to stop.

While the blonde frantically worked on the violin, Luca turned to the conductor and said, "What do you expect when the orchestra is so loud?" The comment was as surprising as Luca's demeanor. One of Zellingari's most well-known skills was his ability to play with soloists in a concerto, particularly violin concerti. Leon looked at Luca, scratched his forehead, and gave an almost imperceptible nod. Eric's second was still tuning the replaced string.

The conductor turned to his orchestra and said, "Okay, let's pick it up four bars before the cello reenters … *mezzo piano*, please." Leon gave the downbeat. When it was Luca's turn to join Micaela, he found the new string was out of tune. He attempted to tune it live, while Micaela and the orchestra played on. Eventually, he quit and walked off the stage.

Leon stopped the orchestra.

"Break!" he shouted. Then he left, stage right. The conductor skittered down the stairs to the dressing rooms. Without knocking, he burst into Luca's pouting sanctuary. Toe to toe, nose to nose, the shouting began. It was clearly heard outside the door.

"What the hell is your problem?" The maestro's voice got deeper, the angrier he was.

"My problem?" Luca's voice got higher, the angrier he was. "Are you deaf? If you played them any louder, we would have to give the front row earmuffs. What the hell are you doing to me?"

"Bullshit, Luca, you're just scared."

"Scared! You're crazy, what would I be scared of?"

"Scared of playing with someone who might be better than you."

"Fuck you!" The shouting turned into a stare-down, which Luca lost. "Goddamn it!" he said, as he turned away from Leon and sat down at the dressing table. Leon looked at his friend, who was staring into the mirror surrounded by bare bulbs.

"She really *is* gorgeous, isn't she?" Leon teased.

"Go fuck yourself," said the exasperated Luca, lowering his head into his own hands. Leon put his hand on Luca's shoulder.

"Gianluca, my friend, she is not better than you … not yet. But she might be in a few years. You can either help her get there or go home. If you go home, I will play Eric, and you will have fucked yourself."

Luca nodded his head in resignation and said, "I don't know how to do this."

"Sure you do, it's in the concerto." The maestro was interrupted by a knock on the door. "Who is it?" asked Leon.

"Excuse me, Maestro," Allen said. "I have a message from Mrs. Campbell. Leon opened the door, and Allen handed him a note. Leon read it and then passed it to Luca.

"It is difficult to hear the cello when it is facing the podium." – EC

Luca stared at the note for a moment and then stood up and put it in his pocket. Mustering a smile, he said, "Okay, I'm ready."

Leon patted Luca on the back and said, "Break's over, Allen, get 'em ready."

The conductor and the soloist reentered the stage together. The audience and the orchestra were silent. Micaela could not look at anyone.

When Leon mounted the podium, Luca asked, "Maestro?"

"Yes, Luca."

"You know, I don't want to tell you how to do your job."

"Since when?" Leon said, spawning a few chuckles.

"It's just that I don't see how the audience, particularly that side," pointing to audience right, "can properly hear the cello when it is positioned towards the podium like that."

Leon smiled back and said, "Quite right. My mistake. Allen, will you properly position Micaela for a double concerto?" Allen and a stage hand arrived on cue to move her chair to stage front, the same distance to the podium as Luca's. This position allowed her to see the conductor, Luca, and the audience. While Allen's crew was executing the change in staging, the cellos started to tap their bows on their music stands, while looking at Luca. They were followed by the violins, violas, clapping from the rest of the orchestra, and then from the audience.

Luca smiled and laughed.

As the applause diminished, he said, "Wow, that's the first time I've gotten an ovation for not playing." The orchestra laughed with him.

Luca then held his hand to his face like the lecherous Groucho Marx holding a cigar and said, "Micaela, wanna do some Brahms?" During the concerto rehearsal, the private thoughts of more than a few orchestra and audience members caused coloration equal to the blonde violinist from San Diego.

— 27 —

Excerpt from eulogy for Addie Mae Collins, 14, Carol Denise McNair, 11, and Cynthia Diane Wesley, 14, three of the four victims of the bombing at the Sixteenth Street Baptist Church in Birmingham on Sunday morning, September 15, 1963.

"... God still has a way of wringing good out of evil. And history has proven over and over again that unmerited suffering is redemptive. The innocent blood of these little girls may well serve as a redemptive force that will bring new light to this dark city. The Holy Scripture says, 'A little child shall lead them.' The death of these little children may lead our whole Southland from the low road of man's inhumanity to man to the high road of peace and brotherhood. These tragic deaths may lead our nation to substitute an aristocracy of character for an aristocracy of color.

"May I now say a word to you, the members of the bereaved families? It is almost impossible to say anything that can console you at this difficult hour and remove the deep clouds of disappointment which are floating in your mental skies. But I hope you can find a little consolation from the universality of this experience. Death comes to every individual. There is an amazing democracy about death. It is not an aristocracy for some of the people, but a democracy for all of the people. Kings die and beggars die; rich men and poor men die; old people die and young people die. Death comes to the innocent and it comes to the guilty. Death is the irreducible common denominator of all men." — Martin Luther King

"Civilization is defined by the reasons we kill each other." — Lyn Gullett

SEPTEMBER 20 FRIDAY

Dinner at Krishna Banji – Indianapolis

Music: Copland, Rodeo – Corral Nocturne

On Friday, after the second rehearsal, Micaela, Hugh, Eric, Martha, and Luca were gathered near stage front talking shop. The mood was decidedly upbeat, and there was much logrolling concerning everyone's contribution to the concerto.

"Luca, you may not know this, but it was actually Martha's idea to do the *Double*," said Micaela. Martha smiled at the recognition.

"I didn't know. I thought it was my evil friend's idea," Luca said, gesturing at the podium. "Martha, that was inspired and brave. I thank you."

"Inspired maybe, brave hardly. I had my own reasons." The group slowly started to break into smaller conversations. Luca turned to Micaela and invited her to dinner.

Eric overheard and said, "That's a great idea. Let's go to the Krishna Banji. Hugh says it's the second-best place to eat in Indianapolis. Right, Hugh?" As much fun as Micaela had had playing with Luca the last two days, she was grateful for Eric's rescue.

"Absolutely," confirmed Hugh. "The Lamb Vindaloo is out of this world. But watch the fish curry; it is hot, hot, hot. I know the owner. I'll make you a reservation."

"Can't you come?" Eric asked.

"I wish I could," Hugh said. "But I have to be at the maestro's house tonight."

"As usual, it's not what ya blow, but *who* ya blow," Martha said, true to form. Only Eric was disturbed by Martha's vulgarity. The rest laughed out loud.

After picking up Luca at Leon's house, Eric collected Martha, then Micaela, and drove to the Krishna Banji. The restaurant was located in a remodeled Victorian home. The owner was an Englishman who served as manager, host, and also waiter. His Indian wife did the cooking, and their children filled in for bussing, serving, and cleaning.

Along the jawline, the owner had a closely cropped beard that neatly separated his neck and cheeks, which appeared sore from shaving several times a day. His facial muscles were permanently frozen in a smile that made one wonder how he could actually speak. Nevertheless, he spoke with cut-crystal diction. Likewise, it was never misunderstood whether the smile denoted sincere friendliness or officious formality. He was not fond of surprises. This characteristic did not serve him well in the food service business.

The owner was in the foyer, waiting. On the banister above his head hung a tapestry that said in large needlepoint letters, *A day without lentils is like a day without sunshine.*

He stood behind a lectern that held the reservation book. There was only one reservation. It was for Morgan, party of five. He had written down "Lamb Vindaloo" next to the name, at Hugh's suggestion. It would be good to see Hugh, he thought.

The foursome walked into the foyer. He greeted them with sincere friendliness.

"Welcome. Do you have a reservation?"

Eric stepped forward and said, "Yes, Morgan. Party of four."

"I have a Morgan party of five." In an instant, his warm welcome had transitioned to officious formality.

"Mr. Morgan will not be joining us. He had a previous engagement," Eric said.

"I see." The owner paused as if there were nothing else to say. Then, he broke his comatose silence. "I am sure we can accommodate the change. You will please wait here while I have the table reset."

After he left, Martha said in her best British accent, "Bit of an odd duck, I'd say."

"Yes … quite," Eric joined in, "but so civilized." Everyone nodded in amusement as they listened to the owner bark orders in Hindi to his children in the next room. The owner returned.

"We are ready for you now," he said, with sincere friendliness creeping back into his voice. He escorted them into the dining area. There was no one else in the room except for the two children, who stood at attention near the kitchen door. The boy, who was eleven years old, held a pitcher of water. The girl, fourteen, held a plate of pappadam and a small bowl containing a mix of chutney and mint curry. They had the crisp jawline and sharp nose of their father, but the skin tone and soft eyes of their mother.

Once the diners were seated, the owner passed out the menus.

"The special this evening is Lamb Vindaloo. Would you care for an aperitif?"

"What do you recommend?" asked the concertmaster.

"Our food is somewhat spicy, so I generally recommend cocktails that prepare the stomach as well as the palate. G and Ts, ginger beer, Pimm's cup all would do nicely."

"What is G and T?" asked Micaela.

"Gin and Tonic," the owner answered.

"G and T for me," Eric said.

"Same here," Luca said.

"I will have the ginger beer," Micaela said.

"Schlitz," Martha said.

"I am sorry, we don't carry that brand. Would you care for a Heineken?"

"Do you have any American beer?" Martha asked.

"No, we do not."

"Then bring me a Heini." Martha did not look at the Englishman when she ordered. The owner left to get the drinks, and the children marched to the table to pour water and present the Indian flat bread. As the little girl started to leave, Micaela touched her arm to delay her.

"What do you call this?" she asked, sweetly. The little girl returned the smile.

"Pappadam, ma'am." The little girl's accent was as English as her father's.

"Do I dip it in the sauce?"

"Yes, ma'am. Break off a piece. The sauce is sweet and spicy."

"Thank you."

"You're welcome," said the little girl, as Micaela followed her instructions and tested the appetizer. Her enjoyment was obvious, and the rest of the table joined in quickly, still trying to decipher the menus. Soon the owner returned with the drinks. He brought a chilled glass for Martha's beer, but before he could pour, she was drinking from the bottle. The owner put his tray down and returned with pen and notepad to take dinner orders. Luca spoke first.

"What fish do you use in the Fish Curry?" he asked.

"It is a local bass. You should know that most of our dishes are toned down for the American palate. However, the Fish Curry is authentically seasoned."

"I assume that means it is pretty hot?"

"That's exactly what it means."

"Good. I'll have that."

"Very well," said the owner. "And you, ma'am," he said to Micaela.

"I would like Beef Korma, please." The owner nodded his head as he took her order.

"And?" turning to Martha

"Chicken Vindaloo," she said.

"*Chicken* Vindaloo?" the owner asked.

"Yep, I can't stand lamb."

"And you, sir?"

"Vegetable Curry," said Eric. The owner went into pause mode again. Returning from his special place, he reviewed the order.

One Fish Curry, one Beef Korma, one Vegetable Curry, one Chicken Vindaloo and no Lamb Vindaloo. Is that correct?" The table agreed. "Your lentil soup will be out momentarily." He turned on one foot and walked to the kitchen. The children returned, each carrying two bowls of the lentil soup. As they passed though the doorway, the owner could be heard, sharply issuing the orders to his wife. Luca asked the children if they could bring more pappadam. The little girl nodded and then hesitated.

"What is it?" asked Micaela.

"Ma'am, we also have Naan. My mum makes the best Naan. It will also help quiet down the spice."

"I have had it before. It is also a flatbread. Not so thin as the pappadam, comes in flavors like cheese, garlic, onion, correct?" Luca asked. The girl nodded. "By all means, then, bring us some, all flavors," Luca said. Micaela added a thank you. The lentil soup was earthy but surprisingly mild. Eric and Micaela described it as elegant peasant food. Luca and Martha thought it was boring.

"But so civilized," added Martha, sarcastically. Luca drained his G and T.

"Civilization is myth," he said.

"What do you mean?" Eric asked.

"I mean we masticate, fornicate, urinate, and defecate and then get together in tribes to fight over meaningless issues."

"Get that man another drink," Martha laughed. "By the way, you forgot procreate." Martha finished her beer and waved at the owner, who was fiddling with his reservation book. Even though it appeared he was not looking at them, he responded to the signal and came over to the table,

"Yes?"

"I need another beer, and he," pointing at Luca, "needs another drink," ordered Martha. "Anyone else?" Micaela and Eric said yes.

"Another round, then," said the owner, and he turned to the small bar on the opposite side of the room.

"Meaningless issues?" asked Micaela, returning to the conversation.

"Yes, like the color of someone's skin, what part of the country they come from, or various political systems, none of which work very well, anyway."

"So it was meaningless to fight Nazis. And now it is meaningless to fight the communists?" Micaela asked.

174

"Necessary, yes, meaningful, no. We have to fight to survive, but it is sheer hubris to assume that there is a greater good involved. It is our good versus their good."

"So you don't believe in evil?" asked Eric.

"*I* believe in evil. But that's just my abstraction of someone else's point of view."

"Hitler was not an abstraction," Martha said.

"No, but fascism is an abstraction. So is communism, nationalism, and patriotism. All of the isms are just the *names* we give our tribes, so we know who we are fighting and who is on our side. Ideas don't kill us, tribes and tribal leaders do ... like Hitler," Luca said.

"What about religion?" asked Eric.

"Nationalism of the spirit. A method of tribalizing the tenets of civilization that are proposed by spiritual leaders," Luca answered.

"Spiritual leaders?" Martha turned cockeyed to Luca. "Like Jesus?"

"Sure, and Moses, Mohammed, Buddha, Martin Luther, as well as the Rev. Martin Luther King, even the Hindu God Krishna." Luca was delighted with the timeliness of his last example, since the owner had just returned with the drinks. He looked at the owner.

"Wouldn't you agree?"

"It is not my place to agree or disagree, sir," said the owner, as he served Luca last. "However, if you are talking about the name of the restaurant, it is named after my father-in-law, who, if there is a God, will never be reincarnated." The table chuckled at the comment and the disappointed look on Luca's face. The owner returned to the reservation book in the foyer.

"Okay, Mr. Smarty Pants," Martha said to Luca, soliciting a duet of guffaws from Eric and Micaela. "What about salvation, hope, faith?"

"Merely marketing artifacts of the tribes. Join us, and we will save you from the inevitable. Join us, and your hope will be restored. Once joined, only the wayward lose their faith. It is their fault, not the fault of the tribe."

"So you have no hope?" asked Micaela.

"Hope is the frail wish for success. And I have faith that tomorrow will be very successful. My faith and hope for tomorrow are based on the experience of the last two days, not a tribal belief."

"Bullshit," said Martha. The children arrived with the main course. The table went silent, embarrassed by Martha's language in front of the children. The boy and the girl quietly served the main dishes, a large plate of rice, and a small saucer containing an oily red paste. Micaela smiled at the little girl.

"What is that?" Micaela asked.

"It is hot chili oil. We call it the Red Death. Use only a very small amount," she answered.

When the children left, Martha continued badgering Luca. "You belong to a tribe of musicians. Musicians are only autistics who can carry on a conversation. It is your faith in them that allows you to succeed. The music is your salvation." Luca stared at Martha as he unwittingly spooned Red Death onto his fish curry. He began to eat as Martha continued, "But I do agree with you. Civilization is a myth ... in the sense that it is poetic truth more significant than fact."

Luca started to speak, but stopped, eyes bulging, and took out his handkerchief.

"I don't understand. Certainly, you would consider Brahms to be civilized," said Micaela, as Martha sampled her Chicken Vindaloo. Luca was gobbling up Naan.

"Brahms the music, or Brahms the man?" Martha said with her mouth partially full. "Gawd, this is good," she spoke to her plate. Eric and Micaela nodded.

Micaela finished her bite before asking, "Are you saying there is not one civilized being?"

Martha hesitated to answer and then said, "I know of one." Everyone waited for the name. "Jesus Christ."

"Ahhhh," smiled Eric, smacking his lips and wiping away the excess vegetable curry. "Which tribe of Christianity do you belong to?"

"Lutheran ... the best one," Martha smiled as she took another swig of beer.

"Do you think He could save Luca from the Red Death?" Eric asked. They all looked at the puddle formerly known as Gianluca Giarrizzo. His handkerchief was soaked. Perspiration streaked down his face, and tears streamed from his eyes. The Naan was gone, but there was plenty of fish curry left. He opened his mouth several times to speak, but no noise came out. His culinary distress was comical and scary. The owner came over with cloth napkins, ginger beer, and more Naan.

"Drink this," he commanded, patting the sweating soloist with napkins. Luca obeyed numbly, while the rest of the table alternately expressed concern and amusement. Slowly, between bites of bread and sips of ginger beer, Luca regained the ability to speak.

"You should know I just prayed for the first time in my life." Everyone laughed.

"To whom?" Eric asked.

"Anyone who would listen," Luca answered.

— 28 —

SEPTEMBER 20 FRIDAY

Stoner BeBop – Alison's Studio

Music: Porter, I Get a Kick Out of You

The Friday night before the Saturday night opening, Alison, Maria, and Hugh were holed up in Alison's remodeled studio. Maria brought the joints, Hugh brought the champagne, and the three of them were getting pleasantly toasted. It was Maria's idea. She and Jason had arrived yesterday and Luca the day before that. Maria marveled at how well Alison was handling the week, full of pre-opening details, moody musicians, and her own opening, which was the unveiling of the limestone busts. Nevertheless, Maria thought that the maestro's wife could use a good unwinding, and Alison obliged easily. She agreed the week had been long and knew tomorrow would be longer. Jason and Leon had gone to Shabbat services, and Luca was out with Eric and Micaela.

Alison used to look forward to opening night. But the excitement had worn off, leaving only the infinite lists and details that must be monitored and tended. In addition, she had to be hostess to the houseguests, Jason and Maria, as well as Gianluca. She had to tend to the maestro who, despite his experience and skill, became increasingly edgy until he walked out on the stage for the performance. When she married Leon, no one told her that he would need so much maintenance and that it was her job to provide it. Alison was effectively his "dresser" and secretary for the performance. He had twenty-one articles of clothing in two cases, scores, notes, and a list of people to talk to just before the performance.

She was uniquely skilled for the job. As a queen of the Proteus Ball in New Orleans, she had organized proms and pep rallies, regales and regattas. Her own coming-out party was an event at least as complicated as what she was dealing with now. Alison and her fellow debutantes had to manage hairdressers, makeup, manicures, endless articles of clothing properly pressed and protected, transportation, and beaus.

When she went away to college in Colorado, Alison found some *new* friends. This group of wannabe ski bums was infused with dangerous doses of Kierkegaard and Kerouac. Her previous education in the social graces seemed embarrassingly pointless. She became fascinated with *Ars Gratia Artis* as well as several artistes. After frequent bouts of endurance drinking, it became clear to her that an artist — a sculptor, in fact — had been lurking inside her and was ready for its own coming out. Her past was simply that, over and done with. Her old friends and, to a large part, her family belonged to another person, someone she remembered with amusement. Then she met Leon.

Falling in love with a world-class artist was as easy as diving into a cool pool on a hot day in the Garden District of New Orleans. Marrying, living with, and dealing with the mood swings of such a celebrity was not nearly as romantic. But it was exciting, and she was certainly prepared for it. Alison slipped into the role seamlessly, bringing all of her previous training to bear, and started to live on top of the social heap in "India no place." Aside from the color of her beau's skin, she was the envy of all her friends from the Big Easy. Surprisingly to her, she was still respected by her newer friends from Colorado, who were impressed by the artistic circles in which she was traveling. The problem was, her goal was no longer to be a socialite, artistic or otherwise. She did not want to be the woman behind the man. She wanted to be the artist.

Alison looked around her studio through these hazy reflections and evaluated the work that had been done during the summer. The studio had turned out very well. Given the large array of windows, one could imagine they were in a loft in New York, a luxurious loft, but a loft nonetheless.

Her friend, Maria, had turned out even better. Even though their backgrounds were different, their situations were comically identical. Both of these sacrilegious souls had married practicing Jews, and right now they were taking full advantage of the situation. Up in the studio, they were watching Alison's brand-new *color* TV and, with considerable help from Hugh, making fun of *Sodom and Gomorrah*. The movie was tedious, overacted, and perfect for their inebriated sarcasm. In addition, all three of them found Stewart Granger, who played Lot, very attractive.

"I have never read the original, but was Lot really such a ... ?" Maria paused, searching for the word.

"Dim bulb?" Hugh said.

"Yeah!" said Maria.

"What do you mean?" Alison giggled.

179

"Look. He has misinterpreted every sign from God. The poor guy blows it over and over. Why would anyone ever listen to this jerk?"

"Because he is quite pleasing to look at," said Hugh.

"And because he is the nephew of Abraham," said Alison.

"And Abraham is?" asked Maria.

"The father of the Jews." Alison smiled.

"No shit." Maria was genuinely surprised.

"No shit. Actually, Lot is not that important. He was more of a messenger than a main character. What you are seeing here is entertainment, not scripture," explained Alison.

"And marvelous acting," Hugh said. The girls laughed at his affection for the star.

Maria took a big hit from the joint and said, holding her breath, "How come you know so much about this? You don't look Jewish, dahlink." Then she forcefully exhaled the marijuana.

"Same book, different religions. I grew up going to Sunday school and married a Jew. I wonder if I can get retroactive credits in my comparative religion class." It was Maria's turn to laugh, while Alison inhaled.

"Honey, if they allowed that, we would all get PhDs," said Hugh, causing Alison to lose her smoke in a coughing fit.

"Look, Lot's about to get another sign," said Maria, pointing to the TV.

"Yep, the Big Guy is making a personal appearance," Alison said. "Guess He doesn't want anymore screwups."

"Here it comes: 'I'm pissed, better get out of Dodge, and don't you dare look back or …'."

"Human salt lick," said Alison, finishing Hugh's commentary. They watched as Lot's wife inevitably looked back and was turned into a pillar of salt. Stewart Granger did his best to show his horror at the event.

"Don't worry, Stewey baby, you can do better. She was kind of bitchy, anyway." Maria said. Alison turned the TV off.

"What I can't stand about these Hollywood religious movies is that they are so safe," Hugh said, guzzling some bubbly. Alison and Maria looked at each other, bleary-eyed and then at Hugh.

"What I mean is, they tell the safe stories. No one wants to risk Cain and Abel, Abraham and Isaac, or the story of Joseph and Mary. Now, that was a great story," Hugh said with conviction.

"What's the big deal about Joseph?" Alison asked. "He couldn't even find Mary a decent place to have a baby."

"I am seriously out of my depth here," Maria said.

"Figures that a Sunday school for girls would skip that poor man's angst. First, he proposes and then, not long after that, finds out his fiancé is pregnant," Hugh said.

"Yeah, and like any man, he decides to dump her," Alison said.

"But nicely, quietly, honorably, so she won't get stoned," Hugh said.

"Stoned?" came the muffled question from Maria as she held in another toke.

"Different kind of stoned, honey," Hugh said. "Here, gimme that." He grabbed the reefer and began a series of inhales as if he was blowing up a balloon from the inside, while Alison continued the argument.

"Yeah, well, if he was so honorable, how come he didn't stand by the woman he loved?"

"He was cuckolded!" came Hugh's raspy answer.

"Cuckolded by God, for Chrissakes," said Alison.

"Exactly," said Maria. Hugh and Alison turned and looked at Maria who stared back, proud of her insight, and the giggling started.

When the giggling had ramped into laughter and then faded back down again, Maria said, "Alison is a Crescent City Christian and I am a New York nothing. What are you Hugh?"

"Ex-papist Mick."

"Altar boy?" asked Maria.

"You betcha, and choir boy, too. Any excuse to wear those lovely white dresses. I also had a crush on Fadda Nolan."

"Didn't he have a crush on you, too?" asked Alison.

"Sadly, yes. Perhaps that was one of the reasons I left, or at least my parents made me leave."

Hugh started to hum. Maria and Alison leaned closer to him to try to hear what he was humming. When they got really close, he broke into song, tapping his foot and moving his shoulders to a rock beat.

(sung to the tune of Be bop a Lula)
Be bop a Jesus
He's my savior
He's the cat with the clean-cut behavior
Be bop a Jesus
He's my savior
He's the cat with the clean-cut behavior

> *He's the joker from Mary's womb*
> *The resurrected roger with the flip-top tomb*

Maria was on the floor laughing, while Alison was trying to clean up champagne she'd spit when she heard 'resurrected roger'.

> *He's the one who's got that beat*
> *He's the one with the nails in his feet*
> *They say his mama was a virgin, but I don't know*
> *He had a real hip daddy, and his name was Joe*

"All together now," Hugh said, now standing and directing.

> *Be bop a Jesus*
> *He's my savior*
> *He's the cat with the clean-cut behavior*
> *He's the joker from Mary's womb*
> *The resurrected roger with the flip-top tomb*

Continuing to sing, Hugh pulled Alison and Maria to their feet.

> *He's the one who's got that beat*
> *He's the one with nails in his feet*

Alison placed her hand on the back of his right shoulder, and Maria did the same for Alison. Moving to the beat of the song, Hugh bellowed.

> *They said he done miracles and walked on the sea*
> *That's our swingin' Daddy from Gallileeeeee*

Hugh led them out of the studio, down the stairs, and to the kitchen.

> *Be bop a Jesus*
> *He's my savior*
> *He's the cat with the clean-cut behavior*
> *He's the joker from Mary's womb*
> *The resurrected roger with the flip-top toooooomb.*

"I'm hungry," said Hugh. Maria and Alison laughed at his predictability but were also victims of THC-induced appetite.

"Hugh, you may only eat what I tell you. We have a reception tomorrow, and I don't want them starving," said Alison. She opened the fridge and took out Skippy smooth peanut butter, celery, kosher salami, cheddar cheese, and milk. While Maria got the glasses, Hugh took a large spoon and filled it with peanut butter, creating a ball about the size of a large ice cream scoop.

"That's too much!" Alison yelled as Hugh open his mouth wide and inserted the spoon. Maria and Alison stood transfixed as he slid the spoon out trying to smile. Hugh tried to chew the enormous ball in his mouth. The difficulty was obvious. His eyes started to widen in incremental panic.

"Don't chew, Hugh. Take it real slow," Maria said, grabbing his wrist to get his attention. "That's right, breathe through your nose, short breaths at first." Hugh started to respond to her directions. "Take your time, it will dissolve, keeping breathing through your nose." Maria was stroking his arm now, and Hugh started to nod his head. He began to calm down, and the mouthful diminished.

"Don't smile, and don't laugh," teased a relieved Alison. Of course, Hugh started a muffled giggle.

"Yeah, that's right. After all, you don't want tomorrow's newspaper headline to be *Conductor's Wife Kills Principal with Peanut Butter*," Maria said. This sent Hugh over the top. He was able to laugh hard with the remaining wad blocking the noise. His eyes cried through the silent convulsions.

"*No More Blow Jobs for Oboe, film at 11*," added Alison.

"*Woodwind Chokes on Conductor's Nuts,*" one more from Maria.

Eventually, Hugh was able to open his mouth, and Alison gave him a glass of milk, which he guzzled down.

"That was fantastic," he said, with stoned delight. Maria and Alison looked incredulous. "No, really, it was amazing. You should try it. Once you get over the panic, you become one with the peanut butter."

"I knew we would get to a stoney baloney, 'everything fits' speech," said Maria.

"I am putting this away before someone gets hurt," said Alison. She picked up the peanut butter jar. In the fridge, she found a whole chicken. "Here we go." She placed the bird on the kitchen table. "Mary's roast chicken. Try not to hurt yourselves." The chicken had been browned and seasoned with rosemary, mixed peppers, thyme, and lemon rind. Maria and Hugh started to rip at the bird like they hadn't eaten in days and turned up their heads in rapture as they gnawed away. Alison joined them in this wanton consumption. The first bite was delicious, as the seasoning invaded her nostrils. The second bite was less so. On her third bite, she stared at the chicken. The meat seemed to be muscular and sinewy. The meat looked too much like meat. The bones looked too much like bones. The trio seemed to slow down simultaneously, as if they shared some dope-inspired, cannibalistic hallucination. They became disgusted with their own savagery and the carcass on the table.

"I need to go home," Hugh said.

"I need to go to bed," Maria said. Alison started to clean up, and Maria got up to help her.

"Go home, Hugh, we'll take care of it," said Alison. Hugh nodded numbly and saw himself out. Alison and Maria were asleep in their beds before anyone else returned.

— 29 —

"Cubs Beat Milwaukee 1-0 but are 17 Games Out"

"Cold War Pause" – subhead of NY Times referring to JFK speech

Excerpt from JFK speech to UN September 20, 1963:

> *I would say to the leaders of the Soviet Union, and to their people, that if either of our countries is to be fully secure, we need a much better weapon than the H-bomb — a weapon better than ballistic missiles or nuclear submarines — and that better weapon is peaceful cooperation.*
>
> *We have, in recent years, agreed on a limited test ban treaty, on an emergency communications link between our capitals, on a statement of principles for disarmament, on an increase in cultural exchange, on cooperation in outer space, on the peaceful exploration of the Antarctic, and on tempering last year's crisis over Cuba.*
>
> *I believe, therefore, that the Soviet Union and the United States, together with their allies, can achieve further agreements — agreements which spring from our mutual interest in avoiding mutual destruction.*

SEPTEMBER 21 SATURDAY

Opening Night Day – Zellingari Home

Music: Mozart, Le Nozze di Figaro, Overture

The next morning Alison was up early. This was not unusual for Alison, particularly on such a big day. Mary would be coming in soon, grumbling about working on a Saturday, but she'd make a great breakfast for the houseguests. Opening night weekend was difficult for everyone. Alison had just finished brewing the coffee and was reviewing her lists for the day when Maria came down. This was early for Maria, and it showed. She poured herself a cup of French Market blend, sat down across the table from Alison, and started to read the morning *Star*. Both of them felt the proximity of last night.

"How'd you sleep?" asked Alison.

"Great, after I threw up. Super dreams," Maria answered. Alison giggled weakly.

Mary arrived. She expected to see Mrs. Zellingari but not Mrs. Foster so early. She looked at her watch to see if she was late.

"Good morning, Mary," said Alison, without looking up.

"Good morning Ma'am, Mrs. Foster." Mary shed her light coat, tan hat and put on her apron over her uniform. "Mrs. Foster, what can I make you for breakfast?"

"I would like some lightly toasted bread."

"That's all?"

"That's all."

"No butter?" Mary pressed.

"Uh uh," Maria grunted, shaking her head.

"Orange juice?"

"Yes please," Maria said. Mary opened the fridge and took out the juice. She also pulled open the wrapper on the chicken.

"Mrs. Zellingari?"

"Yes, Mary?"

"Who ate half a raw chicken last night?" Alison and Maria locked eyes in astonishment as the vision of last night's debauchery came back to them with full force. Eventually they laughed. Alison remembered that she had instructed Mary to brown a chicken to be cooked later tonight for the concert's reception. She looked over at Mary, who was still waiting for an answer and was clearly perplexed by the laughter.

"Well, Hugh was over…"

"That explains it," Mary said.

Maria shuffled through the paper until she found the society section.

"Have you read Corbin yet?" Maria asked Alison.

"Nope, go ahead."

Maria read aloud.

Symphony Beat – by Corbin Blomster

The calm conductor has everyone climbing the walls at the Zellingari house as opening night approaches. Between rehearsals Saturday morning and the evening performance, maestro requires absolute quiet. This will be difficult for Alison Zellingari, the conductor's wife, to accomplish with all the preparation she is responsible for. The phone rings constantly, as she makes

*sure the governor gets his tickets, that everyone will make it to the Woodstock
Dinner honoring the guests in the Zellingari box, that the women get their
orchids, that someone will meet the plane of the visiting critic from the* New
Yorker.

*And, while worrying about the weather and attendance, she must make
sure that all 26 items of the maestro's dress clothes are packed properly.
Everyone else in the house turns into a peacock, too, including the Zellingaris'
house guests, Mr. and Mrs. Jason Foster and opening night soloist Gianluca
Giarrizzo. They will need help with their travel-mussed finery. No doubt the
women will be dying shoes and doing their hair with trembling fingers.*

*On top of all that, Mrs. Zellingari must be nervous about her own
opening. During the intermission, her first work commissioned by the
Campbell Foundation will be unveiled. The work consists of two limestone
busts for permanent display in Campbell Hall. One is of benefactor Edith
Campbell and the other is of the Maestro. Word is that the latter is hauntingly
realistic.*

*Last Sunday, the Zellingaris took one last vacation before their intense
season of 140 concerts in 28 weeks. With a small group of friends, they visited
the quarries near Oolitic. The refreshing swim in this last gasp of summer was
accompanied by a picnic of caviar, cucumber soup, beans vinaigrette,
homemade bread, salami, Chianti, and cheese. It's been said before in
Naptown, and I'll say it again. If you are lucky enough to get one, never pass
up an invitation to eat with the Zellingaris.*

*Speaking of food, there is rumor that certain members of the orchestra let
off some steam at Indianapolis' only Indian restaurant, the Krishna Banji, last
night. Apparently, after a shaky start at Thursday's rehearsal, our new star,
cellist Micaela Miklos, and this week's spicy soloist Gianluca Giarrizzo have
become fast friends. Let's hope so, since Miss Miklos' American debut tonight
will showcase the cellist paired up with the famed violinist Giarrizzo for the*
Brahms Double ... *fireworks in September, how nice!*

"I hate reporters," said Alison. "I wish Corbin could see the 'calm
conductor' upchucking twenty minutes before show time."

"So he's a puker, eh?" Maria laughed.

"Like clockwork. How about Jason?"

"Every once in a while. You'd think they would get used to it," Maria
answered. "Well, at least he didn't get *our* story about last night."

"That'll be in tomorrow's column," Alison said.

"Whatever happened to Micaela's other 'fast friend'?" asked Maria.

"Jed?"

"Is that the guy from Oolitic?" Alison nodded to Maria.

"They broke up in August. Kind of a surprise. They were getting along *quite* well for a couple of months. I think she was instrumental in getting him promoted to principal. Rumor was that he was practically living over there and then, all of sudden, poof, they act as if they don't know each other."

"A summer fling," Maria said.

"Guess so."

"Well, summer's over. Are you ready to dye some shoes with trembling hands?" Maria kidded.

"That's highly unlikely." Alison laughed. Then, on second thought, she said, "If you need help with anything like that, Mary would be happy to oblige, wouldn't you, Mary?"

"Yes, ma'am. I'm here all day … and all night, I guess." Mary's agreement was anything but gracious.

"Thank you, Mary, but I think we're in pretty good shape," Maria said.

The rest of the day followed the track of the Corbin article, with only a few variations. When Luca showed up for breakfast, he didn't look well. He complained about a sore mouth. After a couple of bites of Mary's eggs benedict, he disappeared into the bathroom for a very long time. When he returned, Alison look at him with concern.

"Fish Curry?" she asked.

Luca nodded.

"You poor boy. Mary, Mr. Giarrizzo will have two pieces of lightly toasted Wonderbread, no butter, no jam, cereal with skim milk, no juice, no coffee, and a glass of Alka Seltzer."

"No coffee?" whined Luca.

"Nope."

Later, Leon and Luca came back from the morning rehearsal, happy and keyed up. For lunch, Luca was served a baloney and cheese sandwich, no mustard, no mayo. The maestro had a light antipasto of prosciutto and melon.

"But I wanted spinach gnocchi," Luca whined again.

"Maybe later tonight, if you behave yourself," scolded Alison. At two o'clock, a masseuse came over for the maestro. Afterwards, Leon took a nap. A massage was offered to Luca, who declined. He then had another long stay in the bathroom.

The rest of the day was routine. The maestro would get upset at the smallest detail. At the concert hall, Alison helped him get dressed. First were the shorts, dress socks with garters, jersey t-shirt, pants, and shoes. The first stage was followed by a visit to the vomitorium. Leon would not be gone long but he would be loud. Afterwards, she would clean his face. He would rinse with Listerine and begin stage two of the dressing. Like lug nuts for the spare tire, the shirt studs would get misplaced and then found again, adding to Leon's irritation. Then came the white tie. Alison tied the bow tie by hand, suffering the usual complaints of "hurry up" or "it's too tight." Once the tie was done, Leon put on the vest, gold watch with chain, and the tails. A long look in the mirror, a brush of the hair, and he was done.

"Five minutes, Maestro," came Allen's voice with the knock on the door.

"Come in, Allen," directed the conductor.

"Yes, sir," Allen said, poking his head in the dressing room.

"Timers ready?"

"Yes."

"Water ready?"

"Yes."

"Is Winthrop seated?" Alison asked.

"Yes, ma'am, just now."

"And the house?" Leon asked.

"Full, sir."

"I'll be up in a minute," Leon said, and Allen left. Leon turned to Alison and held both her hands, smiling broadly.

Before he could speak Alison said, "You're welcome, now break a leg." The maestro and Alison left together. The stage was one flight up from the dressing rooms. At the top of the stairs, they parted. Leon went to the doorway at the edge of the shell to wait for his cue, and Alison took her seat in the conductor's box. Inside the shell, the orchestra was warming up. It was a little quieter than usual because only the strings would be playing the opening piece.

Allen waved his hand to the principals, and the orchestra quieted down. Eric came on stage to the applause of the audience, and proceeded to tune the orchestra. Then Leon proceeded on stage to start the season.

— 30 —

SEPTEMBER 21 SATURDAY

From the Violas – Campbell Hall Stage

Music: Schubert, Symphony No. 8 B Minor, D. 759 Allegro Moderato

In 1905, Galatoire's Restaurant opened at 209 Bourbon Street in the French Quarter of New Orleans. For fifty-eight years the family-owned Galatoire's has been serving classic French Creole cuisine. Galatoire's does not take reservations. Patrons wait in line for hours for their Shrimp Clemenceau, Crabmeat Ravigote, Lamb Chops Bearnaise, and Sazarac cocktails. Everyone is treated equally, provided they have the money to pay for it.

Jed had never been to Galatoire's and probably never would go. He knew about it, though. He heard about it on the local radio station (WIBC), in its weekly pre-concert interview with his boss.

WIBC – Maestro Zellingari, next week you will open the '63- '64 season with the Indianapolis Symphony.

MAESTRO – Yes, we are all tremendously excited. (Leon's radio voice was higher-pitched than his normal basso, and exceedingly friendly.) *We have a great season ahead of us with great musicians, both old and new.*

WIBC – This will be Miss Miklos' American debut, correct?

MAESTRO – Yes, and she will be a busy young lady. We open with Tchaikovsky's Andante Cantabile *from his first string quartet and then she performs the Brahms* Double Concerto *with Gianluca Giarrizzo.*

WIBC – My goodness. That will be a long weekend for her. It must have been a long summer as well.

MAESTRO – Like most professionals, she is a hard worker. During the summer, she studied the concerto with our concertmaster, Eric Solomon.

WIBC – Isn't it a bit of a surprise that Giarrizzo agreed to do the Double?

MAESTRO – Nothing that Gianluca does is a surprise. (Leon paused for moment) *Or, to say that another way, everything Gianluca does is a delightful surprise.* (Leon let out his deep chuckle, which was echoed by the interviewer.)

WIBC – Maestro, can you describe what it's like to walk out on that stage for the very first concert of the season?

MAESTRO – (Leon paused.) It's hard to compare ... It's like going to Galatoire's.

WIBC – Excuse me?

MAESTRO – Galatoire's is one of the world's great restaurants. It's in New Orleans. You have to wait outside for a table. It can be dark and somewhat wild out there on Bourbon Street. It's not unlike waiting in the wings before a concert.

There is a set of very small French doors that open into an equally small vestibule. Once inside the vestibule, you are faced with another set of French doors that open occasionally, giving you glimpes of the brightly lit interior. Eventually, they let you in, and you are immediately startled by how bright it is. There is no soft décor or lighting to diminish the experience of the food. It is loud and happy. It sounds like applause. You are seated and then get to enjoy some really fine food.

WIBC – So the only difference is that you're standing?

MAESTRO – And I'm eating with the cooks. (Leon laughed.) *When Justin Galatoire founded the restaurant in 1905, he said, "Il est au sujet de la nourriture," which means, "It's about the food."*

WIBC – I see. Then for you it must be "Il est sujet de la musique."

MAESTRO – Exactly.

Actually, the stage lighting was brighter and the set sparser than the décor of Galatoire's. From his backstage experience in high school, Jed knew that stage lighting for an orchestra is visually simple, but technically complex. The musicians need to be able to see their music, each other, and the conductor. The audience wants to be able to see the musicians in bright light. The trick is to provide enough ambient and display light to meet these requirements without blinding the orchestra. At Campbell Hall, the orchestra shell was painted an ivory color to help accomplish this, and the louvered ceiling hid banks of fresnel stage cans for all the indirect lighting. At stage front, there was the traditional floor lighting. For plays, operas, and modern musicals, the footlights were so bright that the performers could not see the audience. For symphony concerts, they were only a hint bright.

Balancing the spots at the rear of the hall among the clouds was the trickiest part. There were no highlights or following spots, even for the soloists. Nevertheless, an array of spotlights was used gently to bring out the "face" of the orchestra, without distracting the performers. After these spots were set, they would remain unmanned and unchanged for the season. Most of the setting occurred during rehearsal. Final settings would be done opening night, live, to adjust for the black-and-white formal clothes of the musicians.

As Jed warmed up his instrument and gave some last-minute encouragement to his section, he saw the conductor's spot move and diminish slightly. He followed its line from the podium, above the audience, to the catwalk outside the control room. He smiled as he remembered meeting Micaela there, their second meeting. She'd been so glad to see him. He followed the light line back until he was looking at an imaginary seat thirty feet behind the podium. She'd called it the angel's seat.

Jed turned in his chair so he could watch Micaela warming up. Her focus was absolute. Undoubtedly, it was uncomfortable to have to split her thoughts between the *Cantabile* and the *Concerto*. He wanted to comfort her. The feeling was unexpected and unwelcome. After the night at the bar, he'd called to tell her that he had hired someone else to finish the painting. She agreed that it would be a good idea. Her response confirmed the break-up.

His shattered heart did not linger on. It died quickly … or so he thought. Maybe he had been sublimating the pain in all the extra work he'd been doing. Professionally, it had been quite a summer … the quintet, being hired to finish the Gershwin arrangement, the promotion to principal, oh yeah, and nailing the new cellist. The resentment *was* a welcome feeling. It was a lot better than pain, and a little better than no feelings at all. He found it curious that his success was occurring when he couldn't care less.

The hall lights were slowly dimmed. The rear of the hall, the catwalk, the control room, the golden clouds, the audience, all faded to darkness as Eric came on stage.

— 31 —

SEPTEMBER 30 MONDAY

Eagle Crest Reservoir

Music: Debussy, Prelude a l'apres-midi du'un faune'

It was nine in the morning on the last day of September, one concert and one week since opening night. The day after the Cubs' final game of the season, an 0-2 loss to the Milwaukee Braves. Leon was walking along the shore at Eagle Crest. It was his day off, or at least his morning off. It was a Monday, always a quiet day out at the reservoir, and he was alone. Indiana was in its full fall glory. For the first time since summer began, the thermometer would not rise past 69 degrees. It was currently much colder than that. The dew remained on the grass, and a mist hovered above the dead-still water. Leon rounded the point and returned to the nearly empty parking lot, but he wasn't ready to leave. He pulled an old Cubbies sweatshirt from the trunk of his car and found a bench that faced the water. Using the back of the sweatshirt, he wiped a spot dry, then settled onto the bench with his elbows on his knees and his chin in his hands. As the mist began to burn off, he watched the reflection of the fall leaves appear on the surface of the water. The mist evaporated in a gentle rhythm that gave movement to the still leaves, making them appear to move closer, then farther away.

Last weekend's concerts came and went without much notice. Opening night was already ancient history. Local reviews had been great, but they faded as quickly as the mist was lifting. The reception was fun but anti-climatic. And Winthrop simply disappeared at the end, without speaking to anyone. He still hadn't heard a word about the Kennedys coming. He wondered how he could be so tired, so early in the season. Lifting his head from his hands, he leaned back on the bench, slumping his shoulders. A small breeze rustled the dry leaves like a distant applause. Looking up, he saw the mist of someone's breath in the cool air. Leon smiled.

"Hi, Thomas," he said, without turning around.

"Hi, Leon," said Thomas Flynn, walking around the edge of the bench.

"You know, you are the sneakiest person I have ever met," Leon said.

"Thank you."

"Have a seat."

Flynn used the back of his suede jacket to make a dry spot for himself and his briefcase and said, "I am sorry I had to miss the concert. I understand it was a smashing success."

"I don't know about that. At least no one got hurt walking out," Leon said.

"Ah, come on, Leon, you're too modest. I read *all* the reviews. By the way, I also heard the radio interview ... a unique perspective. Have you ever been to Galatoire's for Sunday brunch?"

"Nope, but I have heard about it from Alison. Sounds spectacular," Leon answered.

"It is. Perhaps you should go with Winthrop sometime."

"Pardon me?"

"William Winthrop. You know, the music critic for the *New Yorker*."

"I know *who* he is. But I sure don't know why I would go to lunch with him."

"*Brunch,* Leon, brunch. They say if you spend less than three hours there on a Sunday, you're rushing it."

"Okay, why would I want to go to brunch with Winthrop?" Leon asked.

"Because he likes really good food."

"I suppose you know *him,* too."

"Never met the man. I just learned about his culinary predilections by reading his review of your concert."

"His *what*? What review?"

"The review that I have right here." Thomas opened his briefcase and handed Leon a stack of eight typewritten pages, double spaced. The title read,

Magician in the Midwest
by William Winthrop

"How did you …?" Leon gaped.

"I know his publisher." The Irishman winked. "It's due out in a couple of weeks with cover art of the Indianapolis Symphony. As you might expect, this makes our arrangements for Jack and Jackie attending more difficult but, at the same time, more desirable. Such is the double-edged sword of fame."

"I take it the review is positive," asked Leon.

Thomas laughed, "The review is unique. I will leave you to enjoy it. Remember, *Il est au sujet de la musique, mon ami.*" Flynn left quietly and unnoticed, while Leon read the review.

When Leon returned home, he phoned Allen.

"Allen, I want a closed-door rehearsal tomorrow. I want Edith and Alison in the audience. And find a way to get rid of BoBo."

"Is there something wrong, sir?" asked Allen.

"No, I just need to speak to all of them privately," Leon answered.

"I understand, sir," although he really didn't. "What should I do about Mr. Johannesen? Is he invited, too?"

Leon had forgotten that the pianist Grant Johannesen was coming early this week.

"Damn! No, he is not. We need to delay him until the second half of rehearsal. Maybe someone can have a late breakfast with him at his hotel."

"Maestro, I believe he is arriving at your house tonight … and will be staying there.

Leon groaned.

"Would you like me to take him to breakfast?" Allen offered.

"No, I need you in the hall."

"How about I ask Mr. Delmonico to come over to your place for breakfast, and Mary can keep them there as long as you want."

"Perfect. Have BoBo show up at nine. Alison and I will be gone by then."

— 32 —

On October 1, 1963, Hoover received and then approved a combined COMINFIL-COINTELPRO plan against the civil rights movement. The approved plan called for intensifying "coverage of Communist influence on the Negro." It recommended the "use of all possible investigative techniques" and stated an "urgent need for imaginative and aggressive tactics . . . to neutralize or disrupt the Party's activities in the Negro field."

Georgia Desegregates All Public Facilities

President Kennedy Welcomes Haile Selassie, Emperor of Ethopia

OCTOBER 1 TUESDAY

The Review – Campbell Hall Stage

Music: Dukas, L'Apprenti Sorcier

Leon mounted the podium and held up his hand for silence.

"Folks, I need to talk about last month's opening night concert for a moment. I want you to know that I felt it was one of the most remarkable events I have had the pleasure of being part of. Each of you did an outstanding job. As you know, there was a critic from the *New Yorker* magazine in

196

attendance. I have received an advance copy of his review and will read it to you now."

Magician of Midwest for the New Yorker
by William Winthrop

It will come as a surprise to none of my friends that I am a snob. I am a snob about music and food. But mostly I am a snob about New York. I consider New York to be *the* cultural center of the United States. I consider it to be one of the three or four cultural centers of the world. The standards of artistry here are second to none. All other efforts are either indirectly or directly compared to what we do in New York. Bearing that in mind, when I gave a favorable review to an out-of-town orchestra from the Midwest last year, in my mind, I attributed some of their success to the fact that they were in Carnegie Hall, and some of that New York magic had rubbed off on them. At the time, I rashly expressed a desire to see the same orchestra on their home turf, Indianapolis, Indiana. I really don't know why I did that. I hate the Midwest. The food is atrocious, and the music is worse. When I have to travel there, I live in constant fear of hearing "On the Banks of the Wabash," or "Stardust." What kind of name is Hoagy Carmichael, anyway?

Nevertheless, I went. Perhaps I felt I was overly flattering in my praise and wanted to correct it. Yes, I am sure that was part of my New York motivation, to take down these upstart Midwesterners a peg. Every reviewer needs to pan something from time to time to maintain his credibility and to satisfy other personal needs.

Or, perhaps it was the lingering, lyrical memory of the Schubert's Ninth that I'd heard at Carnegie a little less than a year ago. It's a symphony I have heard enough times from enough orchestras to be uninterested in any new performance. Yet, that night, something special happened under the hands of Maestro Zellingari. Something had made Schubert's "Great One" sound fresh and complete. Could he do it again? Or, more of a concern to my New York arrogance, *does he do it all the time?*

The Indianapolis Symphony Orchestra (ISO) plays at the one-year old Campbell Hall. This is a limestone and cement

behemoth designed to service two masters, large stage
productions and the symphony. Skeptically, and with snide
smile in place, I took my seat in the center of the
cavernous auditorium. *This will never work*, I thought to
myself as I looked around, up and down at a space far too
large for the delicacies of good music. This feeling was
exacerbated by noting that the antipasto for the evening
was the *Andante Cantabile* from Tchaikovsky's *String
Quartet No. 1*. String section only for this ballpark?
Zellingari must be crazy. I smelled blood in the water.
The satisfaction of a good panning was not far away.

The lights dimmed and the concertmaster, Eric Solomon,
came out to the friendly, full-house applause of a
hometown crowd. As he started to bow the concert A for his
fellow strings, I was saddened to hear the clarity of his
instrument. The hall began to grow smaller. When Solomon
was done, the maestro strode onstage and mounted the
podium to the same appreciative applause, followed by
quick and respectful silence. Immediately after the
downbeat, I got an auditory preview of the steep and
slippery slope to my impending demise. I was no longer in
a limestone auditorium. I had been transported in time and
place to a gilded and tiny hall in Vienna, suitable for
chamber orchestra only. Furthermore, Tchaikovsky came with
me, risen from his grave, mouth agape at the
interpretation of his rich and delicate work.

I wish I could complain about the tempo being faster
than I am used to. But the result was so glorious, other
interpretations now sound like dirges. The difference
between good music done well and done extremely well may
be subtle, but it is noticeable even to the uninitiated.
The precision and strength of these strings was
extraordinary. Their responsiveness to subtle changes in
dynamics was delightfully evident. Zellingari has
assembled some fine and disciplined musicians here. If the
string section can be considered the heart of any
orchestra, then the ISO has the strength of an Olympic
athlete. This performance was world-class, indeed,
otherworldly class. There is more to Zellingari than his
magical hands.

At the end of the opening, I took some deep breaths to
recover my hard-nosed composure, mentally thumbing through
my litany of orchestral flaws as they reset the stage for

the Brahms' Double Concerto. Finding none to apply, I ignored how they somehow fit a full orchestra into this impossibly small venue and focused on the foolishness of the second course.

Of course, it is not the Brahms that is foolish. In fact, the Brahms is a remarkable work that focuses on melody for violin, cello, and orchestra equally. For the concerto to be played properly, virtuosity must give way to sensitivity, an objective that seems far beyond the prodigious technical talents of the guest violinist, Gianluca Giarrizzo. Furthermore, for this difficult duet, he was not to be paired with another famous soloist, but with the untested first chair of the cellos, Miss Micaela Miklos. Frankly, I was surprised that Giarrizzo had agreed to this. It is not in his nature to share the limelight. Perhaps he was looking to share the blame. If I have anything to say about it, there would be plenty for everyone.

Zellingari has a specific reputation for keeping his orchestra under control during concertos. This is why many soloists look forward to playing with him on stage or in the recording studio. But the Brahms Double requires far more than control. The orchestra is the third soloist on this stage. The first movement would tell the story. Early on, there is a moderately challenging cello solo that is fiendishly difficult in the dynamics. Certainly, any first chair could muddle through it for this audience, but there would be flaws galore for me to gobble up and spew through the pages of the New Yorker.

There is a backstory concerning Miss Miklos. It is a story of a beauty and commensurate tragedy. I will leave it to others to tell this tale because, for me, nothing could be as sorrowful as the sublime excellence of her bowing. As I gleamed in anticipation of impending failure, Miklos took her bow and stabbed me with unbelievable romantic force. The throaty vibrations of the initial cadenza resonated like the lower quadrant of a Rubens painting, holding all the earthiness of the world. As she traveled along the solo, so did she move up the quadrants of the Rubens, from the earthy to the ethereal in smooth, unanticipated transitions.

This tragic, sonorous transportation was interrupted by the leering lyricism of Giarrizzo. Foregoing his comfort zone of the impossibly difficult Paganini Caprices (which he saved for the encore), Giarrizzo dedicated his every attention to the intertwining of his tiny Guanerius with the Baudiot vibrating between the clenched knees of Miss Miklos. He was gracious, he was sensitive, he was delicate, he was titillating. He showed a depth of performance that has been too long overlooked. Was that me or the over-baubled fat lady sitting next to me that gasped? I know I stared, I smiled, I ogled, I grinned like a shameless voyeur as Miklos and Giarrizzo linked their individual melodies into a single song.

There was nothing else in the world at this time - two people, two instruments, one voice. Nothing else in this world except the dark man on the podium hunched over his music stand. His stillness provided the illusion of invisibility. When he moved, I only dreaded what new musical level I would be levitated to. The orchestra arrived without interruption, not in background, but as the part of the whole one hadn't known was missing. The sorcerer on the podium was the leader of a ménage a trois; violin, cello, and orchestra. It was no longer the Brahms Double Concerto, it was the Triple, and I had to suffer through its pleasure for three movements.

At the end, I stood up with the rest of the stadium, numbly clapping my hands with the surrounding thunder. Hopefully, there was something stronger than champagne available at the intermezzo. But first, I had to endure Giarrizzo's smiling and deceptively easy playing of the Caprices. The reason this violinist has been pigeonholed into the "technical virtuoso" category is because he is so damned good at it. His expertise was no surprise. His stamina after the intense rendezvous with Miklos was intimidating, to say the least.

It would be a good time to leave this fiasco, and I considered it. I did not want to endure any more musical success in the Hoosier heartland. By the time I moved through the herd to the bar and quaffed two quick scotches, I was accosted by a local rube of the first order. He introduced himself in some official capacity; he must have been the janitor. Never have I met a man so dressed up who knew so little of what he was talking about. His ignorance and fumbling was refreshing. At last, some mediocrity in the state where it should reside. He got me another drink and took me to some unveiling ceremony, which I barely observed, with a waxed smile that only moved me to sip more scotch. I started to feel better and glanced at what was in store for the second half, all Copland. Zellingari was clearly pandering to me. I had him now. There was no way this magician could pull three rabbits out of his hat. I would crucify his interpretation, imprecise tempo, and general effrontery to America's greatest composer, a New Yorker, no less.

My idiotic escort pointed out the obvious lobby light flashes, which meant it was time to return. I excused myself to the bathroom to get away from him. He followed, which forced me into a stall, which finally sent him on his way. Sneaking out of the facilities, I peeked to make sure he wasn't lurking outside the door and rushed to my seat, stepping over everyone, since they were already seated. Finally, I was down and ready to pounce. The lights dimmed, and Zellingari came out. Again, as he arrived at the podium and raised his hands, the orchestra was instantly ready. And the final downbeat of my continual downfall ensued.

Fellow New Yorkers, I am shattered. Copland is not as hard as Stravinsky, but it is close. It certainly requires a similar level of precision, and perhaps a greater, subtler attention to the melody. After all, it's not supposed to be a hootenanny. But Copland can be that kind of caricature if it is overplayed. The music must be allowed to speak for itself and not trifled with - easy to say, enormously difficult to do. It requires talent, discipline, and leadership. Maestro Zellingari took another step beyond and conducted *Billy the Kidd* and *Rodeo* as if *he* weren't there. The orchestra sections behaved as barely tethered puppets. He gently pulled on their strings, only when necessary, allowing his talented ensemble the luxury … nay, the delight, for it showed on the musicians' faces … of listening and reacting to each other. There is a deep happiness to these pieces. They stir the American patriot in all of us, no matter how deeply hidden that tendency may be. Believe me, I know. At least I do now, and wish I never did. Tonight I have been broadsided by greatness.

After the concert, I slinked away unnoticed and caught the first plane back to La Guardia. Safe in the security of my brownstone, I am trying to resurrect my Manhattan pride. I need to go to the Waldorf Astoria, the Russian Teahouse, Katz's Deli, the Metropolitan. I need to avoid the light and glass of Lincoln Center until this malaise wears off, if it ever does. Located at the crossroads of the Midwest, the heart of basketball, flatlands and flatheads, motor heads and mush mouths, is some of the best music in the world. Unfortunately, I am not making this up. The center of this magic is an absolute wizard of a maestro named Leon Zellingari, who uses his hands, not a baton, to cast musical spells that have only rarely been heard in the Big Apple.

Now, I know that my New York brethren will attribute this story to some sort of temporal anomaly of poor perception to which I have fallen victim. Perhaps there is something in the Midwestern diet that automatically lessens one's standards. Actually, having had the displeasure of sampling the local cuisine, I suspected that as well. However, those suspicions (hopes) were dashed when I heard the musical scoop of the year.

In November, just after the publication of this article (assuming that the *New Yorker* allows it to be published), Vladimir Khazar begins his first American tour. He will not start this tour in New York, nor Philadelphia, nor Cleveland. Yes, that is right, … horror of horrors, this phenomenal pianist will debut with Zellingari in the new musical mecca of India No Place. I will, of course, not go. I wish to remain with the illusion, if it can be recovered, that the standard of musical excellence still resides in Lincoln Center. Plus, I can take solace in the fact that the food in the land of Hoosiers is still ghastly.

To understand the joy of the ISO at this moment, one would have to imagine hitting a two out, full count pitch in the bottom of the ninth inning at Wrigley and waiting over a week to find out that it reached Waveland Avenue. Amidst the cheering and mutual congratulations, Hugh stood up and shouted, "Maestro!" The shout quieted everyone.

"Yes, Hugh."

"I am absolutely mortified at this terrible review!" Hugh was doing his best to fake indignation. "I have never been more embarrassed for the great state of Indiana and its cuisine." The orchestra was giggling.

"What do you suggest I do, Hugh?" Leon played along.

"I want you to promise that the next time Mr. William Winthrop comes to Indianapolis, you will entertain him with one of Mary's soufflés."

"An excellent suggestion, I will see that it is done," agreed Leon.

"And…"

"And what, Hugh?"

Martha interrupted Hugh's response. "And afterwards, Hugh will take him to the Krishna Banji for Fish Curry." Hugh laughed and nodded. Then Hermann Wangler started singing and playing "Kill the Critic" to Wagner's *Die Walküre*. Some joined in, the rest laughed. No one was able to get it back together, even when Johannesen arrived. Everyone knew there was going to be a Bad Friday rehearsal this week, and no one cared.

1036th Day of the 35th President

Friday Rehearsal 1pm

This rehearsal was the second Bad Friday rehearsal they'd had, and the season had just begun. The first was during the week that Johannesen was there. It was Leon's own fault for breaking the news of the review the way that he did. This week's symphonic errors were probably due to a general state of anxiety among the orchestra members about the Khazar performance coming up next week. Coincidentally, that would cause another Friday rehearsal because they would have Thursday off for Thanksgiving. Whatever the reason, they surely needed more rehearsal for this weekend's concert.

Normally, Leon would arrive on a Friday in a surly mood in order to convey the seriousness of the situation. But today that was impossible. By plan and permission of Thomas Flynn, the news that the first family was coming to next week's concert had been leaked to Corbin Blomster the day before and was the headline in the *Star* this morning.

"JACK & JACKIE TO ATTEND SOVIET DEBUT"

Leon had been taking calls all morning from friends, well-wishers, press, critics, and his own orchestra members, who thought it must be April 1st. He had also received congratulatory telegrams from George Szell, Eugene Ormandy, and Leonard Bernstein of the Cleveland, Philadelphia, and New York Philharmonics. He also received a few threats. Any concerns he had about the threats were easily submerged in the tidal wave of good will coming his way.

Walking on stage, he saw the smiles and excitement of his orchestra, and his painted-on frown melted away. Some members of the orchestra were hearing the news for the first time at rehearsal would not believe it. Before Leon could begin, he was asked if it was true.

"Yes, it is. We have a lot to be thankful for next week. And no, I don't know what Jackie will be wearing," he said, with wide smile.

"How long have you known about this?" asked Martha.

"Why, Martha, I get my newspaper the same time you do." The maestro winked.

"Okay, folks, let's get started so we can get out of here. I want to start with the 3rd movement. Hopefully, some of you have had time to practice it since our last meeting," scolded Leon. He sat down on his stool, raised his hands, and the orchestra scrambled to get ready. It didn't take long before he had to stop.

"You guys are like the Mets infield," he shouted. "Once again, from the beginning." Subsequent attempts showed incremental improvement. He made some adjustments to the dynamics and then started over one more time. Halfway through, he was smiling to show his approval when Allen walked on stage and stood next to the podium. Allen's presence there was as surprising as it was impossible to ignore, and Leon stopped the music.

"Allen, there must be an incredibly important reason for this interruption." The Maestro was not happy.

"There is, sir," Allen said.

"What is it, then?" asked Leon impatiently. Then Allen did something even more unusual, he stepped onto the podium and whispered into the conductor's ear. When he was done whispering, Allen held Leon's arm tightly. Leon's expression was as frozen as his limestone likeness in the lobby. Allen held Leon's arm until Leon could move. Turning to Allen he said, "I'm okay," and stood up from the stool to speak to the orchestra.

"Ladies and gentlemen, about an hour ago, President Kennedy was assassinated in Dallas." The orchestra responded with disbelief, pain, and a litany of questions asked simultaneously. The conductor held up his hands. "Friends, I have no answers for you. Please go home to your families and the television. This week's concert is canceled. God bless you, and God bless America."

— 34 —

NOVEMBER 25 MONDAY

Black-and-White TV – Jed's Home

Music: Stravinsky, The Firebird – Lullaby, Awakening of Kaschei, Death of Kaschei, Deep Darkness

Like most Americans, Jed was sitting on the sofa watching the TV. The rich Indiana fall colors had given way to the starkness of approaching winter. That starkness had been consummated over the weekend by the black-and-white world of Walter Cronkite, Chet Huntley, and David Brinkley. Only in death are all abstractions removed. They are replaced by the sheltering details of processing a body to its resting place, right down to the boots facing backwards on a riderless horse. National grieving had been punctuated by the uniquely American event of Jack Ruby assassinating Lee Harvey Oswald on live TV, just two days after Oswald had assassinated President Kennedy. The television had become the reality, and the former reality, with all of its color and hope, had taken an indefinite vacation.

Jed wasn't grieving. He was hungry. The national tragedy had closed up most everything in town, including Frisch's Big Boy. The only thing still open was White Castle and Hoosier Buddy Liquors. His diet for the entire weekend had consisted of Sliders and Schlitz and it was getting old. Thanksgiving was just two days away, but he had no place to go and no one to have Thanksgiving with.

Jed wasn't moved by the death of the president, but he was fascinated. He had limply voted for Nixon, but he was glad Kennedy had won. Kennedy was much more interesting. His whole family was interesting. Jed even enjoyed their Boston accents, especially when the comedian Vaughn Meader made fun of them. In August, the nation had held a TV vigil with Kennedy for his newborn son, who died two days after his premature birth. The assassination was just another fascinating chapter in the Kennedy soap opera, broadcasted at irregular intervals to your very own home.

Even though Jed was still wearing the same T-shirt and jeans that he had on most of the weekend, he was one of the few people expecting visitors today. Lou Flesher and Mrs. Stalcup showed up sharply at eleven. Jed opened the door, holding a can of beer, and waved them in. It was cold and damp outside, so Jed shut the door quickly. Stalcup wore a hat, frumpy gray coat, and the ever-present horn rims on a chain. Jed handed over some sheets of paper, hoping they were not staying.

"Here is the itinerary and the rest of the information I could get. Since Friday, I have not been able to find out anything," Jed said.

Betty Stalcup took the papers and looked them over as she unbuttoned her coat.

"Very nice, Jed. Thank you. This looks useful. Although a little thin." As Stalcup handed her coat and hat to Jed, she added, "Do you mind turning the TV off? I didn't vote for the bastard."

Lou laughed. "Good morning, Jed. Starting a little early, aren't we?" he said, pointing at the beer. Jed shrugged his shoulders, turned off the TV, and threw Stalcup's overcoat on a chair. Stalcup made herself at home and sat down on the couch. Lou stood behind her. "Have a seat, Jed," said Stalcup. "There is something we want to talk to you about." Jed sat down in the easy chair. Stalcup continued, "Jed, we are reconsidering the leaflets and ads. In light of the assassination, this may not be the best time for the John Birch Society to be politically visible. We think we should wait for things to settle down a bit."

"Sounds reasonable," Jed said.

"Yes, we thought you would agree. On the other hand, Lou has come up with an interesting idea." Jed turned his head slightly to Lou.

"Is the commie still coming to play?" asked Lou.

"I assume so. It is a big event for the entire music world," answered Jed.

"Well, considering our national loss, we think the timing stinks," said Lou.

"Yes, it is in very poor taste," agreed Stalcup. Jed's body language was noncommittal as he waited them out.

"So we think it should be stopped," Lou said.

Jed chuckled a little and asked, "How do you propose to do that?"

"We got the idea from you, actually. What would happen if there was no conductor?" Jed became stiff.

"What?"

"Relax, Jed, we aren't going to do anything to your boss. Just answer the question. What happens if the conductor can't perform, he gets sick or something?" asked Stalcup.

"Then the assistant conductor or the concertmaster would take over," Jed answered.

"You see, Betty, I was right, they have a back-up system just like the presidency." Lou was very pleased with himself.

"Okay, so they need a conductor for the performance. They can't just do it without one?" Lou asked. Jed nodded.

"Now, here is the $64,000 question. Can they do the performance without a conductor's score, like you showed us last time we were here?" Lou smiled and waited for the answer. Jed thought for several moments.

"It would be disruptive. They would have to replace it."

"What if it was missing at the last minute?" Lou pressed.

"I am not sure what would happen. But, yes, that would cause a big problem. Plus, it is valuable artifact. Are you planning to steal the score?" Jed asked in disbelief.

"No, we are planning for *you* to steal the score," said Stalcup. She then picked up the papers that Jed had given her, scanned the second page, and said, " … say, Saturday, after the rehearsal?"

"Forget it. Why would I do that?" Lou and Stalcup were silent and unsmiling.

Eventually, Stalcup answered, "There are lots of reasons you might want to do this. For example, you might want to do this for the good of the cause …"

"You're confusing me with someone who gives a shit," Jed said.

Stalcup ignored him and continued, "… or you might do it as a patriotic American. You might even do it to get back at an organization that, until very recently I understand, treated you like dirt. However, you will end up doing it simply because you want to keep your orchestra job and the nice new position that you have worked so hard to earn," Stalcup explained.

"You're crazy. This will get me fired," Jed said

"Only if you're caught. But if you don't do it, the fact that you're stealing information about the whereabouts of visiting soloists so they can be harassed will most certainly put you in hot water with your boss and possibly John Q Law." Stalcup held up the papers in her hand. Jed was pissed. "And since you DON'T GIVE A SHIT!" Stalcup paused to regain control of her temper "… why don't you just pick up the score after rehearsal, find some place to throw it away, and be DONE WITH IT!"

Stalcup's anger was scaring Jed. He stood up and paced. He thought about the mechanics of lifting the score. That wasn't a problem; it would be on top of a stack outside the shell after rehearsal, waiting to be returned to Leon's dressing room. Just walk by and pick it up. Besides, Allen will have a backup score and the show will go on. He really wanted Stalcup and Lou off his back.

"Okay," Jed said hesitantly.

"That's great! I knew you were up to it," smiled Lou. "Betty here didn't think you had the spine for it. But I told her about how you jumped first into that quarry with me and Gar."

"But …" Jed said.

"But what?" asked Stalcup.

"But this is the last thing. I am not doing anything else for you or the Society."

Stalcup looked at Jed firmly, smiled and said, "Don't worry, hon, we don't have any more interest in you either."

Stravinsky: The Firebird – Disappearance of the Palace and of Kaschei's Spells

After they left, Jed returned to the TV. His appetite had vanished. He sat on the couch for hours watching the funeral proceedings in Washington, D.C. Both his body and his spirit were sinking into a comforting numbness. When the phone rang, he slowly wallowed to other side of the sofa to pick it up on the fourth ring.

"Hello," he answered, as if speaking underwater.

"Jed?" Her voice yanked him to the surface.

"Hi, Micaela."

"I miss you," she said. Jed felt his chest tighten and his breathing become short.

"I miss you, too."

"Are you hungry?" she asked.

"Could eat a pig twice," he answered. Micaela laughed.

"Don't have any of that, but the maestro's maid brought over fried chicken and rhubarb pie. Would you like some?"

"You're kidding me."

"No, I'm not kidding, please come over."

"I thought you'd never ask. I'll be there in two shakes of a horse's tail," he said. About to hang up, he interrupted himself. "You know, I have to clean up. It'll be a little longer."

"I'll be here."

— 35 —

NOVEMBER 29 FRIDAY

Torah – Indianapolis Hebrew Congregation

Music: Dvorak, Rusalka — Mesícku na nebi hlubokém (O Silver Moon)

Leon was standing outside the temple carrying a black canvas bag, waiting for Vladimir to arrive, when a black car with tinted windows drove up. The car door opened, and out stepped Thomas Flynn.

"He's not coming, is he?" asked Leon.

"No. He couldn't get past security. I was able to meet with him in private. I suggested that he delay his defection until his trip to London. He had already made that decision. But he was very disappointed that he could not come here tonight. He sent you his blessings," said Flynn. Leon shrugged and nodded at the same time.

"Are you going in?" Flynn asked.

"Yes."

"May I join you?"

"Feel the need for some of that old timey Old Testament?"

"I need something. It's been a long couple of weeks," said the weary Irish Catholic. Leon put his hand on Flynn's back and escorted him into the synagogue. After entering the outer doors and before entering the temple itself, Leon stopped and opened his bag. Inside was his prayer shawl and skullcap.

He put them both on as he said, "The shawl is called a *tallit* and the cap is called a *kippa*. I also brought Vladimir's."

"So that's what was in the other package." Flynn said.

Leon nodded, just as the Rabbi walked up to them.

"Hi Maestro. I'm glad you could make it. Is this the friend you spoke about?" asked the Rabbi.

"No, I am afraid not. He was unable to come. Rabbi Davis, may I introduce Thomas Flynn. He will be joining us tonight."

"Pleased to meet you, Rabbi."

"My pleasure as well, Thomas. It is important to me that you feel welcome. Don't be bashful about asking Leon questions during services."

"Thank you, Rabbi."

Before the Rabbi could leave, Leon said, "Rabbi, my friend is very disappointed that he could not come. I wonder if you could bless these." The Rabbi looked at the *tallit* and *kippa*.

"These are quite beautiful," he said. "And quite old, it appears," he added with respect. "Tell you what. Why don't we trade for this evening? You hold onto these." the Rabbi took off his shawl and *kippa*. "And I will return your friend's to you after services." The Rabbi exchanged them without waiting for an answer and proceeded up the aisle to the *bima*.

"Was that unusual?" asked Flynn.

"I've never seen it before," Leon answered.

The conductor and Flynn took a seat in the back row near the aisle. During the opening prayers, Flynn followed the Rabbi's advice and asked a series of questions concerning the service. Leon was happy to answer what he could.

"The stage is called a *bima*. Behind the lectern is the Ark. Inside the Ark is the Torah, which you will see later, after the opening prayers." As Flynn asked more questions, Leon became pleasantly aware of the audio irony of Flynn's accent juxtaposed with the Dorian mode chants.

After the prayer over the Challah, Rabbi Davis walked from his chair on the *bima* to the lectern.

"*Shabbat Shalom*."

"*Shabbat Shalom*," answered the congregation. The Rabbi continued.

"Welcome, everyone, as we welcome Shabbat into the sanctuary of our temple. Shabbat is observed in three stages. First is the welcoming of Shabbat. Second, the reading of Torah, and tomorrow evening we conclude with the separation from Shabbat, the Havdalah. In the welcoming, we have observed three blessings: the blessing of light, which symbolizes the love which awakens the mind; the blessing of wine, which symbolizes the love that awakens the heart; and the bread, the love that awakens in the body. This week we get a fourth blessing, and that is an additional pre-Torah sermon from me." The congregation chuckled.

"It has been a mournful week in the history of the world. Tonight I would like to offer some words of comfort and advice to you and to myself, as we continue to deal with the loss of a great man who happened to be an Irish Catholic. Tragedies like the event of November 22 seem to be caused by the differences in mankind. Our differences in beliefs. Our differences in background. Our differences in race. Sometimes, simply the differences in where we live. Nevertheless, when we heal, and heal we will, we use our similarities as medicine. It is a magical cure. Indeed it is a spiritual panacea that ignores the boundaries of Judaism, Christianity, Islam, Hinduism, or Buddhism."

"In a minute, we will take the Torah from the Ark and walk up and down the aisle. We celebrate Torah and even touch Torah because we want to be more closely connected with Torah. And, in doing so, we become more closely connected with all of mankind. Torah means guide. Torah is a guide book to our beginnings. Its stories tell us where we came from and give us signposts for behavior. Torah tells us that Abraham was not only the father of the Jews but also of Islam, and that Adam and Eve were the parents of us all. When we read tonight's Torah portion, Vayishlach — also known as Genesis 32, Chapter 4 — I want you to remember that Jack Kennedy studied Torah, too ... the King James version."

After more blessings, the Ark was opened, and then the Torah was carried through the congregation, as members touched the fringes of their *tallits* to the Torah and then kissed the fringe. Members who did not have *tallits* used their prayer books. Members who could not reach to touch held on to members who could.

When the Torah returned to the *bima*, Reb Davis gave another blessing and touched the fringe of Vladimir's *tallits* to the Torah and then kissed the fringe.

— 36 —

NOVEMBER 30 SATURDAY

The Conductor's Score – Campbell Hall

Music: Brahms, Symphony No. 4 E Minor, Op. 98, Fourth Movement, Allegro Energico e passionate – Piu Allegro

The only similarity between a piano and violin is that they both use strings. The violin has four. The piano has eighty-eight. The piano is actually a member of the percussion family because its hammers strike the tone. It is obviously the most complex of that family. Nevertheless, it is not uncommon to see pieces originally composed for piano rearranged for strings. The *Goldberg Variations* by Bach, which were originally created as a keyboard "practice-piece" for his talented protégé Johann Goldberg, have been delightfully adapted to various ensembles that include violin, viola, and cello. This type of adaptation is not a simple transposition. The Gershwin *Preludes* for piano are, from a melodic point of view, simpler. However, that does not mean it is easy to rearrange the Gershwin *Preludes* for violin. Such an arrangement requires interpretation, creativity, and a certain chutzpah to assert the correctness of the interpretation. Jed had never been in this position before and was completely surprised at how much he was enjoying it.

Despite the pall of grief that still lingered like weak rain, the rehearsal week was a lively storm of activity and intensity. Because Jed was the arranger for the Gershwin *Preludes*, he found himself in the center of that storm. He was in constant consultation on stage or backstage with the maestro, Eric, and the other principals concerning his interpretation. Their consultations were frequent lively debates, but he was always treated with the respect of a contemporary composer. The debates would be interrupted by the soloist's rehearsals, which were events in themselves.

There was the coming and going of Vladimir and his entourage of KGB security. Since the Kennedy assassination, the Soviets had doubled their planned security. In addition, Thomas Flynn had arranged for the presence of the U.S. Secret Service. The Soviet and U.S. agents were comically similar. They were tall men wearing thin black ties, earpieces, and tight-fitting suits that poorly concealed rectangular bulges near the hips and shoulders. In fact, if you didn't hear them speak, and you rarely did, the only way to tell who was on which side was by the small lapel pin/microphone. For the U.S. it was a flag. For the KGB, it was a hammer and sickle. During rehearsals, they stood out like marine honor guards. Hopefully, during the performance, their presence would be less obtrusive. Currently, they were literally tripping over each other trying to protect, and frequently conceal, the diminutive Soviet soloist.

Once security had settled in and the concerto rehearsal began, there was extraordinary music. Leon and Vladimir were bonded in and with the *Rach III* at a mystical level. On Tuesday, Leon introduced the orchestra to Vladimir. Despite having just met for the first time backstage, the pair displayed a remarkable familiarity, as if they had been friends for a long time. Leon also introduced the score to the orchestra, walking it up and down the aisles and rows so that each orchestra member could see it and touch it. During the course of the week, that familiarity was reinforced by the ease of communication they displayed during rehearsal. Broken English and broken Russian were not impediments during the rapid and in-depth rehearsals of the concerto. When discussion occurred from either the soloist or the conductor, understanding was immediate and then exemplified in the playing.

Likewise, orchestra members had no trouble keeping up with the bond and participating at levels they had never before experienced. Most of the concerto rehearsal time was occupied by playing the concerto, enjoying the concerto, reveling in the concerto. At the end, Leon, Vladimir, and various members of the orchestra would chat until security would come and escort Vladimir offstage. Allen would then collect the score and put it in Leon's briefcase just outside the shell. Before breaking for the day, Leon would sum up other issues of the performance with the orchestra. There had been much discussion and many last-minute program changes for the performance.

Impromptu, one-on-one discussions would occur onstage, and then Leon would get to leave as well, taking his briefcase to his dressing room, where he would towel off before going home for lunch.

On Saturday, the rehearsal ended earlier so everyone could have their individual preparations for the evening's performance. Many members stopped by to get a final handshake from Vladimir and communicate their enjoyment of the week. Around the podium, it was a like a locker room celebration, and it continued after Vladimir had left. Leon was one of the last to leave. As he exited the shell stage right, he looked down at his *open* briefcase.

"ALLEN!" The sound of the conductor's anger in the hall, onstage, and backstage was painful. Downstairs in the locker rooms, the roar was frighteningly audible.

Micaela could not hear Leon. She had left quickly after the rehearsal to get home for a long, hot bath. Outside the door of her home, she heard the phone ringing. She rushed with the keys but did not catch the phone in time.

"Damn," she said. She was hoping it was Jed. Until this morning, the week had been glorious. The music had been fantastic. She enjoyed, with quiet pride, witnessing her man so integrally engaged with the orchestra. She reveled in his affection and attention every night. She was in love again. As usual, he left early without saying anything. And, as usual, she pretended to be asleep, waiting for that kiss so gently applied in order not to wake her. But today, he just left. At rehearsal, he was oblivious to the secret signals of recognition and affection. A shell had grown over him during the night, and it seemed treacherous to try to penetrate it. Maybe he was just nervous about the Gershwin. Who wouldn't be? If he would just call, she could reassure him, comfort him, as he had wanted to do for her. She tried his house, but there was no answer. She started the bathwater and began to undress.

"**Any word from** Micaela?" Leon asked.

"No, first there was no answer, and then it was busy. I'll try again later," Allen answered. Leon, Eric, Martha, Hugh, Hermann, and Thomas Flynn were gathered in the small conference room.

"Okay, we will have to start without her. Let me introduce you to Thomas Flynn. He is with the State Department and is responsible for the Secret Service agents who are with us this week. As you know, the *Rach III* score has been stolen. Thomas?" Leon deferred to Flynn.

"We don't know who stole the score. More importantly, we would like to know why. It could be a prank. It could be because someone is trying to disrupt the performance. Or it could be a diversion."

"Diversion, for what?" Leon was surprised.

"We don't know that, either. We are pretty certain that the Soviets had nothing to do with this. It would not be in their interest at all. Therefore, it is probably someone in the orchestra ... any ideas?" Flynn looked to the group.

"You mean suspects," said Martha.

"Yes," Flynn said. "There are over eighty in your orchestra. Certainly there are some who are not politically happy that a member of the communist party is playing music from a Russian composer ... perhaps even more, considering the assassination." The group nodded, but none were willing to offer any names. Flynn went on.

"I understand your reluctance to suggest anyone. It is admirable, but possibly dangerous." There was still no response.

"Do you have anyone in mind?" Eric asked the question that no one else would.

"Miss Miklos and Mr. Norton have obvious motives. On the other hand, it appears that they would have the most to lose as well," Flynn answered. "It doesn't help that they won't pick up the phone."

"Not possible!" Eric defended them. "They care too much for the music." Everyone nodded except Hugh.

"Mr. Morgan?" Flynn said.

"I agree with Eric. But something was up this morning. Maybe it was just a lover's quarrel," Hugh said.

"Very well," said Flynn. "We'll check it out. Anyway, like they say in the mysteries, it's usually the one you least suspect."

"Guess that makes you guilty, Maestro," Martha said, inciting nervous laughter. Flynn turned to Leon.

"By the way, how much will this disrupt the performance?" he asked.

"No more than it already has," the maestro answered. This was not just an answer but a command to his principals.

Micaela was stepping into her bath when the phone rang again. She quickly withdrew and ran to the phone. She caught it this time.

"Jed?" she asked expectantly when she picked up the phone.

"No, this is Allen."

"Oh," said Micaela, with obvious disappointment.

217

"Micaela. We have a problem."

"Yes?"

"Someone has stolen the score to the *Rach III*." The news broke apart the logjam of morning mysteries. Immediately, she knew that Jed had the score. At the same time, she noticed the black sedan across the street with two men sitting in it and covered herself with a towel. She summoned years of performance poise.

"Unbelievable! Do we know who took it?"

"No," Allen answered, a deliberate intonation. This type of conversation … coded by inflection … was a skill that Micaela had practiced for years behind the Iron Curtain. She knew immediately that Allen had a pretty good idea who took it.

"How is the maestro handling it?" she asked.

"He is as mad as I have ever seen him. He wants to fire somebody in the worst way. I just hope it's not me."

"He would never do that. Is there anything *I* should do?" She intoned perfectly.

"Other than making it magically reappear, I can't think of anything," answered Allen.

"I was never good at magic. But I will be home until performance. Let me know if there is any news."

"I will," Allen answered, and then hung up. Micaela got dressed. She wrote a note that said, *Please do not disturb, concert preparation.* She put a stack of records on the turntable and started the music, then grabbed her coat and a large shoulder bag. She taped the note to the front of the door, ran down the stairs to the ground floor, and knocked on the door of the landlady's apartment.

"Yes," the landlady answered, opening the door.

"I need favor," Micaela said. The landlady smiled and nodded.

"I need to go out your back door and, if anyone asks for me, you need to tell them that you haven't seen me." The landlady nodded again and opened the door wide so Micaela could pass through.

Micaela took the bus to the intersection near Jed's duplex. She entered the back yard from the alley and came in through the unlocked back door. Jed was seated at the small, square walnut dining table. He was looking at the score open in front of him. Micaela sat down at the right side adjacent to Jed, without saying anything. Jed turned the page and continued to read the score.

He was in the beginning of the second movement. It was a long, orchestral introduction of mournful strings, briefly interrupted by woodwind solos. Micaela saw a tear appear and glide down next to the salty track of a previous one. Jed moved back from the score so the tear would not fall on the page. He wiped it away with the back of his sleeve.

"You know, this is a really sentimental piece," he said, with a small laugh.

"Yes, some say it is overly so."

"They're wrong," he said. Jed was still engrossed in reading the score. "Look at the notation when he brings back the piano." He turned the score forty-five degrees so she could see, too. "See how the ink almost quivers as he descends the scale?" Micaela nodded at Jed's excitement. "Look here, you don't even need the crescendi symbols. You can see the pressure he applied when he wrote this. And, look here, when he slides into D major, how light the flags are on the eighth notes."

"It's as if you can see Sergei's hand moving across the page," Micaela said.

"Exactly." Jed looked at Micaela. He then turned his gaze from her and sat back in the chair.

"Why?" Micaela asked.

"I have been passing information to the Society. They were going to expose me if I didn't steal it," he said to the opposite wall. "I have had so much fun this week." Micaela took his hand and squeezed it tightly. Jed turned to Micaela and enjoyed her comforting look.

"You know what's really funny?"

She shook her head.

"Well, about halfway through the first movement, I realized I had to take it back. But now, I want to keep it just so I can read it from time to time."

"I will take it back for you," Micaela said.

"Thanks, Micaela, but no. I have to clean up my own act. Besides, I'm tired of the bullshit."

Micaela shook her head. "You clean up bullshit after the matinee on Sunday. For now, it is better I take it." She was not asking as she held out her hands for the score. Jed obeyed, closed the score, and handed it over. She stood up, leaned over, and kissed him deeply.

"I will see you at the Hall tonight and my house afterwards." Again, she was not asking. Jed nodded weakly and said, "Break a leg."

"Why does everyone always say that?" Micaela asked.

"It's considered good luck in the theatre." Jed answered. "The theory is that if you break a leg, what else could possibly go wrong?"

"I see. Well, considering it's *your* Gershwin tonight. You'd better break two." Micaela smiled and slipped out the back door.

She took the bus down away from Jed's and the maestro's home to a small hotel near downtown. At the hotel, she took a taxi to Leon's home. She told the cab to wait, got out, and knocked on the door, hoping that no one was home and that she could just leave the bag at the door.

"Good afternoon, Miss Micaela," Mary said.

"Hi, Mary. I have something I want to leave for the maestro." Micaela offered the bag to Mary.

"Ma'am, you can give it to him yourself. In fact, he will be glad to see you. Seems like there has been a lot of commotion today. Just a moment, I will go get him." Very quickly, Leon was at the door himself.

"Micaela, come in. We have been looking all over for you. We were very concerned. Note on the door, bathtub full of water, music playing. Are you all right? Where have you been?"

"You have been in my apartment?" she asked.

"Well, not me … exactly," the maestro stammered. "Please." He ushered her to his study. As they walked through the living room, they passed some men in black suits with earpieces. Once in the study, Leon closed the French doors to the room. Leon sat in his large easy chair, and Micaela sat in the same straight-back chair she used for the audition. Micaela began speaking before Leon could start with the questions again.

"I have your score, Maestro." She reached in her bag and handed it over. Leon took the score in both hands, looked at it, and laid it on the counter next to the chair.

"I don't believe you took this," he said. Micaela didn't say anything. Leon started to speak but stopped and stared at the rock-silent Micaela. Music teachers often say that silence is the hardest thing to play. Micaela was quite good at it.

"Perhaps we should talk on Monday," Leon half-asked and half-commanded.

Micaela nodded.

"I'll have someone take you home," he said, concluding the meeting.

— 37 —

NOVEMBER 30 SATURDAY NIGHT

Tribute Concert – Campbell Hall

Music: Bach, Sonata No. 1 for Violin, Sibelius: Symphony No. 5, Rachmaninov: Piano Concerto No. 3, Gershwin Preludes

Alison had never seen Leon so calm before a performance. The obligatory act of vomiting was foregone, and he dressed without one complaint. Allen stopped by during his last performance check.

"Hello, Maestro, how are you this evening?" asked Allen.

"Well, Allen, quite well. Is the spot ready for Eric?" For the tribute, it was decided that the orchestra lights would be dimmed, and a spotlight would be on the concertmaster.

"Yes, sir. We will dim the orchestra lights on your cue. I am planning to operate the spot myself, if you don't mind," replied Allen.

"I don't mind at all. Timers ready?"

"As always, sir."

"How's the house?" Leon asked routinely.

"Maestro, it's … full," Allen said with a deliberate pause and smiled at his boss.

"You're kidding?" Alison said. Leon's face matched her surprise.

"No, ma'am, I am not. In fact, there are people outside waiting for no-shows." Leon's face turned to quiet delight.

"Let'em in, Allen," Leon directed.

"But sir, the fire codes."

"Will be overlooked tonight."

"Yes, sir. Ten minutes to go."

"Would you get Eric for me, please?" Leon asked Allen, who nodded and left. "Darling, you must go now," Leon said to Alison. She kissed him and gave him a gentle hug so as not to wrinkle his clothing. He hugged her back forcefully, clothes be damned. As she left, Eric arrived at his dressing room.

"Maestro, you wanted to see me?"

"Yes, please come in and close the door." Eric did as directed, and Leon continued. "How do you feel?"

"Okay … the butterfly count is as one might expect," answered Eric.

"Stretch the first measure, to control your tempo."

"I know, Leon."

"Yes, of course you do."

"Don't worry about it. It's a strange evening," Eric said.

"Yes, it is, Eric. Did you hear the house is full?" Eric shook his head in surprise. Leon continued. "I know that this not the debut you envisioned. That will come later. Tonight is not about you, me, the orchestra, the publicity, or even the audience. It's about one thing … the music. Just listen to the music, my friend. It will play *you* tonight."

Eric shook hands and left.

When the orchestra finished warming up, the large audience was unusually quiet … and dark. There were no white dresses. Black arm bands were prevalent everywhere, including in the orchestra. The first box, stage right, first level, was empty except for a very large arrangement of flowers. The flag, stage left, was at half-mast. To accomplish this, Allen had to have a new, taller flagpole constructed.

Eric came onto the stage to polite applause and bowed. He turned and gave the signal to Hugh to sound the Concert A. The orchestra tuned. Then Leon came out on stage to the same polite applause, to which he gave a half-bow while walking but held his hand up to stop it. The audience responded to the conductor. Mounting the podium, he turned to the audience, not the orchestra, and spoke without microphone in a deep, clear voice that could be heard by the last person standing behind the last row in the third balcony.

"Ladies and gentleman, thank you for coming this evening. I know that your decision to do so was not automatic." Leon paused, looked down for a moment, and then continued. "It is frequently said in times like these that 'the show must go on.' I don't believe that is true. That is not why I am here, that is not why the orchestra is here, and I don't think it is why you decided to come here tonight. One week ago (gesturing to the empty box), we lost a leader, a statesman, and for some, a great friend. We also lost a representative of human evolution, a man who held in his thoughts, his words, and his deeds the tribal passion of humans as well as the honor of a better humanity. He was a sanctuary of civilization. It is appropriate that we are here tonight, for the medium of music is a set of rules for exposing the passions of our soul. Music allows us to see the great beauty that exists in every tragedy. We (gesturing with both hands to the entire hall and orchestra) are not here tonight because 'the show *must* go on,' but rather because we *want* it to go on."

After a long pause, Leon continued, "We have made changes to tonight's program. The piano concerto and the Gerswhin *Preludes* have been moved to the second half. The Sibelius will be played before the intermission. In addition, we will have a tribute." Gesturing for Eric to stand, Leon said, "In honor of John Fitzgerald Kennedy, and with our condolences to his family, Eric Solomon will play the Adagio and Fuga from *Sonata Number 1 in G minor for Solo Violin* by Johann Sebastian Bach.

The house lights and orchestra lights dimmed, as the spot illuminated Eric.

Stage lights always reduce the performers' ability to see the audience. This effect is diminished for the first row of violins and cellos, the conductor, and standing soloists. They are closer to the lights and can effectively see over them. A spotlight is, however, simply blinding and took Eric by surprise. He stood still for a moment, vainly hoping for his eyes to adjust and waiting for the audience to settle down. He suddenly realized that the audience was, and had been, silent.

With a shot of adrenaline, he quickly put the baroque violin to his collarbone and assumed the ready position with his bow. Without counting, he started the first measure. The single shot of chemical fear was now spreading through his body. The tempo was too fast. Although his hands were moving, he was unconnected to the music, like an orchestra and conductor out of sync. While his hands continued to play, his mind raced ahead through the music to a point where he could again take control. Finding the spot a mere three measures ahead, his mind willed his bow hand to hold onto a note it had practiced hundreds, perhaps a thousand times, for an extra beat. The bow hand obeyed its master, and he was once again in control. The fear evanesced, leaving only the reservoir of adrenaline to be drained with dynamic deliberation.

Now that *he* was playing the music and not his limbs, he used the bright light to focus on his left hand. The harsh light put his fingers into a black-and-white contrast with the fingerboard. He could see the grooves in the pads of his finger as they locked onto the catgut. He actually *saw* the music before he heard it. The individual vibrations of the strings were visible. He could see them as they lifted off the strings, pushed and carried by the vibrating wood of the violin, carried into the light.

Perplexed but unafraid, he continued to watch and listen until he realized that once again he was no longer in control. This time it was a pleasant realization. He was simply a very willing participant, negotiating and translating the commands of Bach to his fingers and bow. Every note and expression arrived at its rightful place.

Then a remarkable thing happened. He heard the music. It was not "hearing it like he had never heard it before." It was like he was hearing it for the first time. This new sensation was not limited to his ears. His chest tightened, and he had to work to breathe evenly. It felt familiar, like falling in love. But instead of a sensation fueled by joy, it was fueled by sorrow. Like a broken-hearted lover, he played through the pain.

During the pause before the Fuga, he waited in the bright spotlight and, for a moment, realized that his face was wet with tears. The cavernous silence and the spotlight spurred him to continue. He stayed in that light and state until, to his surprise, the piece ended. The audience did not applaud. As the lights came up, Eric sat down and, without looking, handed the baroque to the second chair, who dutifully took it and, in return, gave him his Strad for the rest of the concert. The second chair whispered, "I have never heard anything like that before." "Neither have I," Eric replied.

Even from his perch among the golden clouds, Allen knew he had just heard something special. He nearly forgot to kill the spot. Allen deftly made his way along the catwalk to return to the stage. Silently, he opened the door to the auxiliary lighting control room. Just as silently, he eased it closed. He turned to the right and saw an open trombone case on the floor. He had enough time to understand that something wasn't right. He had enough time for the hairs on the back of his neck and forearms to tingle. He had enough time to open his mouth to say something. But he did not have enough time to figure out what to say or to defend himself. The blow came to the back right of his head, a painful starburst, extinguishing consciousness as it spread through his skull.

The audience was extremely well behaved. They had been silent after Eric's solo. They did not applaud between the movements of Sibelius *Fifth Symphony*, though they were sorely tempted. From Martha's flawless opening horn to the complicated, crashing ending, they remained appropriately silent. Then, their pent-up delight exploded. The hall sounded much like the Butler field house next door, during the Indiana State basketball championship. They were not just standing and clapping amid intermittent shouts of *bravo*. They were cheering, yelling, uncontained. After bows from the conductor, the orchestra, and several members highlighted in the symphony, there was a tiny subsidence in the volume, at which point Leon made Eric stand and bow alone, which fueled a new round of raucous applause, as everyone remembered his heart-ripping tribute. This new wave of volume directed at the concertmaster placed Eric in an unusual state of embarrassment. As Leon escorted Eric off the stage, the audience finally gave up and the intermission officially started. Offstage, Leon put his hand on Eric's shoulder and said, "That was a unique beginning for a most remarkable performance." With watery eyes, Eric looked sheepishly at his conductor, who was full of smiles. "Thank you, Maestro. I doubt that I will ever do the beginning like that again. For that matter, I may never replicate the rest of it either," Eric said, laughing at himself.

"Perhaps not," Leon agreed. "But all of us will remember tonight." They shook hands gently and parted.

Leon became immediately aware that Allen was not there to give him the water that he desperately needed. Frustrated and visibly irritated, he grabbed the first stagehand he saw and asked where Allen was. The stagehand said that no one had seen him since he'd left for the spotlight bay. In disgust, Leon stomped off to his dressing room.

The news of the maestro's mood traveled through the backstage like an unwelcome wind. Everyone's elation was muted by the knowledge that something was wrong. The question "Where's Allen?" had reached every member of the orchestra and backstage crew within minutes.

Mrs. Zellingari arrived at her husband's dressing room, elated in equal measure by the performance and the audience reception. As she opened the door and saw him guzzling glasses of water from the tap, she knew something was amiss.

"What's wrong?" she asked.

"Allen's disappeared."

"Jesus, what else can happen today?" Alison said. "Do you still have the score?"

"Yes. And we have a piano, a soloist, and a very fine orchestra. So I shouldn't complain. But I am worried. It is not like Allen." Alison nodded.

"Let's get you changed. Then I will look for him," she said.

"Yes on changing. No on looking. I need you in the audience. It'll work out," he said, handing her his soaked formal shirt and taking off his undershirt.

Jed was washing his face and hands when he heard the phrase, "Where's Allen?" By the third time he heard it, he was drying his hands with a towel. He stared at his frozen face in the mirror. He felt a chill of fear and anger scream through his body, locking it down. "That bastard," he eventually uttered. Jed was out of the bathroom before the towel hit the floor. He bolted through the back stage door and leaped up the stairs to the third tier. Lou had played him from the very beginning. He never wanted to sabotage the concert or the maestro. He wanted something more permanent, more devastating, something with more impact. The score was just a distraction, while he kept everyone moving to their rightful place. Lou was going to shoot someone tonight, probably Zellingari, and Jed had helped set it up.

The orchestra was nearly assembled, but a new question started to circulate. "Where's Jed?" While warming up for the concerto, Micaela glanced frequently at the empty chair, her distress mounting as time passed. Backstage, the atmosphere was charged with annoyance at Jed's disappearance. "Where the fuck is he?" said Eric, pacing around the opening he should be going through by now.

"Tell you what, Eric. Let's get started before we lose anyone else," said Leon. The conductor's levity was reassuring, even if he was actually serious. He had been watching Micaela's increasing concern. Eric immediately proceeded onstage. After the applause, he went to the piano and keyed the

Concert A for the orchestra to tune to. Offstage Khazar spoke to Leon, "I see you have the score in hand."

"Yes. It is a great gift. Too great a gift to misplace," Leon said.

While Eric was tuning the orchestra, Lou placed two small sandbags on the platform that supported the spotlight. He rested the barrel of his Winchester on them. Snuggling his right cheek on the stock, he checked the view through the Weaver telescopic site. He moved the crosshairs around the orchestra, getting his upper body settled and comfortable, and enjoying the strapless formal wear of the female musicians. The rifle had been sited flat for one hundred yards. Considering the down angle, about twenty degrees, he would have to aim three inches low. He had four soft tip rounds in the magazine, one for the target and the rest to assure panic in the concert hall so he could escape. He loaded one into the chamber and then continued his voyeurism. While checking Micaela's breasts, he noticed that she repeatedly looked to her right. He guided the site upwards to the empty chair, Jed's chair.

He lifted his head from the site and said calmly, "Well, it's about time." Lou laid the rifle on its side and went back into the control room to wait.

Once the orchestra was tuned and Eric sat down, the soloist and the conductor proceeded onto the stage. Leon carried the score at his side in his right hand so that both the orchestra and the audience could see it. Vladimir took his place at the piano and Leon at the podium. Vladimir bowed to the audience, and then sat down. Leon turned from Vladimir to the orchestra, put the score down on the music stand and never opened it. Checking his principals' readiness, he saved Micaela for last and looked sternly at her. She nodded and then looked at Vladimir to show him that they were ready and, with the maestro's downbeat, the concerto began, with the orchestra first and then the simple one-handed theme from the Russian echoed by Hugh's oboe.

When Jed arrived at the door to the control room, he stopped to catch his breath. He turned the handle slowly and opened the door only wide enough to slip inside. He let his eyes adjust to the dim red light, then walked toward the door on the opposite side that led to the catwalk. On his way, he tripped and fell hard. With his cheek pressed against the cool corrugated metal floor, he saw Allen's face. Allen's mouth had been covered with duct tape. His eyes were open and moving, but otherwise he was motionless. Jed heard's Lou voice.

"Glad you could join the party, college boy," Lou said. He kicked Jed in the stomach. The force of the blow collapsed Jed's diaphragm, leaving him gasping on his side. Lou raised his leg up and slammed his foot down on Jed's chest, cracking two of his ribs. While Jed was gasping for air, Lou duct-taped Jed's wrists behind his back. Then he rolled him over, held down his legs, and tied his feet together. Lou sat down on the lighting manager's swivel stool, looked down at Jed and waited for him to catch his breath. When Jed recovered enough to speak, he pleaded hoarsely, "Don't do it, Lou. Don't kill him."

"Which him, Jed? The nigger Jew or the commie Jew?"

"Zellingari. Khazar is only a temporary problem."

"I like the way you think, Jed. You're right, we get a much bigger bang by putting down a local celebrity. That was Gar's problem. He couldn't see the bigger picture. He just wanted to kill them all. Not a horrible idea, actually, but not an original or timely one either. Poor Gar. He was just too out of control. You should have seen him drop. After we went stump shooting, he just passed out in the back of the pickup. Once I got the rope around his chest, it was easy to tie him to the hoist. I was a little worried the Dodge couldn't support him." Jed laughed. "Anyhow, he didn't come to until he was hanging out there over the water. His eyeballs started to bug out. Before he could start kicking and screaming, I let go of the rope, and he fell with his mouth wide open just like that first time we jumped." Lou paused wistfully. Jed was shaking. "Why do you want to save the other one?" Lou asked, pointing at the stage.

"It's not right, Lou, this has got to stop." Lou shrugged his shoulders. Jed pleaded, "He's a great man, you would only be creating a great martyr."

"You're right! Okay, I won't shoot him." Lou stared at Jed and smiled. Jed's confusion was as obvious as his fear. "You know, for a college boy, you are dumber than a box of rocks. Landsakes, what do you think RW meant when he said ..." Lou paused, half stood, and adopted an imperious voice as if he were speaking to a group.

"'We can no longer afford to fuel the fire of misplaced sympathies. We need to put the blame where it righteously belongs ... at the foot of the communist horde.'" Lou turned his head back down to Jed.

"Misplaced sympathies," Lou mused. "Sounds like a PR problem. Perhaps we need correctly placed sympathies." Lou grabbed the duct tape and tore off six inches and, with two hands, taped over Jed's mouth. Jed's eyes widened as the realization crept over him like an evil shadow.

"That's right, college boy. Who is the most revered and loved out there right now? Who do *you* love?" Jed began screaming into the duct tape. Lou started to sing the Bo Diddley tune…

Walked 47 miles of barbed wire
Used a cobra snake for a neck tie.
Got a brand new house on the roadside,
Made out of rattlesnake hide.
I got a brand new chimney made on top,
Made out of human skulls.
Now come on darlin' take a walk with me, tell me,
Who do you love,

Lou leaned down with both hands beside his face fanning his fingers

Who do you love, Who do you love, Who do you love.

"You know what is even better than sympathy, Jed?" Jed was still moaning into the tape. "Now, pull it together boy, this is important." Jed started to whimper. "That's better. What is more important … is anger. If someone you love gets hurt, you feel bad for them, but it also gets you angry. And, if you have something to get angry at … it's even better. It was so convenient when I heard that the Russians were coming; so many people to get angry at. And everyone just loves Micaela."

Jed groaned. Lou stood straight and slid his hands down the side of jacket.

"How do you like my suit? Do you think I look like one of those KGB hanging around your commie soloist? I sure hope so. I added this hammer and sickle lapel pin. Yeah, I know what you're thinking … no one will see it. That's why I got this." Lou pulled his pant leg up, revealing a dagger and sheath strapped onto his calf. He pulled the knife from the sheath and held it close in front of Jed's face. "It's called a Spetnaz Blade. Used by Russian Special Forces, who sometimes masquerade as KGB masquerading as attendants for famous commie artists touring the free world. It's razor sharp from end to end on either side. It's especially useful for dealing with the enemy quickly and quietly. It's a fine piece. I hate to leave it behind. But that's the whole point, wouldn't you agree?"

Lou knelt over the face-down Allen and turned him over.

"Don't bother closing your eyes, fella. I didn't hit you that hard."

As Allen opened his eyes, Lou plunged the knife just below the rib cage. A duet of muffled cries filled the sound-resistant control room.

"Ah, quit whimpering, Jed, you still have a few more minutes. About seventeen minutes, according to the book that this guy had on him." Lou pointed the bloody blade at the timing ledger that Allen had brought. "I won't take the shot until the final applause. After all, the show must go on. Would you like to watch it? I'm sorry, I should have been more considerate. Here, let me help you up." Lou put the knife down on the table next to the ledger and lifted Jed up onto the stool so he could see the stage from the control room. "There, that's better. Notice that smug bastard isn't even using the score? Guess that was a dumb idea from the beginning, eh, college boy?" Lou started to sing again, rocking his shoulders to the Bo Diddley beat ...

> *Micaela took me by my hand, she said, Lou boy, you know I understand*
> *I got a tombstone hand and a graveyard mind,*
> *Just 22 and I don't mind dying.*
> *Who do you love, who do you, who do you love, who do you love*
>
> *Rode around the town, use a rattlesnake whip*
> *Take it easy girl, and don't give me no lip*
> *Night was dark, and the sky was blue*
> *Down the alley, the ice wagon flew*
> *Heard a bump, and somebody screamed,*
> *You should have heard just what I seen.*
>
> *Who do you love, who do you love, who do you love...*

Lou walked to the catwalk, winking at Jed as he opened the door. Momentarily, the sound of the piano concerto passed through the door. Lou slid out. The door closed, and Jed watched from the silent room. Lou made his way to the perch and snuggled up to his rifle and sandbags.

Jed squeezed his eyes closed so tightly that his cheeks almost touched his forehead. Then he opened them and looked down through the control room window at the orchestra. They seemed so far away. The concert grand piano took up much of the stage and pointed directly at Micaela. He could not hear the concerto. From the snippet he caught as Lou left the room, he knew they were in the third movement, but he didn't know where. In the center of the console in front of him, he saw a toggle switch marked monitor. Bending over, he flipped the switch with his nose. The room filled with the sound of the *Rach*

III. They were about halfway through the movement. How much time was that?

"Time!" he sputtered into the duct tape. By contorting his shoulders and pushing on the foot rest with his bound feet, he was able to rotate his swivel chair 180 degrees to view the time ledger … and the Spetnaz that Lou had left next to it. Jed extended his feet to the floor and tried to push himself over to the table. He succeeded in only turning himself another 180 degrees to face the orchestra and control panel. He put his feet up to the control panel to push backwards, but the wheels stalled on the corrugation, and the swivel stool started to tilt backwards, dangerously close to falling. He turned the stool again, extended his feet to the floor, and threw his torso forward to stand up. The stool gave way behind him and he rocked back and forth to gain balance. Stabilized, he hopped pogo-stick style to the table and turned to pick up the knife with his hands. Only able to get it blade first, he sliced his fingers as he turned to grasp the body of the blade. He tried turning it in his hands to put it in position to cut through the tape, but it was slippery from the blood. He dropped it.

Jed screamed into the duct tape and jumped up and down in an odd rhythm to the concerto crescendos. He fell down into an expanding pool of blood and found himself staring into Allen's eyes. He rolled away, and his tied hands felt the cold handle of the knife. Grasping it deliberately with his right hand, he used short wrist strokes to saw through the tape where his wrists met.

Lou glanced at his watch, although it was not necessary, for even he could tell that the concerto was nearing its end. He had been considering whether to shoot her while she was sitting during the applause. This would be a conveniently motionless target. On the other hand, her torso would be sideways to him and provide a smaller target area. He could easily accomplish a head shot, but that wouldn't make for a very pretty news picture. He decided to wait for her to stand. The full frontal torso would be easy enough to hit, plus the soft-tip hollow-point would mushroom inside her and do all the necessary damage to assure a kill. And if she didn't die instantly, all the better for martyrdom.

Khazar's animated finish was as elaborate as the beginning was subtle. With the final strokes of their hands, the pianist and the conductor concluded the concerto, and the audience roared its approval. The orchestra clapped or tapped their bows on the music stands. Leon stepped down from the podium and gave Vladimir vigorous hug. The completion of any concerto is a milestone accomplishment, anywhere, anytime. When a concerto as complex as this is done so well, it becomes a permanent record in the memory of the music world.

Lou slowed his breathing as he lined up the crosshairs on Micaela. "Stand up, bitch," he whispered to himself. As if commanded, and indeed she had been commanded by the maestro, she stood with the rest of her section and the orchestra to receive her share of the ovation, turning slightly to face the audience. Lou exhaled and squeezed the trigger. As the firing pin of the .3006 released, Lou felt two intense sensations simultaneously. One was the burning pinpoint pain as the Soviet steel penetrated between his spine and right shoulder blade. The other was the full weight of Jed falling on his exhaling body, voiding his lungs of any air. Both sensations caused his body to arch and, in turn, push the rifle stock down. As the rifle belched out a yard of flame, its lone bullet sailed through the golden clouds and then ricocheted around the spotlights until it put one out in a shower of sparks.

The explosion of the 170 grains of gunpowder in that rifle created a sound inside the limestone hall that was simply not understandable by the human psyche. Every sense of every member of the audience and orchestra was assaulted. As loud as the actual rifle shot was, it was more clamorous as an event. For those who experienced this sound, nothing that had gone on before would ever be the same, marking a portal of personal life change. Previous concepts of beauty, safety, security, power, leverage, future, and expectations were shattered and reconstructed in a singular instant.

The applause stopped as suddenly as it had begun. For a moment, the entire concert hall played a game of freeze. Then came the pandemonium and screams. Khazar's attendants rushed on stage, barking commands, and provided a human shield for the soloist as they shuffled him into the wings. All around the hall, more and more fingers were pointing to the catwalk near the control room. Lou was wheezing, but slowly getting to his feet. Jed stood and kicked him in the ribs to keep him down. Lou collapsed again, knocking the rifle off the perch. It fell into the seats below in the front tier, which was rapidly emptying.

Micaela had been frozen at attention, peering into the darkness around the catwalk. She screamed, above all other screams, Jed's name. He heard her and turned to look at her onstage. Lou tried to rise again. Jed kicked him in the face, and the kick shoved him towards the end of the catwalk, propelling him off the edge. Lou was holding on as best he could, but his grip was slipping. He was going to fall. Jed kneeled down close to Lou.

"This time I will watch *you*, asshole." Jed spat in Lou's face. Lou's bloodied face managed a weak smile. With his right hand on the scaffolding, Lou jerked up with all of his strength and then grabbed Jed by his tux lapels and pulled them both from their lofty perch.

Cartwheeling down, Lou hit the metal railing of the second tier, which smashed his skull and broke his grip on Jed. At the same time, Jed hit the outer limestone wall, breaking his left arm, ripping his shirt, and scraping his skin in the process. The impact of hitting the middle tier caused them both to bounce past the boundary of the lower tier railing. The audience below had already scattered at the sound of the rifle. Lou was dead before he hit the ground floor. Jed was completely conscious as he landed between the seats with most of the force on his left leg, breaking tibia, femur, and pelvis. As his leg collapsed, his upper body awkwardly folded over the back of the seat, and his left clavicle snapped. Micaela scrambled down the aisle and stumbled into the row. Jed slid off the seatback to the floor, folded like a garment bag, before she could reach him. Jed was still conscious, but as he bled from the compound fractures and internally, his world tunneled with the diminishing view of Micaela's face.

— 38 —

DECEMBER 1 SUNDAY

Emergence

Music: Schubert, 8 Piano Impromptus

Jed penetrated the surface tension of the water headfirst. Plunging deep into the quarry, he could feel the water pressing along the surface of his skin. He turned to look up. The water was as clear as air, except at the surface, where the view mottled and dappled those above the surface. He saw Micaela looking down on him. He waved. She waved back with the bow in her hand, as if to say "deeper."

He followed her direction and turned downwards. It did not get colder or darker. For a moment he panicked, 'What about air?' Odd, he could hear himself breathing, but he couldn't feel it. It was an industrial sound. He opened his mouth. Water came in and out. There was no air and apparently no need of it. I must be a fish today, he thought and went deeper. The water continued its embrace of pressure, a comforting embrace that invited him to go deeper still.

He looked up again. Micaela was much farther away now. She was playing ... playing beautifully. Why was she crying? He wanted to go back and see her and comfort her like the warm water that was caressing him. Just a little farther, and then I'll go back up.

A large albino carp swam by and said, "This will only sting a little." The carp smiled broadly, showing vampire teeth. It grabbed Jed's left arm with its

fins and sank its fangs into the bulging vein. Jed felt the pain of the fangs and tried to pull away, but the vampire carp was too strong. The carp puffed up on Jed's blood and eventually released his arm, wiping its swollen lips with a fin.
"You rest now," it smiled, and swam away in a rustle.

Micaela had been close to tragedy but never next to it. They pulled her away from Jed, past the lifeless body of Lou. They did not allow her in the ambulance. They did not allow her in the emergency room, where Jed's heart stopped beating and was subsequently resuscitated. They did not allow her in the operating room where they cut, punctured, sawed, stitched, and plastered all of his broken and shredded body parts together. But they did allow her access to the Campbell Intensive Care Unit at Indiana General Hospital.

She stood next to his bed as the nurse was adjusting the drip from the IV bottle. It was really a matter of identification. She knew this person lying before her to be Jed. And she knew Jed intimately. But those two pieces of knowledge could not intersect. This person was bigger than Jed. Swaddled in bandages, plaster casts, connected by cables and tubes, this being was a medical exacerbation of Jed. His eyes were puffy, but not entirely closed. The nurse applied some cream to exposed slits of his eyeballs.

"Comatose patients' eyes are slightly open. The Vaseline keeps them from drying out," she explained. His face was rounder than it should be. In his mouth, there was a tube attached with white tape, keeping *him*, whoever he was, alive. She knew he was alive because he was breathing ... loudly. She looked across the bed and realized it was the sound of the machine breathing for him.

Aside from his respirator-supported breathing, he was motionless. She had never seen Jed still, even while sleeping. Not that he was hyperactive. But he was a man in motion, and this person was not. In ironic confirmation of that stillness, his arms and unbroken leg were securely strapped down. This last observation was the first reassuring fact. If he needed to be strapped down, then someone thought he could move again. She began to reassemble Jed by first remembering the details of the fall and then by an incessant series of questions to the nurse.

"Na co mà tu trubičku?" she asked, pointing to the tube in his mouth.
"Pardon?"
"What is the tube for?" she asked again in English.
"It is called an endotracheal tube. ET tube for short. So he can breathe."
"What is the tube in his nose for?" asked Micaela.

"Nasogastric tube. NG Tube, to take care of gastric secretions. His bowels have shut down."

Micaela asked questions concerning the IV, the stitches, bandages, leg traction, foley catheter, the connections to the EKG, and the sine wave display on the EKG. She only partially understood the answers from the nurse, who was becoming exasperated by the tenacious quiz.

"Is there anything wrong with his hearing?" It was Micaela's final question.

"No, I don't believe so," the nurse answered.

Micaela held Jed's unbandaged right hand and shouted, "Jed, this is Micaela, can you hear me?" There was no response except from the nurse, who admonished Micaela to be quieter. Micaela glared at the nurse, then turned on her heels and left the room. When she reached the hall, she was greeted by Leon, Alison, and Hugh. The maestro tried to hold her, and she gently pushed him away.

"Thank you, but I can't. Not yet." She brushed away the tears from her eyes.

"How is he?" asked Alison.

"He is a disaster," Micaela answered, while looking away.

"Can I get you anything?" asked Leon. Micaela thought for a moment.

"I want my cello."

"I will have it brought here immediately." Leon left to find a phone.

"They won't let me play it in here," said Micaela.

"I'll take care of that," said Alison. "In the meantime, you must sit. I will be back shortly. Hugh, take care of her 'til I return."

"Please, sit," said Hugh, gently directing Micaela to a seat in the hallway. "I will be back in one minute with some water. And then you will drink it," Hugh said more firmly. He returned with the water, sat down in the chair next to Micaela, and made sure she drank the entire glass.

"Thank you," Micaela said. Hugh took the glass back and stroked Micaela's upper back. Micaela started to speak but broke down sobbing. He continued to stroke her, saying nothing, waiting her out. Eventually Micaela's sobbing subsided. "Everyone is so nice," she said.

"Not everyone," Hugh said. Micaela nodded. "Your man saved someone's life today. I am not sure whose, but he is a real live hero."

"Fuck heroes, just give me the 'real live' part."

Hugh laughed, "My goodness, your English has improved."

Within fifteen minutes, Leon returned, followed by Alison.

"Eric is bringing your instrument," Leon said to Micaela. "He should be here soon. Micaela, there are an extraordinary number of police and federal agents asking questions. I need to go speak to them and someone else. I'm going to leave you with Alison and Hugh. But if you need me for anything at all, they can get hold of me." This time it was Micaela who got up and put her arms around Leon.

After Leon left, Alison said, "I spoke with the staff and the doctor on call. There is a suite next to the ICU, and the doctor agreed, with some help from a phone call from Edith Campbell, that Jed is stable enough to move that far. The room is large and has its own doors. Micaela, I assume you want to play your cello in there?" Alison asked. Micaela nodded. "Very well. There is also a larger anteroom for visitors. Hugh, you get to do what you always wanted." Hugh looked at Alison curiously. "You get to order Mary around. Go to the house and have her … and help her bring all the food and drink for the reception here." Hugh nodded and appropriately hid his delight. He left to call Mary. Alison led Micaela to the new room.

On his way to where the police were being held back by a squad of nurses, Leon stopped at a payphone. He took Thomas' card of out of his wallet and began to dial. A hand appeared from his right and pulled down on the phone cradle, disconnecting the call.

"I got here as fast as I could," said the man with the familiar accent. "What do you need?" Leon put the handset back and looked at Thomas Flynn. The surprising thing about Thomas was not his unexpected arrival but that he was the first person Leon had seen tonight out of uniform. The maestro was still in his tails, although his tie was undone. The women were still in their gowns, the nurses in their whites and the police in their blues. Thomas was dressed as a civilian in regular coat, tie, and trousers. Leon lifted his right hand towards the police down the hall. Thomas understood the cue.

"Okay. I am sure they will want to speak to Jed most of all. Is he conscious?"

"No."

"Will he live?" Thomas asked. Leon shrugged. "I will handle them, but you will have to make a formal statement before long. And I will need to debrief the target."

"Vladimir is already gone," Leon said.

Thomas turned to look Leon in the eye and put his hand on Leon's shoulder. "I know he's gone," Thomas said. This time Leon *was* surprised. Of course you do, he thought. He tried to solve the puzzle, but Thomas interrupted him with the answer.

"Micaela."

"What? But I thought…"

"The assassin was Soviet Special Forces. We found his service knife. Apparently, he was masquerading as part of Khazar's KGB guard." Thomas said. "We are assuming that they wanted to finish the job that they did on Micaela's parents and send a message to Vladimir. The message was received. That is why Vladimir is on his way back."

For Leon, the relative horror of what could have happened was something he could not have handled. For a twisted moment, he was glad it was Jed who was in that bed fighting for his life and not her. The image of a bullet-mutilated Micaela flashed inside his mind in nauseating clarity. Thomas held his shoulder more firmly.

"Steady now," Flynn directed. Leon started to recover. "He saved her life," Thomas added.

"I don't think Micaela knows," Leon said.

"Go tell her. I will deal with the police." Thomas proceeded down the hall, and Leon collected himself and went back to Micaela. They had moved Jed to his new room, and the nurses were busy making sure that all his monitoring and support systems were in order. Micaela was watching every detail. Leon refrained from interrupting her until the nurses were done.

"Micaela." She turned to face him.

"Yes?"

"I have some important news."

"From the doctor?" she asked.

"No, from someone else." She waited for him to continue. "Micaela, the assassin was Soviet Special Forces." Micaela said nothing. "The man was not trying to kill Vladimir. He was after you." Micaela turned away, looked at Jed, then laughed quietly.

"What's so funny?" asked Leon.

"Did you get that from your state department friend?" she asked.

Leon nodded.

"Well, he is only half right. The assassin is not Soviet. His name is Lou Flesher. He is from Oolitic, Indiana. The first time I met him was last spring. He and another friend of Jed's were in the lighting control room in Campbell.

"The first time?" asked Leon.

"I saw them again at the 500 and then at some political meetings." Micaela bit her lower lip and then continued. "They seemed like nice people. But they are not. They are as bad as the people who murdered my parents — worse, I think. At least the KGB do not claim that God is on their side. Jed was forced into helping them to sabotage the performance."

"He stole the score," Leon said.

"Yes, although, I think he knew you didn't need it. He realized it was a pointless prank and felt ashamed. He had no idea what Lou was really up to." After a few moments, Micaela asked, "Does anyone else have to know about this?"

"Just my friend in the state department. He may have more questions for you. You just take care of Jed now."

There was a soft knock on the door of the anteroom. Leon left and closed the door of Jed's room. Eric, Mary, and Hugh had arrived. Mary and Hugh set up the food and liquor. Mary also brought changes of clothes for Leon, Alison, and Micaela. Eric had brought the cello, a music stand, and a briefcase full of sheet music. Leon told Eric to go on in. Quietly, Eric opened the door and slid into the room with Jed and Micaela.

"Hello," he said. Micaela turned and forced a smile. "Where do you want to set up?" Eric asked, almost inaudibly.

"I want to set up over here, away from that awful machine," she said, pointing at the respirator. Eric opened the case, took out the peg stand, and attached it to the chair. Micaela took out the prized instrument and started wiping the strings. Eric set up the stand and held out some sheet music for Micaela to look at. It was the Bach's *Suites for Unaccompanied Cello.*

"Perfect," she said. Eric put the music in the stand and, for the first time, really looked at Jed. As it had Micaela, the view of Jed's incomprehensible devastation froze him. Thawed by the sound of Micaela tuning her instrument, he left the room, closing the door behind him.

"I need a drink," Eric stammered. Hugh, who was bartending, immediately provided him with a scotch on the rocks. Eric drained it and took a breath.

"What was that?"

"Scotch," answered Hugh.

"I don't drink Scotch."

"I know, but you didn't look like you could wait, so I gave you mine."

"Thanks. May I have another?"

In the other room, Micaela began with the first of six movements in the first of the six Bach suites. The eighteenth-century music wafted through the adjoining doors. The music contained a dance-like combination of minor and major phrasing that supported both the grief and hope of everyone there.

Jed was still descending, but not by choice anymore. He was being sucked down. The pressure was no longer soothing. It became hard. He could feel his jaw ache. He tried to cry out, but his lips couldn't close and his throat couldn't move. He tried to move his limbs to swim up, but they were frozen. He looked down at his feet and saw a rope tied around them. He was being pulled down by something at the end of the rope.

The pulling stopped. Jed's momentum carried him a little farther, and then he started to float back. The rising stopped when he reached the end of his rope tether. On the tether, he bobbed in rhythm with the factory sound of his breathing. The currents caused him to sway back and forth. If he could only get free from whatever the rope was tied to, he could float back to the surface, and Micaela could help him.

The carp swished back and this time was swimming around his waist.

"I have to pee," Jed said.

"Go ahead," said the carp.

"But I don't want to pee on you."

"You won't," said the carp. Jed allowed himself to pee, but didn't feel relieved.

"What's wrong?" asked the carp.

"I am tangled. I need to be cut free."

"Tangled on what?"

"I don't know," Jed said, whining.

"Would you like to see?" offered the carp. Jed did not answer. The carp grabbed him by the shoulders and turned him. Every movement hurt. The water pressure was like a suit of misshapen iron now. The carp forced him upside down. Jed became disoriented. The water began to move up his eyeballs and into his nose.

"Look!" the carp commanded. Jed blinked and did as he was told. The outline of his anchor became slowly visible. It was a limestone bust. Two busts, in fact, joined at the back of the head — the tragic and comic theatre masks. The large, wid- open mouths allowed the actors to speak more clearly.

"C'mon, Jed, jump," echoed the comic mask.

240

"Yeah, faggot, give it a whirl," came the hollow words from the tragic mask, which then changed into a gargoyle.

The first time Micaela saw the doctor was during morning rounds. She slept little during the night. It seemed that when she did, she was awakened by the rustle of the starched uniform of the nurse. The doctor had a small goatee, glasses, and examined Jed without acknowledging her. Micaela thanked the doctor for allowing her to play in the room.

"It wasn't my choice," he said. He continued to inspect the patient, waving a penlight in his eyes, hitting the right leg with a small rubber hammer below the knee, rubbing a small blunt object along the soles of his feet from heel to toe, and frequently referring to his chart at the foot of the bed.

"How is he?" Micaela whispered.

The doctor finally looked at Micaela.

"He is critical but stable."

"What's that mean?" she asked forcefully.

"May I be frank?" asked the doctor.

"Please."

"It means that we, as doctors, have mended everything. It means that all his vital signs are good. His reflexes are fine. His pupils are reacting properly. And given enough time, he can heal up nicely." The doctor paused, looking for reaction from Micaela. There was none. He continued, "It also means that we really have no idea what is going to happen now. He could remain unconscious for days, weeks, or ... never wake up. There are many things that could fail at any time. The fact that his heart stopped is not good. He is like a house of cards. If one thing goes awry, then it might take the rest of him. And there is also the respirator," he said, touching the bellows of the wheezing apparatus.

"The breathing machine," Micaela said.

"Yes," the doctor raised his eyebrows. "The machine has probably saved his life. Unfortunately, the body quickly becomes dependant upon it, like an addict on drugs. It is important that we try to wean him from the machine as soon as we can. But each time we try, there is a risk of complications."

"Complications?"

"Pulling a card out of the house of cards," he explained, while mimicking the gesture.

"When will you start?" Micaela asked. The nurse had returned and was starting to organize the disarray of connections from the NG tube, respirator hose, and IV tubes.

"Now," he said. "It would be good for you to leave the room."

"No," Micaela said. Both the nurse and the doctor stilled for a moment.

The doctor recovered more quickly than the nurse. "Very well. Please come over here, and you can help." Micaela did as she was told and stood next to Jed's left side, while the doctor joined the nurse on the opposite side. The nurse had removed the tape from all the intermediate points along the respirator hose. The doctor pointed to where the hose was still taped to Jed's mouth.

"Do you see this fitting where the hose attaches?" asked the doctor.

"Yes."

"We are going to disconnect the hose. The nurse will turn off the machine at the same time, which will stop blowing air into his chest. If he is able to breathe through the remaining tube, then I will extract it from his mouth. If not, I will reconnect the hose. Your job is to hold his hand, speak to him, and try to reassure him if he becomes conscious."

"Everyone ready?" asked the doctor.

The nurse and Micaela nodded.

The doctor disconnected the hose, and the nurse switched off the machine. A shadow of silence descended. The doctor had his stethoscope placed on Jed's chest. Micaela squeezed Jed's hand. The hand did not squeeze back, but the body started to stiffen and arch against the restraints.

"Talk to him," the doctor commanded.

"Wake up, Jed," Micaela pleaded repeatedly, at different volumes. "Please wake up." Jed's body continued to push against the restraints, but there was no sign of breathing.

"Get ready," the doctor said to the nurse. The nurse had the hose in hand. Then Jed's eyes opened.

"Jed!" Micaela shouted at his eyes. Briefly, he looked in her direction, and then his lids drifted down. The doctor took the hose from the nurse and reconnected it to the mouth tube.

"Back on." The nurse switched on respirator, and air refilled Jed's lungs. Micaela released Jed and held onto herself with both hands.

"It will take several more tries before we can get him off the respirator," the doctor said to the visibly shaken Micaela. "Each time, he will become more conscious."

242

"I think he recognized me."

"I think you're right. I want you here every time we try. This is difficult, and we are not out of the woods. Believe it or not, these are encouraging signs." The doctor spoke with scientific interest and was not trying to mollify Micaela.

"Shall I continue to play?" she asked.

"Yes, keep playing."

The gargoyle separated from its comic partner and started to float up to Jed's eye level. Abruptly it stopped, constrained by the same rope that held Jed. The face was wearing his dark glasses and spun in front of Jed as the rope unwound. On that last turn, the dark glasses flew off, and Jed was looking into the lifeless eyeballs of Gar. The rope continued to unwind, and Jed was loosed from his binding. At the same time, the mechanical sound of his breathing stopped. He had no air.

He tried to kick to the surface but could only float at the speed of his bubbles and inside his air-deprived panic. He felt the surface before he saw it. Breaking the water membrane, he gasped and tried to scream. The gasp was unsatisfying and the scream was inaudible. He saw Micaela and others looking at him with grave concern. He tried to breathe again ... still no air. A large man in a white coat ... was it the maestro? gave a signal, and he heard the sound of the breathing engine again. Relief and blackness soon followed.

Micaela played every day ... all day. Eric and Hugh came by and played too. Soon the anteroom was full of musicians, all taking turns in duets, trios, quartets, and solos. With Edith's support, Alison made sure that the symphony members had carte blanche to visit whenever they wanted. They played Brahms, Mozart Clarinet Wind Concerto, Schubert, Haydn, Prokofiev. They tried some Berg and Schumann, but only in small doses. However, the main course was lots o' Bach. It was an-all-you-can-hear musical marathon. Even Leon sat in from time to time, borrowing Eric's Strad. Mary, under Hugh's constant meddling direction, kept the room well provisioned with remarkable buffets, wine, and liquor. The musicians all consumed as if competing with Hugh. Despite the apparent festival aspect, the tones remained subdued, in deference to the situation. Micaela would only take short breaks for food, rest, and to clean up.

"Anything but Vivaldi," she said as she left the room. Martha Collins showed several times, sans instrument and attitude, but brought clothes and support for Micaela.

There were more attempts to wean Jed from the respirator. Each attempt was equally frightening but also reassuring. Jed was becoming alert during the incidents. The prolonged unconsciousness was now being induced by painkillers, not the physical trauma.

On Wednesday, Leon met Micaela and several musicians in the anteroom. He had brought more music.

"I don't know why I didn't think of this earlier," he said passing out the sheet music for the Gershwin *Preludes*. "You won't be able to do *Prelude No. 1*, it's too orchestral. You should have no problem with *No. 2* and parts of *No. 3*." Leon stayed to hear the premiere performance of the arrangement.

Later that night, Jed woke up in the fluorescent darkness of his hospital room. Restrained by sedatives and leather straps, he mentally connected the sound of his respirator with the rise and fall of his chest. How easy it is to breathe, he thought. In the shadows, he heard a familiar sigh. Turning his head to the right, he saw the silhouette of Micaela asleep in the chair. Smiling against the adhesive tape around his mouth, he fell back asleep, hearing the rhythmic wave of the breathing machine for the last time.

On Thursday morning, the doctor carefully removed the tape from Jed's mouth, causing a small tear to fall from Jed's wide-open eyes. His lips were chapped and swollen.

"Are you ready?" The doctor said to Jed.

Jed nodded.

The procedure for removing the breathing tube was quick and disturbingly forceful. Jed opened and closed his mouth, moving his lips in an exaggerated fashion. Then he looked at Micaela and spoke with raspy voice.

"Would you play for me?"

"I thought you'd never ask."

Acknowledgments:

Limestone Concerto is fictional. However, many facts, quotes, and headlines from that period are used to provide the flavor of that time. Every attempt has been made to accurately cite the source of that material in the context of the story or chapter heading. One exception is the 1950's rock and roll tune *Be Bop a Lula* by Gene Vincent, referenced in Chapter 28. Despite numerous attempts, I was not able to find out who wrote the satirical replacement lyrics used in that chapter. Those lyrics were handed down to me via impromptu sing-a-longs and were believed to have been written by an east coast prep school student around that time.

The picture of the quarry on the cover is used with permission from John McMillen (www.bedfordonline.com).

My thanks to all the fans of Limestone Concerto, who have insisted that it be published.

And, finally, I would like to acknowledge the patience and support of my family and friends, without which this work would not have been published.

Support the Arts – Buy a Fresh Copy

Recently a reader of Limestone Concerto told me that she read it not once, but twice. She said she enjoyed it even more the second time. I asked her if she bought a fresh copy. She said no and wondered why it would make a difference. I explained that it's always important to buy fresh. Pages untarnished by finger oils, coffee stains, and/or heavy breathing impart a special liveliness to the storyline.

She then implied that my artistic goals had been tarnished by more mercenary tendencies and perhaps I needed some sort of intellectual laxative to help remove the build-up of waste matter in my system. I told her that, while her scatological analysis was probably correct, her assumption as to my financial motives was wrong.

Unlike paintings, which seem to have an existential purpose once they are hung on any wall, even if it is your Uncle's, literary work has no real existence unless it is read. Therefore, as an author, it is my goal to get the work read. I am also the publisher; not by choice, but by necessity. The term "self-publishing" has accrued a variety of definitions — from convenient low-investment print-on-demand methods, to assuming all the roles of traditional publisher, just on a smaller scale. I have chosen the latter, which means I have made all the investment of time, money, and energy. This is a riskier proposition. The purpose of this risk is not financial reward. The chances for that are minimal. Rather, it is to maintain complete control, while trying to gain exposure for the novel.

I am only partly kidding when I suggest that one should always buy a fresh copy. I have no desire to be a publisher. I just want to keep on writing. In order to do so, I need to make a little money. If you enjoyed this book, please consider making an investment in the work. Don't loan it to your friend. Buy them a fresh copy. With today's internet, it is easy and convenient and will be so much more appreciated by the author, publisher, and future readers.

When you buy fresh, you are not supporting me. You are supporting the book, indeed the art form. And I am grateful for that.

Thank you,

Wallace Westfeldt

You can order a *fresh* copy and/or gift of *Limestone Concerto* by using this order form:

I want _____ copies of **Limestone Concerto** for $17.95 each.

Include $5.05 shipping and handling for one book (allow one week for delivery) plus $1.95 for each additional book. Colorado customers must add 4.1% sales tax. Boulder, Colorado residents must include 8.16% sales tax.

My check or money order for $ _____ is enclosed.

Ship to:
Name: _____

Address: _____

City: _____ St.: ____ Zip: _____

Ph: _____

Email: _____

Make your check or money order payable and return with this form to:

MudBug Press
PO Box 1316
Boulder, Co 80306-1316

If you would prefer a credit card/online purchase, please visit:
www.limestonconcerto.com

For bulk discounts, author events, or more information contact:
editor@mudbugpress.com